THE ENFORCER

ZARA COX

B

Boldwood

First published in Great Britain in 2025 by Boldwood Books Ltd.

Copyright © Zara Cox, 2025

Cover Design by JD Smith Design Ltd

Cover Images: Shutterstock

A CIP catalogue record for this book is available from the British Library.

Paperback ISBN 978-1-83678-957-4

Large Print ISBN 978-1-83678-956-7

Hardback ISBN 978-1-83678-955-0

Trade Paperback ISBN 978-1-80656-062-2

Ebook ISBN 978-1-83678-958-1

Kindle ISBN 978-1-83678-959-8

Audio CD ISBN 978-1-83678-950-5

MP3 CD ISBN 978-1-83678-951-2

Digital audio download ISBN 978-1-83678-953-6

This book is printed on certified sustainable paper. Boldwood Books is dedicated to putting sustainability at the heart of our business. For more information please visit https://www.boldwoodbooks.com/about-us/sustainability/

Boldwood Books Ltd, 23 Bowerdean Street, London, SW6 3TN

www.boldwoodbooks.com

For my twisted little darlings who like their men armed, unhinged, and utterly obsessed! You came for the body count, stayed for the blood-stained grovelling, and cheered when the girl didn't just survive... she made him beg. Here's to the dirty deals, dirtier kisses, and the kind of love that ruins careers and sheets. You sick, sexy legends, this one's all yours.

1

RAFAELLE

An extremely proficient killing machine.

That was what was written in the 'Points of Interest' section of my military file. The file I broke into my commanding officer's desk to peek at one night when I was bored out of my skull.

I never told another living soul, but I was damn proud of those handful of words. Enough to keep me grinning and killing for months and years.

Hell, I'm grinning *now* as I settle onto my belly on yet another cold concrete floor. And wait.

It doesn't take more than a handful of seconds for the grin to slide off my face though. For fury to erode mirth like battery acid eats through flesh. For memory to tear chunks out of my temporary levity. It always does. Hovering in the wings like some fucking demon vampire, ready to suck the joy out of every moment.

These days, it feels like a competition, this push and pull.

I fight to find puddles of bliss in an abysmal landscape, only for the demons to swing by and take a crap in it.

And lately... fuck, it hurts to admit, but lately I seem to be losing.

Ever since my older brother, Cesare Salvatore, former Formula One racer, underboss of the Salvatore Organisation and heir apparent to our multi-billion-dollar empire, opened his arms out wide and invited the enemy into his bed.

Into our lives.

That enemy is now his wife. My sister-in-law.

As much as I want to hate her, Maddelena Mancinelli, now Maddie *Salvatore*, is good people. She deserves props for holding her own in a family that wouldn't have hesitated to rip her throat out and feed it to the specially built pond of piranhas my *nonno* commissioned as a Christmas present for himself three years ago. The one he salivates about dropping some traitorous schmuck into James Bond style the first chance he gets.

Doesn't matter that we've tried to tell him that's not how piranhas operate. That they don't chomp on human flesh just for shits and giggles.

When it comes to getting what he wants, Don Orazio Salvatore, Cosa Nostra down to his very marrow, lets very little stand in his way.

And for reasons I'm still stumped by, he decided giving Cesare and Maddie's Romeo-and-Juliet-style hookup his blessing was the right thing to do. For the sake of family, and because being on Nonno's shit list was a hard 'no thanks', I had to fall in line.

But as my commanding officer would attest, there's falling in line for regular assholes, and there's the way I, Rafaelle Fucking Salvatore, the enforcer of the Salvatore Organisation, choose to fall in line.

Do I admit the other reason why in my quiet, secret moments? Sure I do. The thing is, Cesare was born first, the heir who knew his place and his destiny. I have zero problem with that. But being born within months of each other meant we could've been twins made us close. So close I became his shadow.

But *that's* the problem with shadows.

People tend to forget they're there until they move.

Or act.

So when the opportunity presented itself to act, to use that shadow for more than standing in my brother's limelight and destiny, I took it. To protect my family against our enemies, against the uglier parts of the world no one liked to talk about.

I became *proficient* at it.

Hence my presence on this roof.

Because I sure as fuck am not lying down and taking all that loved up kumbaya crap. Not when the person who took my *mama* – the most important person in my life – still walks this earth, breathing free air.

And irony of motherfucking ironies, that person too happens to bear the surname of my family's worst enemies.

Giada Mancinelli.

I would've preferred the original eye for an eye but the mother to the Mancinelli brats is of very little consequence. On her best days, Vittoria Mancinelli moves like a shadow of whatever the fuck she used to be. On her worst days she's like a character from *The Walking Dead*.

Whatever Bonafacio, the head of the Mancinelli family, or El Topo as he's derisively nicknamed, and his son have done to the woman over the years, I sense she'll be *very* briefly mourned – if at all – then promptly forgotten about should anything happen to her, like a sniper round to the head from my rifle.

And, hell no, that won't do.

I need this to hurt.

To sear and torture and torment.

I want it indelibly marked on their souls as Mama's loss is marked on mine. I need them to never take another breath without knowing the person they love is no longer breathing the same air.

And with Giada Mancinelli having vanished off the face of the earth, and Vittoria not worth the effort, here I am, playing eenie-meenie-miney-fucking-mo.

The most obvious choice is Matteo Mancinelli.

El Topo's first born son, underboss and heir.

I have a feeling I'd be doing everyone a favour by taking him out. Because he too is an oppressor and abuser of women. He stood by while his own father signed off on his daughter's attempted assassination at her wedding. And the weasel has shown zero signs of remorse since then.

Hell, he's boldly stepped into his father's shoes once El Topo realised his plans had failed spectacularly when we handed them their asses at our compound in Fallbrook, Upstate New York on that wedding night a year ago.

With the FBI officially on El Topo's tail, ditto the Russians he foolishly got into bed with thinking he could best us, and us Salvatores hunting him down on the qt, he'd made like the rat he is and scurried underground.

No matter. I have Matteo. His various siblings.

Or El Topo's other grandchildren.

Jacinta, his third granddaughter. The lawyer who bends over backwards to get all the Mancinelli shitheads routinely out of the jail cells they seem to land themselves in on a regular basis.

Or Narciso, Matteo's last born and El Topo's only grandson. Baby of the family and the piece of shit who tried to take out not just Cesare but my younger brother Renzo during the Las Vegas Formula One Grand Prix last year. And it isn't like that was his only attempt. At every turn, the Mancinellis have brazenly and consistently attempted to do my family harm, in the name of the family feud that's either murky or heavily embellished depending on who was doing the narrating.

And last but not least – and I absolutely refuse to acknowledge the fireworks popping beneath my skin when I think of *her* – Sofiya Mancinelli.

The second Mancinelli granddaughter.

The one Orazio asked me to keep an eye on, not having a clue she's been on my radar for the better part of five years now. The woman my grandfather calls 'strange' because she doesn't quite fit the mould of an obedient Sicilian progeny of a family steeped to the eyeballs in Cosa Nostra.

The woman I'm loath to admit has become a subject of rabid interest which has gained near obsession status in the last year.

Moving her to the top of my revenge kill list will solve a host of problems.

First, I'll feel a damn sight better than the hellish nightmare I've endured since finding out that the circumstances of Mama's death weren't as clearcut as I'd thought. Shit, I might even be able to finally sleep more than a forty-five-minute stretch.

Second, it would be doing my family a favour and depriving the Mancinellis of a key threat in their admittedly shoddy protection, leaving them even more vulnerable and ready for the death blow that should've taken them out decades ago.

Who cares that she fascinates me beyond reason? That the whispers I heard two years ago, the little traps I left on the dark web that she walked straight into, and the final confirmation in the last few months of just *what* Sofiya Mancinelli is would've had me salivating under different circumstances?

If she didn't have the fucking surname she wears so proudly.

And all of this even before that gut-punch of a fuck-hot body she loves to display with jumpsuits and catsuits, as if daring any red-blooded man not to stop and stare at the juiciest ass without losing their fucking minds.

None of that matters, stronzu!

As the enforcer of my family's continued security and well-being, none of that *should* matter. I already dropped the ball once, allowing my mother to fall prey to our enemies.

This is my chance to set things right.

I breathe out.

Adjust the scope of my sniper rifle with the ease of long practice, my finger brushing over the trigger like a lover's caress.

The lens sharpens, and there they are. Narciso Mancinelli stepping out of his Ferrari F80 – a little obvious in the boys'-toys-zero-class department if you ask me. Beside him, Matteo.

Both oblivious to the monster watching from the rooftop a quarter of a mile away. They walk around the car, lost in their love of fast, showy cars, giving me ample time to weigh their fate.

At the thought of avenging every single soldier we lost last year at Cesare and Maddie's wedding when these assholes unleashed their cowardly carnage, my lips curve into another slow grin, snatching this piece of joy straight out of my demon's mouth.

'Eenie.' I tilt the barrel towards Narciso, brash and mouthy, immature but with the potential to be a wildcard and a pain in my ass down the road. 'Meenie.' I shift to Matteo, older, slower, soft-spined yes-man. 'Miney...' I flick back to Narciso, who's laughing about something, cocky as hell in his loud designer gear. 'Moe.'

My pulse doesn't even tick up.

A strange kind of stillness lives inside me – cold and precise, dark as the shadow I was born into. This is what I made myself into, after all. The useful tool to deliver consequences. To balance the *famigghia's* bloody ledgers.

My brother may be the golden boy who wins in the light. I do my winning in the dark with little applause. Just the comforting silence of a job done right.

I'm the perfect yang to his yin.

Does it grate sometimes, being painted that black? Sure, but knowing I'm keeping him and everyone I love safe? There's no greater honour.

So I study their faces, the curve of their jaws, the way Narciso shoves his hands in his pockets and smirks like the world owes him a favour.

Matteo glances behind them once, hand instinctively resting on his son's back, guiding him like he still believes he can protect him.

I roll my neck and exhale slowly. I could end them both. Right here. Right now. *Pop pop.* One breath.

And yet... I hesitate.

Will it feel different once it's done? Will the ache inside me dim, the ghost of my mother's final screams quiet? Or will I just be another man who traded one corpse for another?

I should feel rage. Fire. Triumph, even.

But all I feel is the soft breeze on my face and the slight sting of memory behind my eyes. Killing a Mancinelli *will* settle the score. But will it ever make the silence less loud?

For fuck's sake. Who the fuck cares about the storm of silence?

Breathe in. Out. Blink away the peppering stings behind my eyes.

For you, Mama. I hope you'll rest peacefully after this.

I settle the crosshairs on Narciso, but again I hesitate. Think about the son *I* was to my mother.

Out of the five children she birthed, I'm the only one she gave her brown eyes to. The only one she shared her talents of cooking with.

So yes, I'm fucking *special*. She told me every day and I wore that shit with pride.

So fuck a treasure for a treasure.

And if one death doesn't appease, I'll spree my way through the whole clan, wipe them off the face of the earth.

They spilled precious blood. They took my mother. Now I take the baby of the family. *And* one of the remaining siblings? Why the hell not.

An eye for two. A tongue. A hand. A heart. I'm not fussy.

Maddelena's a Salvatore now and therefore off limits.

There was a silent rule about old women and children. El Topo broke that when he killed my mother.

Every Christmas I stare at the empty seat she'll never again occupy. The kitchen haunted by the echoes of her happy humming and deep laughter as she made my favourite meal while I told her dirty jokes.

It'd been no less painful when we remained in the dark about who killed her.

Now we know.

I'm the Enforcer, the necessary hand of Salvatore justice. Tonight I'm bringing vengeance that's as inevitable as breathing.

The fallout will need careful handling, of course. Maddie would be upset. But she'll have Cesare to comfort her.

But better to ask for forgiveness than permission, right?

And who comforted me when Mama died? In a house full of hard men she was our soft centre, a soft place to land.

A warm hug and a hot meal. The customary ribbing about when I'd give her grandkids. My solemn promise that I would start actively working on it... next week. The squint of her faintly wrinkled eyes before she kissed my crown and pressed second helpings on me. El Topo ripped it all away.

I never even got to hear her last words. And that, perhaps most of all, is what flays my insides when I think of her loss. It's what Giada Mancinelli, the sister I've been unable to locate, is keeping from me. The one who holds the last piece of the puzzle surrounding my mother's death. Including her last words.

Last year when Maddie told me she didn't know her third youngest sister's location, I'd believed she was covering for her family, protecting Giada from my righteous wrath. They still could be.

So regardless of what happens here tonight, who I kill, my hunt for her can't stop. *Won't* stop.

My phone buzzes in my pocket and I grimace. I silenced it but didn't turn it off.

Rookie mistake that's very unlike me. Sliding my hand into my pocket, I correct that error. I know who it is.

Cesare. Calling to check up on me.

Not out of some protective mother-hen routine gone overboard, but because of the bullshit promise he'd made to his new wife about peace-making.

We'd all barely recovered from discovering that he'd gone over to the dark side. Fuck was I going to honour some vow he'd made because he was eyeballs deep in his feelings.

He's forgotten that I, too, had made a vow. As I stared down into Mama's beautiful, lifeless face.

I'd vowed to bring her killer to a very gruesome end. No way was I going to renege on that.

Purpose reaffirmed, I let out a slow breath. I've pissed around long enough with which way to go with this.

Both, I decide.

A bullet to the old man's spine. Keep him alive but take away his mobility, his *joie de* fucking *vivre* long enough for him to watch me take down a couple more of his brood before I finish him off.

Three? Four? How many bullets would it take to salve the gaping wound in my chest? Innumerable, I suspect. But this is a start. A solid target instead of the blanket retribution my brothers and I had rained down on the city six years ago.

Five minutes from now I'll light up my cigar and feel the brief glow of warmth. It's my first vice. Well, maybe my only. Pussy really isn't a vice since it doesn't rot your lungs.

It might rot other parts for other men, but I keep my choice prime.

I take an imaginary deep pull and grin in the dark. Feel the smoke swirl in my lungs.

Just as the cold butt of a silencer kisses the space behind my right ear.

Okay.

Well, shit. This just got interesting.

2

RAFAELLE

The butt of the gun isn't a light, friendly kiss.

It's Frenching my skull in a way that means dirty, sordid business.

My hand doesn't move from the trigger, my eye still trained on Narciso Mancinelli. 'At least buy me a drink first?' I murmur, wondering why my heartbeat still hasn't picked up. Am I already dead?

'Nah, you don't deserve a drink. I was hoping you'd make this more of a challenge. Thanks for making it so easy.'

I exhale more than imaginary smoke. I exhale a lungful of shock.

Because it's not a man standing behind me, making conversation before firing a bullet into the back of my head.

It's a woman. With a sexy as fuck voice I want to play in a loop.

She scoffs softly. 'I know what you're thinking. You believe your chances have improved because I'm a woman.'

Since that was exactly what I was thinking, I shrug.

I'm itching to turn around, look at her, just to confirm the absurd hope that the breathtaking body I've seen many times from a distance matches the sultry, cock-stroking voice I've never heard before... until now.

Because if this is how I meet my end, then I'd rather it be at the hands of someone as beautiful as she is.

My lips curve as I contemplate what could be my last moments. I've led an interesting life, as far from mediocrity as I could get. And the biggest bonus of all, I'll get to see Mama again.

'Thinking of your last words?'

I chuckle. 'I was, but I'm thinking, what's the point? There's no one around to impress with poignant prose. I'm much more interested in who the angel is ushering me into the afterlife.'

The nuzzle presses harder into my skull.

Clever girl.

'You think I'm an angel?' Her voice turns harsh. Still insanely sexy.

'Oops. Have I offended you?'

'Don't kid yourself,' she tosses back, but the irritation is still there. 'But yes, I'm curious as to why you think I'm remotely angelic.'

I contemplate my answers, then stick to the truth. 'I hate to be cliché, but you don't sound like my idea of the Grim Reaper. Not to say you're not the angel of death, but I prefer to imagine you as an insanely beautiful angel instead of a hooded pile of bones.'

I catch the barest hint of a snort before I'm prodded harder. I'm not going to tell her – because I'm not *that* much of an idiot – but her harsh treatment makes my dick hard. I wonder if she'll dally long enough for me to nut one last time before she kills me.

Yeah, I'm not normal. Far from it.

'Who were you planning to kill tonight? And don't even think about bullshitting me.'

Ah. Back to being all business. 'I hadn't made up my mind,' I answer truthfully. 'One definitely. Both, possibly.'

A sharp inhale. Giving herself away. If she's who I'm beginning to think she is, for the hints of a reputation she's gathering on the dark corners of the web, she's too emotional. But then she's a rookie, I remind myself.

'You really want to die so badly?'

'On the contrary, I enjoy breathing very much. And I would never lie to an angel. What I said is the truth.'

'You want me to believe that the infamous Enforcer just turns up with a random target in mind?'

Surprise stalls my breath for a millisecond.

'Yes,' she says with a hint of a gloat. 'I know who you are. Just as I knew you'd be here.'

I haven't been betrayed because I've shared this side mission with no one. But I'm seriously impressed by her contacts and how she anticipated my being here tonight. Whatever surveillance she has in place is top notch.

Remarkably, that knowledge makes me even harder. Bringing me one step closer to my goal of rubbing one out before I go. 'In that case, will you do me the honour of telling me who you are before you blow my brains all over this rooftop?'

Silence. The gun doesn't move from the back of my head, but I feel her waver.

'A dying man's wish,' I say, pressing my luck.

'No,' comes the firm reply.

'Fine. So... what now?' I take my finger off the trigger and relax further into the cold ground. 'You want something, or you would've killed me by now. And don't ask me the same question again. My answer won't change.'

'I know you're the Enforcer. And I know he always has a back-up plan. Tell me what you planned to happen if you didn't succeed tonight.'

My chuckle turns into laughter. 'If I'm the Enforcer, under what circumstance do you believe I would divulge that?'

Silence stretches again. 'Under the possibility that I might consider not killing you... yet?'

Okay, that's... almost anti-climactic. Because the second I turn, it's game over for her. 'Hmm, and what do you intend to do to me in the meantime, angel?'

'I have other means to take you out of commission without killing you. And don't call me that.'

'Tell me your name, then. Or at the very least, let me see your face.'

'You're more concerned about seeing my face and knowing my name than you are about dying?'

'We're all destined for death. And in our line of business, we meet our end sooner rather than later. If you're not reconciled to that fact, then you're not as clever as I think, *duci*.'

She inhales sharply at the endearment.

It wasn't a slip. While she'd been delaying what I'm beginning to think may *not* be my inevitable demise, I've been collating every scrap of information I have about her identity.

I'm certain I know who my potential killer is.

'You... you're...' she sputters.

Her reaction all but confirms it.

'Yes. I am. Sicilian through and through,' I say. Just like you, *Sofiya Mancinelli*.

My pulse jumps, half-elated, half-resigned. With a shovel of danger-etched arousal thrown in.

Because this just got exponentially more interesting.

'Turn around,' she snaps. Her voice has altered, as if she too senses the stakes have shot up higher than ever.

I turn around slowly, ensuring my gloved fingers are splayed open and well away from any dangerous object I could use to defend myself. She might yet shoot me, but she has questions.

And I need to scope her out.

I sense her surprise when she sees my masked face.

I take my time in dragging my gaze up to hers. And *sì*, there are so many entrancing things to admire on the way to meeting her searching eyes.

Those killer boots she's wearing, for example.

I want one lethal heel pressed against my balls. Or those mile-long legs wrapped around my head as I eat her out like she's my last supper.

Supple hips I want to sink my fingers into. A narrow waist I can easily encompass with my bare hands. And... fuck, she's wearing a catsuit, black as midnight, deadlier than the sniper's rifle resting above my head.

As for her tits, well, they're simply a work of art.

Michaelangelo would weep at the sight of them. I just want to slap and bite and worship and suckle them until my jaw falls off.

'Are you being serious right now?' she snaps.

'I'm not dead yet, angel. Don't ask me to ignore a master-piece in motion when it's right in front of me. Fuck, you're beautiful,' I breathe when my journey ends on her face. And yep. *Angel.*

Deadly. Determined. Divine. But angelic, nevertheless.

The silky black hair frames her face perfectly as she leans forward, the gun now cupped in her expert hands aimed directly at my heart. I want to tell her to aim it higher. But I hold my tongue.

'Take off your mask,' she orders.

'No can do, sweetheart. You want it off, come over here and do it yourself.'

Her eyes burn unholy fire. 'How stupid do you think I am?'

I smile. 'I don't think you're stupid at all. But this isn't the movies. I'm not going to kneel or beg or dig my own grave or lift a motherfucking finger to make your job easier. So you'll have to satisfy that particular curiosity after you kill me. Besides, if you're just wanting to confirm my identity, I think you already know. So stop with the fucking games, Sofiya.' I say her name softly. With the reverence it deserves, this once, for getting one over on me.

Her breath shakes out. But her finger remains steady and deadly over the trigger as my words and disclosure sink in. 'You know who I am. So I guess my question is, did you really come here to kill my family?'

There's dishonour in lying about *this* of all things. So I don't. 'Yes.'

The gun wavers a little more. A look flashes though her eyes. 'Then I can't let you live.'

Her lips part. She breathes out to steady herself.

Then she pulls the trigger.

3

RAFAELLE

My body jerks, more in surprise than in pain, although the two shots to my chest hurt like the *bejesus*.

When this is over, *if* I make it out alive, I might give her props for pulling the trigger. Not once, but twice. For having the balls to do what it takes to protect her family, even though in the end she'll lose.

For now, I hold my breath, absorb the pain with my eyes shut. And wait. Wait. *Wait*. Thanking fuck I'm wearing a custom-made bulletproof vest that cost me upward for three-quarters of a mil.

Playing dead now is far easier than it was that fateful day six years ago. Back then I was terrified out of my mind, filled with fury and horror because I knew I'd lost her. I screamed for a straight hour afterwards, cradling my mother's lifeless body in the aftermath.

A helluva lot more terrifying things have happened since then, also requiring me to play dead from time to time. But those things have been at my hands.

Things I've had to do as the Enforcer but *on my terms*.

So will this be.

I sense her approach. Hear her juddering breaths as adrenaline leaves her body and the full repercussions of her actions kick in.

Does she regret it? Is she relieved?

She's close enough that I hear her gulping swallow. Smell her sublime perfume carried on the soft breeze.

'I'm not sorry. I'm not sorry,' I hear her whisper under her breath. 'Not for protecting my family. Especially not if I think you're who you are.' Through the tiny slits of my eyes, I see her reach for my mask, still whispering, 'I'm not sor—'

I punch the gun out of her hand.

It skitters across the concrete floor. She yelps in surprise and pain, her mouth gaping in shock. Before she can recover, I jackknife upright and lunge for her.

Her reflexes are impressively sharp.

My fingers graze her arm as she jumps back, slips out of reach.

But the move sends her off balance. I sweep out one leg to knock her off her feet, but she anticipates that too. She backflips so perfectly, I want to stop and applaud. But I want my hands on her more than I want to praise her antics.

Luckily for me, she doesn't know every square inch of this rooftop the way I've learned it. She lands on the uneven floor and for a split second, she's off-kilter again.

I'm on her before she can take her next breath, blocking the punch she aims at my throat. I catch her fist in mine and use her momentum to yank her forward.

She slams against my chest and the sensation of firm softness is divine. But I don't have time to enjoy it. Her other hand shoots out, connects a punch to my jaw.

I shake off the pain. I've suffered way worse, days of torture in unmentionable hell holes.

I capture her other hand easily and within a second the tables have satisfactorily turned. The zip ties I carry in my back pocket come out and I have her secured before she can blink.

Only then do I wrap my arm around her shoulders and pull her back flush against my body. And yes, I'm the filthy bastard who nudges my cock into the small of her back, salivating as the top of her lush ass caresses my balls.

'Ah, *bedda mia*,' I croon in her ear. 'You should've gone with your original plan and shot me in the head. Now look where you are. My captive. Mine to do with as I please.'

She struggles to free herself for a full ten seconds before she stops.

Breathes out. Shoots me a venomous glare over her shoulder. 'You're deluded if you think I'm going to beg for my life.'

'Nor should you, angel. You should only beg for pleasurable things, like my hands around your throat when I fuck you harder than you've been fucked in your life. Or after I've edged you for hours and you can't stand it any more. Only then should you beg. With enough tears running down this pretty face I can lick clean.' The image of it is hot as fuck. And I don't hold back a depraved moan.

She laughs, a delightful but mocking sound that tunnels straight to my cock. 'Are you sure you're not high? Because you seem to be hallucinating things that will never happen.'

'Hmm, we'll see. I am curious though about you not begging for your life. You know why I'm here on this rooftop. And yet you're not asking for me to kill you in place of another member of your family. You love them enough to save them from me but apparently not enough to die in their place, huh?'

I hear her teeth grind, and fractured emotions dart across

her face. 'Fuck you, you know nothing about me. Just get this over with.'

'All in good time. Where were you planning to take me?'

'What?'

'You mentioned other means of taking me out of commission without killing me. That means many things but I'm guessing for you it involved stashing me somewhere until you decided what to do to me. Possibly torturing me for information on what other contingencies I had for your family. You'll take me there.'

I'm watching her closely enough to see her reaction. She gives nothing away. Impressive.

'I have no idea what you're talking about.'

'Take me there,' I repeat, my voice now a deadly blade. 'Or I'll tie you up right here, and you can watch as I finish the job you so rudely interrupted.'

She stills, watching me from the corner of her eye, gauging to see if I mean it.

'Will it help if I counted down from ten?'

'Fuck you.'

'So impatient.' I tut. 'All in good time,' I whisper, right before I give in and draw my lips down the soft skin beneath her ear, letting out the moan that's been building in my chest since she first spoke.

'Jesus. Get the fuck off me,' she snarls, but I catch her shiver. See the way her nipples peak against the stretch of her catsuit.

'Five... four...'

'What happened to counting from ten?' she snaps coldly.

'You wasted it. Two...'

'Fine! I'll... I'll make you a deal.'

'One. Sorry, sweetheart. The window for deals just closed.'

She swallows and I follow the line of her silky throat, saliva pooling in my mouth as hunger rips through me.

The depth and ferocity of it make me frown.

This feels more powerful than mere attraction.

Sure, she's come closer to killing me than anyone else has all my life bar the massacre that took my mother. Yeah, that heightened state of being close to death turns me fucking hard. Always.

One of the other 'points of interest' noted in my file, though that was recorded with more... PG language.

And yes, now I know her identity, the stakes are even deliciously higher.

But I shouldn't be *this* aroused. This keen to fuck. And not just anyone.

Her. The Salvatore nemesis.

And yet... I lean closer, breathing in her scent again.

Fuck, she smells incredible. And she's also confirmed my suspicions of being an amateur. 'You've already blown through the first few essential rules of effectively taking out your enemy. But seriously, don't you know you shouldn't wear identifying scents unless you want to be caught in two fucking seconds?'

She stiffens for a moment, then shrugs. 'What does it matter? I shot you. If not for that vest you're wearing, you'd be dead.'

There's a little snag in her voice at the end of her response that gives her away.

'How many kills do you have under your belt, angel?'

'Enough! I told you not to call me that. Can we get on with whatever this is, please, or do you plan to kill me with chit chat?'

'So eager to die? So eager to show off this insane body to the Grim Reaper?' Okay, why the fuck does saying that make me want to track down the lord of the afterlife and tear him limb from limb?

Did I miss toxic fumes emanating from the cement on this rooftop? Because I must be losing my fucking mind.

She swallows but doesn't speak.

So I go to work. My fingers dive into her hair.

So *silky*. Not enough to make a rope to hold her still while I ram into her, but more than enough to keep her trapped while she swallows my cock.

Down her nape to the collar of her suit.

'What the hell are you doing?' She strains to get away from me.

'Looking for hidden weapons.' I watch her carefully as I speak. 'Or tracking devices.'

Her face remains passive.

She's good.

I shake my head at the trickle of pride and sadness that washes over me. Sofiya Mancinelli would've made a decent assassin with the right training.

Shame she's fucked up tonight and a few flaws that could've been corrected have sealed her fate.

Because, sadly, there's no way I'm letting her go.

Or letting her live.

She delivered herself into my hands like a message from hell. Or heaven. I can finally do what I've bided my time in doing.

Avenge my mother.

* * *

My hands travel down her arms and up again to her armpits.

I follow the line of her body and swallow a groan when I

confirm that yes, my hands indeed *can* span her waist. This fixation would be fucking hilarious if she didn't have serious curves in seriously heart-stopping places.

Hell, she makes Halle Berry look like a stick figure.

My lower lip catches between my teeth when I reach her ass. Firm. Supple. My dick swells thicker when I imagine it between them. Has she ever been fucked in the ass? I would kill to find out.

My pants strain painfully when I drop into a crouch, and from this angle she's even more glorious. 'If you're thinking of using these heels on me, *duci*, think again. Because I won't be best pleased.'

'You're wasting your time. I'm not carrying anything,' she hisses when my hands drag slowly down one leg.

I laugh. 'You could've said that before I started. I wouldn't have believed you but now I *know* you're lying.'

Two seconds later, I hit the jackpot.

In her left boot, an ankle strap containing six lethal-looking sheet-thin throwing knives. In her right, I find something more interesting. A sleek black fob that looks like an electronic key with two tiny buttons.

'What's this for?'

'Nothing you wanna know, asshole.'

'Dammit, that just makes me want to know even more.' I pocket the weapons and fob, then whipping another zip tie from my pocket, I tie her ankles together.

'What the hell?'

Rising, I cup her nape. 'I suggest you stay very still. I'd hate for you to fall and bump your pretty head. I also suggest you don't do anything stupid, like scream. You dressed the way you are is already giving me filthy ideas. Toss in a ball-gag and we'll stray into unchartered territory where your safe word better be on standby.'

She glares holes into me as I stalk over to where I kicked her gun.

I pick it up, examine it and whistle. 'Glock 17 with an expensive suppressor. Not bad, *bedda mia*. Not bad at all. This must have cost you a whole lot of pocket money, especially if you had it custom made?'

At her mutinous silence, I look up.

She's teetering on her feet, struggling with the urge to remain still.

Keeping her in my sights, I go over to where I set up my own gear, quickly break down my sniper rifle and stash it in my bag. I toss her gun in there too.

Bag in hand, I return to her.

I stand close enough that she has to tilt her head up to meet my eyes.

Slowly, I reach for the bottom of my mask and peel it off.

My hair flops into my eyes but I ignore it, more interested in her reaction. As I did with her, she suspected my identity from the Sicilian I dropped into our conversation.

But perhaps, like me, she'd hoped she would be wrong.

Her pupils dilate with part shock, part resignation as she sees me for the first time.

I smile in that way that's terrified many souls in their last moments. Unlike her, I'm a fallen angel of death.

And I fully embrace my role in this life.

'*Ciao, duci*. Shall we start our adventure?'

4

SOFIYA

I barely have a moment to get over my shock of confirming the Enforcer's identity before he's bending low, tossing my bound body over his shoulder.

Dear God.

Rafaelle Salvatore. Not just the Salvatore enforcer but the *Enforcer.*

For the best part of a decade, a name that usually meant little more than the mafiosi's epitome of a 'big scary guy' had gained cult status on the pitch-black areas of the internet and the world.

Before he'd ever carved out a rep as the world's most untraceable assassin very few knew him to be, Rafaelle Salvatore was already a legend. Scarier than Luca Brasi, deadlier than most 'made men' ever dreamed of becoming. He didn't just enforce, he *dismantled.*

He disappeared men without leaving bloodstains behind. Because unlike the brutes who relied on muscle and mayhem, Rafaelle operated on precision, patience, and a terrifying kind of restraint that only made the explosion worse when it came.

As the shadow to his older brother Cesare, he'd never claimed a definitive title, had been seemingly content to assume the usual enforcer role for the ruthless delivery of justice and pain for the Salvatore Organisation. Entire crime families whispered about him like a curse word, a bedtime story gone wrong.

And absolutely no one wants to see the unhinged assassin – the true Enforcer – in their rearview mirror.

I heard the whispers, of course, had gone looking for myself and failed many times.

But I kept going because usefulness is currency in my family. One mistake, one weakness, and they cash you out.

Maybe that's why I kept looking for the Enforcer. Who else to learn from but the best? And I *had* to learn to be better. To carve out something sharp and terrifying in myself so I wasn't disposable.

So no one, not even my grandfather, could look at me and see the lesser daughter. The girl who wasn't born first, or male, or enough.

I didn't want admiration. I wanted immunity.

But never in my wildest dreams did I think...

Shit. I was bluffing before, hoping he'd show his hand one way or another. While fervently praying the most lethal assassin in the world wasn't really on the rooftop a quarter mile away from my family's hideaway house, aiming his rifle at my brother's head.

God, what if I'd been five, ten seconds late?

Would Narciso be dead right now?

I swallow, will myself not to shake as the most sought-after assassin on the dark web walks me off the rooftop, taking me God knows where.

When I got the alert from the mole that I pay eye-watering

sums to keep me informed that the Enforcer was sniffing around my family, I thought... *hoped* it was a cruel joke.

The confirmation that the threat was credible sent me rushing from my hideout in Queens.

I'd spent the past two days utilising my most prodigious skill and analysing every possible place the assassin could hit from, leaving the clever little gadgets that would alert me of suspicious movement within a half-mile radius of my family home.

It'd been a wild shot in the dark, but worth it because I knew the general movements of the bodyguards my father employed. And the fact that since my grandfather attempted to assassinate his own granddaughter and her new husband, none of my sisters were allowed outside after 9 p.m. Having them all in one place helped because I knew the Enforcer would strike here.

When the sensor sounded, my heart dropped through the floor.

Now it's somewhere near my ankles as he carries me off the roof and down several flights of stairs like I weigh nothing.

My dry mouth turns to sawdust as he takes the stairs with the ease of a man confident of his surroundings. Confident the predator has conquered his prey.

'Where are you taking me?' I hate the tremor in my voice and pray he thinks it's because I'm upside down. I squeeze my eyes shut when a wave of dizziness washes over me. But I force them back open. Remain alert.

'Come on now, you know better than that, *duci*.'

I grit my teeth at the lyrical endearment that rolls so smoothly off his tongue. *Duci*. Sicilian for sweetheart. A term for lovers and benign relationships.

Not toxic, decades-old vendetta-craving characters in a macabre play that has seen several members of both our families dead in the ground, some as recently as a year ago, at the wedding of Cesare Salvatore to my older sister, Maddelena.

Bitterness sweeps through the dizziness, souring my stomach.

I'm not sure who I blame more for this – Maddie for deciding that, out of the billions of men on earth, she would fall in love with Cesare Salvatore, first-born grandson of our family's enemy, or my grandfather for the bloodlust he's kept stoked, even though it's ripped our family and countless others apart.

To be fair, Orazio Salvatore holds more than his fair share of the blame.

Between those two bone-headed, old-fashioned men, they've perpetrated the eye-for-an-eye *vinnitta* which shows no signs of dying anytime soon. And conveniently, Nonno has gone into hiding, leaving the rest of us to bear the brunt of his actions.

Would they mourn me or would I become just the latest casualty of their war? If my poor mother dropped dead from the years-long stress she's been carrying, I'm 100 per cent sure my father will barely mourn her for a week before he's back to carrying out Nonno's commands.

My sisters would mourn me. Sure, we're not as close as other siblings, probably on account of the divisive nature and the sheer hell of living under Bonafacio Mancinelli's roof and thumb.

But we don't hate each other. Which is a plus, I guess.

And I'm certainly not the warm and fuzzy type. A plus in my line of work and *essential* in the role Bonafacio dropped me into on my fifteenth birthday.

While other girls were fumbling with makeup and crushes, I was learning how to break bones and fake identities.

From the moment my grandfather realised my ability, my

life's goal was made clear. Every soft edge was to be filed down until I was all blade.

I was different. I was useful. Sentiment was a liability. Empathy was weakness.

Even now, when I catch glimpses of the girl I might've been – laughing freely, trusting easily – I shove her back into the shadows.

Because that girl wouldn't have survived.

And the woman I am? Who lately attempts to flex wings that have long been nailed down? She's still not sure she's allowed to want more than survival.

I drag my morose thoughts from my family to the more dire situation at hand. 'You're going to kill me, aren't you?'

He doesn't reply, but I sense him contemplating the question. Is he pondering how he will do it?

My heart lurches again when I relive squeezing that trigger.

It isn't the first trigger I've pulled.

But it's the first one that's been strictly personal. A decision made with fear and terror in my heart instead of on orders from my father or grandfather. And it's also a kill – a *failed* kill – made without first verifying my victim's identity.

Victim.

I swallow a hysterical snort.

Rafaelle is as far from a victim as Jupiter is from Venus.

'Why didn't you do it on the roof?' I push.

'Too messy, sweetheart,' he rasps.

I lift my head when I realise we've reached the quiet street three streets away from my home.

My sensor went off at 1 a.m., which means it's approaching 2 a.m.

Years ago, Nonno bought all the properties bordering our family home in Connecticut and either gave them to his men who held positions in the family business or razed it to the ground in the name of security.

The advantage was that no one could approach our home without being spotted by security.

The disadvantage was that deadly assassins like the Enforcer could stroll in and out without encountering another soul. The house we've just left belongs... *belonged*... to one of the lieutenants who was brutally massacred by the family of the man holding me prisoner now.

Maybe even *he* did the killing.

Desperation unravels down my spine as I fight the urge to ignore his warning and scream.

'Don't,' he warns, his tone soft and deadly. 'Seriously. Let's not ruin this adventure just yet, *si*?'

I open my mouth to tell him to fuck off. With my ankles and arms bound, my mouth is the only tool at my disposal right now. But he's lowering me to the ground. Next to the electric sports car I drove here.

Another wave of shock cannons through me.

I'm not sure how he found it. I thought I'd hidden it well beneath the weeping willow a quarter mile away. Apparently not.

Shit.

In silence I watch him pluck the fob from his pocket, accurately guessing which one of the buttons opens the car.

He examines it, then arches his eyebrow at me again.

When I don't answer, he pushes me to the ground with a callous shove. I land on my ass in the grass with an *oomph* and glare at him.

Asshole.

Insanely, stupefyingly *hot* asshole, with a body created for death and sin.

My face heats at the recollection of the imprint of his cock against my ass.

The Enforcer is packing a different kind of heat in his pants. The kind destined to leave a woman bow-legged and screaming for God and deliverance while secretly hoping both never come.

He slides behind the wheel of my car and flicks on the interior light.

I can't look away from his profile.

The light shines on his jet-black hair sexily rumpled from the mask he took off. There's a neatly trimmed stubble gracing his strong, square jaw, and his mouth... fuck me, his mouth is made for the dirtiest kind of depravity.

The feel of his hands tracing my body replays for the dozenth time and I have to clench my belly to stop the shiver tickling into being.

To distract myself, I side-eye the bag he dropped ten feet away.

He catches me looking. 'Ask nicely and I might just show you my toys, baby,' he says, his voice far too sexy.

Before I snap a killer response, he turns serious. 'Programming the location of your stash house is amateur, even for you. So I'm guessing it's somewhere you visit often enough not to need a GPS?'

My lips flatten, refusing to dignify his smirking observation with a reply. The bastard is right, and we both know it. I underestimated him. Just a little. I was focused on his body count and his battlefield history, not the fact that he's wickedly clever in that unhinged, whiplash way that makes his smile feel like a blade slipping beneath my ribs.

Above all, I didn't count on him being a *Salvatore*.

He watches me for a moment, quiet, too quiet, then nods – like he's just made a decision I'm not going to like.

'You know,' he says conversationally, 'if I didn't know better, I'd think you *wanted* to get caught. I mean, roof access without a backup exit? Really? I've seen rookies with more survival instinct.' He gestures to the passenger seat. 'Get up. Get in. Or I carry you like a bride, and we both know I'll enjoy that way more than you will.'

I hesitate, then climb to my feet.

I calculate distance, the knives I strapped to the undersides of the driver and passenger seats, how quickly I can free myself from the ties, grab one knife and shove it under his ribs if he blinks wrong.

But the eyes watching me mock my every strategy. He'll come out on top in every scenario and fuck if he doesn't know it.

Revel in it.

His hand taps the top of the passenger door, and he hums a jazz tune under his breath as he waits, all sexy deadliness and maddening calm.

I don't speak. I can't afford to. Not until I know where he's taking me. Then again, maybe I already do.

I drop into the seat, my hands trapped under my ass.

He grins as he secures my seatbelt. And I swear he takes a quick sniff of my hair.

He drives, says nothing for ten minutes, right until we've left my family's compound far behind. Then he pulls over, glances at me with that wolfish grin.

My heart jumps into my throat. He's not going to kill me here.

He's not, he's not, he's—

'I need you conscious, but pliant. Cooperative's too much to hope for this early, I think. But we'll get there, won't we?' He smirks, then his hand lifts, fast and deliberate. I barely have time to scream before his fingers press against a pressure point beneath my ear with surgical precision.

I can only buck against his hold, my heartbeat roaring in my ears as my vision turns dark. Darker.

As the world fades in slow, humming spirals, his voice is the last thing I hear.

'Don't worry, *bedda*. I'll take good care of you.'

5

RAFAELLE

She's laid out like something I stole from heaven and have no intention of giving back on the double bed in my Upstate New York safehouse, lit only by the crackling fire and the low glow from the kitchen.

My phone's been buzzing ever since I turned it on.

I should answer Cesare.

As the Salvatore underboss, he has the right to reasonably demand my whereabouts.

But these aren't reasonable circumstances.

Certainly, my inability to take my eyes off the captive beauty in my bed isn't reasonable. And Cesare... well, he owes me. He knows that. For the better part of a year, I've kept my word. Not harmed a single Mancinelli capo, except the few who've made the error of stepping into Salvatore business.

Sure, I've been tracking Giada Mancinelli's whereabouts, but it's as if she's turned into a ghost. But even ghosts can be hunted down. Eventually. With the right tools. And I'm starting to think I've just found the perfect tool tonight.

Unfortunately for both of us, Cesare is also an unreasonable fuck. Especially with Maddie expecting their baby in the next month.

So I intend to avoid him for a little while longer.

I stare at Maddie's little sister. Attempt not to stroke my cock to the rise and fall of her full chest like the pervert I most definitely could be. Hell, I could even convince myself I've earned it. She did try to kill me, after all.

I shake my head as my thoughts crash into each other.

Her beauty is a study in contradiction – soft curves wrapped around concealed violence, long dark lashes fluttering against high cheekbones, even in unconsciousness.

Deadly. Divine. A little too still, even now.

I checked her for weapons again and still I don't trust that she doesn't have a vial of poison shoved in her pussy or an invisible garrotte wire braided into her hair.

It's kind of turning me on, the possibility that she could wake and try to kill me. Again.

I sit in the armchair across from her, sipping espresso as if I haven't just kidnapped a woman who aimed a gun at my skull less than two hours ago.

Cristu. She tried to kill me.

My pulse spiked for all of two seconds, and then it got... fun.

I've interrogated enemy soldiers, tortured cartel traitors, broken war criminals who screamed for hours. But this? This is delicate. Intimate. Like trying to hold a cobra without getting kissed by its fangs.

I know she's awake before she even opens her eyes – her breathing changes, just a little. That predator stillness tightens in the air.

And then—

'You drugged me,' she spits, sitting up too fast and wincing.

Good. She's disoriented.

I grin around the rim of my cup. 'Nah, you don't remember? It was just a little pressure-point trick. Old army thing. No hangover, no fuss. I'm thoughtful like that. I can teach you if you want?'

She glares at me without speaking but I know her senses are on full alert. Trying to catalogue the room, the exits, *me*. I can practically see her calculating how long she'd last if she lunged for the fireplace poker behind me. The answer? Not long. But I let her keep thinking. Because the longer she plays the game, the deeper she sinks into it. And I'm going to enjoy every second of watching her unravel.

She shifts on the bed like a cat waking from a nap, all grace and veiled danger. Or maybe she knows exactly what she's doing to me, capitalising on her admittedly priceless asset.

Her fucking allure.

I've been pistol-whipped in the past.

I sense I could be in the throes of discovering what it feels like to be pussy-whipped. And I haven't even seen her pussy yet.

Eyes wide open now, those cold, calculating depths already trying to charm, to manipulate. God, I admire her hustle.

'I have places to be,' she says, voice smooth, just a hint of husky from the pressure point knock-out. She shakes a lock of hair off her forehead, glances towards the windows like she's mapping every route out of here. 'You don't want to keep me too long, Salvatore. I'm not exactly low-profile.'

I let the silence stretch, let her think it's working.

Then I set my espresso down and lean back in the chair, smiling like a wolf who just found a rabbit burrow. 'Nice try, *bedda*. But you seriously underestimate me if you think I'm some chump you can sweet-talk. You go off-grid for days without a trace. No calls. No contact. Not even to your sister or that cry-baby brother of yours. You're really poor at that by the way.'

She lifts her chin, eyes glinting. 'Off-grid doesn't mean off-line. Not these days. Aren't you worried someone will come looking for me?'

I grin. 'Really? I hope they do. I'm all for turning this into a party.' I drag my eyes over her, feeling another series of hot throbs when I watch her full, sexy mouth. 'I'll have to insist it doesn't get nasty though, *bedda*. I'm not sure I'm willing to share you with another guy. Not now. Maybe not ever.'

Her eyes widen at my soft, deadly warning.

Then she shifts. One hip juts out, slow, deliberate, showing me her weapons. Showing me she's still in control, even if she's not. 'So what's the plan then? Tie me up, torture me, get your revenge right here? Or in one of those rooms you're keeping as a happy surprise? You going to make me beg, Rafaelle?'

I rise from the chair, slowly, not rushing the moment.

Enjoying it far too much that she's watching me like she doesn't know if I might strike or kiss her.

Maybe both. I cross the room and stop at the edge of the bed where she's stilled now, eyes narrowed, tied hands fisting the blanket like she's debating how fast she can use it as a weapon. I tuck my hands in my pockets and lower my voice.

'I'm prepared to spare Narciso,' I say. Her brows lift, but she doesn't interrupt. 'The women in your family. Hell, even your father if he doesn't make any stupid moves to inconvenience the Salvatores. But only if you give me one thing.'

She waits.

'The location of your sister, Giada.'

She pales a little, then fury and fear fill her eyes for one intense second before she snarls, 'You might as well kill me now because I'll die before I tell you anything about Giada.'

I suspected that, knew from Maddie's own reaction last year that the siblings were fiercely protective of one another. And from what Maddie also said, they might not have any idea where their sister is. Although that might be more lie than truth.

'Fine, then give me El Topo. And I'll think about giving you a reprieve from my wrath.'

It's a short-term win.

Won't bring my mother back, won't satisfy the blood screaming in my bones. But it's a move Cesare can live with.

And right now, my big brother's been calling nonstop, breathing down my neck like the damn Pope waiting for confession.

I need results. I need progress. And maybe, just maybe, I need to see what this lethal, beautiful enemy of mine does when the line between family loyalty and survival starts to blur.

Something flickers in her gaze. Anger, or guilt, maybe both, but she covers it fast. I lean in slightly.

She studies me with those glacier-cut eyes, silent long enough that I almost hear the gears grinding in that beautiful, brutal mind of hers. Then she settles back, a queen reclining against the pillows, like she owns this place, like she didn't wake up ten minutes ago, drugless but stolen, helpless in my bed. At my mercy.

Fuck, the way she's acting, it's like *I'm* at *her* mercy.

Her chin tilts, her mouth curving with mocking sweetness.

'You expect me to believe that killing Bonafacio will satisfy you?' she asks, voice like silk dragged over steel. 'That you'll just... walk away after that? Spare Narciso, spare my sisters, my father, spare *me*?'

I don't answer right away. Let the silence thicken. Let her stew in it.

Finally, I give a small shrug, the kind that says, *You already know the answer*. 'No assurances, *bedda*. None. That's the nature of vengeance. It grows legs. Tends to evolve.' I take a slow step towards her. 'But let's be honest, you're not exactly in a position to bargain.'

She stiffens but doesn't move. I watch her pupils dilate just slightly as I stop a few feet away – close enough to feel her breath start to hitch.

God, she's electric. Like standing too close to a storm and daring it to strike. Her tongue flicks out to wet her lips. It's a reflex, maybe, but it draws my eyes there. My body reacts, and I don't hide it.

'You're bluffing,' she says, voice lower now, not quite so sharp. 'You'll kill him and still come for the rest of us. I know your type, Rafaelle. You're the fucking Enforcer. You don't stop. You burn everything down.'

I chuckle, low in my chest, and crouch slightly, bringing my face to her level, out of headbutt range, but just invading her space like smoke curling through a locked door. 'You're right,' I murmur. 'I don't stop. I don't forgive. And I sure as hell don't forget.'

Her jaw clenches, breath catches. I can see the tremor just beneath her skin. A combination of fear and tension and want tangled with warning.

'But,' I continue, voice softer, crueller, almost gentle, 'even fire has to breathe, Sofiya. Give me your grandfather, and maybe I decide to let the rest of you Mancinellis breathe free air for now. Maybe I let the rest of your world keep spinning.'

She doesn't flinch, but I see it in her eyes, that flicker of doubt, the calculation already shifting.

'And maybe I don't,' I add, smiling darkly. 'But isn't that a risk you're used to taking?'

We hover there, war and want between us, the air thick with it, and I wonder, not for the first time, how something this dangerous could make me feel more alive than war zones ever did.

'I still call bullshit,' she eventually murmurs.

My stubborn, beautiful angel.

'Take your time, you have until I finish taking my shower to give me your answer.' I straighten, then grin. 'Before I go though...'

* * *

Sofiya

I shouldn't be surprised at all when Rafaelle peels off his T-shirt.

But I am. I feel my eyes widen as the breathtaking landscape of inked bronzed flesh is exposed.

Jesus fucking Christ, he's gorgeous.

Mouthwatering.

Furiously sexy with twin silver barbells piercing his male nipples that holds far too much fascination.

God, everything about this man is bending my brain.

Heat punches me sideways, then keeps punching me so hard that I barely hear what he says as he tosses the scrap of fabric away.

'Look what you did to me, baby. Are you going to kiss it better?'

I have to blink a few times – drag my eyes from the deep V framing his pelvis and the sudden need to run my tongue along both lines, feel his blood sing beneath my licks – before I grasp what he's saying.

The area he's drawing my attention to.

The large, palm-sized bruise covering his left pec. Put there by the force of the two bullets fired from my gun into his Kevlar vest.

I stare at the red mark with a mixture of horror and filthy fascination.

Until I notice he's watching me with equal rabid interest. I clear my throat. 'Sure. I'll be happy to use some teeth too, if you like.'

He laughs, and holy fuck me if it isn't the most beautiful sound in the universe. I hate that it settles over me like a warm hug, shoving back the nausea of confronting the damage I've inflicted. Which in itself is absurd. I've never been squeamish about blood, gore or viscera, much less a bruise, albeit an impressive one.

But... he should be livid, digging out the torture tools whispered about on the dark web. Instead he's... he's...

He's toying with me.

To what end?

'What do you want from me?' The words fall out, land heavily between us. We're both aware I'm asking about much more than his bruise. I wish I can take it back. But I can't. So I choose silence.

He stops, his hands still on the bruise over his heart. As I watch, his fingers dig into his skin and he flinches.

It's a slightly sickening act. As if he wants to remind himself of the pain.

I should be revolted by what he's doing. Instead, a different sensation takes hold, curls insidiously through me.

Heat. Curiosity. Elevated heartbeat. *Lust.*

What the hell?

My belly rolls as his hand drops and all traces of humour leave his face. 'Where is your grandfather?'

6

SOFIYA

I shake my head, almost disappointed at the abrupt return to what seems to be his favourite subject. And my least favourite one. But at least he's dropped the subject of Giada. An idea which terrified me for a full minute.

And I won't admit it even under torture, but my grandfather's disappearance hasn't exactly been devastating.

There's a flicker of guilt in that. Shouldn't I feel *something* for the man who taught me to clean a Glock?

But then I remember that he tried to have Maddie, his own flesh and blood, killed *at her own wedding*.

Still... does it make me a monster if I sleep better with him in hiding and silent? Maybe. 'Why do you want him, anyway? I thought... I thought...' I press my mouth shut.

He shrugs. 'Someone should've put him down like the rat he is a long time ago. I volunteer as tribute.'

Fear and fury sizzle through my veins. 'You're right. I should've aimed for your head.'

'Nah, sweetheart. That shit is nasty. There's no coming back from your first head shot. I'm told there's something quite visceral about watching brains splatter all over the floor.'

'What do you care?'

He studies me in silence for a minute. 'How long have you been doing this?'

'Doing what?'

A smile twitches his lips. 'Good answer. You've learned the basics at least. But it's clear you're a sapling. You'll need to go for a head shot at some point but don't rush it.'

'Are you seriously giving me advice right now?'

His smile gains wings and my belly swoops wildly as it soars. Every single one of the Salvatore men are handsome.

Unspeakably so.

But perhaps it's this new discovery of who Rafaelle truly is or this crazy circumstance we're caught in. I can't look away from him.

And the more I look, the hotter my pelvis gets. Until, to my horror, I feel myself getting wet. Slippery. Gushing.

Fuck.

It's a stupidly inopportune time to be reminded I'm a virgin. That as a rule, I despise guys, especially hot-as-fuck guys like Rafaelle Salvatore.

But also... I never really had the chance to rid myself of my V-card.

From fifteen, my body was trained for kill shots and leverage, not pleasure. It became a weapon before it was ever allowed to be a sanctuary or a thing of pleasure. A thing to be worshipped and adored by a man worthy of it.

And trust? That's a currency I never learned to spend. You don't undress in front of someone who might put a knife in your back five minutes later. Or worse, expect something in return.

Then there was Bonafacio. My grandfather made it clear that women were meant to be pawns or property. He once told me love was a leash, or worse, a death sentence, and I believed him.

So no, I've never been touched in a way that wasn't tactical. Never been kissed without calculating the angle of escape. I've never let myself want.

Until now.

I battle through the disarming sensation and focus on what he said. *...at some point but don't rush it.* That alludes to a future scenario that precludes me being killed by the Enforcer. Despite everything he said before, I didn't think he really meant to let me live beyond tonight.

But now...

He wants to find my grandfather. A man as talented and resourced as the Enforcer doesn't need me for that, but if he thinks he does... if keeping me alive is a subconscious thing, I don't want to draw his attention to it. Maybe the idea needs to steep a little before becoming a reality. For both of us.

'What do you mean by "I'm told"?' I ask instead. 'Did you not feel it the first time you... umm... did that?'

'*Did that?*' he mocks with another grin. 'No, *duci*, I did not. I tend to go for whichever way downs my target the quickest. Unless I want them to suffer. Then a gut shot works a treat. Or disembowelment with my favourite hunting knife.'

I wait for the nausea to return. For horror to arrive at the nonchalant way he discusses taking a life. But... it doesn't.

My breath catches all over again. Am I... am I like him?

I shake my head. No. No, I'm not. 'You actually enjoy it, don't you?'

He seems to think about it for a moment, his hand absently returning to the bruise. Once again, his fingers dig in, prodding the contusion. 'Enjoy it? No. Perfect my skill so I'm the most proficient I can be? Absolutely.'

'So you grew up thinking, "I want to be the most proficient killer I can be"?'

He saunters over to where I'm laid out, his bare feet, bare chest, taking up too much room, too much of my oxygen.

My breath snags somewhere on its way to exhaling when his fingers slide into my hair to cup the back of my head. His fist slowly tightens, and I wince from the discomfort as he drags my head up to meet his gaze.

The glint in his eyes is almost manic and I know I've pressed a specific, possibly deadly button.

'No, *duci*, I had a different set of dreams entirely, but my sweet, lovely innocence was ripped away from me. So I did what Salvatores have been doing since the dawn of time. I rolled the fuck with it until I came out on top.'

There's a solemn mournfulness to his voice, but weirdly I sense he's not inviting sympathy.

He's simply stating a truth.

Before I can respond, his gaze rakes my face, settling on my mouth. Sizzling. Assessing. 'You owe me a kiss-it-better, baby.'

My throat moves in a swallow in readiness to tell him to fuck off. But the words remain locked deep inside. My own gaze drops to the bruises over his heart. This close, the skin is livid, stark even against his bronzed skin. And next to that, his flat nipple is pebbling.

He draws me close. *Closer.*

My breath feathers over his skin and I watch goosebumps break out over his chest. I've never had a great fascination for male nipples, but watching my captor's harden beneath my gaze, the flesh around his areola rising in a constellation of bumps makes my thighs clench.

'Remember, no teeth. Or there will be consequences.'

'Will you let me go if I kiss it?'

'Fuck no,' he growls. 'But it'll be a start of... something.'

'Something in my favour?'

'Kiss it and find out,' he replies.

My gaze drops back to the bruise.

He cradles my head in the palm of his hand, a nod towards mercy or violence. One snap and I'm dead.

But he doesn't push me into obedience. He wants me to do it.

Or refuse.

My heart beats faster until it's a roar in my ears. My body seems to lurch closer of its own volition. I smell his skin, a hint of sweat and man and nothing else. I'm reminded of his admonition of wearing a scent to a job.

He's wearing nothing and yet the headiness of him hits me like a wrecking ball. I want to bury my nose in that succulent divide where one muscle pack separates from the other.

I force myself to concentrate on my destination.

The bruise I put over his heart with bullets from my gun.

An unexpected wave of gratitude and relief wash over me. That I didn't kill him. I might well live to regret it sometime in the near future. But for now...

I brush my lips over the sore... *hot*... spot. Feel his fingers convulse in my hair as he hisses. Empowered by that reaction, I repeat it, lingering a little longer this time, my mouth on his skin. Another hiss. A clench of his pecs.

A rush of pleasure arrows through me.

I part my lips and this time stay for one, two, three seconds. Then tease my tongue over the starburst that must have been agony.

Agony he withstood while playing dead.

I lick him again, barely bite back a moan at the taste and texture of his salty, warm skin.

'Fuck yeah,' he breathes when my tongue catches the edge of his nipple.

I look up. He's staring at me with an untamed look in his eyes.

I don't know what comes over me.

Call it madness. Recklessness.

Maybe at the back of my mind, I don't rate my chances of leaving this place alive and subconsciously want to hasten my end.

Whatever.

My eyes remain locked on his as I part my lips wider, swipe my tongue over him once more. Then... snag the bruise between my teeth.

Bite down. *Hard*.

'Fuck!' His hand drops from my hair and he staggers back a step. I'm yanked forward by my teeth until I'm forced to release him. The taste of leather and salt is still on my tongue. I stare in part horror, part fascination, *all horny, pre-orgasmic desperation*, at the teeth marks I've added to the bruise.

A part of me celebrates the idea that he'll bear my marks for a least a week, maybe longer. Long after he's tortured and killed me and put me in the ground.

I'm not even sure why my gaze drops lower when I should be watching his face, his hands, anticipating his next move even though there's very little I can do.

But when I do, and when I spot the thick bulge in his pants, the bulge growing thicker at my fascinated stare, a fractured moan escapes me.

I can feel his coiled tension, still taste him in my mouth,

hear the low groan that rumbled out of him like it startled even *him*.

Jesus, I was meant to soothe the bruise, show the tiniest act of contrition. Instead... I *bit* him?

Rafaelle is still standing over me, chest heaving, eyes locked on me like he's trying to decide whether to fuck me or finish me off.

The Kevlar vest that saved him lies on the floor next to the chair he was sitting on, and I know his weapons are nearby too.

With my ankles still bound, and the ties on my wrists replaced with metal cuffs – presumably when I was asleep – I'm a sitting duck if he decides to end everything now.

He looks down at me, a wild glint behind his eyes, his lips curling into something sharp.

'Jesus, *bedda*,' he rasps, voice low, nostrils flaring, full of heat and warning. 'That mouth of yours is a liability. You ever bite me like that in a different context...' He leans in, slides one hand between my clamped thighs. 'You better be ready to deal with the consequences.'

My breath stutters.

I *should* look away.

Should say something cutting, regain the high ground. But I don't. Can't. I just watch him, every nerve in my body humming with confusion and heat. 'You – you said to kiss it,' I manage, my voice thinner than I want it to be.

He laughs, the sound dark and rough. 'Didn't say *maul* it, *tigra*.' His gaze flicks over my face, hungry, unsettled. 'You trying to get yourself punished? Or are you just reckless by nature?'

I don't answer. My mind is spinning with too many variables, too many consequences.

What the hell is wrong with me?

He's still watching me like I'm something he can't quite

figure out. Then he exhales through his nose and shakes his head, like he's trying to break a spell. 'You've gone and done it now, baby.'

'What are you talking about? Done what?'

He grins, lopsided and lethal. 'Need a fucking minute,' he mutters, and he turns, walking towards the door on the other side of the room.

I collapse back on the bed, pulse pounding, body aching in all the wrong and right places. The flesh between my legs throbs with a tension I've never known, sharp, frustrating and utterly humiliating.

Seriously, what the fuck is *wrong* with me?

And worse – did he *like* it? Because if he did... what else would he like?

The thought sizzles through me. I'm a virgin. A trained killer. I've broken bones, sliced arteries, looked evil men in the eye while they bled out. But *this*? This game between us?

If Rafa doesn't kill me first... I'm not sure I'll survive him either way.

The sound of running water yanks me from my thoughts.

My breath catches when I realise he left the door open. A bathroom door that swings open and *stays* open. On purpose.

Because of course it is.

I tell myself it's because he wants to keep an eye on me, but even I don't believe that. The Enforcer is unhinged enough to get a kick out of... whatever this new game is.

I lie here, still restrained, my body buzzing from too many things I can't name.

Don't look. You don't need to look. He wants you to. Maybe.

Which is exactly why I *won't*.

But my eyes betray me the second I hear the low, unmistakable groan.

God... he's not. Is he?

The glass is fogged just enough to blur the details, but not enough to hide the shape of him. The hints of sculpted back and tapered waist. Of an ass carved from marble and mouthwatering enough to make my fingers spasm.

One hand rises, braces on the tile wall, and even though his back is turned, I've watched enough porn and TV shows to know the other is working himself in slow, sure strokes, the timing between the back and forth estimating his impressive length.

My thighs clench and I gasp before I can stop myself.

Don't fucking look!

He groans, and the sounds of Rafaelle Salvatore's fist working his cock crests over the water and fills the room.

His head tips back under the spray. His mouth parts. Another groan, this one rougher, darker. My whole body tightens with heat.

'You planning to keep watching or just memorising the sounds?' His voice, low and rough, cuts through the steam.

My mouth goes dry even as my face flames. 'I wasn't watching,' I snap.

He laughs, a low, satisfied sound. 'Liar,' he says, turning just enough that I catch the flex of his forearm, the ripple of muscle down his inked back. 'I can *feel* your eyes on me. Normally I need a minute to get in the zone, but knowing you were watching... *fuck, bedda.*' He shakes his head slowly. Pins me with his dark brown, deeply unstable gaze. 'Keep watching, baby.'

As if I can tear my eyes away. Sweet holy heaven. Save me.

Or not. In one unhinged thought I know I'll fight... *kill* anyone who tried to stop this.

'*Sì,* just like that,' he rasps, eyes locked on me. His arm works faster. *Faster.* 'Just like that.'

My pussy spasms, weeping with an alien emptiness, while my nipples protest their pain and lack of attention. For years I've convinced myself I'm missing nothing special by batting away male attention. Hell, even going as far as to teach a few assholes the meaning of *no means no*.

'Nothing special' is smashed to smithereens as my depraved would-be executioner uses me for his visual pleasure as he jacks off. As I lie there, needy and powerful and pissed off and enthralled, my hips commencing shadow rolls, chasing a high that is destined to be thwarted.

'Fuck,' he groans. Spins so his back is to the wall, the water hitting his powerful throat as he throws his head back, his eyes never leaving mine. '*Fuck!* I'm going to come so hard for you, *duci tigra.*'

He seems to choke on his own words, then his jaw sags on a gasp.

Then with a savage roar, Rafaelle's body spasms as he unloads, grunting and groaning for a full minute.

And hell save me, it's the most beautiful, hypnotic string of music I've ever heard, accompanied by a visual of steam and man so stunning I couldn't look away if a nuclear countdown commenced next to my face.

I'm so caught it in it doesn't even occur to me to make a move. Attempt escape. I'm lying there, stifling my gasps, when he steps out of the shower a moment later, towel loose around his hips, droplets clinging to his chest like he's straight out of a sin-soaked fever dream.

My face flames higher, hot enough to burn. I want to disappear. Dive into the mattress and never come back out. *God.*

He catches my eyes and grins. 'You be my good girl and I promise you'll get yours too, *bedda.*'

I swear, I've never wanted to kill or kiss someone more.

7

SOFIYA

'You're an animal.' A little too late to hide behind insults, but it's all I have.

'*Sì*. And it also looks like I'm an exhibitionist.' His head tilts in contemplation. 'Guess I'm learning new things about myself.'

I grit my teeth at his nonchalance. I'll bet my Cayman Island nest egg that Rafaelle Salvatore knows *exactly* who he is. What his role is in this insane life we both exist in.

'I need the bathroom,' I announce, even though the need is manageable for now. Not so manageable is how wet and sticky I am. How infuriatingly turned on, all it'll take is a whisper of a touch to make me explode.

He watches me for a moment, and I think he's going to call bullshit, but he nods. His eyes settle on the cuffs. Then on my attire.

Without speaking, he turns and heads to his closet and returns with a black shirt. It looks expensive.

A dress shirt with long sleeves and pearl buttons. The kind of power shirt men like my father wear to business meetings. Par for the course for a billionaire gangster.

'There's minimal trust between us so for now I'm going to help things along, *sì*?'

There he goes again with hints at the future. I try not to react to it even though my heart jumps. 'What does that mean?'

'It's means you stay tied while I undress you—'

'Fuck no.'

'Or you stay in bed,' he finishes as if I didn't speak.

'Look, Salvatore...'

His slow strangling of his shirt until his knuckles turn white whittles away my response.

He's visibly struggling with something. Something big and ugly and terrifying.

After a moment he exhales, then grimaces. 'Call me Rafaelle. Or Rafa. Salvatore makes me think you're referring to my father. Or my grandfather. Or any of my uncles or brothers. Thinking you are makes me imagine your mouth and your teeth on one of them. The same mouth you just put on me. The mouth I imagined sucking my cock just now. And, newsflash, it drives me a little nuts, *capisci*?'

My mouth has dropped open.

Something wild and electric is moving through me at the blatant display of rampant, unhinged jealousy on his face. 'But... that doesn't make sense,' I stammer anyway. Even though very little makes sense at this point.

He exhales noisily. 'Let's establish a baseline of trust, *tigra*. You know who I am and have a fair idea of one or two things I can do. Be assured you have very little inkling of the full extent of my role in this life. But I will never lie to you. I'll withhold a fuck lot of things which will probably drive you insane and make you want to bite me some more. Probably want to kill me too. But until we decide which way things go, you have my word on uncut honesty. In return, when I ask you to take a thing seriously, I never, ever don't mean it. Now, are we doing this or do you want to lie in bed and piss yourself?' he asks, blithely ignoring my shock. 'I'll be surprised as fuck, but I promise I won't judge you. Different kinks for different folks and all that.'

It's my turn to draw frantic oxygen. Hope for clarity of thought.

Remind myself that he knocked me out, yes, but he carried me in here, patiently waited for me to wake up and did it all without touching me inappropriately. And call me insane, but that little speech just now? As much as some parts were batshit crazy, I believe him. For the most part.

Whether out of some warped sense of unstated assassin's creed bullshit, I don't want to question.

My gaze flicks up to meet his. 'Fine. Go ahead.'

His nostrils flare briefly, then he places one knee on the bed. He produces the keys to the cuffs and places it next to my pillow.

Then he reaches for the fastener to my suit.

The sound of the lowering zipper fills the room.

His eyes stay on mine long after it's stopped at my navel. Heating. Heating. *Sizzling*.

Then they drop.

He slowly parts the sides of the suit without touching my skin and I watch a near feral expression flicker over his face. 'You always go on a job not wearing a bra?' There's a deadly edge in his voice. A resurgence of that neon-green jealousy. Making my tightening nipples turn pebble hard.

'What's it to you?' I taunt, ignoring the husky throb in my voice. The low simmering in my pelvis. The plumping of my pussy as he keeps parting my suit, baring me to his livid gaze.

'You better be wearing fucking panties, *duci*,' he warns, the shimmer of madness now in his voice too.

That manic light flashes once more and I almost regret the

scrap of fabric getting steadily drenched between my legs. Because that insane *something* that made me bite him wants to see his reaction to seeing me without panties.

He finishes parting my suit with a little less care and he exhales audibly when he sees my black thong. He stares at my body for an age before he reaches for the key. He frees one hand and draws the suit off my arm before freeing the other.

The cuffs go back on before he repositions himself at the bottom of the bed and peels the catsuit over my hips and down my legs.

He tosses it away and settles back on his legs.

'You're fucking breathtaking.' His voice is low, thick with savage hunger he's done pretending to hide.

Dark eyes rake over me, slow and deliberate, like he's memorising every inch of skin, every shiver. There's a roughness to his tone now, a raw edge that sends a jolt straight through my core. He steps closer, heat radiating off him in waves. 'I can't wait to fuck the hell out of you,' he murmurs, gaze locked on mine. 'No games, no weapons, just your tight body wrapped around mine, giving in.' There's no mistaking the promise in his voice – or the restraint he's barely holding on to.

It's the third time he's given me hope, and I can't stop myself. 'Does that mean you don't plan on killing anytime soon?'

He drags his gaze from where it was fixed between my legs. I'm thankful the thong is black so he can't see how wet I am. How turned on by the need in his eyes. He can probably smell me, but I can't help that.

Those eyes are almost unfocused when they rise to stop at my breasts, linger on my gem-hard nipples before locking on mine. He breathes out long and hard. 'That, *duci*, is entirely up to you.'

'What does that mean?'

He grabs the shirt without answering and goes through the process of feeding my arms through the sleeves before he folds them back so I'm not drowning in it.

I sit up properly for the first time in *hours* and sway with mild dizziness.

'Bathroom,' he says.

He grips my arm, helps me up.

It crosses my mind that now is a good time to break free and make a run for it. But I have no idea where I am and I'm 100 per cent sure the Enforcer has dozens of contingencies in place to thwart any attempt I make.

He leads me to the bathroom and over to the toilet.

My face flames as he drags my thong down to my knees. Then, to my surprise, he turns and walks out of the bathroom and shuts the door behind him, leaving me to do my business.

* * *

Rafaelle

The call connects on the third ring.

'*Finally.*' Cesare's voice crackles through the line, tight and sharp. 'I was about five minutes from sending the capos to drag your ass out of whatever hole you've crawled into.'

I lean against the window ledge of the hideaway. The air outside is blue with the hush of impending rain, a storm pressing at the horizon. But it could be the apocalypse for all I take note.

My gaze doesn't move from the bathroom door.

I saw her surprise when I left her alone to use the facilities. Even if she could miraculously contort those killer curves between the bars of the bathroom window, the sheer drop beneath it will kill her. So it's a good thing I've got state-of-the-art alarm bells and whistles to alert me of a breach.

'Rafa,' Cesare snaps.

'Busy week,' I say.

Understatement of the fucking millennia.

'You don't answer for two days straight, not even to tell me you're alive, and all you have to say is *busy week*?' His voice edges from irritated to genuinely strained. 'Rafa, Maddie's not sleeping because of the baby and worrying about whether El Topo's going to pop his fucking rat head out of the woodwork and try something. You ignoring your phone isn't helping.'

A pinch forms in my chest. Guilt, maybe. The real kind. Not the lazy sort I usually let drift through me before brushing it off. 'I'm alive,' I tell him. I look down at the bruise that's beginning to purple and fuck if I don't feel a punch of *something*. Elation? Pride? 'Mostly intact. Can't promise anyone else is.'

'You're being cute.' His tone turns colder. 'I'm not laughing.'

My own tension ratchets higher. 'Wasn't cracking jokes, *frate*. And I didn't ask you to.'

He exhales slowly. The scrape of a chair on tile comes through the line. He's sitting down now. Tired. Probably rubbing that spot above his brow like he does when the pressure builds behind his eyes. 'Where the hell are you, Rafa?'

'Upstate. Lying low. Watching some things unfold.'

'Lying low like recon, or lying low like cleaning blood out of your fingernails?' There's suspicion now. Familiar. Brotherly. Sharp as a blade just before it's sunk into someone's gut.

He knows me too well. A blessing and a curse.

I pause too long. Cesare picks up on it like a wolf scenting blood. 'What the fuck is going on?' he snaps. 'Don't lie to me.'

'I'm not,' I say, which technically isn't a lie. 'It's... complicated.'

'Fuck, tell me you didn't go after Narciso?' His voice drops, suddenly low, deadly quiet. '*Rafaelle.* Tell me you didn't make a move without a family green light.'

'Fuck you. I didn't kill anyone,' I reply.

'Not what I asked.'

I drag a hand down my face. 'Look, we agreed I would let things be. This is me, letting things be. But if you must know, I have... someone who might be useful. Temporary leverage.'

'Someone?' Cesare is silent for a beat too long. 'Jesus. Don't tell me it's *her.*'

I don't respond.

His breath comes out ragged, furious. 'Fucking hell, Rafa. Tell me you didn't kidnap Maddie's *sister*? You were supposed to watch her. Report back. Nothing fucking else.'

'You act like I'm a puppet dancing to your strings. Am I?' I let him catch the glint of the blade in my voice. He knows what that means. Hell, he's wielded it via me for the *famigghia* countless times.

And that's the crux, isn't it? He was born to lead. Groomed, primed, anointed. I was born to follow orders. Clean up the mess and be the blade, never the hand holding it.

I gladly accepted that role. Went the extra mile to create a niche for myself so it mattered more. So it didn't feel like the spare was just a simple, ordinary tool but an exceptional one.

And whether my brother likes it or not, I also remember the vow I made at Mama's grave – that I wouldn't rest until she was avenged.

So what the fuck are you doing, making deals with Sofiya Mancinelli?

'Just... make it make sense a little? If for nothing else so Orazio doesn't cut off my balls when I have to explain it to him.

He already blames me for how lax I am with you breaking ranks, especially more than usual these days.'

I snort but not altogether kindly. Because it is partly Cesare's fault. Granted, he's protecting his wife and the siblings Maddie loves, but still... I can't help if I'm deeply aggrieved it's at the cost of my rightful and righteous *vinnitta*. 'Long story short? She came after me first. I practised restraint and spared her life. You're welcome.'

'Oh, well done. That'll look great on the family Christmas card.' He's yelling now.

Icy fury rolls through me, an avalanche of packed emotions crackling, seeking a trigger to rain carnage. 'You calling me a *quarara*, black pot? Didn't you throw out the rule book with some outlandish shenanigans with the sister you now call wife?'

'And look how close I came to blowing everything up. We barely came out the other side alive. You *know* what kind of shit that could stir up!'

'You don't think we're long past stirring? El Topo flipped on the fucking woodchipper when he tried to blow your head off in front of your wife at your own wedding,' I snap, pulse spiking. 'Don't act like I'm the unhinged one here.'

'She's pregnant, Rafa. *Pregnant*.' His voice breaks around the edges, raw in a way I haven't heard since the day we buried Mama. 'And yes, every day that bastard walks free, I wonder if he's out there planning to finish the job. But you holding Maddie's sister hostage is just gasoline on the fire.'

'Which is why I'm going to find him,' I bite out, straightening at the sound of water turning on in the bathroom.

'What?'

'I didn't stutter, brother. It's either I find Giada for the answers I need or go after El Topo. And I know how you feel about me looking for the sister.' *Forgiveness, not permission,* I affirm silently.

'Go after El Topo,' Cesare growls, as I knew he would, but after a beat, he adds, 'Are you sure it's for the family or because you're pursuing your own ends?'

'Fuck you, *stronzu.*'

The silence between us stretches, thin and dangerous. I can feel his eyes on me even through the call, that old steel-cut gaze he used to give me when we were kids – when I took extra glee in rearranging some shithead's face or took a beating from Orazio meant for him.

What the fuck are you doing, Rafa?

He'd never understood then that I welcomed the pain, and still doesn't. That violence brought an inexplicable high. One I've accepted I'll chase for the rest of my time on this earth. That it's the only thing that ever made me feel real, more than a shadow behind Cesare, more than the spare son with nothing but blood on his hands.

'You and Nonno asked me to keep an eye on her. Things have fallen this way. Besides, she might be the only way to Bonafacio,' I say at last. 'So unless you've got a better plan, maybe don't burn the only lead we've got.'

Cesare doesn't speak. I hear the subtle sounds of him pulling himself back, checking the rage, tucking it behind the mask he wears so well.

Finally, he asks, 'What's the status on the dock shipment? And the Romano deal?'

'Dock shipment's delayed. Romano's waiting for the go-ahead on product out of New Jersey.' I rattle it off because I'm still me. Still efficient. Still loyal. That part of us doesn't get to break, no matter what chaos surrounds the rest. I give him a full update on the Turks, Armenians and the new unexpected angle developing with the Triad.

'Let's go slow with the Triads. Those fuckers are nuts, and yeah, I know saying that to you is exactly as ridiculous as it sounds but—'

'Yeah yeah, I get it. And stop calling me names. You're hurting my feel—'

I stop when hear it then – the soft click of the bathroom door opening. My head turns instinctively.

Sofiya steps out. Damp hair. Wearing my shirt. Caution and calculation in her every movement like a panther pretending not to stalk.

Fuck she's sexy. And that little bathroom scene is going to feature in top billing on my spank bank list for all eternity. Unless I replace it with something even hotter.

Goals and aspirations, for the win.

Cesare hears it too.

His voice drops. 'Is she there?'

'*Sì.*'

'Watch your back, *frate*. You're a fucking shithead pain in my ass, but I'd hate to lose you.'

'She's not a threat right now.'

'She's *a Mancinelli*, Rafa. They're always a threat.'

I don't bother to call out the obvious because to Cesare, Maddelena is now a Salvatore, not a Mancinelli. In his eyes, his beloved has changed her every spot, from the inside out.

A year on from their Godfather-carnage-like wedding day, I haven't made up my mind whether I pity my brother or envy the sheer balls on the fucker. A little from column A. A little from column B.

There's a pause. Just breathing, and that old, choking space between us where Mama's memory used to fit like a jagged tooth. One you worried with the tip of your tongue while nursing it like a loving friend.

'She'd have hated this, you know,' Cesare says quietly, intuitive as fuck. 'You and me on opposite ends of a mess like this. Especially over *them*.'

I close my eyes. 'Yeah. And fuck being opposite. We're just—'

'She made you promise to stay in control.'

Ah, now we're in big guns territory. I don't tell him I've got the biggest guns in any room. 'I'm in control,' I say, keeping my voice easy.

'No, you're in denial.' Another pause. Then, 'Come home soon, *frate*.'

He hangs up before I can answer.

Sofiya's watching me like she can read everything in my face. Every crack. Every shake of my carefully kept foundation. And maybe she can.

Because for the first time, I wonder if the pulse, the fire, the maddening need to keep her close, is what Cesare felt when he was chasing Maddie.

But no. I shut that shit down hard.

I'm not him. And this Salvatore sure as hell won't fall for another Mancinelli.

One was bad enough.

Two is... well, psychotic. And I should know.

According to my military file, I'm the biggest motherfucking psychotic this side of the planet.

8

RAFAELLE

'First things first,' I say, clicking my phone off and slipping it into my back pocket. 'Get back into bed.'

She crosses her arms. 'That your way of avoiding telling me who you were talking to?'

I arch a brow, closing the distance between us with slow, deliberate steps. 'It wasn't your name on the screen, was it, *picciridda*?' My tone dips low, the leash on my control back in my fist. 'So I suggest you don't make it your business.'

She hesitates. That fire in her eyes still simmers, but I can see the tight coil of awareness in her body, how every inch of her is wound up, tense and alert. Her tongue wets her lower lip before she finally turns away from me, climbs back into the bed without another word.

Good girl.

I fasten the cuffs to the headboard again, just tight enough to remind her where she is. Who she belongs to, for now.

'I'm giving you a timeframe and a truce,' I say as I pull up a chair beside the bed. 'For six races starting with Monaco next week. Ending in Silverstone. That's about two months, give or take.' My gaze rests on hers. 'That's how long you have to make yourself useful.'

She sits up straighter, cuffs pulling faintly as her wrists shift above her. Her expression is pure steel. Controlled. Regal. Like the bratty princess she was born to be. Like the killer she became instead.

I feel myself scale another rung of fascination. My cock, once again at half-mast, thickening. Eager for the green light to *go go go*.

'Useful how?' she asks.

'You help me find Bonafacio. You make calls, drop hints, open old doors. You cooperate. And if you do that...' I lean in, close enough that our breaths mingle. To see her pupils dilate deliciously at our proximity. Fuck, she smells incredible. 'No one dies. Not you. Your sisters. Not Narciso. Not your father. Not even that distant aunt of yours who runs that overpriced vineyard on the Sicilian coast.'

'And if I don't?' she asks, her voice low.

I smile. 'Then I stop giving a fuck about collateral.'

But she doesn't flinch.

She tilts her head, her eyes sharp. 'Who signed off on this, *Enforcer*? The heir? Does Maddie know about this? That I'm here? Or are you going rogue again, chasing shadows and dragging me along for the fallout?'

Straight from my conversation with Cesare, that pisses me off.

I lean back slowly, the heat in my chest flaring as I drag my tongue across my bottom lip, keeping myself in check. 'Watch your mouth, *picciridda*. Just because I haven't gagged it doesn't mean I won't.'

She narrows her eyes, reading me. Calculating. 'You really expect me to play your little sidekick for two months without knowing who the hell gave you the green light to abduct me? You think the Mancinellis are going to look the other way when they realise you've got one of *them* shackled to your bed?'

I laugh, low and dirty. 'Careful, Sofiya. You sound like you're worried I'll get in trouble. Haven't you lot had your asses kicked enough for a lifetime? I know to a rounded-up dozen how many active soldiers you have these days. Shall I embarrass us both by stating the figure?'

Her fury intensifies but colour stains her cheeks. She *is* embarrassed by the state her grandfather left them in.

But that's not all.

'Or is this about something else? Is this your way of asking if you'll be staying in my bed the whole time?'

She huffs, eyes sparking with rage and something hotter underneath. 'That wasn't a question.'

'No?' I rise from the chair, slow and deliberate, letting her see every inch of control I'm wielding. 'Because the way you're looking at me? It's not like someone who wants to be cut loose. It's like someone who's curious if next time... she'll still be cuffed. Is bondage your thing, *tigra*?' I lick my lips, slowly. To rile her, yes, but fuck, because I want to taste those lips more than I want my next kill. And that's saying something. It's been too fucking long since my last one. I vow to change that. *Soon*. I need something to take the edge off.

Her breath catches just a little. Barely noticeable, unless you're trained to catch weakness mid-strike.

I lean closer, hands on the bed, towering over her as she glares up at me.

'You've got eight weeks, *bedda*. Be smart. Be useful. And maybe, just maybe, you'll walk out of this with your pride intact and your family breathing.'

Then I lean in, my mouth brushing her ear.

'Or maybe you'll still be in my bed. Legs open. Wrists free. And begging me to make you forget you ever doubted how fucking serious I am when it comes to pursuing my goals.'

She doesn't answer. But she's not looking away either.

Good.

Let the fire burn.

* * *

Sofiya

It's sick that a part of me wants to test that edge. To see how far he'd really go. To feel that sharp blade of danger press a little closer. But my body betrays me with every shallow breath, every flutter in my chest.

I nod once. 'Six races.'

It's not surrender, I tell myself. It's strategy.

A notion dressed as compliance, buying myself time. Time to study him, to locate weaknesses in his armour and in his obsession. Time to plan for what comes after the truce ends, when one of us will have to choose between blood and betrayal. And if I play it right, he won't see the knife until it's already in his back.

'Smart girl. You hungry?'

'No.' It's a gut reaction. Truth is, I don't remember when I last ate. Hunting down the Enforcer on the dark web and chasing him down to within a mile of my family's compound will drain anyone's appetite.

He rises anyway, walks over to the small kitchenette and returns with a plate.

It's not fancy. It's some bread, figs, cured meat, olives, and a wedge of cheese, a bottle of water and... two candy bars. My favourite.

Because, of course.

It's arranged with a care I wouldn't have expected from a killer. But he's the Enforcer. Meticulous to the last.

'You should eat,' he says casually as he sets the tray on the nightstand. 'You've had a rough few hours. Can't have you passing out before the fun begins.'

'You mean more threats?'

'I mean,' he says with a grin, his fingers brushing over a slice of prosciutto, 'you're going to need your strength. For plotting. Scheming. And maybe a few other things.'

His voice dips on that last part, laced with heat, but it's what comes next that disarms me.

He glances at me, a flicker of something – *not* hunger this time – passing across his face. 'You got the same thing your sister has? The low blood sugar thing?'

I blink.

That... I didn't expect. Not that I'm surprised he knows.

'I know Maddie's hypoglycaemic,' he adds when I don't answer. 'She gets faint if she doesn't eat properly. Had a scare once, a few days before the wedding. Cesare lost his fucking shit.'

There's a pause. One beat too long. He's watching me, waiting.

I could lie. Could say no just to avoid the deceptive softness in his tone. That strange, unwelcome undercurrent of *concern*. It's a ploy. Has to be. But the truth slips out anyway, because it's just instinct. 'Yeah. Mine's milder than hers but it's genetic.'

He gives a small nod. 'Then eat.' He reaches for the sandwich, tears a piece of bread and cheese and holds it out. I shake my head, stare pointedly at the candy.

He smirks. 'Clever girl.'

Rafa unwraps it and I take it, more out of irritation than obedience.

He doesn't press the point. And somehow, that unsettles me more. Because for a split second, he stopped being the devil dragging me into his twisted war and started looking like someone who *noticed*.

Someone who cared enough to *ask*.

I chew slowly, keeping my gaze anywhere but on him. The food looks good, annoyingly so, because I know given the same set of ingredients, nothing *I* do will come out like this. But I stick to the candy.

And my body, traitorous as ever, is grateful. My stomach unclenches. My head clears a little.

But I shove the rest of it down. That flicker of warmth? It means nothing. It's just strategy. The same way you feed a hunting dog before unleashing it again.

He wants me strong so I can perform. For his mission. For his revenge.

That's all I've ever been good for, isn't it? Strategy. Precision. Calculated violence. I see threats before they move and I neutralise them without flinching. It's why my father kept me close, why my grandfather trained me, a woman, harder than his own capos and lieutenants.

Is this why Rafaelle hasn't killed me yet? Because I'm *useful*?

Just... a weapon with a pulse? No one spares a thought for just me.

Dammit, if I let myself think too long about what that means, about what it feels like to be needed only when there's blood in the water and a kill order on the table, then the steel I've built around myself might start to crack.

He tears a piece of the candy and brings it to my lips. I hesitate, just long enough for his eyes to narrow in warning, before opening my mouth. The salty chocolate melts on my tongue, and I hate that it tastes like something I'd crave again.

Another bite follows, his fingers brushing my lower lip as he feeds me. I feel heat uncoiling low in my belly, unwanted and wicked, and I curse myself for the flicker of a moan I don't manage to hold in.

He hears it. Of course he does.

Fucking hell. What is wrong with me tonight?

'Careful, *picciridda*,' he murmurs, dragging his thumb along the corner of my mouth. 'You keep making sounds like that, I'll start thinking you like being tied up in my bed.'

I narrow my eyes, but the air between us is thick and humming, and I can't lie, to myself or him. My thighs clench. My nipples ache. My mouth is wet for more than the treat he's feeding me.

He knows.

He fucking knows.

And when he tears off the last piece and leans in again, his breath brushing my jaw, I don't resist.

'Open,' he commands gruffly.

I open for him like a fool.

If this is what feeding feels like with Rafaelle Salvatore... what the hell will it feel like when he finally decides to devour me?

* * *

Rafaelle

It's close to four in the morning when I hear it.

The soft rumble of her stomach in the dark. The candy she

had before was nowhere near enough, but I gave her rope to hang herself.

Now she shifts in the bed, probably hoping I didn't catch it.

But I do. Of course I do.

My senses are like razors, and hers – hers are starting to hum on the same frequency. I turn from the window, where I've been smoking the end of a Cuban I shouldn't be wasting on a night like this, and toss it into the glass tray.

'You hungry for proper food now, *picciridda*?' My voice cuts through the silence, low and rough.

She doesn't answer, but I see the way she stiffens. Pride, always that spine of steel.

I pad into the small kitchen.

The place is spartan with concrete floors, exposed beams and heavy shadows, but I pay discreet people to make sure the fridge is stocked with things I like.

I slice more crusty bread, layer cold prosciutto, mozzarella, a smear of truffle mustard. Add a few sun-dried tomatoes for flair. Not because she deserves it. Because I want her mouth wet again. Want to watch her chew and know I did that. Maybe I want her to wonder who taught me how to make the best fucking sandwich in the world.

Mama.

I clench my jaw and push her from my mind. I need my every guard sharp, and I already lost control in the most sublime way tonight.

Maybe time to give testing saints a rest.

By the time I return, her eyes track me with that guarded expression. She hates that she's beginning to trust me with these things – food, warmth, attention. And I hate how much I like watching her lower her guard.

I sit beside her, pat her inner thigh through the sheets like I have every right to, and hold up the sandwich.

'No biting, *capisci*?'

She glares but her eyes drop to the sumptuous layers of bread, cheese and meat. I tear off a bite and bring it to her lips. 'Eat. Before I decide you're more fun gagged.'

She glares at me with her beautiful eyes, but her lips part. She takes the offering without molesting me.

'Good girl,' I croon.

Faint colour stains her cheeks.

She eats. Chews slowly, jaw tight like she resents every flavour I've curated for her. I smirk and feed her another piece. And another.

My dick's hard again. It never really went down.

'I should be sleeping,' I mutter, licking olive oil off my fingers. 'But it's hard when I've got this tight, slippery virgin tied up in my bed, being so damn well-behaved.'

She swallows, audibly. Very un-ladylike. Adorable colour flows up from her neck until her face is a delicate pink. 'That's a you problem,' she snaps. 'And which particular hallucination told you I was a virgin?'

I give her a lazy smile. 'That cute as fuck blush devouring your face right now? The fact that you were much too curious before when you watched me get off. You should've seen your face, *tigra*. Hunger and wonder. A fuck-hot combination. Fuck, I could jerk off again just thinking about it. Or maybe we should make it mutual? You want a hand job too, *cara mia*, so we can both sleep like babies?'

'Dream on,' she hisses.

'I do,' I murmur, lifting the glass of water to her lips. 'And they're always filthy.'

She gulps down a mouthful through the straw. Another.

And then she freezes.

I smirk. 'Oops, too late, baby.'

'You're joking,' she says flatly, nostrils flaring. 'You drugged it?'

My lips twitch. 'Just a little insurance.'

Her jaw tightens. I tense and wait for the flare of panic, the pleading. Maybe even a frantic finger down her throat to induce retching. Nothing comes, and fucking hell, my dick jumps and fills and begs me for a taste of forbidden pussy. *Just the tip, baby.*

'What the hell did you use?' she demands.

'Nothing terminal,' I murmur. 'Something I get from a chemist in Palermo who moonlights for rescued trafficked victims and trauma clinics. You'll sleep like a corpse but wake up fine. No hangover. No nausea. Maybe a wet dream if you're lucky.'

She glares at me, eyes glassy already. 'You fucking asshole. You think I wouldn't notice the bitter edge? The density shift?'

'You noticed,' I say, smiling faintly. 'And yet...'

Her hand trembles slightly within the cuffs as she watches me set the glass on the nightstand. 'I didn't drink enough,' she murmurs. And I think it's more in hope than confirmation.

And I know when that hope dies.

I watch her fight it. With the tilt of her chin, the effort to keep her spine straight while her lashes start to flutter.

'You son of a bitch,' she mutters, her words already slurring.

'Careful, *picciridda*. You'll wound my delicate pride.'

Her head lolls a little. She forces her eyes to meet mine. 'I hate you.'

I lean down, brushing a kiss to her temple.

I remember what this woman, her family, did to mine. To the one precious person who meant the world. Who didn't deserve it. And I welcome the flood of fury.

I can feel all sorts of chemical reactions for this woman who proudly lauds the Mancinelli blood flowing in her veins, but fuck if I'm going to let that blind me to my ultimate goal.

'Right back at you, *tigra*.'

She exhales sharply, and then she's out.

Just like that.

By the time her lashes settle on her cheeks and her mouth goes soft, I brush a strand of hair off her face, draw a blanket over her and whisper, 'Sleep tight, *picciridda*. Tomorrow we start playing dirty.'

9

RAFAELLE

Out in the cold moonlight, I open her car.

It's parked under the trees, its matte finish blending into the shadows. Inside, I go methodically. Glove box, under seats – knives, panels, trunk, spare tyre compartment. Two Berettas.

Her bug-out bag's slick and light. The kind I'd pack. She travels lean. Efficient. The girl was born into chaos and has learned how to dance through fire. I feel my obsession-tinged fascination rear its head once more.

I reach for the fob that opened her car door and press the second button. A small pop sounds. It takes a minute to find the compartment.

It's subtle. Heat-shielded, locked behind an invisible panel behind the passenger seat most wouldn't think twice about. But I've spent my life gutting cars for disposal and ghosting clean through safehouses.

I pop it open and there it is. Her real prize. And it's not the burner phone or the obligatory passport stack tied with a pile of Benjamins.

It's a single tablet, cold, new and clean.

I boot it up. Takes me ten minutes to break in – she's got three layers of encryption, an AI-randomised code-shuffler, and a self-wipe failsafe.

Smart. Meticulous. Like everything she does, it's engineered to vanish without a trace.

I peel it open, one barrier at a time, until her sins spill into my lap. A trail of dark web inquiries and cryptic intel buys. She's been hunting me. Not by name – she's not that stupid – but by trace and timestamp.

She's paid out crypto from multiple ghost wallets. She's traded favours and sold data. Scraped rumours from encrypted boards. All to find the moment I'd be on that rooftop ready to take out my wrath on her family.

And... fuck, she got it right.

I'm torn whether to be more impressed or fucking furious. My hard dick jerking against my fly makes the decision for me.

A hit I spent weeks lining up... and she walked into it like it was her fucking playground.

I let out a slow breath, half a curse, half a laugh. Damn.

Then I scroll lower.

My gut clenches, with disappointment and with a touch of dismay, when I see the search for Giada. Sofiya truly doesn't know where her sister is. And she—

I freeze. Read and re-read the next thread.

Fuck.

She's been digging for something else too. Something bigger. Something she probably doesn't fully understand. She's like a child skipping after a gaily dressed stranger at the fair, not knowing a monster lurks underneath. I stare at the reams of feelers. Probes. Code drops in the right message boards. Looking for a dangerous door she can't name, but I know it instantly.

Aegis.

Most federal agents don't even know it exists. Those who do? They don't say the name out loud. But I've seen what it does. I've killed for it. Survived because of it.

After tonight, after watching her drop me with a clean shot and handle chaos like it's coded into her blood – I know one thing.

She has the makings of a good assassin, but she's nowhere near Aegis level.

But if I don't reel her in, they'll eat her alive for knocking on doors she was never meant to find.

I could sit back... let this happen, but I need her to find El Topo.

Or I could... *Fuck no.*

I don't want to train a Mancinelli.

Do I?

Well... I could.

It wouldn't hurt to see how far her instincts go, what I'm dealing with as both the Enforcer for the *famigghia* and the Enforcer for Aegis.

One mission. No more. Just control the chaos by bringing it closer?

My pulse jumps with more than a thread of rare, unsullied excitement.

Cesare will shit himself. Orazio will rain Armageddon on my head. But fuck it, if you're living on the edge, you're taking up too much room. Right?

So I step off.

Slide into the driver's seat and grab my phone, thumb hovering over a contact I haven't used in over a year. When the line picks up, I speak one name.

'Sofiya Mancinelli.'

No explanation.
I hang up. It's done.
Ghost or a more lethal rival in the making?
Either way?
Game fucking on.

* * *

My phone vibrates once, a sharp pulse against the silence as I sit in the dim corner of the room. Sofiya's tablet sits on my bent knee like a shiny piece of a puzzle I'm yet to solve.

The message is encrypted, cloaked in the same layered code I've used since my first black-ops assignment in Karachi. Only three people in the world can reach me through this channel. I tap to unlock it.

> Operation at handler's discretion
>
> Failure will be dealt with accordingly.

And there it is. My jaw tics as I read the message twice.
The fine print written in blood.
Translation: *If she cracks, I bleed for it.*
'Yeah, I know what you're thinking,' I mutter to no one. 'Let the fucker with the hard-on for chaos babysit the daughter of his sworn enemy. What could possibly go wrong?'
Typical Aegis. No medals for foresight – just a bullet when instincts go bad. I should pay them back by going freelance.
Train this Mancinelli and go rogue with her.
If Cesare and Maddie are Romeo and Juliet, Sofiya and I can be Bonnie and Mutherfukin' Clyde.
I let the screen dim, middle finger raised to the shadows watching from whatever bunker hell they operate in now.

But I don't toss the phone. Or delete the message.

The burn that's been riding beneath my ribs since I dragged her unconscious ass to this safehouse flares hotter. I should be furious. Should feel the weight of every dead Salvatore whispering warnings.

But what I feel instead makes me want to punch through concrete. Not out of rage entirely. Because this already feels more dangerous, an almost relieved thrill.

Because deep down, beneath the sarcasm and resentment and the sick twist of loyalty to the family I love, a buzz is building.

Swelling my mind, and yes, my cock, with the possibilities of utilising her raw talent. Seeing what else her clever brain can do. How she can be moulded.

Her loyalty may be fractured, her blood tainted with Mancinelli sin, but her bones? Her reflexes? Her instincts?

She's mine to train.

Or bury.

I push to my feet, stalking back to the bed like I'm not about to cross a line I can never uncross.

She's curled where I left her, cuffed to the headboard, wrists slack, lashes dark against her cheeks. But even drugged, she's not defenceless. There's tension in her limbs, a current under the surface. She's still fighting me in her dreams, in her blood.

Good.

She should know exactly what I am. Because now I know what *she* is.

Mine.

And maybe this sick, fucked-up world just handed me the excuse I've been craving – to keep her close. Closer. To study her. If necessary, break her.

To make her feel the slow, consuming agony of loss the way I have.

I sit beside her, fingers brushing her bare arm. Her skin's warm. Velvet-soft. Alive. I should hate that my cock jumps from that tiny contact. That the thought of her working her way into the dark corner of the world I've built for myself like a parasite makes me want to take her again and again until she forgets who she is in the first place.

But further down all the layers I'm uncovering tonight, there's something *wrong* and raw. A sick, almost tender twist in my gut that maybe I'm not elated because I get to train or punish her.

Maybe I'm elated because I get to *keep* her.

For as long as I want.

* * *

Sofiya

I wake slowly.

The sheets smell like cedar smoke and him. I blink through the bleary fog, limbs heavy and my mouth cotton dry. My wrists are sore where the cuffs held me, but it's not the pain that jerks me fully awake.

It's the weight of his stare.

Rafa sits in the leather chair near the bed, his legs spread, another mug of coffee in his hand. He's already dressed in black pants and a half-zipped hoodie, his dark hair damp from a shower. The way he's watching me makes my stomach curl into knots. It's not fear. It's something worse. *Anticipation.*

The events of last night trickle in slowly. Then gush in a torrent.

I frown. I shouldn't remember it all so vividly. And yet I do.

'You about to drug me again?' I ask hoarsely, sitting up, yanking at the tangled sheet to cover my chest. 'You fucking psycho lunatic – *madunnuzza bastarda.*'

He grins like I've just paid him a compliment. 'I told you I'd take care of you. I didn't say I wouldn't drug you a little.'

'Just a little?' I snap. 'I want to know exactly what was in it.' It was too effective. I've been drugged before. Part of my later training in the Sicilian hills under Bonafacio's orders. *That* had been brutal. I'd retched my guts out for twenty-four hours straight.

Not this time though. I feel no after-effects. Not even the faintest hint of nausea. I bite my tongue against asking for his dealer.

He shrugs, maddeningly casual. 'I told you. It's a black-market sedative. It didn't hurt you. And it's not like you didn't need sleep.'

'I don't trust what you put in my body,' I hiss, heat flushing up my neck the second the words leave my mouth.

His brows lift, and a wicked grin spreads across his face like a slow drag of silk over bare skin. *Shit.*

'Oh?' he says, voice suddenly low and gleaming with promise. 'That's a shame, *bedda.* Because if you did... I'd put a hell of a lot more in your body. And I guarantee, you'd beg me for it as you die with pleasure.'

My breath snags and my face *ignites.* My knees draw together under the sheets, a pitiful reflex against the throb that hits me low and hard. He didn't even touch me – didn't *need* to.

Just those words, that voice, and my body's reacting like I've already let him in.

He stands now, looming, all dark heat and command. 'You should trust me,' he continues, calm again – *too* calm.

'Why?'

Then his gaze sharpens, flicking from my mouth to my eyes with that blade-edged focus that makes him so dangerous.

'Last night, on the roof, you were kinda... decent. Definitely edges that need smoothing, but you've got training,' he says, tone shifting – still smooth, but with a new kind of edge. 'Who trained you? Let me guess, those sadistic bastards up in Bosco di Malabotta?'

I freeze.

That's the real game now. Not sex or power. Information.

'I train myself,' I reply, deliberately cool. 'Late-night YouTube binges and a few too many Bourne movies.'

He stares. Waits. He's trying to get under my skin again, but I keep my face still. My pulse betrays me, but barely. I've spent too long learning how to lie without blinking, courtesy of a cruel and frigid tormentor in the Sicilian hills.

'Hmm.' He studies me like I'm a puzzle with one missing piece. 'Cute. But not true.'

I tilt my head. 'You going to cry about it?'

His jaw tics. He didn't expect me to pivot. But I don't let up. I smile. Saccharine sweet and lethal. 'Nice try, *Enforcer*. But I'm not green enough to hand you my entire life history just because you made me blush a little.'

His eyes darken with interest. And *that*, more than anything, makes my skin prickle. Because I might've thrown him off. But not nearly far enough.

Still, I manage a glare, but I can feel the blush painting my skin from collarbone to cheekbone, feel the sting of it in my scalp, my chest, between my legs. I hate that he sees it. Hate more that he *likes* it. And I *really* hate that a twisted part of me wants to find out exactly what else he'd put in my body if I let him.

Just when I think the silence will stretch my nerves to the breaking point – a feat in itself since I'm usually unflappable – Rafa pulls something from behind his back and tosses it onto the bed beside me. *My tablet.*

The sight of it makes my throat close. That was supposed to be locked and hidden. Untraceable.

He's seen everything. The search trails. The fake aliases. The breadcrumbs I stole, borrowed, and begged for, which led me to him.

And the other searches?

'You've been digging in places you shouldn't, *bedda mia*,' he says, low and quiet.

I avoid his gaze, stare at the screen. 'So?'

'You need to stop.'

My jaw sets. 'Or what?'

He doesn't answer.

The silence that follows is loaded, coiled tight like a noose. It stretches long enough that my pulse starts to thrum in my ears. I hate not knowing.

So I look up, my voice quieter when I ask, 'Are you one of the people I've been trying to find?'

His dark caramel gaze doesn't waver. He doesn't say yes. He just repeats, 'You need to stop.'

The air turns heavy with things unsaid.

I look down at the tablet, fingers itching to snatch it back, destroy it, pretend it doesn't exist. But it's too late.

A thread of sick realisation curls low in my gut.

I was hunting shadows and stumbled into something real. And now... now I wonder if *he* is the key. If this brutal, unreadable man might be my way in.

But at what cost?

I force my expression to stay still.

Rafa watches me too closely. I can feel the weight of his stare like a palm on my skin. Waiting for me to flinch. For me to speak. He doesn't offer interpretation. He doesn't need to. He's measuring my silence, reading every micro-shift in my expression like a language he's fluent in.

'You know what I've been looking for, don't you?' I murmur, eyes narrowing.

He raises a brow, all lazy challenge.

I nod at the tablet still resting between us. 'Anyone with half a brain and access to the dark web could mimic an encrypted interface. The information could be fake. I haven't had a chance to verify it yet.'

His eyes glint. 'Careful, *picciridda*. You're two seconds away from making me show you just how real this world gets.'

I snort. 'That supposed to scare me? I grew up at a table where the dessert spoons were bugged and the steak knives came engraved with kill orders.'

He leans in slowly, gaze fixed on mine. 'I do scare you, baby assassin.' His grin sharpens. 'And it's a very bad idea to challenge me while you're cuffed to my bed.'

'I've had worse ideas,' I shoot back. 'At least they didn't involve trusting a walking hard-on with a murder record.'

That earns a low, dark laugh. 'You're dying to find out if that murder record extends to orgasms? The answer is yes, *tigra*. I can in fact kill you with how well I fuck you.'

I roll my eyes. 'Confidence looks good on a man, Salvatore. Pity you keep mistaking it for a god complex.'

He leans in slightly, smirk curling at the edges. 'Ah, *bedda*. You keep poking the monster, and you'll find out just how complex I can get.'

I hate the way my breath catches. Hate more that he sees it.

His smirk deepens, fucking *glows*. 'That got your attention.'

'Shut up.'

He straightens, turning serious in a blink. 'I'm going to uncuff you now.'

My body goes still.

'If you try anything,' he says softly, like he's sharing a secret, 'I'll put you down. One shot. Back of the skull. Be rid of my Mancinelli problem' – long fingers snap, sharp and lethal – 'just like that.'

'You won't get away with it. My family won't let you get away with it. And I suspect some factions in your family won't be too happy.'

His jaw clenches and I know I've hit a raw nerve. 'I'm not some common capo they can demote, Sofiya. I'm the blade they send when diplomacy fails. The secret they bury before it breathes. Half the *famigghia's* scared of me, the other half owes me their lives. So no – no one's coming to rein me in.'

'And you thrive in that, don't you?' I look a little deeper, spot the hairline fracture. 'Or do you?'

He laughs, but there's an edge to it. 'Sure. I'm living proof that if you're not born first, you better be born mean. I carved a place for myself the only way that counted – in blood.' His voice dips lower. 'I may be a fucking spare, *bedda*, but I'm still a much bigger deal than you'll ever be. Don't forget that.'

The silence stretches, a taut wire strung between us, humming with things unsaid. His jaw tics once.

I've definitely touched a nerve. I should be rejoicing. Instead I'm struck so hard by how much it echoes in me – this desperate need to prove yourself when no one handed you the crown.

I know what it is to live in the shadow of the heir, to be the insurance policy, the pawn trained for sacrifice. The one they praise only when you bleed for them.

I don't want to find common ground with Rafaelle Salvatore.

No, no, no!

I grit my teeth so hard I taste copper. 'Are you, though? Remember how we kicked your asses and won six races before you got your thumbs out of your asses last year?'

'Minor inconvenience which we squashed like bugs. Remind me again who won both the Drivers' and Constructors' Championships?'

'One shot. That's all that's ever needed.'

'And you had yours last night and failed. So. Before I unlock you, I want to hear it. Say it.'

'Say *what*?'

He smiles, like he's savouring every syllable before it even leaves my mouth. 'Promise not to be a bad girl and make me use the handcuffs for something *less* benign.'

'I hate you.'

'That's not a no.'

I hiss in frustration – but the truth is, the throbbing between my legs is turning molten again, and he knows it.

And I hate myself more that part of me... *wants* to be the bad girl just to find out what he'd do.

Even as my mind races through training scenarios. There *aren't* any for this – being tied up and drugged by an enemy who wants to screw me *and* kill my grandfather.

He walks to the bed and unlocks the cuffs, fingers grazing my skin. I pull away from the contact, glaring up at him. 'You think finding a few traps I may or may not have put in place changes anything?'

His mouth curves, but there's no humour in it. 'No, but the one string of dead-end forum threads, dark-web bounties, stolen key logs and digital footprints so clean it makes most analysts look like apes in mittens? That changes things.'

I go still. 'Are you saying I'm *good*, Rafaelle?' I drop my voice, tease him with sultriness.

His nostrils flare as he drags the cuff off my other wrist and straightens, voice low. 'You have talents, Sofiya. Talents I'm willing to explore. While you help me find your grandfather.' He steps back, giving me just enough space to breathe. 'It's another condition for keeping you alive. For now.'

My heart thuds once, loud and suspicious. 'That's not the only reason you're doing this, though. What's the angle?'

He studies me for a long beat. Then shrugs, infuriatingly vague. 'You've been sniffing at the feet of monsters, *duci tigra*. I might give you a few more breadcrumbs if you stop trying to get yourself killed.'

I narrow my eyes. 'You're still not telling me what they're called.'

'What who are called?'

A growl of frustration escapes before I can stop it.

His smile is all wolf now. 'I'm trusting you, Sofiya. Which means you're coming with me to Monaco tomorrow.'

'Excuse me? The race isn't till the weekend.'

'I have some business to take care of. Billionaire with a taste for girls barely out of puberty. Human trafficking. The Grand Prix this weekend while I supervise Renzo and Dante will be the perfect cover. You're coming with me.'

A part of me, the part I rarely let surface, sparks with something dangerously close to anticipation. I've heard stories about the Enforcer. Rumours sharpened by blood and myth. Now I get a front-row seat to watch him work?

I should hate the idea – being dragged along like a tool in his arsenal. But my pulse says otherwise. 'And if I say no?'

'You won't. Those breadcrumbs I mentioned? You're already fucking wet about the thought of them.'

I slap him. It's automatic, instinctive, hard enough to sting my palm.

He barely flinches. Then grabs my chin, not rough but not gentle either. He leans close enough that I can pick out the gold flecks in his eyes. Beautiful. Mesmeric. Pulsing with the promise of derangement that shouldn't fascinate me this much. But, God, it does.

He stares at me for the longest time, then he blows a breath over my mouth. It's almost a kiss. A promise. Enough to harden my nipples, carve a path of hunger through my body.

He stays long enough for my brain to short-circuit with the drug of his proximity.

When he pulls back, he's breathing hard. So am I.

'The next time you bite me or slap me, *picciridda*,' he growls, 'I'm going to fuck you. Slowly. Deeply. Until you forget every reason you ever had to think you hate me.'

I'm shaking, but it's not fear. It's... heat. Confusion. My thighs press together under the sheet.

God, I hate how my body reacts to him. 'I'm not yours,' I whisper.

His eyes drop to my mouth. 'Not yet.'

I swing my legs off the bed, trying to focus. Trying to shut out the throbbing between my legs and the twisting in my chest. This isn't just another mission. I know weapons. I know kills. I know strategy.

But I don't know *him*.

And I don't know what the hell I'm going to do if I start wanting things I've never been trained for.

10

RAFAELLE

The hum of the Mancinelli jet is low and constant, a soft growl beneath my boots as I lounge in one of the cream leather seats, fingers curled around a crystal tumbler of Scotch I don't remember ordering.

We're flying over the Alps, en route to Nice, where a chopper will take us to Monte Carlo. The sky outside the cabin windows is bruised gold, sharp with late afternoon light.

Across from me, Sofiya buckles herself into her seat like it's war prep. Chin high. Mouth tight. Legs crossed in that unconscious, regal way that belies the fact that she's been raised in senseless violence and knows how to bite harder.

I take a sip, let the burn coat my throat, then settle in. Time to play.

'I have questions about your grandfather. You're going to answer them.'

She doesn't look at me. Doesn't blink. 'You want to start this now?'

I smile lazily. 'We've got air miles to kill, *bedda*. And I do enjoy killing.'

A flash of anger tightens her jaw. Good.

'When?' I press. 'When's the last time you laid eyes on Bonafacio?'

She exhales hard through her nose. 'Laid eyes on him? The day you trigger-happy Salvatores laid waste to our warehouses and killed our men a year ago.'

'Hardly trigger-happy. It was in retaliation of what El Topo thought he could get away with.' My eyes drop to her chest which isn't quite as calm as she tries to project. 'Pure tat for tits.'

'Seriously. Is everything sexual innuendo with you?' she demands through another sweet blush.

God, I love watching that. I'll give my pinkie toe to witness a full-body pre-climax flush as I pound her cunt hard enough to make us both taste heaven.

I shrug. 'I like to fuck, *tigra*. And a beautiful, willing woman front and centre always brings out my basic instincts.'

'Willing? I guess I'm adding delusional to your fourteen-year-old out-of-control hormonal tendencies.'

'You think you're not willing?' I nod at her chest. 'Maybe you should tell that to your fuck-hot body.'

She starts to look down. Catches herself and lances a glare at me.

I smile. Then switch it off as the subject at hand slams back home. 'So you haven't seen him. Have you talked? FaceTimed? Smoke-signalled?'

She purses her lips, a tell I'm beginning to recognise and would need training out of her. Unless that siren's mouth is pursed around my cock, sucking me off like I'm late with rent and she needs it from my balls.

'Four months ago. Somewhere in Sicily.' She stops.

'And? You don't want me to drag every piece of info out of you, baby.'

'It's not worth writing home about. He was drunk and paranoid and mumbling about rats and unfinished business.'

The lethal blade of my rage sharpens. 'Unfinished business in what way? Did he mention Fallbrook?'

'No.'

I lean forward, elbows on my knees. 'Out of interest, where were you the night of Cesare and Maddie's wedding?'

Her head snaps towards me, eyes blazing. '*Excuse me?*'

'You heard me.'

Her hands clench on the armrests, knuckles whitening momentarily, before she gains control of herself. 'You think I helped orchestrate an ambush on my own sister's wedding night?'

'I think I've seen betrayal take prettier shapes than yours.'

Her seatbelt unsnaps and she's on her feet before I can blink, hands yanked forward like she might strangle me with sheer fury. '*Vaffanculo.* You think I'd put Maddie in the line of fire? She made her choice and I respected it long before she walked down the aisle and married your brother. Be an asshole about everything else, but not that.'

Her voice cracks, just once. A fault line in her otherwise perfect rage.

Something hot and irrational coils low in my gut.

Because she means it. She's not lying. And it hits me harder than it should – how beautiful she is when she's furious, how fierce and loyal and *real* she looks with her eyes bright and voice shaking.

I want to soothe her. *Touch* her. Push her back into that plush seat and kiss every ruffled inch of her.

The thought alone unsettles me. Deeply.

So I shut it down and pivot.

'We land in an hour,' I say, smoothing my voice back to neutral. 'After that, we're dealing with the other problem.'

Sofiya doesn't sit. 'Tell me about the trafficker.'

'Guy collects passports like trophies and little girls like vintage cars. Keeps them drugged in a villa up in the Monte Carlo hills. Pays off police to keep his filthy habits. He will not live to see another sunrise.'

She shivers. I don't miss it.

I rise too and close the space between us, not touching but just standing close enough that she'll feel my body heat. Her perfume's soft and unassuming – white orchid and citrus – but beneath it, I smell *her*. Salt and adrenaline. Gunmetal.

'I take him out,' I murmur. 'You watch and learn. Unless you want to make it a team effort.'

She glares up at me, lips parting like she might say something else – might scream or kiss me or both – but the pilot's voice comes over the intercom.

'We have a little turbulence ahead. Please take your seats and fasten your seatbelts.'

* * *

The chopper waiting for us in Nice is sleek and black, Salvatore power disguised as discretion. She doesn't speak the whole ride to Monte Carlo, and I let her stew in it.

Let her feel the weight of my control and intent like a noose.

The suite Furia Racing booked for me is on the eighth floor of the Hôtel de Paris. One bedroom, one shared living space, and a marble bathroom big enough to drown in.

Sofiya walks in, her spine ramrod straight.

She pauses when she sees the single suite key in my hand.

'Where's yours?'

I toss it into the air, catch it. 'This is *ours*.'

Her brows snap together. 'You've got to be joking.'

'Nope.' I lean in, grin sharp. 'Two bodies. One bed, if you play your cards right.'

She growls something in Sicilian that sounds like a death threat.

And God help me, I hope she tries.

Again.

* * *

Sofiya

'This is a joke,' I mutter, stepping into the suite like I've walked into a trap. Because I have.

Opulence drips from the walls – plush velvet chairs, a balcony overlooking Monte Carlo's glittering coastline, a bed far too large and far too central in the master bedroom. One bed. One key. One goddamn walking hazard.

I've lost count of how many times the Enforcer has come close to kissing me. Taunting me. Messing with my body chemistry. Making me wet enough that I'll need to visit one of the many boutiques on Avenues des Beaux-Arts to replenish the three panties I usually pack in my bug-out bag.

Rafa tosses his duffel onto the chaise longue like he owns the entire principality. 'You want me to sleep on the floor, *picciridda*? Because I'd still make it look good.'

I spin on him. 'You think this is funny?'

The worst part is he clearly does.

That crooked smirk, that infuriating glint in his eyes like he's waiting for me to throw something at his head just so he can catch it mid-air and call it foreplay.

And *God help me*, there's a part of me that doesn't hate it.

His crude, brazen, completely unfettered attitude should make me want to shove him off the balcony. But instead I'm pinging between shock and the urge to laugh. Or slap him. Or both. I don't recognise myself at all.

Because for the first time in my life, I'm not tempted to deck a guy for calling me beautiful. I used to shut that shit down back in high school with a sharp fist and a sharper tongue.

Now? I just stand here, pulse hammering, fighting a smile like some starry-eyed idiot in a cheap romcom.

And he knows it.

The bastard *knows*.

'I think this is *convenient*.' He's already unzipping his jacket, tossing it aside to reveal a black T-shirt that clings to every brutal, gorgeous line of muscle. 'It's Monaco on race weekend. Suites book fast. Unless you want to share a bunkbed with Renzo and his twelve hair products, this is the best you'll get.'

I fold my arms tight. 'How exactly am I supposed to explain this to my family? My *father*, the lieutenants? That I'm shacked up with the Salvatore Enforcer in a luxury suite while my grandfather's still MIA?'

He raises a brow. 'Don't explain it. Let 'em squirm.'

'They'll think I've switched sides,' I snap. 'They'll think I'm like Maddie.'

That stings more than I want it to.

Only a year ago, I was the one disrupting the quiet whisper campaign. *Why would Maddie run away with Cesare? Why would she sleep in the same penthouse, breathe the same air?*

Sure, I was stumped as hell at her behaviour, but I never turned against her.

When Bonafacio raged about Maddie's betrayal, when he demanded blood and strategy in equal measure, *I stalled him.*

Lied. Delayed. Fed him false leads while Maddie slipped deeper into Cesare's world.

I wasn't the reason the wedge split our family – I was the one gripping the cracks, holding them together with shaking hands.

But it wasn't enough.

Bonafacio unravelled anyway. Spun himself into paranoia and fury. And when he finally snapped, it wasn't me he blamed.

It was *her*.

And he tried to kill her. His own granddaughter. The one person I'd fought – quietly, desperately – to protect.

He tried to kill someone he knew I loved, even after I bent over backwards for him. Over and over. Even after I bled and obeyed and turned myself into exactly what he wanted – a weapon.

I never chose this destiny, but I still broke myself trying to be perfect in it. It still wasn't enough.

And now here I am.

Living a fucking echo.

I could ask Rafa to keep it quiet, but that would be like asking a wolf not to howl under a full moon. Just planting the idea would be enough for him to announce it to the whole damn world.

Instead, I quietly excuse myself, step into the marble-clad bathroom, make a single call that, fully leaning into my *mafia princess* persona, delivers me a second room in my name.

One floor down. Just in case.

I message Russo, the most senior of the bodyguards that I know are travelling with the Mancinelli Racing Team this weekend. Then, biting my tongue tip, I send one more to my father.

Here to keep an eye on Narciso for the
weekend. He's distracted. Stefano doing a piss-
poor job on keeping him focused on the car.
Just making sure he doesn't get blindsided.

It's half a lie with enough truth sprinkled into it to make it believable. Stefano, my father's half-brother, the oops product of a sleazy back-alley hookup with a stripper from one of Nonno's strip clubs, was born with a Baltimore-sized chip on his shoulder.

His constant clashes with my father and aunt, and wild power-grabbing antics, had forced Bonafacio to find him a role within the Mancinelli Racing Team just to get him out of New York and out of his hair.

Of course, there'd been very little regard to whether Stefano was good for this or any other job. And shocker, Captain Shit-show turned out to be all about the glitz and glam of Formula One racing and bupkis about the hard work that went into keeping the team running like the relatively well-oiled machine Maddie had kept it before she'd given it up to go play house with the Salvatore heir.

In a rare moment of nostalgia, Narciso had admitted last week that he wished Maddie was still the team's CEO instead of Stefano. That he wasn't stuck with *Ziu Strunzu*.

So I'm praying my father buys my reasons for being here this weekend, and not read more into it.

I return to the living room and my feet stall, my breath strangling somewhere in my midriff.

Rafa's shirt is off.

Not just off. *Discarded.*

He's strutting across the suite in nothing but low-slung black sweatpants, barefoot, towel drying his hair from a recent shower.

His abs gleam, cut and wet, and my brain short-circuits just a little. Every movement is deliberate, smug, *male*. The kind of man who knows the effect he has and exploits it mercilessly.

Don't engage. Don't engage. Don't— 'You always put on a show?' I mutter, trying not to stare.

He tosses the towel onto a chair and stretches, arms overhead, full *mouthwatering* gladiator. 'Only when the audience is this hot. You blushing again, *bedda*?'

'I'm *not*—' I start, too fast, too defensive.

He smirks. 'Oh, you're so blushing.'

He prowls closer, eyes flicking to my lips, my throat, the quick rise and fall of my chest. The air between us hums, thick with something unstable and heavy. He reaches out, his fingers barely brushing my jaw, and dips his face close. *Too* close. His breath is warm and spiced.

My lips part. God, we're a breath from kissing. Again.

From *disaster*. Again.

But I don't move and neither does he.

Until he whispers, 'You ever been kissed like you deserve, baby assassin?'

I swallow. 'Don't call me that.'

He grins. 'Why not? I have a bruise right here that tells me you're deadly. But you look like you'd come apart the second someone touched you properly. It's a fucking sexy combination.'

My cheeks flare again, and it's not from embarrassment this time. It's from the low ache between my thighs. The pressure I can't ignore or control.

He watches me, steps back just slightly, but the mood doesn't lift.

Then he cocks his head. 'Wait... don't tell me you're actually a—'

I don't answer.

His grin falters.

'Holy *fuck*,' he breathes, his eyes darting between mine. Alight with glimpses of something I'm terrified to name. '*You're actually a virgin*. I wasn't really serious before because... but you are, aren't you? The real fucking thing. How's that possible?' he mutters with a frown.

The silence between us grows teeth.

Because there's no way I'm baring my truths to him. No way I'm telling him that I learned very fast that pretty girls got noticed. Noticed meant targeted. In high school, on the street. In every workplace across the face of the earth. I made myself useful instead. Safe. Unbreakable.

Nor am I telling him that I'm terrified of anyone making me feel helpless like the way the men in my family made the women feel, especially my mother. Why would I start in bed?

Something *primal* flickers in his gaze – raw, masculine, hungry. The playful arrogance is gone, replaced by something deeper, darker. He steps forward again, slower this time, like a man tracking prey.

And I should be scared.

I *should* be.

But *Diu miu*, I'm not.

I'm wet. I'm shaking. And for the first time in my life, I feel like prey that wants to be caught.

'Left or right?' I snap.

'Left or right what, *bedda*?'

'Your balls, Enforcer. Which one are you more attached to?'

A slow, sublime smile spreads across his face. 'You asking me to choose a favourite? That's like asking me to choose our favourite child. I love them both equally. Unconditionally.'

'Then I suggest you keep that thought front and centre the next time you decide to call me beautiful. Or angelic. Or cute. Or whatever the fuck cliché labels sprint into that tiny mind.'

He staggers back a step, clutching his chest. 'Ouch. I'm not sure where to start with that one. That you're calling me cliché or that you think I have a tiny mind.' The smile slowly wipes off. 'Or that someone's taken a hammer to your self-esteem and done such a good job. Who did that, baby? Just give me a name and they'll cease to exist by sundown.'

It's my turn to stagger. I barely manage to catch my jaw before it drops and smashes my sprinting heart. Because that hammer he just mentioned? He might as well be wielding it because he's just smashed through the outer layer of a terrifying truth.

I yank my gaze from his. 'You're insane.'

'Undisputed. But just because I'm mental doesn't make it not true,' he slides in softly, deadly as a poisoned dagger. 'I'm waiting, *bedda*.'

'And you're testing my fucking patience.' I reach for rage to cover the flanks he's torn wide open.

He folds his thick arms over his thicker chest, a hint of a smile returning. 'It's okay if you need time to regroup. But I'll have the name one way or another. In the meantime, feel free to come for my balls. I'll be my pleasure to introduce them to that beautiful, hot little mouth.'

The sound that ripples from my diaphragm feels just as unhinged as the man planted before me. Absurdly, it widens his smile. Like I've just given him exactly what he wants.

'No, *duci*, I'm not going to stop showering you with sentiments from our beloved homeland. You're fucking beautiful. Fuck diamonds and pearls. You deserve worlds conquered and laid at your feet.'

'And let me guess, you're just the man to do it?'

He stops, shrugs. 'In another life, maybe. In this life, we have the small problem of you being my mortal enemy. And my maybe mentee.' His face hardens a little and his brown eyes dim. 'One of you lot over on our side is fucking bad enough.'

My skin chills with the naked fury pulsing in his words. 'That better not be a threat against my sister I hear in your voice, Salvatore.'

My voice is ice. Sharper than it should be. Sharper than I feel. But something about the way his eyes shuttered when he said 'one of you lot' sends fear crawling up my spine like it's wearing a silk dress and stilettos.

Rafa's jaw flexes. A long pause hangs between us, charged and brittle. Then he speaks, his voice lower now with something dark threading through it.

'Maddie is an Untouchable now,' he says. 'She's Cesare's wife. That means she's under family protection, for life. No one touches her.'

My mouth opens. Closes. I feel relief slam through me so hard my knees nearly buckle. It's instinct, pure and irrational – the same protective reflex that used to have me sneaking into Maddie's room when we were kids after one of Papà's rages, curling against her back and whispering made-up stories until she stopped shaking.

And he sees it. He sees *all* of it.

His gaze sharpens like a scalpel. 'You didn't know if she was safe, did you?'

I try to school my face. To recover. But the damage is done. The little flicker of raw, involuntary emotion has already sliced through the wall I spent years building.

Rafa steps closer. There's no smile now. He's just watching. Way too closely. 'You thought I'd hurt her.'

'I didn't know what you'd do,' I snap. It comes out too defensive, too quick.

'No,' he says, deadly quiet now. 'You thought I was a fucking monster. And you're right in every aspect but one, *bedda*.'

I suck in a breath, but he's already shaking his head, jaw clenched like he's swallowing something bitter.

'I don't harm women. Or children. Not even when they deserve it,' he says. 'I'm not El Topo. I don't terrorise. And I sure as fuck don't use my fists to feel powerful.'

Something about the fury in his voice makes my throat tighten. Because he's not just angry. He's... *wounded*. Like the thought that I might've lumped him in with the real monsters eats at him deeper than it should.

'I didn't think that,' I lie. My voice sounds small, even to me.

He doesn't answer. Doesn't have to.

His silence is punishment enough.

* * *

Rafaelle

I shouldn't be thinking about it.

About her.

About that one devastating fact now burned into the folds of my fucking brain like a brand.

Not after the nasty assumptions she made.

But... *Sofiya Mancinelli is a virgin.*

Unbedded. Untouched. Unclaimed.

I've tortured men for intel. Disposed of bodies so thoroughly their own mothers couldn't recognise them. But nothing – nothing – has ever possessed me like this.

I don't want to be the next man who fucks her. I want to be the *first. And the fucking last.*

The one who ruins her for anyone else.

And if some other bastard even *thinks* about touching her, I'll carve them into pieces, dump them into a pine box and bury them under the Monaco circuit.

She steps out of the bathroom now, lips glossed, dark sunglasses perched on her head, her black slacks hugging every inch of those hips like they were made to test me. The silk blouse she's chosen dips at the collar, just enough to show the faint flutter of her pulse.

'We need to head to the track,' she says, pulling her blazer on with military efficiency.

'I know,' I mutter, still watching her like a man starved.

She looks up. Sees it. *Feels* it.

Her expression tightens. 'I'll go separately.'

'*Fuck no,*' I growl before she can take another step.

Her hand freezes mid-button. 'Rafa—'

'No. You're not walking out of here or going anywhere without me.'

'Like hell I'm not. I'm not a child.'

'No, *picciridda,*' I say, stepping into her space. 'You're worse. You're *mine.* Under my control and my supervision. And I'm not letting what's mine fuck off anywhere alone.'

She glares. 'Then I'll walk in front of you.'

My eyes drag down the length of her body. 'Fine. I'll stare at your ass the whole way like a pervert.'

'You *are* a pervert.'

'How are you going to stop me?'

She opens her mouth. Closes it. And fuck me, it's another near-kiss with her breath hot, that chin tilted, those perfect lips a heartbeat from mine. My blood surges.

I don't touch her. I can't or we'll never leave this suite.

So I let the truth slide out of me instead. 'This little news about your virginity's driving me insane.'

Her eyes widen, shock and... something else in her eyes. Intrigue?

Fuck, now it makes sense. The way she blushes. The pockets of wonder when she looks at me. When my natural don't-fuck-around-ness adorably disarms her.

I'm not sure why I'm shocked as fuck. She bears all the hallmarks of a natural rebel with the sometimes pixie haircut and the constant disappearing acts and the fire and the utter lack of self-preservation that makes her slap a deranged psychopath with very little thought of consequences.

And... fuck me... but her purity just flings another log onto the obsession inferno. At this rate I'll be entirely under her thrall by nightfall.

'It's front and centre now,' I admit, voice gravel dark. 'I want it. I want *you*. I'll do anything for it.'

She recoils slightly. 'It's not a piece of *panaru d'u mercatu* you can bargain over at the local market.'

'Then I'll give you something more,' I say, dead serious now. 'A villa in Lake Como. A racing yacht. *My next kill.* Whatever currency makes you feel like you're not being bought.'

She stares at me – and laughs. Sharp. Disbelieving. 'You're *serious.*'

I don't blink. Surge closer. Revel in the warmth of her delicious skin. 'Deadly.'

The laughter fades. She's not smiling any more. Because she knows I'm not talking about something as trite as sex.

I'm talking about claiming. Conquering. *Fucking pillaging.*

The kind that comes with a predator's roar and white sheets unfurled at sunrise to show virgin blood.

And it shakes her.

No one's ever offered her anything like that, I know.

Not with reverence or with desire.

Her father and grandfather are the old-school assholes who would only ever offer her body like a blade – a deal to be forged, a prize to be used.

I've done my own research on Sofiya Mancinelli in the last year. I know her skills are frequently farmed out to other Cosa Nostra families for money. Know that she firmly stipulated maiming on those jobs, never kills – a shot-out kneecap or lost fingers here, a low-calibre gut shot there.

Which is why her body count is relatively low.

But regardless of the dubious intent, it's the same way they tried to trade Maddie like cattle last year. The same mistake that led to her rebellion. That pushed her into Cesare's bed and ignited the latest Mancinelli-Salvatore powder keg.

And now here I am.

A Salvatore.

Doing the same thing.

But it's not for power.

What I'm offering doesn't end with a ring and an old Sicilian *padre* mumbling words from the Old Book.

This is just for the one prize. For her.

Sofiya tears herself out of my space, her breath ragged, her cheeks flushed. 'We're supposed to be at *war*,' she hisses, like saying it aloud will undo whatever the fuck is happening between us. 'And you think I'm going to hand myself over to you to conquer? Dream the fuck on.'

My head drops against the wall she just vacated. Chasing her scent. Savouring possibilities.

But I don't chase her. I don't need to because I can already feel it. The inevitability of it. And the panic rising in her like smoke.

She's not running from *me*.

She's running from *herself*.

And she has no idea that I've already started hunting.

11

SOFIYA

I feel like I'm choking.

The air in the suite is too rich, too close, filled with Rafaelle Salvatore's scent and the echo of the words I can't unhear.

A villa in Lake Como. A racing yacht. My next kill.

I'll do anything for it.

The force of my desire to scream 'yes' rocks me long after I've pushed him away and fled to the bathroom.

Yes. Yes. Yes.

Not for status or to leverage a treaty.

But for *me*.

And it terrifies me more than any sniper's scope ever has.

Because I know what it means to be offered like a deal. My father and grandfather do it often and blatantly with pride.

I watched Maddie wither and smile stoically through the sting of her body and self-worth being traded like a bag of blood oranges at the Palermo docks.

I listened in silence while they debated *what she was worth* – and what they stood to gain by tethering her to some crusty old yes-man from the Old Country.

And then I silently condemned her when she didn't appreciate my efforts in stalling for her. My shock and disappointment when she lit it all on fire and jumped into bed with Cesare Salvatore.

Now I understand the look in her eyes that night in Singapore, when she set the trail of gasoline and threw the match the next morning.

Now I know what it means to want something you're supposed to hate.

Because when Rafa said those words – *my next kill* – something cracked open inside me.

Deranged and full-blown psychopathic as he is rumoured to be, the Enforcer's reputation is second to none. With a record he meticulously, jealously and lethally guards.

So for him to offer that... for me... it was heady in ways very few people on this planet would understand.

And I want it. God help me, I *want* it.

I stride farther away from him like it'll stop the spiral, like distance can undo heat, want, madness. But it clings to me anyway, thick and wet between my legs, high in my chest, buzzing under my skin like Salvatore *sorcery*.

We're supposed to be enemies. I'm supposed to be loyal.

But my loyalty was forged in violence. In fear. In expectation.

This... *whatever this is*... feels like something else.

Rafa doesn't move. He watches me with that dark, consuming stillness I've come to dread and crave in equal measure.

And I know, if I stay here one more minute, I might let him touch me.

I might *ask* him to.

So I flee.

Because if I don't, I won't be able to pretend any more.

Won't be able to deny that the war I'm fighting now isn't between the Mancinellis and the Salvatores—

It's inside me.

I toss my phone onto the bed and stand. 'I'll go to the track later. I'm going shopping.'

Rafa's still at the window, shirtless, the kind of shirtless that should be outlawed. He glances at me over his shoulder, slow and amused. 'Where?'

'Avenue des Beaux Arts. I need clothes. Unless you want me attending the Grand Prix in filthy boots and a tactical vest, explain to a bunch of Mancinelli capos where I've been for the last twenty-four hours?'

He gives a low chuckle and turns towards the armchair where he discarded his shirt. 'Shopping it is, then.' He slides his arms into the sleeves like he's putting on armour. 'But I'll be close.'

'Stalking me again?'

'Shadowing,' he corrects. 'It's sexier.'

I don't dignify that with a reply.

The cobbled stretch of Monte Carlo's elite shopping district gleams in the late morning sun, boutiques lined up like polished jewels. I move from store to store, aware of the eyes on me. The staff's, the other patrons who assess my net worth and satisfy themselves that I'm good for it.

But most keenly, I feel *his*.

Because no matter how far ahead I walk, Rafa appears. Leaning against a mirrored column, inspecting a silk belt, watching me from across the boutique with that slow, unrushed predator's gaze.

In Chanel, he murmurs behind me, 'Try the black. It'll hug your ass in ways I won't be able to ignore.'

In Dior, he holds up a set of strappy heels. 'You should wear these while straddling me. Nothing else.'

Somehow, when I find myself in Agent Provocateur without meaning to visit a lingerie shop, he prowls even closer, sending lethal glares to husbands and partners who even dare to glance my way. He doesn't say anything. Just plucks a blood-red set of lace and silk and holds it out to the saleswoman with a smile. 'Wrap it.'

'No. Don't,' I counter. 'It's not my type.'

'It's mine,' he retorts. Whips out a black card with no visible writing. A card I've only heard whispers about.

I want to slap him. I want to kiss him. I want to scream. I want to claw the saleswoman's eyes out for the flash of unadulterated fuck-me-now look that glazes her eyes.

By the time we're back at the suite, my skin feels too tight, my pulse a metronome of arousal and disbelief.

'We leave for the track in twenty minutes,' he says, already shrugging off his shirt again like the world has given him full permission to drive me insane.

I start unpacking the bags, trying to breathe, trying not to think about how wet I am.

The lingerie bag slides free first.

I stare at the tissue-wrapped bundle of lace and silk like it might detonate. Agent Provocateur – blood-red, barely there. The exact set he chose without hesitation and with implacable certainty. Like he *knew* what would make me come undone.

And I let him pay for it.

I let him pay for *everything*.

Designer bags and shoes and lingerie I didn't even ask for or need when I have my own bank accounts – accounts fatter than some governments'. I've been the Mancinelli's protector as well as their seven-figure-gun-for-hire for the better part of a decade.

I've protected rogue diplomats. Once bribed a Turkish border agent with a Breguet watch I had on loan from an oligarch's mistress.

I can pay my way around the world a thousand times and not feel a dent in my bitcoin wallet.

But here? With *him*?

I just... let it happen. Like I'm playing a part. Or worse, *falling* into one. By the time I tuck the last bag into the closet, I'm flushed and unsettled and bone-deep aware of every inch of my body.

'You hungry?' he asks behind me.

I jump a little, whip around to find him lifting the lid off a tray he's somehow managed to coax from room service. The smell hits me instantly – seared salmon, herbs, warm couscous and citrus, grilled vegetables still steaming.

He pulls out a chair. 'Eat.'

I narrow my eyes. 'Is it drugged?'

He quirks a brow like I've just accused him of poisoning a kitten. Then he picks up *my* fork, stabs a piece of salmon, and pops it into his mouth like a man who's too damn comfortable being accused of anything.

He chews. Swallows. Licks his bottom lip.

'If it is,' he says with a grin, 'I guess we're going down together.'

I hate the flutter that low, gravel-dark voice stirs in my chest. I should toss the plate but my stomach betrays me with a vicious growl.

He scoops another bite and gestures towards the food. 'Trust me, *bedda*. The next time I want you sedated, you'll want it too.'

My fork pauses halfway to my mouth.

He sees it, of course he does. Like a striptease in reverse, I layer on everything he's intent on laying bare, but I'm losing.

He leans in, lowering his voice until it's a breath against my skin. 'Who knows, you might even ask nicely.'

The temperature between us spikes. My cheeks flush and my stomach twists, but not from fear. I eat while fixing him with a glare sharp enough to slice open bone.

He chuckles, slow and rough, and leans back, watching me eat like it's the most erotic thing he's ever seen.

I force another bite down, even as my pulse punches through my veins.

Because I don't trust him. But worse, I'm starting to trust myself around him even less.

And I have no idea which one of us is the bigger threat.

* * *

Rafaelle

The Furia Racing garage smells like sweat, fuel, and adrenaline – the trinity of speed. Mechanics swarm like hornets around Renzo's car while Dante, his identical twin, leans against the pit wall with his helmet off, grinning like the cocky bastard he is. They're first and second on the timing sheets, eager pit groupies and celebrities hanging on their every word.

They're in heaven.

I nod to the capos doing their best to blend in and failing. I don't mind that too much. The show of power will deter any fuckers who think of messing with what Cesare talked us all into building with him four years ago. What's now becoming a legitimate way to rake in hundreds of billions.

Of course, the *other* Salvatore organisation will also play their part in keeping us rolling in money.

Everything should feel good.

But it doesn't. I'm irritated. Restless.

A layer of my sniper-grace precision is missing. And I know why.

It's her.

Or rather, the *absence* of her.

I let her go. Reluctantly. Told myself it was the smart move. She needed to make an appearance at the Mancinelli Racing Team's garage – keep up appearances, stop the vultures from circling, and most importantly, avoid drawing attention to the fact that the family assassin has been shacked up, albeit unwillingly, with the Salvatore Enforcer for the past twenty-four hours.

I said it was strategy. That I needed space to focus on the mission tonight.

But I've checked my phone five times in ten minutes. And yeah, *shocker*, I gave her my number. Like we were on a fucking date or something.

Now my brain won't shut the fuck up.

I don't like not knowing where she is.

I don't like not seeing her.

And I sure as hell don't like the idea of her being surrounded by those inept shitheads masquerading as her family security. It's barely noon and her fucktard uncle, Stefano, from what I spotted when I not-so-casually spied in, is already pissed. The idiot waste-of-skin thinks he can hide his drug and booze habit under *corporate entertainment.*

Maybe I should revert to my original plan – take out a Mancinelli. Specifically Stefano Mancinelli. I'd be doing the whole fucking world a fav—

'Everything okay?' A voice cuts through the static in my head.

Bibiana. My sister. One year younger than me and the only

female among a sea of testosterone, both here and within the Salvatore family. She has scars to prove for that cruel privilege.

She stands next to me, dark curls pinned back, tablet in hand. She's in her full strategist mode – sharp eyes, sharper tongue, and zero patience for bullshit.

'Shouldn't I be asking you that seeing as you're officially in charge now?' She's acting Team Boss seeing as Cesare has his hands full with impending fatherhood, being underboss and designing and selling supercars with a waiting list longer than the Monaco racetrack.

No one can accuse us of being underachievers, for fucking sure.

I nod at the twins. 'Renzo's nailing his lines at La Rascasse,' I say. 'They have another bet going as to who can get closest to the barricade at Turn 15?'

Bibi snorts without looking up. 'What do you think? I've told them whoever crashes gets Orazio's boot up the ass if I have to petition for a whole year for it.'

I smirk despite myself. 'You're scary.'

She finally glances up, arching a brow. 'And you're twitchy. Sure you're cool?'

I grunt. Can't argue. I *am* twitchy. I don't twitch.

Except when a raven-haired *virgin* assassin with a perfect mouth and a smarter-than-you glint in her eye decides to play games with my bloodstream.

I drop a kiss on her temple, earning myself a get-the-fuck-off-me glare, then step away from the pit wall, thumbing open a secure app on my burner.

I wait till I reach the garage and find a rare pocket of privacy.

I tap the screen and the freaky-as-shit black owl does its thing, unfurling slick wings, soaring straight at the screen before disintegrating into a shower of green encryption code.

A year since the mysterious hacker reached out to Cesare out of the blue to help us with our mole issue, we're no closer to discovering their identity.

I stare at the blinking cursor, not sure why I am reaching out now.

They haven't answered any of my messages in weeks.

Trying one more time beats *twitching*, I guess.

> Hey. Anything on El Topo? Possible move near the coast in Taormina?

The blinking cursor mocks me.

Then—

> Playing with shadows when your target's the sun? Careful, Enforcer. The fire comes tonight.

I frown, fingers tightening on the phone. Typical cryptic shit. But I know what he means. He's not talking about Bonafacio. He's talking about the assignment. The billionaire I'm meant to take out tonight. The one who traffics in flesh and secrets.

> Intel. Now. Don't be cute.

> Shadow Watch

Meaning what, exactly?

The message burns behind my eyes, driving my irritation up another ten notches.

I work alone. No backup. No shadow team. Just me. Like always.

Except... tonight. I'm changing my routine, planning on bringing Sofiya with me. Sexy as fuck. Pure as the driven snow. And belladonna deadly.

On paper, the worst idea I could have. Have to give

them props. The fucks at Aegis have a twisted sense of humour for giving me the green light knowing it could all go tits-up.

But it sure won't be funny ha-ha if I end up with a blade in my spine.

I glance at my reflection in the side mirror of Renzo's car. I look calm. Salvatore *mafiosi*. Unbothered. Zero twitch.

But there's a small part of me – the one Sofiya's been chipping away at with every bite of sass and every flash of vulnerability – that wonders if I should call it off tonight. Just this once. Quadruple-check my shit.

Cuff her to my bed and maybe play with her a little instead of slitting a monster's throat.

The fuck's wrong with me?

I'm about to type another response to Nightowl when my senses flare. A nanosecond before a familiar voice rolls over me like thunder.

'Who the fuck are you sexting so hard you didn't even notice me standing here?'

Cesare.

In the flesh.

Right here in an immaculate black suit, arms crossed, jaw tight. There's a tension in his shoulders I don't miss.

Neither does Bibi, who raises her brows from across the room before muttering something under her breath and quickly ducking away with her tablet.

'*Fratuzzu*,' I say, schooling my face. 'What a surprise. Shouldn't you be four thousand miles away, ass-deep in baby showers and gender-reveal bullshit?'

'Maddelena wanted to come. Monaco is her second favourite race. Besides, I thought I'd come look you in the face. See what's what.'

Slate-grey eyes inherited from the Salvatore male ancestors attempt to pierce my layers.

His tone isn't light. Cesare doesn't do 'light' these days. Not with a baby on the way and a host of trigger-happy fucking Mancinellis for in-laws.

I slide my phone into my pocket, fake nonchalance. 'Look around, it's busy as hell,' I say. 'Twins playing Russian roulette with the barriers. Renzo deciding if he wants to shoot a celebrity or ass-fuck them. Usual shit.'

His brow twitches. 'Uh-huh. So I guess we're going to talk about everything else besides the most important subject?'

I blink. 'Which is?'

'Don't fuck with me, *frate*.'

'You keeping tabs on me now?'

'No,' he snaps. 'I'm keeping tabs on the war we're *not* trying to start again, seeing as the timing is...' He snaps his fingers. 'Bad as fucking fuck. And you don't seem to give a flying shit.'

That cuts deeper than it should.

Because I don't have an answer. Not a good one.

Not one that doesn't sound like: *She's sneaking under my skin, and I'm trying to figure out if I want her out or deeper in.*

So I do what I always do.

I smirk. 'Jealous that my life is way more exciting than yours these days?'

His jaw tightens, but the corner of his mouth betrays him. 'It's not. And fuck you.'

I shrug. 'I'm busy tonight. Big job. The Chinese might reach out.' It's not a lie. But it's not the whole truth, of course. I've never betrayed my oath to the clandestine team I serve. Not even for the brother I love more than the blood in my veins. There was a time when my silence almost became an issue. Thank fuck Cesare learned to accept it.

His expression shifts instantly. 'Need anything?'

That's Cesare for *I love you, asshole.*

I shake my head. 'Not unless Maddie's willing to let you out of the palace after sundown.' I can joke about that because she won't. And I'll be long gone with another princess in tow tonight.

'Not a fucking chance,' he mutters.

We stand there for a beat – two brothers, full warriors, lately half strangers, bound by blood and bruised trust that hasn't quite healed from the events of last year.

Then he exhales and claps a hand to my shoulder.

'Whatever the fuck you're doing, don't die tonight. I'd hate to have to add the Triad...' He slants a ferocious look at me as he adds, '...or anyone else to my to-slaughter list.'

I nod.

'Ditto.'

12

RAFAELLE

If I thought Cesare would hightail it to wherever his pregnant wife was after our little chat, I was wrong.

I catch glimpses of him schmoozing the sponsors, discussing strategy with Bibi and the twins, then giving the engineers a taster of the hell he used to give them during race weekends. Basically Cesare doing what Cesare did as a racing driver between practices.

So it's no surprise at all when he returns to me, standing with his back to the track, arms crossed, suit impeccable despite the Mediterranean humidity.

He doesn't look like a man running an empire. He looks like a man who's just watched his younger brother stroll into a fire with a can of gasoline and a hard-on. And yearned for it to be him.

'You miss it, don't you?'

He tenses for a nanosecond, then shakes his head. 'Nah. At the risk of sounding like a sappy dipshit, I love my life now more than ever.' He winces, then slaps my arm. 'No offence, *frate*.'

I don't shrug and for the life of me, I can't find a single joke to counteract the sting. Our months-apart age gap made us near enough peas in a pod growing up. We stood shoulder to shoulder in everything, from taking a pummelling from Orazio's fists to losing our virginities in the same damn week.

'You were spotted this afternoon,' he says without looking at me. 'You slipping or do you just not care?'

I light a Cohiba – ignoring the no-smoking sign and the glares of the Wellness-R-Us freaks who fill their lips with Botox and their tits with fake liquid but object to a little Cuban culture – and take a long drag, leaning on the railing like I'm not the subject of an impending interrogation. 'Define "spotted".'

'Walking three steps behind the younger Mancinelli sister. Remind me again, didn't she try to kill you, like, five minutes ago?'

I shrug. 'Technically, she only tried the once. That shows restraint.'

He turns, eyes narrowing. 'You're seriously doing this?'

'Doing what?' I ask, blowing smoke rings skyward. 'Forming a strategic alliance? Getting intel? Getting head?'

Cesare exhales, slow and sharp, and pinches the bridge of his nose like he's resisting the urge to headbutt me into the next race circuit.

'She's dangerous.'

'So am I, *fratello*.'

'No. You're unstable. That's different.'

I choose not to think he's placing us in separate boxes. After three decades of bleeding side by side, of burying bodies and secrets no one else could carry. Of being mirror and shadow to each other. Is he now drawing a line between us? Making me *other*? Or am I in my fucking feelings?

I snort at the thought that isn't as funny as it should be. 'And yet you love me.'

Cesare doesn't respond right away. He looks out over the track, where Renzo's car gleams under the floodlights. Somewhere nearby, I imagine Sofiya is pretending not to be watching me from the VIP suite like she doesn't want to stab me *and* kiss me in equal measure.

Fuck, I'd give my right nut for that to be happening in real time.

My phone pings the distinct sound we both know. I don't glance at it but I feel Cesare's gaze sharpen.

'Nightowl?' Cesare says, his voice quieter.

I nod.

He frowns. 'They haven't responded to me in weeks. Not even a coded check-in.' He sounds jealous.

I smirk. 'Maybe they like me better now. And what the hell do you need them for? They're hackers, not psychics. They can't tell your future or how great you'll be at fatherhood.'

He glances at me. 'They're not supposed to *like* anyone. They're a phantom contact.'

I don't answer right away. I know what he's saying. What he's *not* saying. 'I'm not trying to cut you out.'

'No?' He looks at me again. There's no heat, just that quiet Cesare stillness that always made me want to throw punches. 'Because it feels like everything's shifting. I used to know every move before you made it. Now? I learn about your little dance with the Mancinelli chick through a damn capo.'

I flick ash into the wind. 'Things change.'

He nods slowly. 'They do. Maddie's belly gets bigger every day. She fell asleep last night with her hand on it, like she could already feel the baby dreaming. You know what that felt like?'

'What?'

'Peace. For the first time in years, I didn't feel like a killer waiting to come back to life. But with you... it doesn't feel like a good change. It feels like you're punishing me.'

I look away. Something stabs beneath my ribs. I can't deny it. Learning Maddelena and Giada Mancinelli were present when my mother took her last breath was a kick in the heart.

Cesare laying down the directive that I wasn't to go after Giada, find out everything she knew? Yeah, that was a kick in the face *and* the fucking nuts.

I scoff. 'You're about to be a dad. That's your big redemption arc. You get to raise a soft, squishy little human and teach them not to be assholes like us.'

He huffs. 'Right.'

I glance at him sideways, smirking, injecting humour into the moment because I'm a fucking team player. 'You gonna be in the room when Maddie pops it out? What if you faint when the afterbirth hits? You want me to hold your hand? Or just take your place and deliver the kid myself?'

'Shut the fuck up.'

'I'll wear gloves. Maybe.'

Cesare glares. 'You even *think* about saying any of this bull-shit to my wife and I'll put a bullet in your thigh.'

'Aw. Just the thigh?' I mock-pout. 'I distinctly remember a gun to my throat when I suggested you do the world a favour and fuck her. You're getting soft in your old age. Also, you're welcome.'

'Fuck off.'

'You first, *stronzo*.'

We fall quiet for a moment. The roar of an engine echoes below, a mechanical scream in the dying hours of *parc ferme*.

When he speaks again, it's softer. 'She may feel like some kind of deranged kindred spirit. Or a means to a necessary end. Just... don't get killed, Rafa. Not by her. Not for her.'

I clap him on the shoulder. 'That's the thing, *fratello*. If I go out, at least I'll die hard and happy.'

He groans. 'You're a fucking caveman.'

'And you love it.'

We stand there like we always have – side by side, chest to the world. But the silence now isn't easy. It's laced with something heavier. A thread we both feel but neither wants to pull tonight.

So we let it hang, the way only brothers can.

Close. Still connected.

But not quite the same.

13

RAFAELLE

I'm buckling a thigh holster over my cargo pants when the secure phone pings – three short vibrations, one long.

Nightowl's signature. The only soul outside my bloodline who can find me anywhere on earth and still vanish before sunrise.

I thumb the message open. As always, it's a riddle:

> Salt on skin. Steel underfoot. The water sings tonight.

'*Fanculo*,' I mutter, already typing back on the encrypted keypad. Either they're going easier on me or I'm getting more adept at Nightowl speak.

I'm not even going to bother to think about how Nightowl knows about a clandestine mission sanctioned from the super-secret bowels of an organisation that's not supposed to exist. I'm not going to question it though.

So far, our little hacker has been all asset, zero liability. And I'm not checking this free fuck for warts.

> My target's villa's empty, isn't it?

> Monsters in tin palaces. Sea legs advised.

Tin palace. Lupo's yacht?

The Nerissa.

Gianfranco Lupo, the silver-tongued heir to a Tuscan dynasty, far too adept at tech laundering, crypto wash pools, and the part that makes my trigger finger itch – child trafficking. A year ago I ghosted his lieutenant in Marseille; the man's Rolex turned up in a shark's belly weeks later.

Lupo doubled protection, dove deeper underground and started staging his auctions last-minute with locations switched at a moment's notice.

I'm not surprised he's moved this one from his villa to international waters.

A quick check with shady sources shows he's anchored off Larvotto like a shark in a koi pond.

I slide the phone into an RF-block pouch. Sofiya doesn't know Nightowl exists, and I intend to keep that advantage.

Across the suite, she's seated on the sofa, combat boots in her lap, tugging the laces tight. Too slow. Testing my patience – or more likely, baiting me for a reaction.

'Change of plans,' I say, strapping my second blade behind my back. 'We're going maritime.'

She looks up, eyes narrowing. 'Since when?'

'Since five seconds ago. Lupo's shifted to his yacht.'

'Source?'

'Unimpeachable.' I hope. I zip a duffel and toss her a black dry-bag. 'I'll adapt,' I say, checking the rounds in my Beretta. 'You keep up.'

She stands. Chin high and defiant. 'I'm not a rookie, Enforcer.'

I give her a look. Cool, precise and deadly.

'To me you are, until I say otherwise.'

Her face tightens.

I close the distance between us in three steps and tilt her chin with two fingers. 'You can take offence if you want. But you're young. Still figuring out where to draw your lines. You chased breadcrumbs but left a trail that I found within ten minutes. What the hell do you think the people you're looking for will think of that? If they exist.'

'Let's drop the act. We both know they do.'

'You still think you have a choice in how this plays out. You don't. I have all the power in this, or it doesn't happen. I lead, you follow. Simple as. *Capisci?*'

She's glaring at me when I continue.

'Change of entry means change of kit. Dive gear underneath, formal on top you can ditch when we get to the water. Minimal metal.'

She unzips the bag, pulling out a sleek wetsuit and a small, custom PPK with an integrated suppressor. 'Nice toy.'

'Stainless. It won't malfunction if you end up swimming.'

Her brow lifts. 'Planning to push me overboard?'

'Only if you slow me down.'

I shrug on a tactical black dress shirt – reinforced button placket with knife plate sewn between the shoulder blades. Over that, a charcoal blazer that drapes just loose enough to hide the holster.

Sofiya disappears into the bathroom with the wetsuit. By the time she returns she's zipped to the collarbone, curves poured into matte neoprene. She tosses her clothes on the bed and peels another jumpsuit from its hanger.

I whistle. 'Careful there, *tigra*. You'll bankrupt the wrong men wearing that.'

'Focus, Enforcer.' She steps into the dress, shimmies it up, then pulls her hair into a sleek knot. 'How are we getting aboard? Guards will scan invitations.'

I sling a dry-bag over my shoulder. 'Side service ladder. Yacht's galley offloads provisions at twenty-thirty. We'll neutralise two stewards, steal the uniforms, stroll straight to A-deck ballroom.' I grab her chin between thumb and knuckle – gentle, but not soft. 'Stay where I can see you. This crowd buys girls less prettier than you. If someone touches you, I break fingers before I break skulls.'

Her pulse kicks under my grip. 'You assuming I need rescuing?'

'I assume everyone but me is a liability.'

She exhales a shaky breath, but her gaze doesn't waver. 'Baseline trust?' She echoes my words.

I nod. 'I have your back, you have mine. Don't get cute and deviate. Run and I will track you. Get yourself hurt' – I lean closer, letting her feel the steel of my promise – 'and I'll carve souvenirs from whoever drew your blood, *after* I lock you some-where you can't bleed again. And I fuck a seven-day apology out of that virgin pussy.'

A tremor flickers across her lips, maybe fear, or desire, or adrenaline. Fuck, probably all of the above. 'If *you* go down?'

'Drag my gorgeous corpse out before the sharks get a taste.' I grin. 'And mourn me for a dozen years. At least. Because make no mistake. I'll make a mean and fuck-hot ghost. And I'll haunt the shit out of you.'

She chokes on a laugh – half scandalised, half aroused. I love that sound. It makes me want to hear what she moans like.

I toss her a thigh sheath for the PPK. 'Over your cute-ass hardwear.'

'Pervert.'

'You noticed.'

* * *

Larvotto Marina – 20:45

Wind carries the scent of salt and engine diesel. Below the pier, a black inflatable with a silent motor idles.

I help Sofiya down the ladder. The jumpsuit adds an extra layer of sin, reminding me of the one she had on when she shot me in the fucking chest; every step flexes neoprene over skin, and my cock's been a steady ache since she zipped it.

We skim across moonlit water, light spray in our faces.

The Nerissa grows from shimmer to hulking white fortress. Four decks and two helipads. Strings of Edison bulbs trace her silhouette and music drifts over the water, a jarring symphony of smooth saxophone and the brittle laughter of deviant assholes.

We cut engines fifty metres off the stern. Two catering tenders bob beside the loading platform. One security guard, pissing about on his phone.

A pop from my silencer and he drops into the water with barely a splash.

Perfect.

I toss a grapnel hook and limb.

Sofiya follows, knives at the ready as two crewmen step out, cigarettes glowing.

'Delivery's late,' one grumbles in French. 'I'm going to catch shit from the fucking diva chef.'

I answer with a palm strike to the trachea. He collapses without a sound. Sofiya slits the other's femoral, her hand clamped over his mouth; the man bleeds out in seconds, eyes wide with a plea to a god who isn't listening.

She meets my gaze, surprisingly steady with no rookie tremble now – and something hot twists in my gut.

Battle-ready looks fucking good on her.

We ditch our clothes, strip the bodies, don white steward jackets over our wetsuits, slip into polished loafers. Blood wipes off the deck with seawater.

Less evidence than a spilled bottle of rosé.

* * *

A-Deck Ballroom – 21:37

From shore, *The Nerissa* glowed. Inside, she dazzles with the over-gaudiness of a fat pervert with too much money and zero taste.

Crystal chandeliers sway with the tide. A string quartet plays Debussy while waiters glide with Dom Pérignon. Guests wear satin masks – anonymity for auction night. Predators always dress in flourishes and glitter and perfume to hide the rotting underbelly.

I drift past oyster towers, scanning.

Lupo isn't on this deck, but VIPs watch from the upper gallery until bidding begins.

Beside me, Sofiya balances a silver tray, moving like she's born for service, though her eyes flick, counting exits, cameras, guards.

We pass a knot of sheikhs. One pinches her ass.

I spin, crack his wrist sideways. A pop of cartilage and he

yelps. His guards move. I flash my Beretta under the tray cloth and they step back fast.

'She's mine,' I murmur in Sicilian. 'Hands off.'

Sofiya shoots me a look, half gratitude, half fury. 'You don't own me,' she hisses when we're clear.

'Then explain the hard-on I've had since you shot me, *tigra*,' I whisper, delighting in the pink stain climbing her neck. 'Business first, hmm?' I add, slipping a micro-camera under the buffet rail, patching feed to my phone. Then we wait.

Three minutes. Five.

Two burly guards weave their way through the crowd, murmuring to guests. One by one, the sleazy players drift towards double doors, their final destination for the auction.

I nod at Sofiya.

We ditch the trays, ascend a maintenance ladder behind velvet drapes and enter a mid-deck corridor.

Lupo's study is ahead.

Sofiya draws, whisper-quiet. Sexy and efficient.

A part of me admits I'd hoped she wouldn't be this good. That I'd have no choice but to make a definitive decision about her, even before she's delivered her grandfather.

And now?

I push the whole fucking thing away and breach.

Behind the desk, Lupo lounges in a silver tux, wolfish grin. Counting money he'll never spend in this life. He's flanked by two ex-GIGN mercs.

They're immobilised in under a minute, and my breath barely rises above forty-two bpm.

I perch on the side of his desk as Lupo reaches for his hidden gun. Another pop and his right wrist disintegrates.

'*Buona sera, signore*,' I hiss. 'Auction's cancelled.'

He opens his mouth to scream. I clamp my hand over it, the butt of my gun shoved under his ribs.

He gurgles, eyes darting. Pleading.

I drop the gun on the desk and reach for my trusted knife as Sofiya empties his safe. USB drives, ledger, stack of passports the size of a Bible.

I glance down at his left wrist. 'Nice watch. You'll be pleased to know your time of death is... 21:49.'

I side the blade between his ribs. One precise upward jerk. Heart pierces and his life ends. No screams. Just the soft sound of a man condemned by his own appetites.

Sofiya joins me as I wipe the knife on Lupo's silk pocket square. 'Efficient,' she whispers.

'It's what they pay me for.'

I feel her sharpened gaze and I smile to myself. I have her hooked. For as long as I want. I just need to decide *that* measure of time.

Lupo's body's still warm when we slip out. Two minutes later we're over the side, splash-silent into black water.

Behind us, *The Nerissa* still sparkles. Music, champagne, oblivious sin cruising towards open sea with a corpse cooling in its study.

Sofiya treads water beside me, moonlight slick on her face. For a heartbeat the world is only salt, and pulse, and shared breath.

I reach out, hook a hand behind her neck, pull her mouth to mine – hard, claiming, salt-sweet. She gasps but doesn't pull away. For three seconds we forget blood, war, family.

Then the RIB inflatable drifts close, a silent reminder that we're not free and clear.

I break the kiss, tastes of sea and danger lingering. 'Baseline trust, *bedda*. I've got you.'

She swallows, and her eyes sparkle in the dark. 'And I've got you.'

I smile and gun the motor towards the lights of Monaco, leaving a dead monster adrift and one very alive temptation at my side.

* * *

Sofiya

I'm still vibrating when we hit the beach, blood-warm water licking at my calves as Rafa drags the inflatable onto the damp sand.

Adrenaline always leaves me jittery, but tonight it feels different – hotter, dirtier, like I swallowed live wires. The salt air can't scrub the iron scent from my nostrils or the sting of Lupo's fear from my tongue.

The easy violence with which Rafa broke that asshole's wrist makes me... hot.

I clutch the waterproof satchel stuffed with passports and ledgers, aware of how my hands tremble despite years of conditioning.

And conditioning started early.

* * *

The Past – Summer
Age Twelve
Mancinelli hunting lodge, Madonie Mountains, Sicily

'You shoot a deer once or twice – okay, five times – from over four hundred and fifty yards during one hunting season,' I mutter under my breath while I walk, half-numb from recoil and teenage outrage, 'and suddenly your dreams of becoming an equestrian champion or a dance instructor are out the window. You *had* hedged your bets – just in case the horses detested you, just in case the stables smelled too strongly of manure.'

But the second Bonafacio saw the grouping in the deer's ribs, something predatory lit behind his eyes. Sealed my fate.

From then on, my summers weren't tennis lessons and learning to swing my hips like my sisters at the country club; they were dawn hikes to isolated ridges, target practice on dangling tin cans, sketchy guerrilla fire-and-manoeuvre drills with ex-soldiers who smelled of sweat and gun oil.

* * *

Winter
Age Fifteen
Palermo docks

First human shot: a smuggler who thought hiding behind a refrigerated container made him invisible. I vomited afterwards – behind a stack of pallets where no one could see.

When I straightened, Nonno ruffled my hair and told me he was proud. That I had a bright future ahead of me.

Pride should have felt warm.

It felt like acid.

* * *

Tonight
Monaco Shoreline

Ten kills in eight years and that acid still burns.

I keep waiting for the guilt to dull or harden into something useful. Or at the very least, something I shrug off when I need to. It never has.

Instead it roams in pockets, manifesting in sudden, unpredictable sinkholes that chew through my composure.

Right now, one of those craters yawns wide at my feet.

I bend, brace my palms on my thighs, breathing too fast as the last fifteen minutes replays on a loop.

As if I need something else to admire about him, Rafa kills clean. I kill because someone told me I had the gift. A gift I couldn't return or give away or even complain about because had it been wielded by a man, he would've been given a kingdom. Instead I got watched, controlled, and even the slightest deviation from total acceptance would've made me a liability in Nonno's eyes.

Why am I thinking about this? Getting emotional instead of emotion-free?

And why does the wetsuit feel like a fucking straitjacket? I swallow rising bile. 'Shit.'

Rafa steps close, dripping seawater, dark hair pasted to his skull. Even soaked, he radiates that unholy mix of easy strength and feral promise.

The Enforcer. My temporary stay-of-executioner, possibly my mentor. My family's enemy. My—

'Breathe through it,' he orders, voice low, calm, annoyingly steady. His hands stay at his sides; he's smart enough not to grab me. 'Dump the flight-or-fight juice before it bottles up. Shake your arms out.'

I do it, rolling my shoulders, flicking wrists, sucking air that tastes of brine and monsters. Still, the memory blurts: Lupo's eyes bulged, lips shaped around a plea that never made sound.

You did that, Sofiya. You helped.

Another pocket of guilt tears open.

Rafa sees it. Of course he does. 'First one's a bitch,' he murmurs. 'Even if it's not your literal first.' He angles his body, shielding me from the glow of a boardwalk café a hundred yards away, giving me privacy without retreating. 'He had girls in cages. You gave them a shot at breathing free air. Let that be louder than the hesitation in your pulse.'

I bark a brittle laugh. 'You give TED talks now?'

'Only the after-dark edition.' A flicker of humour softens his feral edges. 'Come on, *picciridda*. You did good.'

I block out the 'for a Mancinelli' and ride the wave of praise.

Good.

The word lands strangely. I've never sought moral applause. I do what must be done. For my family, eternally at war with someone or something. Because I'm useful, non-hysterical. All the ways that deflect the fact that I don't have the Y chromosome.

Yet hearing it from him – this brutal, deranged, *temporary* guardian angel – sends heat crawling across my skin.

I look up, expecting mockery. Instead I find... concern. Uneasy, reluctant concern in coffee-brown eyes.

It tilts the world.

'You really believe that?' My voice cracks despite my best effort.

He nods once. 'Unfortunate truth – monsters exist. People like us are the tax collectors.' His lips twitch. 'And I hate to say it, but you make an excellent auditor.'

It's absurd, obscene – and oddly comforting. The pocket of guilt stops expanding.

Wind lifts my tangled hair.

Rafa reaches out, tucking a strand behind my ear. The touch

jolts a fresh surge of adrenaline. Less fight, more *heat*. Memories stack back up – his kiss, his body covering mine in the water, a broken wrist in my honour, the constant crackle of tension since New York.

I'm not supposed to want this man. The impulse feels treasonous.

But want throbs low in my belly anyway, ratcheting up as we haul the RIB under pier shadows, secure it, trek to a service lift that dumps us in the hotel's underground garage. A private elevator whooshes us up eight floors. Silence hums between us, thick with unspoken things.

'You okay?' he asks, softer, once we're in the suite.

I nod. Lie. 'Peachy.'

'Prove it. Eat something, hot shower, forty-five minutes downtime for you while I take care of the final touches.' His eyes harden a touch. 'There's also the matter of tracking Bonafacio's last hidey-hole.'

Always planning. He's the blade that never dulls.

And blades can cut the wielder.

'You ever unwind?' I ask.

His grin is all wolf, his shrug utterly unapologetic. 'I either fuck something hard enough to incinerate my spine or find the next walking problem and delete it. Fastest reset button there is.'

It takes a full second for the words to land. 'You get the high from one... call it a "fixed-variable operation"... by jumping straight to another?'

'Adrenaline's a habit,' he says, eyes gleaming. 'You taper it with sex or blood. Keeps the engine tuned.'

I huff, half shocked, half morbidly impressed. 'That's... efficient, I guess.'

He tilts his head. 'Your turn, *picciridda*. How do you come down?'

Heat detonates under my skin. The honest answer is two fingers and the hotel showerhead set to pulse. 'Music,' I start – and under his arched brow, I add in a mumbled, 'And... uh, water pressure.'

His laugh is low, devilish. 'Should've known. Bet you look gorgeous falling apart under the spray.'

My cheeks flare. The tease should annoy me; instead, it sends a pulse between my legs. Damn him for resurrecting that memory. Damn me for liking it.

In the suite, Rafa strips out of his garments, muscles rippling as he wrings water into the sink, then dons slacks and a shirt, unbuttoned.

I peel off my clothes. A silk slip lies folded on the bed alongside towels, energy gels and bottled electrolytes.

He must've ordered turn-down service before we left.

I pop a gel, and sour cherry hits my tongue. Rafa watches, amusement curling his lips.

'Good girl,' he murmurs.

Heat darts under my skin. 'Don't.'

'What? Praise?' He steps closer and drops a towel over my shoulders. 'You earned it.'

Praise again. Makes the guilt recede further, replaced by a frightening blaze of pride. But it's a dangerous drug, rarely offered selflessly.

God, I should retreat to the shower. Instead, I grip the towel like a lifeline. 'I'm still your enemy.'

He brushes knuckles down my cheek. 'So be it, baby.'

I breathe him in – sandalwood, gunpowder, something dangerously male. My pulse hammers. The guilt pockets are gone, replaced by a craving I don't recognise.

He dips his head and his breath skims my lips. 'Tell me to stop.'

I should. The list of reasons scrolls through my brain – families at war, loyalties in tatters, Bonafacio, wounded and hiding but by no means vanquished. Even my sister Giada's hidden existence is now a threat I need to keep a close eye on.

I should step away.

Instead, I fist the lapel of his open shirt and pull.

Our mouths crash. Raw, searching, nothing like the controlled kiss on the yacht. His hands frame my face, angling for deeper. I taste adrenaline, seawater, the lazy bourbon he downed before we left. I moan and he swallows it, responding with a growl that rumbles in my chest.

He walks me backward until my thighs hit the bed.

The towel slips, wetsuit half peeled to my waist. His palms drag down my arms, thumbs grazing the peaks of my breasts. Sparks scatter along my spine.

He breaks the kiss just enough to bite my lower lip. 'Baseline trust,' he rasps. 'I won't break you, yet – but I'll bend you so sweet you'll forget every goddamn rule your family drilled in your skull.'

The promise steals my breath. Shame flickers with how quickly duty dissolves in heat, but the guilt pockets stay closed. Maybe they can't coexist with this wildfire.

I slide my palms beneath his damp shirt, mapping scars. Old knife, bullet, vicious lines near his ribs. Proof of battles fought alone by the mighty Enforcer. It twists something tender in my heart. My fingers linger over the space where I shot him.

With that same deranged impulse, I probe his bruise.

He hisses. Pulls back, eyes black with want. 'Last chance, *bedda*.'

I swallow. 'I get to drag your corpse out, remember?'

A wicked grin. 'Well, okay then.'

He kisses me again, deeper, slower, like he's savouring a victory. I let him. For tonight the monsters are one corpse lighter, and the war can wait outside our door.

Inside, two predators burn the guilt away in each other's arms.

14

SOFIYA

Sour cherry and salt still coat my lips when Rafa backs me against the suite's door and clicks the lock.

The city hum of Monte Carlo fades; in its place, our jagged and hungry breathing that drowns out everything but need.

The wetsuit drags against my skin as he peels the zipper down, inch by inch, like he's unwrapping contraband.

He growls something in Sicilian-laced English about how the neoprene hid 'every sinful inch' from him all night.

My heart jackhammers. I'm proud of my first mission with the Enforcer, wired from adrenaline, but beneath that pride curls an ache I barely recognise.

The suit puddles at my feet. I'm left in damp panties and weak knees. Rafa kneels – *kneels* – and drags his hands up the backs of my thighs, gentle but with a hint of nails. Goosebumps race in their wake.

Up. Down. Up. Down.

Absorbing my every reaction like he's deciphering Sanskrit. Then he pulls closer, drops a kiss on my navel. Higher, to the apparently seriously erogenous zone of the lower curve of my left breast.

A long swipe of his tongue. A thick groan. 'Fuck.'

Several flicks that bounce my breast and make my pussy throb like a drumbeat. God, how did I not know...?

He laves everywhere but the screaming tip of my breast, leaving whimpers and pleas locked in my throat. I'm near mindless when he pays the same infuriating attention the other breast.

My nails dig into his shoulders as I angle mine, seeking deliverance from his mouth. 'Rafaelle...'

A filthy smirk. 'There she is, my little *tigra*.'

He barely finishes speaking before his mouth closes over my nipple, suckling and flicking without mercy while his hand closes over the other.

My head falls back. Hunger stalking me since the second he revealed himself on the roof in New York flays me wide open.

'Look at me, *duci*,' he growls.

My head drops, my eyes finding his even though I sense I should be avoiding them. Masking. He's staring at me as he returns to lapping the underside of my breasts, and sweet heaven, why is that so fucking hot?

'Do you like that?' The question is redundant.

My knees are sagging beneath the onslaught of pleasure. Still, I try to reason it out. 'How... Why...?'

He smirks. 'Your tits are the perfect weight and beautifully sensitive for maximum sensory overload.' Eyes gone dark coffee sweep hot and feral over me. 'You will look sensational all tied up, tits free and ready to be sucked and licked till you come. I won't even need to go near this pussy growing slick for me, will I, *bedda*? Breast play alone will get you off, won't it?'

I want to ask how he knows. Where he learned that. But I've

participated in one murder tonight. I'm not entertaining a potential jealous rage killing.

With a hitched cry, I offer him my tip again. He swoops, a groan torn from his throat as he accepts my gift.

The first inkling of that bending he spoke of is when his hands suddenly grip my legs, his thumbs pressing into my inner thighs to hold me up. I blink. Realise I've sagged halfway down the door.

He splays me wider. Scents me while looking into my eyes.

Then his gaze drops.

And for the first time in my life, I watch a man staring at my pussy. Licking his lips and groaning at what he sees.

'Fuck, you're beautiful.' His voice is a ragged scrape. 'I need to taste how righteous victory made you.' Then his mouth replaces his hands on one inner thigh.

Hot and devastating.

He mutters crude devotion against the inside of my leg. I only catch fragments – something about cherries and spoils of war – before language melts into sensation. Every flick of his tongue up my thigh tightens the coil in my belly.

My fingers tangle in his wet hair, anchoring myself as if the ground might tilt beneath me. When his tongue drags slowly up the inside of one thigh, deliberately avoiding where I'm desperate for him, my back arches, breath hitching.

The coil inside me winds tighter, drawn taut by the way he takes his time, like he's savouring each reaction. He kisses the hollow at the top of my thigh, then does it again on the other side. Soft. Then rougher. His stubble scrapes lightly, a contrast that makes me shudder.

'Rafa,' I whisper, barely recognising my own voice.

He hums like he's amused. Or turned on. Maybe both.

'You taste like trouble, *bedda*,' he murmurs, voice thick and gravel rich. 'And I haven't even had the best part yet.'

My whole body flushes at the implication.

His fingers tighten around my hips just as his mouth finally – *finally* – moves to where I'm throbbing for him.

Then his mouth closes on my clit. *Flick. Flick. Flick.* And I howl, my vision compressing a nanosecond before it detonates.

Pleasure splinters me, sharp and helpless.

'There you go. That's it, *tigra*,' he croons. Fingers dance at my molten entrance, but he doesn't go in. Just draws out my slick and my release. 'I can be patient, baby. Just keep giving me the honey.'

A tortured groan ripples through the room when his mouth finds me once more, hungry licks lapping at me.

The moment the trembling eases, he shifts back.

Reaches for the towel and starts to tuck it gently around my waist like he's already moving on. His hands still linger on my hips, but there's a hesitation in them now. A peculiar restraint.

My pulse rallies, part defiance, part stubborn pride. I push him back and Rafa drops onto the carpet.

'You need rest,' he says quietly, brushing damp hair from my face. His voice is low, rough with emotion – and something else. 'You don't have to—'

I glance down. He's hard. Thick and straining against his slacks.

My chest and pussy clench hard.

But he's shaking his head already. 'Sofiya, there's no need.'

No need.

Like I wouldn't want to. Like I couldn't handle more. The words land wrong. The burn of them flares beneath my skin, sharp and instant. He thinks I can't take it. Because I'm a virgin?

My pulse kicks up again, this time from something fiercer. Lust? Guilt?

No. Defiance.

Shirt loose and chest bare, he's beyond mouthwatering. He stretches beneath me, scarred torso gleaming and feral eyes watching. Danger personified. I want that danger on my tongue.

I crouch and nudge his waistband down far enough to free him and wrap trembling fingers around his thick heat. His hiss is a shotgun blast in the quiet room. 'Easy, *bedda*. Slow or I'll embarrass us both.'

'I'm not as green as you think,' I breathe.

I pull out his thick girth and... oh... God, he's *hung*. And beautiful. Veins I want to lick hands-free the way he just licked my breasts. What did he say?

...the perfect weight and beautifully sensitive for maximum sensory overload.

My fingers snag over a bump and my breath catches.

Silverware. *Oh holy hell.*

Rafa's pierced. At the top and just beneath his crown. The promise of that... inside me, caressing the bundle of nerves I've yet to discover... is a blend of terror and feverish anticipation.

He's watching me. Waiting. Weighing.

Before I chicken out, I bend, slide my lips over the crest of him. I'm clumsy, too wet with climax and nerves, yet his groan tells me clumsy still feels good. He fists the carpet, dropping into mentor mode.

He murmurs directions – filthy, velvet-rough encouragement that sparks my own heat back to life. Possessiveness coils in his words. 'That better not be you telling me you've done this before.'

I don't respond. I'm busy learning the taste of Rafaelle Salvatore's cock. And Jesus. Another first. Because he's addictive. Insanely moreish.

But he snatches my chin, his touch none-too-gentle. I freeze with his crown in my mouth, my eyes pinned by his.

'No one else gets this mouth. Do you hear me, Sofiya?'

My nostrils flare with my exhale. With my delight at hearing my name on his lips.

'Fucking answer me, just so we're on the same page.'

I release him with a decadent pop, jerking when the sound electrifies my bloodstream. 'I hear you.'

His fingers tighten. 'Flirting with semantics, *bedda*? You're either foolish or death-wish baiting. But fuck, you look so good with your mouth wrapped around my cockhead. I'll let it slide. Go on,' he encourages. 'Take me down your throat, *tigra*. Let me ruin you for other men.'

It should scare me.

Instead, it brands something – ownership I should reject – but my traitorous body arches into it. I lick and suck in sloppy greed I can't control.

And he seems to love it. Growing feral by the second, hips piston higher with each push of his length down my throat.

'Fuck!' His control splinters when I hollow my cheeks, and he pulses hard once, twice, spilling down my throat. He mutters a long, guttural '*Cristu.*' I swallow – proud, shaky, a little stunned at my own boldness.

He drags me up over his body, kisses me – tasting himself on my tongue – then rolls me under him, forehead resting against mine. 'You're lethal everywhere, aren't you?'

He doesn't give me a chance to answer. He swoops in for another long, tongue-tangling kiss. And the suite is still humming with the aftershock of what Rafa's mouth did to my body when a sharp rap jolts us both.

Three measured knocks, then the latch kicks.

Rafa swears, snatches his discarded trousers, and stalks into the living room, shutting the bedroom door behind him with a controlled click.

I sit up, clutching the towel to my chest, pulse ricocheting. Voices carry through the wood.

'The fuck—'

'You weren't answering your phone – again,' a voice growls. Deep and unmistakable.

Cesare Salvatore.

He sounds tired and irritated, the way only an arrogant heir and older brother can. 'Thought you might be dead. Should I even bother asking where you were?'

Rafa's answer is dry, a little smug. 'You know better than that, *frate*.'

There's a pause – Cesare probably taking stock: Rafa shirtless, hair wet, no trace of contrition. I imagine his jaw tightening.

'Well, while you were busy doing something you should know better than to do, the Chinese reached out.'

I hear a hiss of irritation. 'Let me guess. They want to meet at the casino?'

'No. In Nice,' Cesare continues. 'We're wheels up in thirty.'

'We? You're coming?'

'Might as well, since I'm in the neck of the woods anyway. Not letting you have all the fun.'

A grunt. Then, 'Copy. But I thought you'd be reluctant to leave Maddie.'

'She's fine. And speaking of Maddie—' Cesare raises his voice, directing it at the closed door. 'Sofiya, if you're behind that wood, my wife's asking for you. She's restless and irritated and pregnant. And apparently you brushed her off this afternoon.

Think you can keep her from tearing the place apart while we go negotiate with some Triads?'

I clear my throat, hot embarrassment crawling up my neck. But I bite my lip for a moment, then mutter back. 'Sure.' It's barely audible but he hears me.

Apparently Salvatore men have bat-sharp hearing.

'Good,' he mutters. 'Because I'm trusting you to keep her calm. Both of you, try not to kill each other while the grown-ups handle business.'

Rafa's low chuckle filters through. 'Speak for yourself.'

Shoes scuff, then the door thunks shut. Silence swells until the bedroom door eases open again. Rafa steps inside, now half-buttoned and wholly predatory.

'You okay?' he asks, sweeping me with a gaze that still burns.

'Peachy.' The adrenaline of combat returns – different flavour, laced with embarrassment this time. 'He knew I was here?'

'He's suspected for days. Now it's confirmed.' Rafa strokes a thumb across my swollen bottom lip.

'Great, now I can look forward to an interrogation from my very pregnant big sister to top off the night? What more can a girl ask for?'

His eyes gleam. Savage and deranged as he crosses to me, fingers trailing from my neck to my shoulder to the top of the towel tied over my breasts. 'I can think of two dozen. Easy.'

I shove at his chest but with not much force, more flustered than in protest. 'Well, unthink them.'

The guilt pockets from earlier? Gone. Burned to ash by a man who devours sin for breakfast and praises my darkness like it's a crown. I don't know if that should frighten me or free me.

Maybe both.

Rafa hangs back at the doorway, watching with that

unblinking focus that always makes me feel skinless. 'Remember the agreement,' he says quietly. 'Do nothing foolish, Sofiya. I'll know.'

Something almost... tender edges his warning. I tamp down the flutter it sparks.

'I'll head out to see Maddie,' I reply, summoning composure. 'Try not to burn Nice to the ground.'

He smirks and it's equal parts threat and promise, then he leans in, pressing a kiss to my temple, surprisingly gentle. But his eyes are anything but when he rears back. 'Be here when I get back, *bedda*. Don't make me hunt you.' His lips graze my ear. 'We'll finish what we started when Nice stops burning.'

When the door closes behind him, the suite feels twice as big and far too empty. I stare at the rumpled sheets, at the wetsuit half-rolled on the floor, and touch the spot his mouth branded on my skin.

Only forty-eight hours ago, Rafa was lining up a sniper's shot at my baby brother. Now he knows what my pleasure tastes like and I'm standing in the middle of his suite, craving him again while my pulse still beats to the rhythm of his name. My skin still tingling where his mouth branded me – a reminder that war has more than one battlefield, and tonight, somehow, I survived both.

But... what kind of war is this – where the enemy feels like the only shelter I want?

15

RAFAELLE

22:47 – En Route to Nice

Rotor wash rattles the cabin windows like hail.

Beneath us, the Riviera is a smear of night-black water stitched with yacht lights. Cesare sits opposite, blazer off, sleeves rolled up, displaying tattoos we've been inking jointly and separately since I was sixteen and he was seventeen.

That punch of memory soothes for a minute and I watch him updating a shared file on his tablet before I return to running a final check on the burner SIMs we'll hand over after signatures.

'Six delegates from the Jade-Dragon Tong,' he reminds me, voice pitched low over the engine thrum. 'Chairman Lu's son runs point, but we treat Elder Tang as the real decision maker. No jokes about age, no eye-contact linger on the facial scar. And definitely no popping kneecaps for shits and giggles like you did to Kamirov's man back in Azerbaijan. Got it?'

I smirk. 'Scar looks like art. I might ask who did the brushwork.'

Cesare flicks me a glare that would freeze lava. 'Try professional tonight, brother.'

Professional I can do. It's emotions that keep tripping the wire.

He exhales, sliding the tablet away. 'We're green on intel, but I need your read on distribution. France wants deniability. Spain'll pay extra for hush routes.'

'We double the transit fee,' I say. 'They're desperate. They'll eat the cost.'

We lapse into silence, but Cesare's gaze keeps drifting – past the clipboard, past the gear bag beside him – onto me. He's working himself up to something.

'Spit it out,' I mutter.

'You slept with her?'

I lift a brow. 'Define "slept".'

'Cut the shit. Did you fuck Sofiya?' He rubs the space above his brow, then carries on before I can deliver the *'none of your fucking business'* I planned. 'I was ready to chalk the past few days to... I don't know... a take-the-edge-off skirmish. But Maddie thinks there's something going on—'

'And how would she know if you didn't tell her?'

His glare sharpens. Deepens. 'I like my balls exactly where they are, which means I know better than to keep secrets from my wife. Her bullshit radar is top class,' he adds with a hint of pride. Then he exhales. 'I know things aren't as copacetic as you and I would like them to be, but if anything happens—'

'Family first. Always,' I cut in. 'Sofiya is, believe it or not, the reason things aren't... a little more fucked.'

He stares, waits. As if I'll crumble under the Underboss routine. 'Care to expand on that?' he snaps after a handful of seconds.

'Nope.' I let the 'p' pop in a way I know will irritate the fuck out of him. 'But I won't screw with the current directive, such as it is. The rest you'll have to take on trust.'

He scoffs, shakes his head. 'You've never let the family down; I'll give you that. Doesn't mean I want a war bride sequel.'

I lean forward, elbows on knees. 'She's a means to an end.' My gut calls me a liar, and I hate how loud it sounds. 'You want reassurances? I'll try not to be the one who kills her.'

'Saints fucking preserve us.' He pinches his nose, half-laughing, half-miserable. 'Maddie'll skin me if Sofiya ends up on a slab. And I'll stay alive long enough to fucking skin you.'

'Then all incentives align, *frate*. Leave it.'

He studies me – old habit, reading micro-tells from our street-fight childhood. Finally he nods once, steel in his spine. 'We get the contract, we exfil, then you go get Sofiya. My wife needs her rest and that sister of hers is...' Whatever he sees on my face makes his words trail off.

I smirk. 'Sure thing. If she's not blowing up my phone first,' I murmur, surprising myself with how much I hope she does.

* * *

23:08 – Nice, Port Lympia – Private Freeport Warehouse

The Tong picked a discreet venue.

A concrete bunker with a mezzanine draped in red silks to hide the cameras. Six men wait at a lacquered conference table flanked by bodyguards in bespoke suits.

Elder Tang rises. Early seventies with a thin silver braid, cheek scar like a white river delta. His gaze pins Cesare, then me. 'Salvatore brothers. Your reputation precedes you.'

'And yours keeps me awake at night,' Cesare answers in flawless Mandarin. Good opening – respect plus implied parity.

I switch to Cantonese, just to showcase another arrow in the quiver. 'Let's talk numbers before dawn steals the luck.'

His eyes slide back to me. Rests. Assesses.

Beyond his shoulders, shadows move in the dark.

'Drink, first.'

I bite my tongue, swallow a trite comment.

I've never understood the need for mobsters to drink before a deal. A sliced throat? A bare-knuckle fight to establish who's got the bigger dick? That I understand. Respect even. Fucking around with alcohol to see if I lose a sliver of inhibition? Bullshit.

But I feel Cesare's silent warning. And I nod.

Chairs slide. Whiskey appears – top-shelf, exquisite crystal-ware, no ice. I grudgingly admire their class.

'To gathering sand and collecting harvests,' Cesare says, glass raised.

The old man's eyes glint with a hint of respect.

We drink.

Then the bare-knuckle negotiations begin. Contracts are offered, weapons manifest, shipping corridors disguised as medical-supply lanes. We haggle over percentages, off-loading sequence, fallback ports if Interpol sniffs too close. Lu's son tries to grandstand; Elder Tang silences him with a single knuckle rap.

Two hours later, the ledger is signed in disappearing ink. And not a single moment do I get a hankering to reach for the long knife resting against my right ribs. More's the pity.

At the final handshake, my palm slides across Tang's scarred knuckles, his thin lips curving. 'To future harvests,' he intones.

'May they be bloody and bountiful,' I reply.

If he's offended, he hides it behind a smile sharp as a scalpel.

* * *

01:32 – Return Flight

The rotor beats feel slower on the way back – mission success kind of calm. Cesare locks the USB ledgers in a biometric case, then buckles in.

He glances over. 'You gonna check in or shall I?'

'Soon as we land.'

'Good.' He taps the armrest twice – our old code for 'watch your six'. Then he lets his eyes close.

I stare out the cabin window at the black sweep of sea. Nice recedes; Monaco neon-flares on the horizon like a pulse. Somewhere in that glow, Sofiya will be pacing Maddie's suite, half-annoyed, half-relieved I'm not dead.

She's worked it out by now. Kill me and another will take my place. There are enough Salvatores to keep our decades-long vendetta going.

I thumb open my phone, type a message I never thought I'd send to a Mancinelli assassin:

> Wheels down in 15. Still breathing. You?

Three dots appear almost instantly.

My chest does a stupid, weightless lurch I pretend not to feel.

> Still breathing. Maddie fed me tiramisu and scolded me. Why are you texting me, Enforcer? You bored?

> Not bored. Far from it. Withdrawal symptoms from the taste of your cunt? Most definitely.

The speech bubble ripples, then dies. As I knew it would.

I pocket the phone, a grin tugging despite myself, imagining her pink cheeks and elevated breathing.

Means to an end, I remind the traitor voice in my head.

Yet for the first time in years, victory tastes sweeter than blood.

* * *

02:05 – Monaco Airfield, Idling on the Tarmac

The rotor whine fades and the cabin hatch thumps shut behind Cesare and me. Before the generators spool down, Cesare pulls out an old-school satellite handset the size of a brick – Orazio swears encrypted cells 'steal your soul through the glass'.

Traditional, stubborn as Sicily. And yet the same man who's addicted to playing Candy Crush on his iPhone.

He hands it over. 'You closed the deal; you get the honour.'

Lucky fucking me.

I pace away from the fuselage and thumb the cranky keypad. Three rings. Click. No hello – only the gravel rasp of the man who ran the Salvatore empire before indoor plumbing reached half our villages in the Old Country.

'About *fucking* time one of you called,' Orazio barks.

'*Ciao*, Nonnu.' I keep my tone even, respectful. I may be a pain whore, but I swear the sting from my grandfather's fist is laced with voodoo to make it hurt more. And I don't believe in the fucking crap. 'We locked the Triad contract. Full container allotment to start, double haul price, delivery windows set.'

His snort crackles the line. 'Guns and powder – good. Money keeps the *famigghia* fat and happy. But where's the *real* trophy? You find that goat-humping Mancinelli yet?'

A sixty-seven million deal is tossed over his shoulder like the husk of a sucked-out langoustine. Onto other... better things.

I exhale. Don't blame him. He was there right alongside me and my father the evening Cesare told us what he'd learned from Maddelena. That contrary to our beliefs, it wasn't the Russians who gunned down my mother and two other innocents in the church in Manhattan.

That Bonafacio and his progeny had a direct hand in it.

'I'm chasing leads,' I say. 'We located one safehouse tonight.'

I catch Cesare's sharp interest at that.

Orazio sputters, 'Leads? *Pah*. You boys used to drag assholes home by their intestines.' He hacks a laugh that turns into a cough. 'You want me to come down there and show you how to twist a knife? I might be eighty-one, but I can still shove steel up a *culo* faster than your TikTok generation.'

I glance at Cesare; he rolls his eyes skyward, mouthing *Good luck.*

Orazio keeps going, Sicilian fire in every syllable. 'That bastard Bonafacio blew up half our home, put your mother in the ground, and now he hides like a church mouse? Unacceptable. I didn't build this family so my grandsons could finger-paint business deals and let old debts rot.'

The jab lands dead centre – *your mother*. The familiar ache hums in my ribcage. 'We'll settle it,' I grind out. 'Soon. You have my word.'

'Soon is horseshit,' he snarls. 'Vengeance grows mouldy if you store it too long. You want a reminder? I'll take the next flight, put a bullet in every Mancinelli I find, starting with that pretty little race boy – what's his name – Narciso? I'll cut his brakes and watch his guts paint the asphalt.'

Heat flashes behind my eyes – a picture of a sniper reticle, my mother's blood, Sofiya's laugh. Confusion tastes like copper on my tongue because those two thoughts belong nowhere near each other, never mind intertwining.

'Nonnu,' I say, voice dropping into the tone that's used to silence lieutenants. 'You raised us. You know I don't let debts slide. But I handle this *my* way. Trust that. Stay in Fallbrook.'

Silence. Then a low, grudging chuckle. 'There's my Enforcer. Fine. I'll give you rope. Wrap it around the bastard's neck quick, or I start yanking.' He sucks in air, softer now. '*Famigghia above all*. Don't forget the oath.'

'I never do.'

'And Rafa—' He pauses, sudden weariness bleeding through. 'Your mother would want his head, *sì*. But she'd want your soul whole. Make this quick. Don't let the *vinnitta* eat what's left of it.'

The line clicks dead.

I stare at the handset, jaw tight. Stunned as fuck. My fucking soul? Since when did he—

Cesare steps up, clasps my shoulder. 'Same speech he gave me when I married Maddie,' he mutters. 'He's fire – burns everything, including us.'

'Fire keeps predators back,' I answer, though my voice comes out hollow. Inside, two truths grind like bone: duty to blood, and the feral pull of a Mancinelli assassin who should be my enemy.

I hand Cesare the phone, walk towards the waiting SUV, and promise myself the same lie I've repeated for the last year – when a Mancinelli bleeds, everything will make sense again.

But the echo of Sofiya's moan still rings in my ears, and for the first time, I'm not sure vengeance alone will quiet the ghosts.

* * *

Sofiya

'Dammit, I need to pee again. BRB,' Maddie grumbles, before hefting herself to her feet and waddling away towards the bathroom.

It's cute. And unsettling as fuck.

I feel as if my life has tracked a steady, near predictable course, only to speed up in the last twelve months.

And the only variable in there? The shattering of the previous never-the-twain-shall-meet-except-on-the-battlefield standards the Mancinellis and Salvatores lived by.

I lean against the suite's balcony door now, listening to Mozart drift through the candle-lit sitting room and letting the past ten minutes replay in my head like slow-motion telemetry.

I'd barely raised my hand to knock before the door swung wide. Maddie – eight months pregnant and radiant in a koi-print kimono – hauled me into an iron-ribbed hug. Pregnancy, it turns out, hasn't blunted her bone-crushing strength.

'You smell like seawater and bad choices,' she whispered against my ear, half scolding, half amused.

'Busy night,' I replied, slipping past her as she engaged the deadbolt.

Candlelight flickered over half-eaten tiramisu, a bodyguard by bullet-resistant glass, Mozart lilting in the background – domestic serenity, mafia edition.

Maddie lowered herself onto the sofa, one hand rubbing the small of her back. 'Cesare told me you were in Rafa's room,' she said, pointing a dessert spoon at me like a gavel. 'Apparently you and he had "business". Translation: my husband is covering whatever debauchery his baby brother dragged you into.' Her dark-lashed eyes narrowed. 'Some secrets I let Cesare keep. The ones about my baby sister and the Salvatore Enforcer? Not so much. Spill.'

I'd sunk onto a cushion opposite, suddenly twelve again under that stare. 'Nothing world-ending,' I'd said, voice too careful. 'Your bro-in-law is as safe as nitro-glycerine left out in the sun. It's my job to make sure he doesn't go bang and take us all down with him.'

She didn't miss my emphasis on the 'your', and yeah, it was a touch bitchy and shade-throwing as fuck, but it was that or admit I'd let the second Salvatore grandson go down on me. And fuck if I was admitting that to my big sister. The same big sister I'd – in a moment of weakness – admitted to that I was a damned *virgin* last year. God, I had a hard time admitting every-thing that had happened tonight to myself.

Understatement of the century, but I needed a shield, and espresso-soaked ladyfinger did the job. I took a slow bite, heat flickering in my cheeks.

'And did you?' She arched a brow. 'Manage him, that is?' There was a peculiar note to her tone, a teasing and a probing.

I'd shrugged. 'We're still here, no?' I returned, trying my damnedest not to think of gaudy yachts, wetsuits, and Rafa's tongue rewriting my moral code.

'Interesting, I've never noticed this before.'

'Noticed what?'

'Your poker face sucks when you're tired, Sof.'

Shit. She saw through the dodge.

'Fine. Evade like you always do,' she'd said, dredging up the perennial guilt of our not being BFFs.

As if there's ever a good time to tell your sister that you were the family assassin. And that while sometimes blood made you queasy, you actually didn't mind watching the life drain out of the eyes of bad guys. Or that you were quietly desperate to expand your horizons. To become meaningful to more than just your family so you could hang onto a fracturing self-worth that didn't entirely hinge on your gender.

'Do you know where Nonno is?' she'd demanded, eyes piercing in a way I suspected she'd picked up from her husband.

Ice had slid down my spine. 'Would I be here if I did?'

'I don't know, would you—'

I tossed the spoon, sugar high souring. 'Stop.'

Maddie blinked. 'Sof—'

'I said stop.' I raised a hand. My nerves were frayed; Lupo's death still clings to my skin, Rafa's mouth still pulsing between my legs – too much. 'If I had a location, you'd be the first to know. Until then, let's not claw each other open.'

Silence. Then Maddie exhaled, guilt softening her features. 'Okay.' She patted the sofa. 'Truce?'

'Truce.' I slid closer. She clasped my hands, thumb stroking the swell of callus on my trigger finger. No judgement – just knowledge even as she'd held my gaze, measuring.

After a beat, she'd sighed, scooped another bite of tiramisu, and let the subject hang unanswered.

Now, I turn away from the balcony after a minute, pause when I hear voices.

Maddie's in the bedroom, talking to the baby in soft Sicilian – promising him or her another piece of tiramisu tomorrow.

I exhale, forehead against the cool glass.

Monaco's harbour glitters below, but my reflection stares back. Flushed cheeks, bruise-dark circles and a mouth still swollen from Rafa's kiss.

'Busy night' doesn't begin to cover it.

And dawn promises worse.

I join Maddie in the bedroom, where apparently she road-blocked after going to the bathroom.

She grimaces when I enter. 'Sorry. My energy needs careful allocation these days. I was just catching my breath, but since you're here...' She pats the bed.

I sit next to her.

And for the next half hour she chatters about nursery paint swatches, how Cesare hovers like an anxious hawk, and baby kicks that feel like 'tiny mafia hits from the inside'.

Her laugh is bright, defiant, proof she refuses to let a simmering *famigghia* feud steal her joy. I sip chamomile tea and listen, something warm swelling in my chest that feels inconveniently like envy. Not jealousy of her, her husband, the devotion or the empire they're building and adding to. Just the audacity to rewrite her script. And fucking succeed at it.

So far, I've hit dead ends in my own audacity journey.

The whispered-about organisation I'd hoped to approach but was actively giving me the cold shoulder. The organisation I'm certain Rafa is a part of. A thought bounces through my brain but I don't give it time to land, never mind find fertile soil. A few filter through nonetheless.

'My next kill for your virginity', he'd offer.

'How about an introduction to the assassin agency you work for?' I'd counter.

I grimace, more than a little disgusted with myself. *Just because the Salvatore enforcer was a little feral about your cherry doesn't mean he'll want it that much.*

Would you even respect him if he did?

Maddie catches my expression, nudges my knee, but thankfully misinterprets it. 'You'll get this too, you know.'

I snort. 'Sure. Right after world peace.'

'I mean it.' She rests my hand on her belly; beneath the silk, a flutter answers. Life, stubborn and loud. 'You can carve any future you want, Sof. Same way I did.'

Could I? Two hours ago Rafa tongue-worshipped me like a conquered country. The euphoria still thrums. But tomorrow – or the next night – he could line my brother in a rifle scope. Violence is bred into us; love is the inconvenient variable that ignited this, after all.

'If I rebel,' I whisper, 'someone has to keep the balance. Father's half-mad trying to step into shoes far bigger than he can grow. Narciso still thinks upheaval is solved by horsepower and tequila. I'd cut my arm off before I pull Jacinta or Mama deeper into this shit. That leaves me.'

Maddie squeezes. 'Balance doesn't mean martyrdom.'

'Maybe it does.'

She studies me, then smiles sadly. 'At least promise you'll let yourself be happy *sometimes*.'

I make a sound that means nothing at all. Thankfully, she lets it go. Just before I'm saved by the ping of my phone.

I rise and rush much too quickly to the door. Tell myself I'm not running from unwanted advice or towards the next skirmish with a certain fuck-hot Enforcer.

'Sofiya?'

I stop. Turn. She's risen from the bed, waddling towards me.

Her eyes are anxious. 'I know there's no variable where we make things right with Nonno after what he did. But…' She rubs her belly, her throat moving in a swallow. 'I also don't want to welcome my baby into the world knowing we had a hand in ending their great-grandfather. So…'

I reach out, and she clasps my hand. 'I don't know how all this will pan out, Maddie. And I can't make promises I don't know whether I'll be able to keep.'

She blinks. Then nods. Presses my hand before she releases me. 'I know. I love you. Stay safe, please?'

'Don't worry about me, sis. Worry about how much tiramisu

you're feeding that kid. And how you're going to pop it out if it's as big as a small cottage.'

She's gasping in outrage when a knock interrupts – two quick, one long. Salvatore code. I open the suite door a crack.

Rafa stands there, freshly showered, black Henley clinging to muscle, eyes softer than they should be for a killer who just flew in from a gun deal.

'Maddie,' he calls over my shoulder, 'your overprotective husband is on his way. But he wants you in bed. Underboss's orders.'

'Tell Cesare he can get his hot ass over here himself and talk to his not-fragile wife,' Maddie shouts back – but she's already approaching the door. She kisses my cheek, whispers, 'Make happiness the goal, Sof. Remember that.'

She waddles to the bedroom. I close the door. Rafa's gaze sweeps my face like he's cataloguing bruises. 'You good?'

'Fine.' I cross arms to hide the way his presence tightens everything low in my belly. 'She interrogated me.'

'Did she use waterboarding or more tiramisu?'

I huff. 'Both.'

His grin is quick, then fades into something almost tender. 'Let's go.'

We head for the suite in silence. I'm not sure what to expect because he's not acting like his last text suggested. The one that made me so hot, I'd had to step out onto the balcony to cool off.

Is this some trick to keep me on my toes? To—

'Go sleep, *tigra*.'

I look around, clocking that we've arrived in the suite.

'We're racetrack bound in a little over four hours.' He pauses. 'You plan to be there, *si*?'

I nod.

He turns but I catch his wrist.

The hallway lamp casts gold over his scars, the ink on his neck and throat, over the vein that jumps in his forearm. 'Rafa.' The name tastes bold on my tongue. 'Don't do anything stupid tonight.'

He steps closer, fingers brushing my pulse. 'Define stupid.'

'Turning that rifle back on my family.'

A flicker – pain, regret, something heavier – crosses his features. 'Not tonight.' He slides a thumb under my chin. 'And if tomorrow I forget why I promised, remind me – preferably with that mouth.'

My breath snags. He kisses my forehead, soft and devastating – then strolls down the hall, danger in every line.

I press my back to the door, heart thundering.

Two days ago he was a nightmare on a rooftop; now his kiss feels like the only oath I trust.

What the hell have I let happen?

16

SOFIYA

Circuit de Monaco – Pit Lane, Race Day – 11:45 a.m.

The garage smells of burned rubber, brake dust, and the bitter espresso our mechanics mainline like holy water. Narciso's fire-engine-red helmet sits on a workbench, visor up, reflecting pit-lane chaos: tyre trolleys rattling, VIP lanyards flashing and grid girls fluttering like tropical birds.

My baby brother bounces on the balls of his feet, race suit half-zipped to the waist and Nomex peeled to reveal a shirt stamped with our team's snarling stallion. He's vibrating as he always does before lights-out. But today his energy keeps rico-cheting towards me.

'Quit staring,' I mutter, adjusting the comms earpiece Stefano insisted I wear 'for emergencies only'. As if he could stop one if it walked up and jammed a butt plug up his ass.

Narciso smirks, his peroxide-dyed curls plastered to his fore-head. 'Tough. You look possessed. Figured I'd keep an eye on the demon in the family.'

'I'm fine.'

'Fine means you haven't threatened anyone in fifteen minutes. You barked at the tyre engineer, nearly took off the data guy's head, and drank three espressos back-to-back – without sugar. That's illegal in Italy, sis.'

I snap the Velcro on his glove tighter than necessary. 'Then it's a good thing we're not in Italy, isn't it? Focus on Turn One. Dust line's worse than last year.'

He winces at the glove, then catches my wrist. 'Sof, what's going on? You've never given me race advice before. Fuck, I didn't even know you liked racing.'

The nickname digs under my ribcage – only he and Maddie still use it. My throat feels raw. I slept maybe two hours, woke to an empty suite.

Rafa was gone, not even a note.

Only a coded text sent at dawn.

> Take care of your engine today, bedda. Mine's running hot and heavy.

Nothing since. No filthy promise to finish what we started.

And because I'm apparently insane, that absence slices deeper than it should. Nothing has changed – the man still intends to spill my family's blood – but my stomach knots because he didn't stay for breakfast?

What the fuck is wrong with me?

Narciso's grip tightens, dark eyes searching. 'Did Pops say something? Is Nonno—'

'Concentrate!' I hiss. 'You're a couple of dozen points off the championship lead – drive like it. We can't keep letting the fucking Salvatores win every fucking thing.' There's more acid in my tone than I intended.

He flinches, surprised.

We don't snap at each other. Not ever.

Guilt prickles, but before I can soften, his engineer signals helmet-on. Narciso releases my wrist, slides the helmet down, and climbs into the cockpit.

His engine fires, a banshee shriek as he drives out, drowning whatever apology I was scrambling for.

I retreat behind the garage wall and watch the cars snake to the start boxes. Renzo's matte-green and black Salvatore Furia on pole, Narciso P3 behind Dante's identical chassis. Salvatore versus Mancinelli – every camera salivates, gagging for a repeat of the violence that's always bubbling beneath our surface.

The next fifteen minutes whistle by in a technicolour of frantic preparation.

Then the grid clears.

The canyon of grandstands vibrates with anthem static.

Five red lights bloom.

My pulse syncs with their glow – one, two, three – Rafa's hand on my jaw – four – his mouth between my thighs – five—

Lights out.

Twenty turbo-charged V6 hybrid engines detonate.

Renzo rockets clear. Dante covers inside and slides into his twin's sweet slipstream. Narciso darts left, wheel to wheel with a Mercedes before Sainte-Dévote. I want to shout into the pit noise, but it's pointless.

Laps blur, the inevitable carbon shards at Mirabeau, yellow flag in the tunnel and pit cycles rolling mid-field. I analyse sector deltas like it means something when I have very little clue, fake calm for the crew, but inside I'm a churn of caffeine and... aching.

Every crackle of team-radio static reminds me of Rafa's laugh. Every downshift pop ricochets like the thump of his heart against mine last night when he helped me overcome my adrenaline fever.

How is it possible to miss someone programmed to destroy you?

Lap 72, Renzo still leads.

Narciso trails in third by just one second, his teammate by a whole seven seconds. But Dante's brakes are fading. Narciso might finish second with luck, although I know Dante won't give up first place without a fight. Monaco is the holy fucking grail for an F1 driver.

Second and seventh aren't bad results if not.

It should thrill me. Instead I'm hollowed out, so distracted I nearly miss Renzo's victory radio scream. He crosses the line; confetti cannons fire and Monaco roars.

Dante, the little shit, managed to nurse his tyres into second place.

The Salvatores have won again. Fuck.

The team erupts in forced cheer and resigned back slaps for not at least performing worse. I drag myself out into the pit lane, and no, I don't search the crowd for Rafa.

Instead I clap, pasting on my own smile, but my chest aches like a bruise. Narciso parks in parc fermé, climbs out and tugs his helmet off.

He finds me instantly, delivers a tentative grin. I nod, apology tucked behind my teeth, and he seems to accept it.

While cameras flash, my phone buzzes. Unknown number – no, encrypted scramble I recognise now without thinking.

Wheels up in one hour. Be ready – R

Relief hits stupidly hard. I type back before sense intervenes:

> Already am. Monaco's fucking loud. I'll shoot
> someone if I have to shout to be heard one
> more time.

Three dots appear.

> Good girl. Keep your voice. I want your throat
> hoarse for me, not the crowd.

My pulse screeches in outrage and arousal as I pocket the phone, heart stuttering, and I lift my face to the spray of victory champagne. The fizz sticks to my lashes like sea-mist. Somewhere nearby, the Enforcer is plotting a systematic power shift, my possible demise.

And all I can think about is his mouth on my skin.

If that isn't treason, I don't know what is.

But as the trophy photographs commence and the anthem plays again, the thought that scares me most isn't that Rafaelle might aim a rifle at my family tomorrow.

It's that he might not – and I don't know which fate would ruin me more.

*　*　*

Rafa
17:22 – Monaco Podium, Parc Fermé

Renzo punches the air, champagne geysering off the bottle.

Dante douses him from behind; the twins slip on the soaked rostrum and laugh like spoiled brats who've never cleaned blood from their boots.

Down on the third step, Narciso Mancinelli forces a tight

smile for the cameras. First–second–third. On paper, a perfect advertisement for 'racing unites feuding dynasties'.

It was a stroke of genius for Cesare to hand his seat to Dante after retiring.

Identical Twin Brother Formula One Racing Drivers.

That thirsty little tagline alone had brought in tens of millions in sponsorship.

Every major public-facing organisation wanted to exploit this possibly once-in-a-generation phenomenon.

Every woman with a pulse hyperventilated every time the twins posted their antics on social media.

Hell, the twins only needed to breathe to have cash thrown at them.

I allow myself a smirk and a nodding accolade in their direction and a wink for Bibi before I step out of view.

The moment I do, my phone hums – a rare *Aegis* code-string.

> Asset 17B neutralisation confirmed. Operational
> result A-grade. New target file inbound.
> Stand by.

Formal praise from Washington's deepest basement, and normally I'd feel the buzz of validation. Instead, a splinter of irritation lodges beneath my ribs. I've barely seen Sofiya all fucking day – just a flash of her sexy legs clad in her favourite tight pants, displaying that cock-hardening ass at the Mancinelli pit wall, the sway of that short ponytail vanishing into a sea of mechanics. Radio silence on every text. She's good at hiding. *Too good.*

Fuck, wasn't that why she flew under my radar for years before her sniffing around in Naples and on the dark web a few years back brought her to my attention?

Another ping, this time Nightowl. No greeting, just a line of hacker poetry, and... surprisingly... *coordinates*. That's a first.

> Old vipers moult in ruined orchards.

I map the lat–long in my head. My pulse kicks for the first time since I walked away from Sofiya last night, even though I'd craved nothing more than to snatch her up by that trim waist, toss her onto the bed and finished what we started.

But I knew for damned sure Maddie had been whispering in her ear, same way Cesare had griped in mine. And the thought of being cock-blocked, *again*, plus the shadows under her eyes, had forced me into a rare retreat.

Yeah, I'm turning into Mr Fucking Sensitive.

I deserved one of those Louis Vuitton crafted medals the twins were waving about.

I forced myself to concentrate on the map.

Rural Sicily – three ridges over from where my drones lost Bonafacio's heat signature six months ago. I'd call him stupid if the old fucker wasn't slipperier than a lubed eel.

But Nightowl never sends junk intel.

And the timing's perfect, too. A righteous hunt, a neat exit excuse.

I swipe champagne spray off my sleeve and catch Cesare's eye on the paddock stairs. He's shoulder-hugging Renzo, but one brow lifts. *What now?*

I gesture. *Need a word.* He grimaces, wipes fizz off his cuff and meets me behind the stage rigging.

'Chinese funds en route,' he says first. 'With usual spa treatment, funds will be snug in their beds by next race.' He stops. Eyes me. 'You look like you swallowed a coked-up wasp – what's crawled up your suit?'

'Nightowl just pinged Nonno Mancinelli's latest burrow.'

Cesare exhales. 'Of course he did.' He checks the crowd, lowers his voice. 'You going solo?'

I pause, then come clean. 'No.'

His glare flickers between astonishment and resignation. 'Naturally. One Mancinelli for intel, one for leverage. Maddie will gut me if you leave without saying goodbye. And be prepared for a grilling.'

'I'll handle the goodbye.'

'Handle my wife better than your phone, *fratuzzo*. She thinks you ghosted breakfast.'

I grunt – no comeback.

He clamps my shoulder and squeezes. 'I'll say it again, *frate*. Don't die.'

'Nah. Bad for business.'

* * *

Sofiya
18:10 – Hôtel de Paris, Eighth floor

I knock once on Maddie's suite.

I hear faint grumbling ten seconds before the door yanks open. But it's not my sister who fills the doorway.

Umberto 'Fist' Lazlo, built like a thousand-year-old sequoia, with the ancient, dead eyes to match, scrutinises me like he doesn't know who I am.

The bodyguard – and cousin of the Salvatore men – used to be Cesare's shadow. But lately, he's glued himself to my sister, probably at the behest of her possessive and unhinged husband – definite family trait, that – who can't leave his wife's sight for more than two seconds.

'Out of the way, Fist. I told you I'd get the door. Get in here, Sof,' Maddie says, more than a little irritably. After another long second of dead-eye staring, the gentle-until-provoked giant shifts. *Towards me.*

I glare and step out of his way before I'm steamrollered.

Maddie's barefoot, her massive bump wrapped in a racing tee. She shuffles backwards to let me in, one hand bracing the small of her back. 'He's driving me insane,' she mutters, shooting Fist a glare. 'Apparently I can't turn a doorknob at eight months pregnant without adult supervision.'

Fist grunts something about 'protocol' and stations himself at the balcony doors.

I follow Maddie to the sofa, where she lowers herself with a soft groan. Her belly pushes the team-logo tee into a perfect dome. She pats the cushion beside her. 'Sit. Surprise of the day – you showed up before I had to hunt you down.'

I drop onto the edge, pulling a throw blanket over my lap more for something to do with my hands than warmth. 'Thought I'd say goodbye properly.'

'That's new.' She smiles, but there's a faint wobble under the tease. 'I'm glad, just... shocked. You used to ghost out between dessert and coffee. Hurt my feelings, in case you never noticed.'

Guilt pricks. 'I noticed.'

Her gaze searches mine. 'What changed?'

I shrug. 'Trying something different.'

Maddie tilts her head, brown eyes sharp. 'Different or *dangerous*?'

'Both, maybe,' I admit, staring at the flecks of half-finished *pain au chocolat* from Le Gemir, Maddie's favourite bakery, on a plate on the coffee table. 'But necessary.'

She studies me a moment longer, then sighs. 'Cesare says Rafa's wheels-up too. Any idea where he's off to?' The question is feather-light, but she watches my face like a hawk, waiting for a slip.

'The heir doesn't share family secrets with me, remember?' I deflect, forcing a neutral smile. 'I have no fucking clue what Rafa's up to.'

'Hmm,' she murmurs. 'Still' – her fingers find mine – 'if you do know, you'll tell me he's not dragging you into something that'll get you killed... right?'

I squeeze her hand. 'You know better than that.' Half-truth, half promise. It's all I can manage.

She exhales, shoulders easing, then brightens as if flipping a switch. 'Fine. Lecture over. Can we hug without the world imploding?'

We hug, her scent of vanilla lotion and baby powder wrapping around me like childhood. She whispers at my ear, voice wobbly again, 'Come see me in New York before the baby arrives. Promise?'

I nod against her shoulder even though the promise sits heavy. I want to believe I'll make it, but I don't know what the hell the Enforcer is dragging me to or into. Besides, with one race down and five more to go, my future remains precarious. 'I'll try, sis. I really will.'

She leans back, eyes damp but shining. 'Trying is a start. Love you, Sof.'

'Love you more,' I say – truth, for once, unvarnished.

I stand, brush her hair from her face, and step towards the door.

Fist opens it without a word.

I glance back. Maddie's hand rests on her belly, her thumb stroking a slow circle while she watches me leave.

In the corridor I exhale, the weight of her worry and hopes pressing between my shoulder blades. If Rafa pulls the trigger on Nonno – or if my grandfather strikes back first – New York baby showers might remain a sweet idea, never real.

But hope tastes better than guilt.

So I tuck Maddie's request next to my flickering conscience and head for the elevator, where the Enforcer's shadow already looms.

* * *

Rafaelle
19:12 – Gulfstream G650, Thirty Thousand Feet Over the Med

The cabin lights dim after we level out, the engines a low growl of background sound.

Sofiya is strapped in across from me, arms folded. She refused the chilled water the steward offered. I dismiss the attendant and hit the privacy switch.

She's quiet and watchful. A beautiful snake circling Adam. I'm down for eating her apple.

I feel a smirk tugging at my lips at the twisted interpretation just as my phone vibrates. Swear to God, if it's Cesare with more words of fucking wis—

Nightowl. A single, maddening line fills the screen.

> Two serpents, hidden baskets; only one knows the venom.

A chill skates my spine. What basket? And what the fuck is his fixation with snakes? I fucking hate snakes.

> Fucking clarify. Which serpent?

I thumb back, knuckles whitening.

Three dots… then the exact same line repeats. No explanation, because apparently Nightowl isn't in the mood. I stare at the message.

Then at Sofiya.

Am I dealing with a warning? A taunt? A secret sitting five feet in front of me, pretending to nap?

Snakes. Secrets. Betrayal?

Heat floods my veins, half fury, half dread.

It's the mother of all Hail Marys topped with conjecture, but I pocket the phone and lock eyes on her.

My pulse jumps. My cock jumps higher.

She's waiting, watchful. Like she knows a secret. All the fucking secrets.

'You have El Topo's coordinates, don't you?' I murmur.

She doesn't flinch. Doesn't react at all. Which for a woman who blushed when I go anywhere near her pussy is disarmingly unsettling. And impressive.

'How long have you known?' I press.

A beat. Then, 'Six days. One of my father's bookkeepers leaked supply invoices – food and meds – headed to the exact village.'

Fuck! There's that loathsome feeling galloping in my chest again. Like I'm hurt? 'And you neglected to share.'

Her chin lifts. 'I had to vet the source.'

'Bullshit. You wanted to keep Grandpa breathing.' I lean forward, elbows on knees. 'You expecting a family redemption arc? He tried to vaporise your own sister. At her fucking wedding,' I seethe.

Colour drains from her cheeks, but she doesn't drop her gaze. 'I was weighing options. So shoot me.'

'Don't fucking tempt me.'

Now she flinches.

'You had that in your back pocket while we were burying traffickers?' I snort. 'While I was eating that beautiful cunt?'

Her colour rises, sure as sin and clockwork.

The plane lurches through mild chop; neither of us blinks.

'I'll make this clear, *bedda*,' I say, voice low steel. 'If you want to take a hacksaw to our baseline trust, that's fine by me. We land, we hunt. If Bonafacio draws first breath in my scope, I squeeze. You can walk away or stand beside me.' I lean forward into her space, let her eyes rush over my face, linger on my mouth. Savour what she's throwing away. 'But do not – *ever* – play me blind. *Capisci?*'

She inhales, fists clenching on the armrests. 'If I walk away, who drags your gorgeous corpse out?'

Despite myself, a grin slips. Possessive heat coils under my ribcage – raw and inconvenient. 'So you *do* remember some things.'

'When it suits me.'

'Three days and I'm accustomed to your noise.' I reach across, my thumb brushing her wrist pulse. 'Don't add silence to that elective list. Silence and deception piss me off. Makes me a little... deranged.'

She shivers but not out of fear. There's fire behind her eyes. The same fire that arced through her when she came on my tongue.

The cabin feels smaller, the air charged. I imagine tugging her into the double bedroom at the rear, starting by pressing her against the door, showing her what lying and withholding from me earns. But it's a short flight, and I can't imagine she'll be in the mood to come on the cock of the man who intends to take out her grandfather.

The man who will happily paint her body in the blood of her family.

A spike of regret bites.

I shake it off.

The mission hisses in my head – focus, kill, clean.

She breaks eye contact first and stares out the oval window at nothing.

I recline, my fingers drumming the armrest, mind juggling Nightowl's new message and the old vow etched in bone: make a Mancinelli bleed for my mother.

Out the window, lightning flickers on the horizon. There's a storm building over Sicily, violent and inevitable.

Perfect weather for a reckoning.

And if the woman across from me thinks she can soften the blow...

The corner of my mouth lifts in a promise more lethal than any bullet.

Tonight, the orchard gets salt, and the serpent loses its head.

17

RAFAELLE

The air in Sicily bites at our lungs like it's daring us to breathe. By late afternoon, the sun has scorched every stone to white-hot.

We pull off the narrow coastal road, our tyres grinding on loose gravel. Sofiya rides shotgun. Silent with expression unreadable behind dark shades.

I keep one hand on the wheel while the other flicks through the pages of my memories. My father disappearing into himself after Mama died, Nightowl's clues, my mother's ghost spinning me into this madness.

All the blood I've spilled to bring me to this point.

I glance at her, ask myself *why* I need two sets of eyes in this thing when I've needed none before. *Sì*, it's more personal than ever.

But she's no friend of the Salvatores.

She's a sexy, deadly Mancinelli predator.

So every mile I drive towards the last moments El Topo has on this earth, I find myself watching her as much as the road. Tonight we may shred his life into cold ashes. I wonder how that feels to her: to hunt her own blood. Whether this level of threat and blackmail is about to backfire in my face.

Because when the time comes, what reassurance do I have that she'll stand beside me against the blood who tried to kill her own sister?

Absolutely none.

So I could very well be stoking a repeat of what she did on the rooftop.

My hand finds the bruise on my chest. The pain is fading. I don't... like that. Its loss feels greater than the mere recalibration of damaged cell and muscle.

By the time we crest the ridge overlooking the village, I've loosened my tie into a lariat around my neck. The cluster of whitewashed houses and terracotta roofs seems still, almost peaceful.

Another half mile and I pull over and stop.

Beneath us, the villa – my target – slinks among olive trees, walled in granite and secrets.

'*Tigra*,' I say over the drone of the engine as a despairing gust rattles the windows. 'Is it worth asking how you're doing?' I drawl, unable to take my eyes off her in the sunlight reflected off the dashboard.

Fuck, she's gorgeous. Not for the first time, I wonder if she was so named after the bombshell young Sophia Loren she grew into.

Those luminous eyes. Her distinctive nose. But above all... that luscious, sexy-as-fuck mouth I still feel wrapped around my cock as she sucked me off with a mixture of siren and ingénue. A virgin already stepping into her power, even before she's given up her hymen.

She lowers her shades and exhales, as though she's been

holding her breath since dawn. 'You can ask but I don't know that this calm is what I deserve.'

The raw admission scratches at me. Which is laughable since I shed chunks of my conscience a long time ago, reserving the remaining for my family.

I grip the wheel tighter. 'Don't give me that. Deep down you know it was always going to come to this.'

She meets my gaze. For a moment, the world stutters as soft light flickers across her cheekbones, and I see that the pain behind her eyes is real.

That scratch deepens into clawing. I roll the car forward to a stop at the end of a dead-end lane.

'You good to go?' I press. Requiring – hoping for? – a resurgence of my baby assassin.

She just shrugs.

'No, *bedda*. Answer me.' In some tiny hole at the back of my mind, I sense I'm being unfair. That no matter what, blood is blood.

Is that going to stop me? Fuck no. For that to happen, I'll need to abandon my *vinnitta*. To betray my graveside vow to Mama.

And that's happening over my dead fucking body.

She swallows. 'Even if I wanted to cut myself open and drag out my feelings, which I fucking don't, it's... complicated.'

We stare each other down for a minute and an age.

Then, accepting we're at an impasse while time sprints away, I step out, the dry earth shuddering under my boots. 'Let's go.'

She follows, pulling her own boots from the floor mat. We weave through a small copse of trees and cross the dirt drive, sun baking our backs.

Ingrained stealth and training guides our movements, but I sense she's not moving as quickly as she can. I can't tell if she's hesitating because she's uncomfortable, or because she's uncertain how to betray her own blood.

Standing in the shade of the villa's cypress trees, I level my gaze at her. 'On the scale of one to fucked up, tell me how much you agree that El Topo needs to die? If for nothing else, for what he's done to your own siblings,' I grate out under my breath.

She closes her eyes, as though the question is a blow. When she opens them, they're red-rimmed. 'I don't know.'

I let that land. Around us, the cicadas hum a Judgment Day rhythm. 'Don't lie.'

She flinches. 'He could already be dead. I saved his life once.' Her voice cracks a little with that admission.

A slow swell of... something fills in my chest. 'You what?'

She meets my eyes. 'He was poisoned, four years ago. A blowfish in a restaurant that may or may not have been an accident – he nearly died. I saved him. Sometimes, like when he went after Maddie last year, I wish I'd let him die.' The admission is brutally honest, cold with a sliver of a tremor.

I run a hand through my hair, tasting bile. 'So you'd let him live.'

She shrugs, wincing as the truth wounds her. 'He's my family, even if it turned out he's capable of trying to blow his own granddaughter's head off. And me... I'm a killer with a sometimes ill-timed conscience. Besides, if *I'd* let him die, who would I be then? He trained me to be more than a granddaughter. More than a soldier.'

She laughs, and it's a nails-scraping-chalkboard of self-flagellation that scrapes something much too... *aware* inside me.

'It was my chance to prove I wasn't the failure they always warned me I'd become just because I'm a woman.'

My breath hitches. What I want to do to her warps my tongue, while her raw admission guts me sharper than a blade.

Because it hints that this Mancinelli has a soul, even for vermin she should hate. And right in this moment, I don't know where to put that feeling.

So I dive into filth and threats. 'Careful there, *tigra*. That's an admission that makes me want to pin you against that tree and devour all your soft spots.'

She shakes her head. 'Somehow I knew you'd say something like that.'

'Are you calling me predictable, *duci*?' I ask as I pivot towards the villa, gears shifting in my mind.

Again she follows, a hesitant step behind.

'Predictable? Maybe, but I like knowing what to expect from you, Salvatore.'

I glance at her, reading her face. Or what she wants to show me. There are many hidden depths, ones I look forward to uncovering and ones I wonder if they'll end me before I do. 'Then let me predictably remind you. We're here for blood. His blood. Don't disappoint me.'

She does not move. 'You think he killed your mother. I have no excuse.'

'I don't think. I know. And so do you. He may not have wielded the weapon that ended her, but he lit the fuse that day. He needs to pay. So for the last time, are you going to stand in my way?'

She reaches out – hesitant, trembling – and I flinch away from her and from the *give* inside my chest. I can't... *won't* be swayed in this.

She stands there, unsure whether to cross the distance.

Eventually, I ignore her and march forward. She trails behind, boots stirring gravel. I pause at the villa's iron gate and test the padlock. It snaps open like dry bones.

We make it to the building and inside without incident, which tweaks all my alarms. Inside, hallways stretch into gloom.

I draw my Beretta, silenced and loaded, and sweep from room to room. Each doorway yawns emptily. The kitchen is pristinely abandoned but the stove is still warm. The trophy room's glass cabinets hold rusted pistols and dried lilies – vestiges of another life.

I meet Sofiya at the top of the marble staircase. 'Empty,' I say, my voice between a curse and a groan.

She breathes in, nails biting into the butt of her own gun.

Her poker face is slipping, morphing into the viper Nightowl warned me about. My alarm flares into klaxons.

Jesus Fucking Christ.

The bruise on my chest throbs and I don't know whether to curse or celebrate the reminder of what this Mancinelli is capable of. The lengths she could go to to protect her undeserving own.

I glare down at her, fury rising. Knowing even before I ask the question. 'You were stalling in the trees with that little speech.' Of course she was. I stopped for a chit-fucking-chat, giving her time she didn't need to adjust to killing her own grandfather because he wasn't here. Giving her a chance to hang my rope around my neck. Fucking A, Rafa. 'What did you do?'

She purses her lips, eyes bold and brazen. Sexy as fuck. Eyes I wouldn't mind looking into as I strangled the fuck out of her.

'Maddie begged me. She doesn't want blood before the baby comes. And maybe when I was double-checking my intel on the plane, I wasn't as... careful as I should've been.'

Rage claws at my throat. 'You fucking betrayed me.'

She flinches at my words, knowing exactly how they cut. 'Do you hear yourself? I betrayed you?' Her voice is a lethal shard of glass. 'He's an eighty-year-old man who's spent decades twisting lives. Blood or not, you don't think he'd kill me first – *or any of his grandchildren* – just to save face? Do you not think I'm twisted up about this?'

My hands tremble where they grip the banister. 'I thought you were in this until we pulled the trigger in the same moment.'

She stands taller, anger flickering in her stunning eyes. 'I'm only in this because you haven't given me anything other than fucked-up choices that don't end up with hundreds more people dying if you start another war.'

I lunge forward, my heart pounding. I grab her by the shoulders and push her into the wall, lips knocking against hers in a furious crush. Her breath hitches. She tastes of honey and defiance.

I draw back but I leave my forehead pressed to hers. '*Tigra*, as fucked up as those choices are, you're either with me, or—'

She slaps me with surprising force. The snap echoes. My fist darts up, palm covering my cheek. She stands, trembling, heat in her eyes. The sting, not where I wanted it on my chest, but in my face… riles me. *Arouses* me.

'Get your hands off me,' she spits.

I swallow and lean in close, voice low. 'Take me seriously, *picciridda*.'

She stares back, her chest heaving. Saying nothing.

I bite down on my lip, nostrils flaring. 'We're leaving. And when we reach our destination, you tell me every goddamn thing you've hidden.'

She swallows past a ragged breath. 'Or what?'

My gaze sharpens. 'Or I drive you into the ground, blindfolded, until you beg for mercy.'

Tears prickle her lashes. She does not look away. 'Bring it.'

I march her out of the abandoned villa and back to the car. There, I whip off my tie, and snap her wrist cuffs in place.

'What the fuck are you—'

'Shut the fuck up and turn around.'

She doesn't.

I grip her waist, feeling the muscle jerk and quiver beneath my fingers as I yank her around and wrap a bandana over her eyes, knotting it tight.

She gasps as darkness swallows her, but her stance is resolute.

I shuffle behind her, secure the silk blindfold, then bind her wrists behind her back with my leather belt. Every motion is controlled, urgent.

She's taut as a spring but doesn't struggle. She knows my threats are never empty.

I bundle her into the back seat, dropping to smell her, drag my nose down her throat. 'Try something, *tigra*. I dare you.'

The halo of bloodlust is both a rush and a poison. I want to fuck and kill and fuck and kill.

But with my quarry having slipped through my fingers, and a pliant Mancinelli sprawled out in my back seat...

Fuck fuck fuck.

A growl builds in my chest as I slide behind the wheel of my black Range Rover.

Like any thwarted assassin worth his salt, it's time to regroup.

And I know the perfect place.

* * *

19:32 – Salvatore Vineyard, Fifty Miles Northwest

The vineyard stretches like a green ocean under sunset.

Rows upon rows of silvery leaves, grapes fat as marbles. Purple shadows pool between the trellises. An old stone villa stands sentinel at the far end, abandoned since my mama and my grandmother died.

I pull up outside that ruin, yank the doors open and drag Sofiya, still blindfolded, out onto the grass. 'Stay.' I step back, letting her breathe moon-warmed air. 'You can fight me, or I can untie you. Your choice.'

She does not move. Her voice emerges, restrained. 'Then let's go talk.'

I release the belt.

She peels off the blindfold, blinking in the humility of twilight. I keep my distance, enough to let the vines between us hold our words.

'You played me,' I accuse, voice rough. 'Again.'

She crosses her arms. 'I have trust issues, especially towards Salvatores. That shouldn't come as a surprise to you. At all.'

I lean against a vine stake, jaw clenched. 'This' – I sweep my arm at the villa, the land, the entire weight of inheritance and betrayal – 'was one of my mother's favourite places.'

She rubs her arms, as if warding off a chill. 'I... I won't apologise. Not for trying to protect my sister's wishes.'

I nod. Smile. 'It's admirable you keep falling back on Maddie's wishes, and not your own. It tells me a lot.'

Wariness creeps across her face. 'And what's that, exactly?'

'That you might not protect the murderer who ruined your family, who tried to ruin mine when the time comes. And the time will come, *tigra*.' The words burn. 'You've saved his life. Twice now. I won't allow a third.'

She flinches at the truth. 'I know. You'll do what you have to do. But...' She swallows, anger igniting. 'I won't predict where

I'll stand. Because he's still my grandfather. My family. My blood.'

I step forward, closing the distance between us. My fingers brush her cheek, warm despite the coming chill. 'And he's my war. The target that will begin to put ghosts to rest. Grant him a safety net again and I'll ensure you both fall through it. *Capisci?*'

She freezes, her eyes wide, the revelation hammering the night air. I stare at her, trying to read who she is behind the mask of sorrow and defiance.

'Where will it end, Rafaelle?' Her voice is small.

'It's bigger than me, *duci*, this thing two old men started decades ago. But I have a part to play, and by fuck, I will play it.'

Her breath catches and her tears pool, but she doesn't pull away. 'I understand. And I'm finding that I want' – she inches closer – 'to be something more than a hostage between two men.'

A crack of thunder rumbles overhead; the sky gapes, ready to break. My chest throbs, raw as if grieving.

I cup her face as sadness and deep intent collide. 'Then don't stand between us. Stand aside. Or beside.' *Beside me. Fucking pick me.* 'Either way, his days are numbered.'

Stars fracture in the night sky and the first raindrops sizzle on my jacket, but I ignore them.

She leans into my palm, her siren-call dragging me closer. My enemy draped in beauty. *Fuck.* I press my forehead to hers once more.

She closes her eyes, and when she speaks her voice trembles. 'He's just an old man, Rafaelle. Can't you—'

I tear myself away. *Surprise.* Sirens and their temptation bullshit.

'No,' I breathe, resolute. 'And before you suggest another way, there isn't one. Your father or the rest of your *famigghia* won't stand by and watch him running about forever. Best he's put down. Now. So we can handle the fall out of that. Until then, don't fucking run,' I whisper.

She grips my shoulders. 'I can't... I won't. As insane as this is, I feel the need to see it to the end, however it ends.'

I lean in, kiss her – soft at first, then urgent, as though we might be the only two living beings in this world. Rain slants sideways, chasing us, soaking us, attempting to cool and cleanse the hot and depraved.

I place a hand on her shoulder, my voice low, and my heart – the same heart that refused to lift above dull thuds – hammering. Another Mancinelli witch, practising her dark arts. 'Then I'll give you the same choice, one last time, Sofiya. Truce or total war, right now.'

Her gaze meets mine, storm-washed and fierce. 'Truce,' she whispers. 'As we search for El Topo.' She swallows, her voice trembling. 'How will I explain it to Maddie?'

I brush a raindrop off her jaw. 'Let me deal with that. He won't die by your hands.'

She studies me for a long moment. 'I don't know whether you expect a thank you... or a knife in the ribs for that.'

'It's fucked up, I know. But are you surprised? We're fucked up.'

She shudders. 'Blood. For blood. For Blood. When does it end?'

Lightning forks. I inhale her scent of olive leaf and gunpowder, salt and sorrow. I want to forget the plan and lose myself in her. Yet if I do, every compromise will bleed into my dreams.

'Not tonight. Maybe not tomorrow.' *Or ever.* I catch her hand, pull her onto the portico as thunder splits the sky. Pin her to the wall.

When I pull back, neither of us breathes. 'But the day after or one after that, we go again,' I murmur. '*Sì?*'

She nods, tears mingling with rain. '*Sì.*'

Under a sky dividing itself in half, we stand – hunter and hunted, captor and betrayer – bound by loyalty, blood, and an impossible alliance that might save us both... or destroy us entirely.

Moments later, as the thunder fades to a distant rumble, a sound tears from her throat – something equal parts grief and relief – and she lunges into my arms.

Our lips crash together, rain and want coalescing into something feral.

The kiss turns carnal, urgent – two predators collapsing into the moment.

18

SOFIYA

If Rafaelle clocks that I haven't asked the geographical location of where he's brought me, he doesn't point it out.

Valle di Luce, so-named for the way the late-afternoon sun spills golden over the hills, igniting the vines in a blaze of copper and emerald.

Nestled between olive groves and the rugged cliffs of northern Sicily, the vineyard stretches like a secret whispered between the sea and sky.

In spring, wildflowers bloom at the borders – crimson poppies, violet irises, and sun-bright calendula – scenting the air with soft sweetness.

At dusk, fireflies blink among the leaves like stars come down to rest, and the wind carries the mingled perfume of ripe grapes and sugar-kissed breeze. It's a place built on blood and legacy, but also beauty – aching, untamed, and breathtaking.

I know this because I'd spent uncomfortably long days scoping the place out years ago as part of my 'training', as Bonafacio put it.

And lately, I'd returned, inexplicably drawn to the rarely used Salvatore estate while I searched for my sister, Giada.

The sister my grandfather had hidden so surprisingly well after that harrowing incident Rafaelle Salvatore was determined to decimate my family for that I hadn't been able to locate even the smallest lead.

The Venetian blinds cast slatted shadows across the suite's king-size bed, lacing us in muted stripes of late afternoon light.

I stand in the centre of the room I snuck into and spent a single night in a year ago. Dreaming dreams that should never come true, yet yearn to be born.

Clad only in a thin silk robe that tumbles to my knees, I wait, my heart lodged in my throat. The sea breeze drifts through the open balcony doors, tugging at my damp hair and carrying the faint scent of salt and earth. Everything about this room – its opulence, its stillness – hangs heavy with the weight of what Rafaelle Salvatore and I are about to do.

What that kiss outside had started. What the deranged push-pull-attack-betray had wrought.

A lick of my lower lip from his clever tongue.

A stuttered roll of my hips.

The feral power of his hardened cock. Branding me. *Owning* me.

Then the untamed, unvarnished words he'd uttered.

'I'm going to fuck you, *bedda tigra*. Tonight. I'm going to pluck that cherry, taste it on my tongue and my cock. Claim one victory tonight.'

His voice, low and dangerous, echoed in me like a summons. Truce, we chose. But truce, in our world, means a different war: the one that plays out between skin and need, power and surrender.

'And you're going to let me, aren't you?' he crooned, infusing mesmeric power behind words that shouldn't command my complete surrender.

But they do.

I close my eyes and remember the raw electricity of our last kiss, standing in the vineyard under the cracked sky. The rain had soaked us, but our hunger had burned hotter than any storm. I had allowed him to taste me in a way I never would have imagined.

A Salvatore man's mouth had drawn me so completely into his world. And now, here I am, near-naked at the edge of everything I didn't know I craved until a mere three days ago.

A soft click on the bathroom door makes me inhale sharply.

Rafa steps out, black Henley clinging to his torso, his pants pressed taut across his thighs. His hair is damp despite using the towel on it, on both of us when we came inside.

The faintest flame of candlelight picks out the angles of his cheekbones.

He watches me, slow and deliberate, his gaze sizing me up. I shiver despite the warmth in the room.

'Come here,' he says, voice low, rough with the promise of violence and rhapsody all at once.

I take a step forward, and then another, until only a breath divides us. He tilts my chin up with a fingertip, and I feel every nerve roaring to life.

'Do you trust me?' His eyes glint with sincerity, but also that feral hunger I can't forget.

'No. I shouldn't. Maybe,' I whisper, though a tremor runs through me.

'I'll take all three. For now.' He lifts a small black box from the bedside table – two leather cuffs lined with soft suede and a blindfold of matching black silk. My pulse reverberates in my ears.

An assassin with a go-bag that contains sex toys?

I would laugh if I wasn't insanely turned on.

He shows me both items, watching my reaction.

I swallow hard. 'You're tying me up for the second time tonight?'

He presses a finger to my lips, savouring unsaid things. 'The first was for punishment. The second could be punishment too. If you ask nicely.'

My breath catches. I hadn't thought of asking. The notion feels dangerous, thrilling, and utterly intoxicating.

He slinks behind me, eases the robe off and lightly loops one cuff around my right wrist. I inhale a stuttered breath. His scent, musky and faintly copper, drifts against my neck.

'Relax.' The voice at my ear, velvet-dark, commands an involuntary shiver. He secures the cuff with gentle but unyielding pressure.

The snap of the closure echoes in the hush. He repeats it with my left wrist, and I close my eyes, tasting the metallic punch of my heartbeat.

The sensation is strangely liberating. My arms are mine in the usual sense, and yet entirely not mine.

'Blindfold next. You ready?'

My pulse hammers. It's a question repeated in my mind. 'Yes.'

He stretches it across my eyes and smooth silk dissolves the room into shade. Then he ties it behind my head, a soft knot I could slip free from – but I don't. The world dims. I breathe in darkness. A darkness we were both born into. A darkness we, from opposite sides of a cursed coin, have embraced.

'Now.' His fingers graze my jaw, trailing down my chest and collarbone like a caress and a charge. 'You can't see me... but I can see you.'

I nod.

My throat is tight, but I want this, even as terror curves my spine. Beneath the blindfold, I peer into my own uncertainty. Tears I cannot stem, butterflies tearing at my stomach.

I'm suddenly aware of every inch of bare skin, exposed and trembling.

A draw of breath behind me, then the hum of him stepping closer. A hand clasps my hip, guiding me forward until my belly grazes the plush mattress. I drop to my knees on the cool carpet, obedient and braced.

He runs his fingertips across the hollow of my back, over the curve of my hips and the swell of my bottom and I catch my breath.

'Don't move.' His voice drips need and command. 'Let me worship you, *duci tigra*.'

I'm riveted by the sound of him removing his belt – leather sliding against leather – and snapping the buckle. The silent click of it falling to the floor makes me quiver.

My womb tingles. I imagine the weight of him behind me, unyielding, all-consuming.

I'm vulnerable, and utterly alive.

Firmer touches drift along the valley between my shoulder blades, sending a shiver through my bones. Then, a light brush of a fingertip along my spine, teasing warmth.

His mouth grazes the shell of my ear. 'Stay with me.'

I nod, breath choked. 'Rafaelle—'

He kneels behind me, the rasp of clothing being discarded echoing all around me. I press forward, opening my thighs ever so slightly, an invitation in the darkness. A mute gasp travels up my neck. I'm caught between the need to pull away and the need to back sink into his naked body.

A single thick finger traces the seam of my pussy, light,

exploratory, mapping every quiver. I bite back a cry. My slickness drips on his fingertip. He smiles against my skin – an echo of blades between my thighs.

Then, just as suddenly, he changes our positions and his breath flares around my navel. He's *everywhere*. Trailing soft kisses, stubble brushing my skin as he lowers himself, tongue grazing the crease of my hip. Every nerve ignites. The blindfolded world is all sensation – the press of his warm breath, the wet pull of his tongue, the steady thrum of his massive cock against my thigh.

'Fuck, you smell incredible. It's driven me insane for over a year. You know that?'

'You mean since you started tailing me, thinking I didn't know you were there?' I rasp.

Another smile against my skin. A kiss. 'I wanted you to know, baby. Where's the fun in hiding in shadows when I could play?'

His tongue delves deeper, flicking up to my swelling clit, my mounting need. I *whimper*, a stupidly feminine sound that would... *should* shame me, but I don't care in this moment. My body is trembling so hard my toes curl. He's relentless, patient, each stroke of his mouth forging me towards surrender.

'Rafa,' I moan into the black. My voice sounds distant, yet too loud – like I'm leaking every drop of control.

He hums, soft and possessive. 'Good girl. Cream for me. I'm thirsty as fuck.'

Heat pools under my ribcage at the utter filth from his beautiful mouth. My back arches, pressing my hips backward. He groans, lips parting, and I feel him gather me to the brink.

'Closer.' His voice is a promise and a claiming.

Heat intensifies, tongue darting, teeth grazing and breath warm and flickering. My breaths come jagged – each inhale an invitation, each exhale a confession of how much I want this. Want *him*, the most forbidden thing in my existence.

God, the way my body floods is shameful and exhilarating and I don't care that I'm blushing even as my muscles clench, my mind abandoning everything but—

He latches onto my clit, sucks it like his favourite candy. I scream as the world collapses into waves of sensation.

'Fuck, you're breathtaking when you come,' Rafa rasps.

He holds me there, riding the end of my need out slowly until my limbs tremble into stillness. Then his mouth lifts to press a slow kiss to the nape of my neck.

'I'm not done.'

I'm so startled when he kisses me my heart flutters. I taste myself on his lips and moan as I nod.

His hands trail from my shoulders down to my ass. He shifts behind me and I catch the weight of his cock, hard and stark and hot against my skin.

I swallow, my throat dry, aching for him as he snatches me up and repositions me on the bed to straddle him.

'Lift your hips.' His command is gentle but absolute.

I rise onto my knees, cursing my trembling even as my hips tilt. He's between my thighs, pressing hard into the wetness still clinging to me. His cock teases the entrance, and I gasp, anticipation and trepidation warring with each other.

I'm unprepared for when he pulls the blindfold off and I tumble into a different kind of darkness, one of feral need and the declaration of ferocious intent in his eyes.

I've seen him in various forms of undress, but this time, gloriously bare, unashamedly aroused, a predator locked on his prey... it's near transcendent.

I can't take my eyes off the hand stroking his thick, veined cock, piercing gleaming in the candlelight. Back and forth. Back and forth.

I'm reminded how belly-clenching, pussy-destroying, impossibly big he is.

Diu miu. What am I—

'Watch me, *bedda*. Watch me claim you. Break you in half so beautifully no man will ever be able to put you back the same again.'

He surges up as he speaks, catching first my mouth in a filthy, tongue-jousting kiss, then lower, flicks over one pebbled nipple, and the other.

Then, satisfied with my incoherent cries, he grips one hip with one hand, the other still stroking, stroking, stroking.

Sanity bounces a feather-light touch on the edges of my brain. 'Wait. Condom.'

He freezes. Nostrils flared. 'Fuck. No. Not happening.'

My eyes flare wide. Both at the desperate edge in his voice and the blatant refusal. 'Rafaelle.'

'You're on the fucking pill, Sofiya. And I'm clean.'

His eyes rage at me, his grip bruising. Daring me to refuse either.

I've long passed the stage of wondering how he knows things about me. Or maybe I never questioned them in the first place. And I've seen the way he takes care of his body. His weapons.

The Enforcer might earn his reputation as a ruthless assassin and Rafaelle Salvatore might appear the deranged second to his underboss brother, but there's a meticulousness to his every act.

If he says he's clean, I believe him.

'I'm. Not. Fucking. Stopping,' he grates. The fires of hell flare at even the thought.

I jump into the flames. 'Then don't.'

He slides inside – slowly, excruciatingly – guiding the tip deep. My slick heat grips him, and I bite my lip to keep from crying out. My chest lifts, bracing as he fills me. Inch by delicious, terrifying inch.

He stops halfway. At the point of resistance.

Both hands anchor at my hips, steadying, his cock slick and chest rising and falling faster than I've seen him.

'I have you shackled and beautifully pinned, *tigra*. But this last move is yours. Break that beautiful cherry on my cock or tell me to claim it. Your choice.'

I adjust my posture, pressing down onto him, a shuddering push that draws him deep. Deeper.

I feel full. So full. Terrified too. I clench around him and he hisses.

'Fuck, *duci*.' He breathes deep, and colour flares across his cheekbones. 'Hurry the fuck up. Or this goes sideways.'

I'm tempted to tease, to titivate. But that fullness? I want more. Need it.

'Take it, Rafaelle,' I gasp before I even feel the words forming. 'Fuck me.'

He groans, voice thick with something like awe. Then he thrusts.

Pain slashes through pleasure. But it's the kind that feels... incredible. Purposeful. A means to a glorious end.

'I have it. Fuck yes. It's mine now, isn't it?' Fat smugness rings through his thick voice. His eyes glaze on mine as he pushes forward, deeper, until another lance of pain catches in my womb. 'There you go. I own every fucking inch of this pussy, don't I, *bedda*?'

A gargled sound escapes my mouth, but he shakes his head. 'Not good enough. Tell me, Sofiya.'

'Y-you own it. Every inch,' I gasp.

'Fuck yes, I do. Now watch. The red flag of your beautiful surrender. Here it comes.'

He pulls out slowly, his voice, his touch, his eyes, primal and possessive. And I watch with him as he shows me the blood of my virginity, right there on his thick cock. I clench hard.

'Sweet fucking God, you feel perfect.'

His words scorch through me as he penetrates me, his mouth fusing with mine as he sets an intoxicating rhythm.

I rock into him, hips rolling, small, exploratory motions that ignite electricity in every nerve. His hands slide around to my stomach, then up to cup my breasts, thumbs pressing into the tight peaks.

'Fuck, Sofiya,' he rasps. 'You're mine.'

A tremor of fear flickers through my skull. His 'mine': the single word that warps everything. But under the weight of his hands, under the pressure of his hips, I melt.

I pick up the rhythm, slipping up and down his length like a puzzle piece finding its home. His breath hitches, chest lifting, and I feel the pulse of his arousal deepen inside me.

'Use your words,' he growls, planting his hands on my waist to lift me higher, force me closer.

I moan low. 'Rafa... harder.'

'There she is. My fierce little *tigra*. My baby assassin, killing me with her sublime cunt.'

He thrusts mercilessly, heat and friction colliding until my orgasm threatens to shatter me again. He's a scale tipping towards oblivion, and I cling to the last shred of his voice.

His dirty talk comes in ragged bursts. 'That's it... Ride me... Show me you need it... No one's ever giving you what I'm giving...' Each syllable strikes me like a brand.

I burn with want, stark need pooling between my thighs,

every nerve slick with pleasure. When I clamp down on him, spasms jerk through us both. He roars, voice echoing off the walls, and I taste the salt of him as he shatters inside me.

We collapse together, chests heaving and sweat gleaming on our skin. My ribs ache where his arms pinned me. His heavy breaths stir hairs at my nape.

'Holy fuck,' he pants, running a hand through my hair. 'You wreck me.'

I rest my cheek against his shoulder, mind foggy, heart pounding. 'We're... fucked up,' I murmur.

He lets out a stuttered laugh, groaning as he shifts to cradle me. 'You can say that again.'

Lightning slashes outside. Thunder rumbles low. He releases the restraints and I press my hand to his chest, feeling his heart thunder beneath my palm.

He strokes my cheek with a thumb. 'You okay?'

I push back, still dizzy. 'I don't know.'

He brushes a thumb across my damp lips. 'Me neither. Guess we're in the eye of the fucking storm right now, *no*?'

I close my eyes, torn between relief and dread. The world beyond this villa waits. Bonafacio still breathing, family loyalties fraying, the truce a fragile promise between two dark souls.

He kisses my forehead, then lowers my head until my ear brushes the silk pillow. 'Sleep,' he whispers. 'No one's going anywhere tonight.'

I manage a nod, fragile trust I shouldn't nurture laced with fear.

As I sink into the dark, I wonder, not for the first time, what it is about the Salvatore men that bewitches and mystifies. What blood-deep hunger they stir, warping loyalties, stealing breaths.

In the sway of his arms, I let the world slip away, clinging to

a moment both impossible and necessary, a promise and a
storm yet to come.

19

RAFAELLE

The villa stands silent except for the rustle of cicadas and the crackle of olive branches outside my window. Light slants through carved shutters, painting beams across my face.

The air is still around me, as if holding its breath. Questioning my actions.

For the first time in weeks, months even, I'm not reaching for a gun, scanning heat signatures. Or stewing in anger – well, not entirely.

There's always a nice simmer going on in the background, the soundtrack to my life since that fateful day in Manhattan.

Instead, I'm tying an apron around my waist – my mother's apron, faded and frayed at the edges, smelling very, very faintly of the lavender and rosemary cuttings she used to keep in the pockets.

I know if I stop long enough to ponder those actions, they'll point to a new strain of madness.

I've spent the last hour gathering herbs from the pristine garden kept by invisible staff – rosemary, thyme, basil – flavours she always said could save a bland dish.

The kitchen is old-world Sicilian – chipped terracotta floor, dark-stained wooden counters, beloved copper pots that gleam even under dim bulbs. Sometimes, I still half-expect her to step in beside me, show me how to split an artichoke or braise a shoulder of lamb until the meat falls from the bone.

But that memory is a double-edged blade, a lesson in heritage, a reminder of loss.

Sofiya stirs through the archway, bare feet soft on the stone flagstones, her hair still damp from her shower.

I freeze at the sight of her.

She wears a scarf around her head, knot tied just off-centre. The careless, almost throwaway attitude to a beauty that blindsides and flattens you the moment you stop to stare. To acknowledge. To fucking *worship*.

A fucking centrefold in the sunlight. Did I think Sophia Loren?

Hell, yesterday, maybe. Today? After she's taken a cock and gotten a taste of the power her pussy wields?

There's new, frightening – if I was some wet-nosed *fanculo*, which I am fucking not – knowledge behind her eyes. I watch her pause in the doorway, her eyes narrowing, as if she's trying to figure out why her assassin partner is wielding a wooden spoon and a butcher's knife instead of a Beretta.

'It's lunch,' I say, voice low. 'I'm making pasta with lamb ragu, and fresh greens from the garden.'

She arches a brow, stepping closer.

The scarf frames her face like it frames a painting – delicate cheekbones, wet fringe of hair at her temple. 'You cook?'

Something shifts. I shouldn't answer.

She's a Mancinelli. She shares the bloodline of the man who left my mother in a pool of it. The fact that I'm even in this room with her – let alone cooking for her – should have me questioning my sanity.

Maybe it was the sex. The obscene, toe-curling kind that drains the blood from your brain and reroutes it to foolish places. Or maybe it's the way she asked, not with mockery, but with curiosity.

Real. Open. Soft.

I don't know why I fucking do it.

But I do.

'I used to watch her. My mother.' My voice is quieter than I mean it to be. I grab a clove of garlic, slam and crush it under the flat of a knife, maybe with a little more force than necessary. 'Help her. She eventually taught me.'

She leans against the counter, arms crossed. 'Your mother taught you to cook?'

I toss the garlic into a skillet of olive oil. It crackles. The scent of garlic and oil flares, bright and homey, with a hint of betrayal for sharing the product of her loving lessons with this woman. But then... Mama loved to feed anyone bold enough to walk through Salvatore doors, trusting that, lamb or lion, her men had a reason for permitting entry.

My brain conjures her up, here with me. With Sofiya. Something jolts inside me. Because that image isn't... as agonising as it should be.

Jesus. Was it only a year ago I called Cesare pussy-whipped? Among other deeply unsavoury names?

I push the taste of shame and reverse *Schadenfreude* away. Answer a question I shouldn't have permitted in the first place. 'She thought a man should know how to eat.'

Sofiya's mouth curves into an odd, bittersweet smile. 'A mother's love – only way to a man's heart, huh?' She flicks her gaze away. 'Funny, I always thought your type preferred training on live targets rather than simmering sauces.'

I chuckle, but it's rusty – like a sword drawn after too long in its scabbard. 'Mama gave me two gifts. One was the blade in my hand, the other was teaching me how to feed myself – and my enemies, sometimes.' I stir the garlic, then add chopped onions, letting the fragrance swell. 'Bones break better on a full stomach.'

She watches the onions sizzle, heat rippling off the pan. 'You really think you can get me to eat a home-cooked meal after everything we've done?'

I splash in crushed tomatoes, season with salt and pepper, then add chopped lamb shoulder. The meat hisses as it hits the pan. 'Too chicken to try, *tigra*?' I taunt.

Sofiya's chest rises, stills, then falls. 'If I choke and you let me die, you'll never find peace. Don't say I didn't warn you.'

* * *

By the time the ragu simmers, its aroma drifts through the villa. I boil water for pappardelle – wide, rough-edged ribbons of pasta that soak up sauce like parched earth. I slide wooden spoons across counters, chop parsley, zest a lemon for a final flourish.

Behind me, Sofiya lounges on the sofa, sexy legs tucked, toes curled.

Occasionally she sniffs the air, a cute gesture of impatience I'm not sure she registers. When I twirl pasta into a shallow bowl and ladle sauce over it, I feel her track every movement.

Watch her inhale, the scent of lamb and tomato floating around her. Guilt flickers – she's seen me drop men in their tracks, seen the same hands ladle red sauce now gliding gently across pasta.

'It's ready. Come here, *bedda*.'

She rises, a goddess gliding, hips moving differently after her first taste of a man between her legs.

I set the steaming bowl on the table, then pour a glass of Salvatore bottled Montepulciano for each of us. The wine swirls darkly, reflecting the sun as it dips towards the horizon.

I sit, eyes on Sofiya. No fucking way I'm admitting that I'm waiting for her verdict.

She lifts her fork. 'To the chef.'

I nod once. '*Buon appetito*.'

The first bite is a baptism: pasta melting against my tongue, the sauce savoury, hints of garlic and basil weaving through tender lamb.

I watch her fingers tighten on the fork.

She chews slowly, eyes fluttering – like tasting a memory she wasn't sure belonged to her.

She swallows, sets the fork down. 'This is... incredible.'

I settle back. Smug. 'Patience, technique, respect for ingredients – she made me believe cooking is a weapon, too. One that heals rather than kills.'

Cristu, Rafa. What next? Hand over your wish kill list?

Silence. She takes another bite. I can see the war in her eyes. A desire for nourishment, dread of vulnerability by chasing this connection... this fucking *witchcraft* between us.

'Did she teach just you or your siblings as well?' Sofiya asks, voice barely above a whisper.

I run a hand through my hair, pull, hoping to reclaim and restore some sanity. 'I was the only one interested. It was... our thing. And maybe she knew where I was destined. Maybe she knew I'd need both the fuel and defence.'

Sofiya watches me with keen intent. 'Sounds like you never had a choice on this... path.'

I stiffen, then force myself to relax.

So what if they handed Cesare the throne and me a gun? I was the second son, the spare who carved out a place no one could take from me, even if it meant becoming the monster they whisper and wonder about.

'Choice is a luxury even in the kitchen.' I lift my glass. Drink. Set it down with a decisive click. 'Tonight, you drink that wine and tell me if you'll help me find El Topo.'

She inhales and slants me a look. 'I will help. But I don't know if I can ever eat like this again.'

I push the salad bowl her way, greens tossed in lemon juice, shards of Pecorino. 'You're a warrior and a wanderer. Like me. Take the taste of home when it's offered, *tigra*. It might not come around again.'

The warning is double-spiked. And I absorb the sensation of pain and grounding it brings. I was at risk of letting fucking sappy emotions get away from me.

She hesitates, then picks at the salad, each bite small, deliberate. I watch the muscles in her jaw work, like she's fighting herself to swallow.

Suddenly she drops the salad fork, pushes back her chair. 'I'm done.'

I set my wine down. 'Done?'

She stands, a little unsteadily, but it's not from wine. It's from the shifting occurring beneath our feet.

'Yes. I'm—' Her voice cracks on the edge of something unexpected, and the rawness of it scorches me.

I screech back my chair, the sound jarring. But if I'd hoped it would be enough to knock some sense into this *pazzo* situation, I'm proven wildly wrong when my arms fall open of their own accord. Or, more accurately, under the spell of her fucking witchcraft. 'Come here.'

She stiffens, then rounds the table. Stands next to me, a vision of bare thighs, newly deflowered Madonna's face and potent killer.

'Tell me what you're thinking,' I mutter. Yup, I'm *jutu pazzu*.

She laughs, grating. In this soup of bewilderment we're both boiling in. 'Where should I start? I'm right here in the middle of this metaphor of you and your mother and everything she loved. I should be appalled.' She closes her eyes.

I lift a hand, trail it up her outer thigh to her hip. Draw her closer. 'But?'

'But right now, I want to stretch out on that sofa, ask a million questions I shouldn't. Not think about the dozen ways I should defend myself if you try to kill me. Or the two dozen ways I should be thinking about how to kill you.'

I smile. Because how can I not?

'No reason why you can't do all of it. Lie down and dream of ways to kill. But while you do that, how about I kill you with orgasms?'

Her eyes drift shut and pink stains her cheeks. 'I shouldn't.'

'Fuck that. I haven't had nearly enough of this body. And I know yours is screaming for mine. Are you going to deny it? Deny this cock in that celestial cunt?'

She shakes so roughly, she has to reach out a steadying hand on my shoulder. And fuck, I love that more than I want to admit.

'God, Rafa...'

'That's it. Keep saying my name just like that,' I murmur as I loosen the tie to her robe. Part it. Reward myself with the dips and curves of her breathtaking body.

'You're fucking beautiful.' I kiss her navel, then before I lose my mind, I pull back. She blinks down at me, rare vulnerability flickering in her gaze.

'You make me... I don't know how to...'

I cup her jaw in my palm, thumb brushing her lower lip. 'Go lie on the sofa, *tigra*. Wait for me.'

Her eyes spark. 'What makes you think you can—'

I glide one hand up her thigh and between her legs, chuckle to hide a groan at her damp cunt.

'Rafa!'

'This is why. Sofa.' I stroke her once. Twice. Her eyes glaze over, even as her nails dig into my shoulder. 'Feet on the table, legs wide open.'

Her colour deepens. 'I'm not doing that...'

'Sure you are. You know why?'

Her lips purse. She stays silent.

'Because you're dying to see what that does to me.'

The truth wars with denial in her eyes. I smile. Again. Then before I lose my mind, I spin her around and smack her ass. 'Go, *tigra*.'

She goes.

I surge to my feet. Scoop up dirty dishes and store away the leftovers. Some would leave the clearing up till later, especially with the promise of tight pussy on the horizon. But my mama taught me better. And if I've chosen to honour her today, I'm not finishing with half-measures.

That's not to say I'm not focused on Sofiya though.

Haven't forgotten that, sublime pussy or not, she's a threat. One who betrayed me only last night. One who's won a second chance where others would've been long dead and buried.

From the corner of my eye, I see her slide Orazio's antique letter opener under the cushion next to her right elbow and hide a grin.

Good girl, baby assassin.

Her robe gapes, displaying her beautiful tits as she perches on the edge of the sofa and my cock swells, my tip spilling with pre-cum and need.

Even though my back's turned, I know the second she props her tiny feet on the table, the short silent battle before her legs spread wide open, displaying her pretty pink pussy.

Saliva rushes into my mouth, a groan building in my chest.

I hurry to finish the dishes, stopping once to grip my dick when it threatens to jump out of my fucking pants.

Leftovers stashed, dishes in washer and table and counters gleaming, I toss the dishrag, snag my half-finished glass of wine, and approach my beautiful enemy.

I have every intention of sitting on the opposite seat. But somehow I find myself stepping into the space between the coffee table and sofa.

Her breathing escalates, right along with her delightful blush as I stare. And stare.

I rest on one hand, glass in the other, studying her face in the dappling light. 'I wish I was a half-decent painter. I'd paint the shit of out you right now.'

'You think I'd let you?' she whispers, arousal slurring her words.

'With the right incentive? Absolutely.'

'*Strunzu spavaldu,*' she mutters under her breath.

'I'm a cocky bastard with good reason, *bedda tigra.* This time yesterday, you were a virgin. Yet here you are, your beautiful, wet cunt spread out for me, your belly full of delicious food I made. Not an ounce of genuine outrage in your body.'

Her face flames and her legs start to shut.

I grip one ankle, rubbing my thumb above the delicate bone. 'Uh uh. No take backsies or you don't get to come.'

Before she can issue the sharp retort burning on her tongue, I dip my fingers into the *vino russu* made from the black clay of the field outside my window and drip it down her inner thigh.

She hisses, but her mouth stays parted, her wide eyes on the twin drips of red heading for her slick centre.

We both watch, fascinated, as the wine drips into her pussy.

I do the same with the opposite thigh. By the time it reaches its destination, she's panting.

I tease the fabric apart, revealing the curve of her waist, the hollow of her belly, the soft swell of her breasts. I pause, thumb drawing a circle around her nipple through the thin silk. She gasps, hips lifting.

'Do you need me, *duci*?' I whisper, voice thick.

She nods, breath trembling. I lean in and press my mouth to hers – slow, searing – letting her taste the insanity, the promise, the hunger. Her arms wrap around my neck, her fingers sinking into the hair at my nape as I deepen the kiss, my teeth grazing her bottom lip until she sighs against me.

I disentangle her arms, push her onto her back. 'Arms above your head. Offer those glorious tits to me.'

The sight of Sofiya Mancinelli in this Salvatore villa, spread out on my sofa, her hands cupped around her heavy rose-tipped tits, my wine dripping down her taut, sexy thighs, is better than any masterpiece in any museum on this earth.

Intensely, obscenely satisfying too is the knowledge that no man will *ever* see her like this.

That notion throbs, loud and depraved and gaining power at the back of my head. Before it bubbles over into the unthinkable, I tip my glass and anoint her breasts with Salvatore wine.

The trails catch on her fingers, overflow and drip down, racing, an eager river, to join the flow drenching her pussy.

Drops glide over her pussy and she gasps. One drop lingers on the tip of her clit.

'Fuck.'

She whines and arches her back, so her glorious rose-tipped globes are pointed at me, ready for my tongue, teeth, my lips and hands, urging me on.

'Tell me how badly you want it.'

'Fuck you.' A ragged inhale. Exhale. 'Please. So bad.'

'Addicted to Rafa cock already?'

A flash of pure murder. I wonder if she's going to use that letter opener on me. Fuck, I hope so. 'Answer me. Beg for it, baby.'

Her exhale is outrage and death.

I set the wine aside, lean down, capturing one drenched peak in my mouth, tugging and suckling until she moans my name. I transfer my attention to the other. She releases her breast, her fingers tunnelling into my hair to hold me to my task.

I torture and tease until her skin is almost as red as the wine.

Then I taste my way down. The smell of exquisite wine and prime pussy hits my nostrils, and I groan. 'I'll never get this scent out of my head now, will I, *tigra*?' I growl against her skin.

She makes a gurgled sound, pushes her hips forward, eager with a touch of lingering innocence that makes me want to pound my chest, mark my territory in the most definitive way possible.

For one unhinged moment, I contemplate the letter opener. A few slashes and my name would be carved on her inner thigh. A claim. A fucking warning.

'Rafa, please. Please!'

I push away the psychotic thought... for now... and I wrap my lips around the pink, hooded flesh, sucking it deep into my mouth.

'Ah! Oh... God!'

Her hips surge up, then instantly retreat, as if she's not sure whether she craves or fears the storm of pleasure. I solve the problem by sliding one hand under her lush ass, the other clamped on the thigh I want to mark with my name.

Without mercy, I feast on Sofiya Mancinelli's cunt. Lap, lap, lapping her up. Dipping inside to collect her flowing juices. Groaning when she cries out over and over, her fingers convulsing in my hair.

It takes every ounce of self-control to pull away when I feel her cresting the edge. To yank down my pants and free my dick.

'No! Please...'

'I know, baby. But I need you too. Need you to come on my cock. You want that too, don't you?'

Her head bobs, her eyes glazed, her beautiful siren mouth gasping.

Dragging her forward to the edge of the seat, I guide my broad head to her tiny hole. Marvel at the sublime sensation awaiting me.

Inch by inch, I watch her take me. She shakes, whimpers and cries, but my brave little *tigra* never stops.

Not until I'm bottomed out inside her, with stars exploding on the edges of my vision.

'*Cristu*, you look so good, stretched around my cock. Tell me how you feel.'

'I n-need you t-to fuck me, Rafa,' she gasps.

'*Sì, bedda tigra.*'

Something cracks and I'm gone. I piston her on and off my cock, darting my greedy gaze between her pussy and her face, her tits and her mouth. Traces of wine reenact her virgin blood and I slide deeper into insanity as thoughts I shouldn't have multiply in my brain.

I don't stop when her shrill cry announces her first climax. When she begs me to stop, right before her nails dig in and she pleads the opposite.

Sweat slicks my body by her third orgasm.

Then, with a final surge, I tumble over the edge on her fourth – her cries echoing in the warm room, my name on her lips, our bodies moving as one until the tremors fade and we collapse into ragged stillness. I press a kiss to her forehead, tracing the scar at her hip.

'Good food, exquisite wine. Your pussy and my cock and no war. One more day. Maybe two. Deal?' I murmur, voice shattered.

Eyes screwed shut, she inhales. Nods. Shudders and clenches around me as I surge inside her, insatiable. On the brink of desperation.

'Deal.'

I stagger up and walk us into the bedroom.

We lie together, tangled in silk and sweat, readying ourselves for the storm waiting outside, but fortified for now by the fierce power of our precarious bond.

20

RAFAELLE

Day Two – Morning

Sunlight floods the terrace.

Olive trees rustle as I set a small table for two.

Late-harvest olives, freshly baked bread, ripe tomatoes sliced and drizzled with sunflower oil. On the burner, a pot of coffee simmers, sending dark aromas through the villa.

Sofiya emerges in one of my cotton shirts. Her hair is braided, pillow-soft, and she's barefoot. She blinks at the spread, uncertain.

I hand her a steaming cup. *'Caffè?'*

She nods, wrapping both hands around the mug. *'Grazie.'*

We sit where the breeze catches just right, the sea a glazed blue in the distance. I watch her stir sugar into the coffee, though the morning light reveals a thin bruise on her upper arm, a souvenir from last night's fucking.

She lifts her gaze. 'I know I shouldn't ask... but how do you keep the... pain... from consuming you?'

I tap my fingers on the table. 'You know how,' I rasp. By slitting throats and squeezing triggers.

'That only fulfils... sometimes, doesn't it?'

That insight is... disarming. And deserving of the truth.

I nod at the table. 'By cooking for people who care. By you eating my food and moaning.' I grin, teasing. 'And eating some more until you almost throw up. Like last night.'

She almost smiles. 'I'll make up for it.' She takes a bite of bread – thick crust, soft crumb – and chews slowly. I watch crumbs drift from her mouth, the way her lips curve around the taste.

When she swallows, she exhales. 'This is... peaceful.'

I nod, heart aching. 'It should be. There's been nothing but peace here.' *Unlike at Fallbrook and the carnage your grandfather visited on my family last year.*

She reads my unspoken words and lowers her gaze, stirring her coffee.

Silence throbs around us. 'When did you start?' I ask.

Her eyes dart to mine and her body goes rigid. After a full minute, she relaxes. 'Too young. Fourteen.'

Fuck. Even I didn't start until I was fifteen. 'Let me guess, you accidentally exhibited a skill?'

I know I've hit the bullseye when her eyes widen. 'Yes.'

My smile feels starched. 'It's always a skill they notice first. They close their eyes to everything but the talent. Like we were made for the blade. Like that's all we're good for.'

She swallows, and her nostrils quiver delicately. 'I was told everything in my life is about survival. The *famigghia's* above all else. It was my duty to ensure I survive and thrive so we all could. So I best death. But I never... rest.'

Fuck, I don't know how to process knowing she didn't choose this path, didn't embrace it as wholeheartedly as I did.

Hell, from what I'm beginning to piece together, she's near-killed herself to mould her soft soul to this, rather than discard it entirely to make room for the darkness. The way I have.

Before I can talk myself out of further insanity, I rise, skirt the chair and crouch next to her. I squeeze her waist. 'Then rest now.'

She tilts her head, searching my eyes. 'I don't know how.'

'I'll show you.' I brush a kiss to her temple, then lead her hand to the table where I've set a small dish of lardo, thinly sliced and translucent. 'Taste this.'

I guide a slice onto her tongue. She hesitates, then closes her eyes. The fat melts like silk. I watch her shoulders unfurl. 'I never knew fat could taste... so freeing.' After a moment, she sets the dish down, leaning into me. 'I'm not sure I deserve this.'

I draw her close. 'You deserve to live beyond the blade.'

She presses her face into my chest. 'Show me how.'

* * *

Day Two – Late Afternoon

We wander the villa's grounds, terraced gardens of lavender and rosemary. The sun is a molten orb, casting long shadows. I show her where my mother planted grapevines – roots nearly fifty years old. She kneels, touches the gnarled trunk.

Then she looks up, a look in her eyes I can't decipher. 'I know who you are. What you are. And yet I can't reconcile it with... everything?'

I slide my arm around her shoulders. 'Stop fucking over-thinking, Sofiya. The shitshow will come soon enough.'

Her head turns to rest on my shoulder. She hesitates, then lifts her face. 'Come inside. I want... something.'

I try to summon a smirk but all I achieve is an eager nod.

We ascend the curving stone steps to the kitchen, the space still warm from yesterday's cooking. She moves to the cutting board and pulls fresh peaches from a basket. She sinks her teeth into the ripe fruit, juice dripping down her chin. I chuckle, then close the gap, kissing the sweet slick from her lips and chin.

She pushes me gently, neck flushed. 'Now *that* is dessert.'

I grin, stepping back, tearing off my shirt, revealing scars and muscles honed by war. She watches, heat building.

'When you're ready,' I murmur, 'I'll take you to bed.'

She swallows. 'I'm ready.'

* * *

Day Three – Morning

A hush falls over the villa. The barometer of conflict in my chest ticks down just enough to let peaceful nerves pulse. I'm chopping garlic for bruschetta – Thursday's breakfast, as her morning-after request. When I glance over, I find Sofiya in the doorway, hair loose around her shoulders.

She cups her hands around a mug of coffee. 'I brought you a refuel.'

I set the knife aside, step forward, and take the mug, breath filling with the earthiness of espresso and cream. '*Grazie.*'

She props a hip against the counter, nods towards the board. 'Looks like I'll be tasting again.'

I lean in, brushing a kiss to her temple. 'Taste all you want.'

She dips a cherry tomato – tiny and sun-warmed – into salt, then brings it to my lips. I taste it, and the sharp salt and sweet burst of flavour spread warmth through me. 'Perfect,' I murmur.

She smiles, but it wavers. 'I'm scared.'

I step back, reach for her hand. 'Of what?'

She lowers her head. 'Of forgetting why we're here.'

I lift her chin, lock eyes, ignoring the shifting sands beneath my own feet. 'Then don't look ahead. Focus on what's in front of us.' I trace a fingertip along her jaw. 'If Bonafacio still hides, we'll find him. But *not* at the expense of this – whatever this is between us.'

Her shoulders relax. 'I think I'm getting addicted to you.'

A flicker of disbelief punches me – horses given wings, bullets turned to butterflies. 'I'd say you're insane but...' I shrug. My insides roil from how hard I want to reach for that.

She winks, impish. 'But you're the expert and you don't think this is insanity? Doesn't mean it's not true.'

I cup her face, thumb brushing over her smooth cheek. 'Don't tempt me with it, *bedda*. I will take and take and take.'

She hums – a purr that ripples through my chest. 'Maybe I want you to.'

She steps close, pressing her lips to mine, brief and tender, proof that even in a world built on blood, there can be sweetness.

I hold her there, and for a moment, my mother's kitchen, my mother's apron, the taste of home, all merge into a single insane prayer.

* * *

Two Days Later – Dusk

We've spent two days in this delicate interlude with meals shared over candles, filthy jokes in the corridors, moments of calm silence beneath the arbour as cicadas thrummed. But inevitably, pressure and time bears the fuck down, marching to the drum of its own reckoning.

I turn from the sink with water dripping from my hands. She's outside, leaning on the railing staring at the orange and violet sky.

I join her and wrap an arm around her waist, this woman I've fucked and gloried in but might have to kill when this clusterfuck is done.

I've never felt the slightest inclination to carve a place in my black soul for those who've met their deaths at my hand.

But for her I might just make an exception.

An exception to death or to life?

I ignore the whispered question. Ignore the jagged path it attempts to carve inside me.

'Sofiya.' Her name catches on my lips – an invocation. A warning to myself not to stray from what needs to be done.

She leans back against me, voice hushed. 'I know. Tomorrow, we go back to the hunt.'

'We've had two extra days.' I press a kiss to her temple.

She lifts her face, eyes haunting in lantern light. 'Peace till dawn?'

I tuck a lock of hair behind her ear, allowing... hell, *disarmed* in the face of her singular temptation. '*Sì*. Then it's war, unless...' I trail off, searching her gaze. Fuck. Am I really doing this?

'Unless what?'

I pull her close, feeling the beat of her heart against my chest. 'Unless we keep doing this, beyond six races, beyond blood. Maybe for the season.' I don't frame it in a question because I'm not sure I can stand the wrong answer. A statement she can take or leave.

Her shoulders tremble. 'I don't know how I can—'

'Then leave it with me.' I summon a wink, which feels heavier than normal. Hell, every single fucking thing feels different with her. 'I'm training you in other things. Why not this too, eh?' I press my forehead to hers.

Her gaze searches mine. 'Don't let this go to your head, but I'm a little terrified.'

I cradle her face. 'I'm not.' Lie. I am. A little. Of what Cesare will say. What Orazio will do. But most unsettlingly, why that organ in my chest seems to be fucking *elated* with this new plot twist. 'And that's all that should fucking count.'

She closes her eyes, and I lean in for a kiss that's equal parts promise and frenzied. Rain begins to patter against the roof, and we stand wrapped in one another, clinging to this fragile peace that probably won't have a hope against the mighty *vinnitta* machine.

Soon enough, we'll choose sides again.

But tonight, there is only us. This shaky bliss, our blood-soaked history, and the stubborn glimmer of hope that two broken souls might find a way to create something beautiful.

Something even Mama would've loved.

21

SOFIYA

My phone vibrates against the marble counter in the bathroom, its screen lighting up with a number I don't recognise.

There's no name, yet I know, with the few people who have this number, that I can't ignore it.

I glance back at the bed I've just vacated. My thighs clench in recollection of everything we've done in the past few days, but especially tonight.

God, the way he *owned* me.

I cling to that memory, a large chunk of me burning with pleasure and shame, when I press the home button.

Bonafacio Mancinelli's face flashes above the line.

Every muscle in me tightens. I lift the receiver and press it to my ear.

'*Nupita.* I suppose I should be thankful that you picked up my call?' His voice is low and ragged, the rasp of a snake cornered, the hatred of a king turned pauper.

'Is it worth asking where you are?' I murmur, keeping one ear out for a change in Rafaelle's breathing. A sign that he knows I'm engaging with his enemy.

'You ask me this, why? So you can betray me?'

I lean back, gripping the edge of the counter so hard my knuckles whiten. I realise abstractly that I'm not even shocked at the accusation. 'Betray you?' I echo. I keep my tone flat – bloodless. 'You betrayed yourself with your sloppiness, Nonno. And even then, I bought you hours to get away. You should thank me,' I snarl, but inside, something claws at my ribs.

How many times have I bled for this family? Bitten my tongue until it scarred? Endured whispers and brushed off groping hands because I wasn't born with a cock? I was good only when I was useful. Feared only when I was precise. Loved... never.

The only thing that matters is what I can deliver. Who I can remove. What secrets I can bury to fatten the Mancinelli bank account.

Fury builds in my chest. I stayed. I killed. I protected him. Even now, I'm the one half-hiding him. Shielding what little is left of our legacy.

My eyes flick back to the bedroom, where Rafa sleeps – careless and unguarded in the early light, dark lashes resting against stupidly fine chiselled cheekbone.

For a terrifying second, I wonder if *he* is my way out. My next move. If Maddie could carve a future with Cesare, against every fucking odd and tradition, then maybe... I... I could—

I shut the thought down like a trapdoor.

Because hope like that tastes like betrayal. And I've got just enough Mancinelli blood left to still feel sick about it.

He hisses through clenched teeth. 'I should thank you? You think you helped me? You sheltered me? You bought me time in a cage you're helping our enemies to build. Why are you in Sicily at all?'

'Because of your actions. Because you've forced me to take

whatever steps necessary to make sure no one else dies! You would already be in the cage if not for me.' I swallow, feeling a shock of guilt flash through my chest. 'And I did that because you're my grandfather. Because I'm remembering who I was before you taught me to kill.' Thanks to the very enemy I've been brought up to hate. A hate perpetuated by a bitter old man. 'My days of being your weapon are numbered, Nonno.'

He laughs, a harsh sound that's evil and dominance and zero remorse. 'You're my granddaughter, Sofiya. My blood runs in your veins. You owe me everything.'

I set my jaw, refusing to let his venom penetrate. 'Not after you tried to kill my sister at her own wedding!' I stop, suck my fraying control back in. 'I bought you time once. It won't happen again. All I owe you is the strong suggestion that you stop running. It's not too late to turn yourself in. A quick confession, and they might show mercy. But if you stay on the run, the enforcer will find you – and you know he won't leave you alive if he finds you.'

He breathes in sharply. 'You dare to tell me to turn—'

'Do yourself a favour,' I cut in, voice firm. 'Save what dignity you have. I'm telling you this because once he's on your trail, there's no coming back.'

Silence stretches for a heartbeat, then he snarls, 'Then do what's necessary. Kill him.'

My blood slows – awash in ice. 'I'm not your assassin any more, Nonno,' I say, soft but lethal. 'I stopped killing for free, and my schedule is full for the rest of your life.'

He seethes, the line crackling with rage. 'You abandon me, your blood, just like your sister did. You choose that Salvatore bastard over—'

A heavy click echoes. He hangs up. I'm left with a sudden emptiness, and the phone's black screen glares at me.

My fingers tremble as I drop the device onto the counter.

'Everything okay?' Rafa's voice is right behind me. Soft, low, and raw with suspicion. I hadn't realised he was there. He steps into view, arms folded, watching the phone as if it's a ticking bomb.

I swallow. 'I know you heard him.'

'Hmm?' His voice is cautious as he crosses to me. 'Not everything. Care to tell me what he said?'

I meet his eyes. Dark and insistent. 'He wanted me to kill you.'

His lips curl, a flash of defiance. 'Old news. To which you said...?'

I place a hand on his chest and feel muscles taut beneath his shirt. 'He should go fuck himself. But respectfully.'

His eyes gleam, even as they peer into mine, dissecting me. 'Tell me what you're feeling.'

Empty. Angry. Terrified. 'Ask me again in the morning.'

'You know what that means, right? He's not going to take this well. It's one thing believing his hand of retribution might come to his aid at some point in the future. It's another thing having that surety yanked away.'

I feel something in my gut twist. 'You mean now he's alone, he's ten times more vicious?'

'*Si.*'

I swallow. 'Yes, I know that.'

He runs a hand through his hair, his eyes narrowing. 'Does he know you're with me?'

'I'm not sure, but he thinks I'm a traitor anyway so...' I shrug, even though half my bones protest. 'I told him you don't leave men like him alive.'

He lets out a short laugh – tension exhaling in a sharp burst. 'You stealing my lines now, *tigra*?'

'Just because it sounds insane like a line from *John Wick* doesn't make it false.' A tremor of relief and terror coexists in my chest. I realise how close I came to – what? To turning on him? The thought makes me cringe. And shake.

He catches it. Steps forward and tilts my face towards his. 'Don't knock it, *bedda*. There's a reason it's a franchise and a fucking cult classic.' He turns serious for a moment. 'You've handled yourself fairly well so far. Whatever happens, we'll handle that too. Together, yeah?'

I close my eyes, leaning into his touch. 'Yeah,' I whisper.

He brushes a thumb over my lips. 'Good.' His gaze softens a touch, and he captures my mouth in a tender kiss. An anchor back to a need I don't even know I need until he offers it.

And, yes, I'm beginning to notice a pattern, *this* pattern, with my enemy.

When he pulls away, I'm trembling, heart pounding.

'Fairly well, though?' I toss in, eyebrows raised.

He holds me by the waist, forehead against mine. 'You're far from top of the class yet. But the night isn't over, *bedda tigra*. You're still mine,' he murmurs, fierce and unwavering and far too possessive. 'So I'll give you a chance to score some much-needed points. *Sì*?'

God, what that name does to me. A silly nickname that I should bat away and yet... '*Sì*,' I answer, breathless.

Rain hammers against the shutters, but inside the villa, the storm is us. Desire and unease and longing entwined.

* * *

Rafaelle

I step into the pre-dawn hush of Valle di Luce and close the villa's heavy stone door behind me to stand alone on the gravel path, the last sun rays warming my cheek.

I should feel triumphant – Sofiya and I extended our truce. My fingers are so close to clamping El Topo's neck I can feel the weasel's heat.

In a few days, a week, tops, I can snatch another victory in this never-ending war between Salvatore and Mancinelli.

More importantly, I can claim an eternity of rest for Mama.

But my chest is tight, my mind racing.

I pace a few steps before a gnarled vine trunk and run a hand across its rough bark. Normally, solitude here – earth and grape must – clears my head.

Tonight, even these ancient vines feel like they're pressing in on me.

I exhale, recalling Sofiya's call with El Topo, her voice breaking when she refused to kill for him, that defiant flash in her eyes as she hung up.

I thought I knew her from what I've learned over the past year. That she's loyal only to blood and family. But last night she stood across from me, bearing her pain, choosing herself instead of someone else's warped version of vengeance.

It shouldn't have surprised me. Hell, I chose myself for something more than my birthright handed me. Found fulfilment that was entirely and selfishly mine alone.

We've done this, separately but so often, drawn comfort in the same kill zones, that it should've eroded any hint of softness, like it has to me.

Now I'm haunted by her words – *I want to be something more than a hostage between two men.*

I shake my head.

I've never been hostage to anyone – always predator, never prey.

My mind flashes back to cooking for her. Copper pots, garlic sizzling in olive oil, the rich scent of lamb ragu simmering under my mother's gaze even though she's been gone years now.

The memory feels absurdly tender. I remember Sofiya tracing the tomato sauce with her tongue, tasting it with an intensity I'd only seen on the cutting edge of our one mission together.

In the past, I'd treated those memories as fuel – reminders of home – but never offered them to another – certainly not a Mancinelli. Yet something warm and alien buzzes in my veins. Something *a lot* disturbing.

I'm beginning to sense a kindred spirit in my enemy. And that's a big fucking problem.

I thumb my burner phone, replay Nightowl's cryptic warnings, coded hideout locations. Wondering why I'm stalling in taking the next necessary step. Violence has always been my life's baseline – I pull the trigger, slit that throat, walk away whistling. But now, for the first time, the next kill leaves me flatlining.

And if *she* were in the line of fire, I know I'd drop my rifle. Walk away.

Not whistling.

Fuck.

I rub my face. Slap a taut cheek. 'Focus.' But the word tastes bitter.

Her footsteps, soft even on gravel – another talent I don't want to notice but do – break the silence. She steps into the last golden light, silhouette caressing the vines. Damp hair curls around her face and she looks both vulnerable and unbreakable.

'You should be asleep. We head out soon enough.'

'I couldn't sleep,' she says, coming to stand beside me.

A fingertip brushes a leaf, half-smile on her lips – like neither of us can believe how we ended up here.

I keep my gaze on the vineyard, hiding the storm inside. Because this is where I make a clever quip. A filthy joke about helping her sleep the best way I know how.

Except I'm all dried up.

Fuck. Fuck. Fuck.

Well, at least I can still cuss. I'd lose what's left of my mind if I couldn't, I'm sure.

She narrows her eyes, reading my tension. 'Before things get fucked up again, you should know my time here has been... not safe like a mission, safe like... an unfamiliar home.'

Unfamiliar... because she'd never known a true home?

My jaw clenches. I don't know what to do with that. And I want it all over me. Repeated in surround sound on a loop.

Classic insanity.

She reaches out, brushing my arm and my pulse spikes. Worst-case scenarios for the first time gaining a foothold in my thoughts. Thought of losing her, seeing her become collateral courtesy of El Topo.

That feels like a blade at my throat. I squeeze out the words. 'I think you should head to Canada,' I say. 'Check on Narciso before the race—'

'No.' She steps closer, clasps my wrist in her hand. 'Nothing changes. I'm in this with you – soul and bone.'

I raise deliberate taunting brows, resorting to tried and tested methods. 'I don't know if I can believe that.'

She blinks. Again. Her eyes shimmer with anger. Disappointment. But she holds my gaze. 'Then look fucking deeper.'

In that moment, I see her pain – raw, open. The girl who

lives in shadows and secretly thrills on the hunt of a kill now stands before me with a crack in her armour.

I realise that in hunting her own grandfather, she sacrificed that part of herself. A part she's desperate to claim back.

For her, the ambiguous line between predator and protector has shifted.

She spared her grandfather's life and refused to finish him off.

I grip her hand, fingers locking tight around hers against the vine's rough bark. 'We came to kill a monster,' I say, voice low. Reminding her. Reminding myself.

I let go of her hand, stepping back. Nights of tenderness are over. They have to be.

I pour steel into my tone. 'If you want to come with me,' I warn, 'you will answer to me every second. I'll have full control over you once more. That won't change.'

Her bottom lip trembles, but she doesn't argue.

I see the hurt flash in her eyes, and it stabs me, yet I harden against it. My vendetta hasn't waned, nor my hunger to protect my family from the monster who nearly destroyed them.

A beep sounds from my pocket. 'I have to take this.' I jump on the excuse.

She nods, vulnerability etched on her face, and something fierce stirs in me, a *protectiveness* I've never known.

I turn away, footsteps crunching over gravel. When I push open the villa door, I turn for one last look.

She stands tall against the dying light, a statue of loyalty and pain. And all around her, the vineyard pulses with what we might have been, two killers who found refuge briefly in each other.

Maybe history is inevitable.

Or maybe this is what grasping at bullshit straws feels like. Because when the hunt resumes, and I'm forced to choose between her and vengeance, I know what I'm choosing.

Right?

22

SOFIYA

Long after Rafaelle has retreated, I stand on the terrace of the villa, inhaling the sweet, dusty air.

I've spent five days here with Rafa; days blurring into one another of wine-dark evenings, home-cooked meals, and nights where I slipped into his arms, feeling something like safety for the first time in my life.

Every vine, every twisted trunk, echoes with memories of a mother's laughter and my own weakened heartbeat.

And yet the world beyond these walls – my family, my duties – won't leave me to this fragile peace.

I've watched him in the garden below, pruning a row of sage with steady, practised strokes. His fingers move with a surgeon's precision, even here. I think back to how he taught me to taste the olives yesterday morning – an almost sacred ritual – and I feel a pang of longing for this moment to stretch on forever. But I know it can't.

My phone buzzes in my pocket, one vibration, then another.

I draw it out, thumb skimming the lock screen. Then with the inevitability of a cage door slamming, I activate it.

PAPA

Where are you? Narciso needs you. Call
me. Now.

My chest tightens. I slip behind a column of wisteria, hiding
my phone from view so Rafa doesn't see the sharp line of worry
etched on my face when I re-read the message.

Why is Narciso asking for me? He never has in the past.
Besides, he has my number.

The thought that Bonafacio is still out there, still breathing
to plan his next move, possibly using my brother, makes my
heart lurch.

My fingers fly, tapping one of the many numbers I've
memorised.

'Ms Mancinelli,' the gravelled voice answers, tight with
caution.

I press the burner phone tighter to my ear. 'Agent DeLuca.'
My voice is steady enough to reassure me there's enough left of
my practised cold-blooded calm. 'You have something for me?'

He clears his throat. 'I assume you remember what's at stake
for me?'

I lean forward. 'I'm not the one with the spotty memory and
sticky fingers. Go,' I bark.

'Last night, Palermo surveillance logged someone under one
of the names on our list,' DeLuca says hastily.

'Which one?'

'Mario Vitale.'

I suck in a breath. 'Location?'

'Apartment 3B, Via Caracciolo.'

I tap the screen, capturing the details. 'What's your
mandate?'

'There's a warrant coming down the wire. We go in at

midnight tonight,' he says, but I hear hesitation. 'My hands are tied until then. If you want him alive... or not, you need to act before then.'

My pulse hammers. 'You won't think of double-crossing me, will you, Agent?'

A slow, nervous chuckle. 'No, *signurina*. I haven't forgotten that I have... personal reasons to be invested in your family's affairs.'

'Good.' I made it my business to procure a file he'd kept about a discretionary fund, the one I 'misplaced' in the loan shark's stash house last year. The ledger I lifted just before the Interpol raid. Proof Agent DeLuca had siphoned Interpol resources into untraceable accounts. Enough to ruin him.

His voice is clipped now. 'I want that file back.'

'Then you know what to do. Keep on my sweet side and you just might get a Christmas wish granted.' I hang up, slide the burner into my pocket.

I let the silence press in for a moment.

My pulse still hums with the weight of that bargain. Duty, blood, and now blackmail. But for the first time in days, I feel something else: a brittle spark of faith. An alien feeling.

Directed at the man who's slowly turning me inside out.

My feet move towards him even before I clock I'm moving. That moment outside when he attempted distance and dominance I push deep down.

To be addressed later, if needed.

I wonder how he'll take this – knowing I've used his leak to my advantage, knowing I'm dragging him back into the hunt partly on my terms. I wipe my palms on my jeans as I approach the bedroom.

He's sitting on the bed, calibrating his rifle's optics.

He doesn't look up when I approach, but I catch a flicker in his shoulders, that tension in his breathing.

'You had a call,' he murmurs, voice smooth as gravel.

I draw the phone from my pocket and lay it on the wooden table. 'A source. Interpol.'

He nods. 'DeLuca.'

Shock punches through me. 'You know?'

'That he's in your pocket?' He lets a mocking smile curl a fraction. 'Maybe.' The rifle hisses as he straightens. 'What did he have to say for himself?'

I step closer, voice low but precise as I relay every word – the alias Nonno's using, the deadline, the blackmail, the threat of exposure.

He stays still, absorbing it all like gravity. For a heartbeat I can't read him. Maybe anger, relief, something softer buried beneath the surface. He brushes the stock of his rifle against his bicep. Then he breathes out. 'So we move now. Take care of things before midnight.'

'Yes.' My voice feels firmer than the quake in my chest. My hand lifts on its own, sliding to his forearm, fingertips brushing over the muscle. He doesn't pull away. Fragile trust flickers between us. Or maybe it's just wishful thinking.

'You sure about this?' he asks. 'You need to be fucking sure, *tigra*,' he insists, jaw tight enough to cut glass.

'I trust you enough with this to tell you the truth.' I look over the bed, still warm with the memory of everything we shared here sizzling beneath my palm. 'And reprieves, by their definition, end,' I whisper, lifting my gaze.

In his eyes I see that same dangerous spark, that fierce protectiveness. But is it for his mission, the vow that brought him to the rooftop in Connecticut, or for me?

He nods once, decisive. 'Go pack. I'll have the car ready in ten.'

Insides shaking more than I want to stop and examine, I turn to go, but his voice stops me. 'Sofiya?'

I whirl back. His rifle is slung, but his attention is all on me. 'I appreciate you trusting me with this. Now you trust me when I say I'll keep you safe, *si*?'

I want to say I'll keep myself safe, but I've never handed someone my blood and bone before.

So instead I step forward, closing the space between us, and press a quick, trembling kiss to his stubble, a benediction of our fragile truce. When I pull back, his hand slides to my waist, anchoring me. Deepening the kiss, turning it into a branding, his tongue sliding over mine like he's already thinking about rewriting the terms, turning this from a partnership into a surrender. Like he's already claimed me, a prize he doesn't intend to give back.

And absurdly, his touch grounds me, steady and sharp as a blade's edge.

This was never a simple mission. But now it's raw, volatile, and real – and whatever storm is coming, I'm secretly, fiercely glad I'm not facing it alone.

* * *

Rafaelle

Trust.

That's what she offered me, and God knows it's a currency I've never been willing to spend so freely.

I brace my hands on the boot of the Range Rover.

Its tailgate is already open, saddle bags and rifle cases

stacked neatly inside by my own careful planning. I haul in a duffel of extra mags, bindle of grenades, and a leather satchel with medical gear. Every click of hardened plastic on metal jars in the dark stillness.

As I snap the lid on another ammo box, my mind drifts back ten minutes ago. Those eyes, wide and vulnerable when she whispered she trusted me.

Sofiya Mancinelli, whose loyalty was never given lightly, has put faith in me where bullets and betrayal reign.

My world of blades, bullets and broken men taught me to work alone. To kill, then vanish. But for five sublime days, she's been as inside me as I have been in her.

I zip the last bag and close the tailgate, heart pounding. The vineyard's walls loom behind me, a fortress of memories – my mother's laughter in the kitchen, our shared confidences, the hopes and bliss we staged between these rows.

No, *bliss* isn't the right word, but the faint warmth of connection is something I never expected. Now violence calls me away, but I can't ignore the fact that this time, I'm not going in alone.

I head inside the villa.

The kitchen is still redolent of last night's braised lamb – peppery tomato, rosemary, fat melting into sauce. I slide my hands over the countertop as Sofiya's voice snaps through my brain again.

I trust you enough with this to tell you the truth.

Packaged within that trust is an unspoken question: *Do you trust me?*

I should take a moment, to figure *that* out. Because she's either the world's greatest actress – better even than her beauty-namesake, Sophia Loren – or...

Fuck. The naked truth simmering beneath the skin threatens to floor me. Without her, this mission – our future partnership, an Aegis possibility which blazes even brighter now – feels hollow, like running an empty chamber.

I fucking hammered her when I thought she'd betrayed me, and yet her trust feels heavier than any rifle I've ever carried.

He's in my pocket now, she said of her spy, DeLuca. But really I'm in hers, and that terrifies the hell out of me.

Responsibility warps my gut. To protect her is to risk everything I've ever known. Everything the Salvatore rule stands for.

Famigghia above all.

The solution is simple, then.

Don't fuck it up.

Sofiya's trust has snared me; whether that's salvation or damnation, I haven't decided. But resolve settles like steel. We face down the coming storm together – or we both go down in it.

I head upstairs to grab my phone.

Nightowl's been silent. But even without new intel, I know what needs to happen. I'm going with her. Side by side, just like the truce dictates, because the thought of her standing alone on that dark street in Palermo gnaws at me.

Every instinct in my being wants to protect her, to keep her here in this villa where I can watch her breathe.

I pace back downstairs. The aubergine-coloured walls, the copper pots – every item here could have been touched by my mother. She taught me to cook, and with every lesson, I buried a piece of her in a recipe. Now, every dish I make tastes like vulnerability, and I loathe it.

But I'm willing to hate it for her.

I grab my keys, sling a leather jacket over my shoulders, and head for the car. As I pass the table, I see my mother's worn apron, folded carefully. I hesitate, brushing the linen between my fingers. In that instant, I know I'll never be the same.

I brought Sofiya to punish her.

Instead she's reached inside me. Broken open a place in me I'd thought hardened by a lifetime of death.

I slip outside, night-time lanterns glowing along the drive, and see her – standing at the gate in shadow, face upturned in dusk's final light.

She steels herself as I approach.

'Ready?' I ask, voice hoarse.

She nods, expression luminous and wary. 'Together?'

I slide my arms around her because I can't resist. And I don't want to. '*Sì*. Together.'

Her sigh is soft, way too tender for my hard edges.

Teeth set, I pull away. 'Let's go find him.'

She nods again, the flicker of determination in her eyes. We turn and walk towards the car, two hunters tethered by something deeper than vengeance.

As the engine roars to life, I linger on the thought. Sofiya, strategist, granddaughter, woman. Could I trust her in this? For now?

The lone wolf inside me growls, *Fuck no*. Seethes at the prospect of walking this dark road with her.

But other howls sound, reminding me that tonight we are no longer just Salvatore and Mancinelli. We are something else entirely – an alliance that neither of us understands, but both of us need.

I shift the car into gear, and we drive into the night, my chest hollow and whirling, wondering what the hell is happening to me.

23

RAFAELLE

The apartment building in Palermo sits on the edge of the coast like a broken jawbone – its balconies rusted, its windows stained with the salt of old sins. I park two blocks down and we approach on foot, slipping past drunk tourists and street vendors hawking bootleg cigarettes. A party rages somewhere nearby, but this place is a tomb.

We climb the cracked stairwell in silence.

No plan B. No backup if this goes sideways. It's just her, me, and the weight of two families' legacies balanced on the edge of a blade.

I test the door and it's unlocked.

Classic fucking arrogance. The Devil taunting the Reaper.

Inside, the apartment stinks of old smoke and spoiled meat. It's dim, curtains drawn.

In the hallway, I glance behind me at Sofiya.

Her eyes are steady, her breathing silent. The only betrayal is the pulse jumping in her throat. The fiercely controlled tension. I raise an eyebrow. She raises hers. Then nods.

Here goes fucking nothing.

Four long strides and we enter the sorry space.

It's almost pathetic, the old man worth billions reduced to this.

El Topo sits at a chipped kitchen table, a pistol within reach and half a bottle of grappa sweating beside it. He doesn't even flinch until I move deeper into the room, silencer raised.

That is until he sees her.

And that's when he freezes. '*Figlia di puta*,' he rasps, like her name is a curse.

Sofiya's already moving, shocking the fuck out of me.

She crosses the room in a breath, knife at his throat before he can blink. One of his bodyguards bolts from the bedroom – big, fast, too loud. I drop him with a clean shot to the throat.

Two more rush from the hallway. One catches a round in the kneecap. The second lunges, screaming. I let him get close, then gut him low and silent.

Three down. Just the old killer of mothers and daughters left.

'Toss it,' I snarl, nodding at his pistol.

Bonafacio slides it towards me, eyes never leaving Sofiya.

'You've turned ugly in the last year, *nupita*,' he says to her. 'Just like your mother in the end. A mouth too big, a spine too soft. Traitor just like your sisters.'

Sofiya doesn't flinch. But I see it, the twitch in her hand, the tightness in her jaw.

'I warned your father not to raise daughters,' he goes on, voice curdling. 'And what did he get for his trouble? Sluts and traitors.'

'Say my mother's name again,' Sofiya says, blade kissing his throat. 'Say it and I swear I'll open you up from gut to gullet.'

'Vittoria,' he sneers. 'Weak. Just like you.'

My fingers tighten on the trigger. 'That's fucking enough.

Or... actually, keep going. Give me an excuse to put one between your eyes ten seconds quicker.'

I'm ready to end him. Have been for over two decades, ever since Orazio sat us down and told us about Bonafacio Mancinelli, the man who killed the love of his life.

But Sofiya speaks. Stunning the fuck out of me. Again.

'Where is she?'

El Topo's eyes gleam with unholy glee. 'Somewhere you'll never find her.'

She?

'Tell me where the fuck my sister is!'

Shock punches through me. Is this why she let the old man escape five days ago?

Absurdly, that makes me feel a little better, while the lone wolf tears into my flesh for believing in her pure loyalty. To me.

Trust comes wrapped in strings. Remember that.

El Topo starts laughing, enjoying twisting the knife of cruelty. 'You'll never find her.'

My fingers caress the trigger, ready to end the man who made monsters of little girls then blamed them for growing teeth. The man who stopped deserving to breathe long before his actions killed my mother.

But she breathes deep. Lowers the knife and takes one step back.

Then she swings the hilt with all her strength. The crack of it landing against his temple is not enough, but it's grotesquely satisfying. He slumps, unconscious.

I stare at him, at the man whose name haunts every empty room I grew up in, whose legacy tried to poison every good thing the Salvatores ever tried to build. This is the moment I honour her memory. *My moment.*

I raise my gun.

One tiny, delicious little squeeze. Barely a flinch. Less than a second. And it's over. I want to draw it out a little. Kick him awake, offer him a chance at last words like some B-movie villain, wasting time with a monologue.

'He deserves to die.' I mean that to the core of my being. I hear the anger in my voice, the edge I don't bother hiding. 'Tell me you know that.'

Her chest rises and falls like she's just finished a marathon. 'I know,' she whispers. *Take one step, then another. Away from him. Closer to me.* 'And I can't speak for you, but you know I can't do it. If I kill him, I become him.'

I don't answer right away.

Because in that instant, I'm not just standing in some rotting Palermo apartment. I'm a fucking wreck again, leaning on Cesare at the funeral, watching my father wither and die in front of my eyes as the love of his life, the air he breathes, is lowered into the ground.

As Orazio swallowed his rage like fire and swore we'd make it right one day. He loved my mother like a daughter, possibly more than his own sons.

That day was supposed to be today.

Now my fucking hands won't work. And even before the gun falls, useless, to my thigh, I know I'm sparing the man who ordered my mother's execution. Or delaying the inevitable. Fuck, I hope it's the second.

Not because Sofiya's eyes and breath and ragged tremors, even as her chin remains high and her courage unimpeachable, wills me to hold off this execution.

Because this woman, this brilliant, budding assassin, this daughter of my enemy, looked a monster in the eye and said *no*. And I... stood beside her.

Fuck.

What will Cesare say? Orazio will tear me several new ones just for the chance to see me bleed before he ends me himself.

What does it make me – if I protect the woman who refused to pull the trigger, instead of delivering justice with my own hands to the man who deserves a fate *exactly* like death?

I don't know.

I just know I can't let her carry this alone.

'We need to go,' she says, shaking, her fingers brushing over the fist still holding the gun.

I stare at her, narrow-eyed, wondering if I'm making the worst fucking mistake of my life. Or the best. 'You think prison will stop him?'

'No,' she says, calm now. 'But it's a start. We hand him over. Let whatever hole Interpol throw him in rot him from the inside out.'

I hesitate. My pride snarls, *Fuck no*.

My oath to my family burns like acid behind my ribs.

'Those assholes can't find their dicks without a GPS and a chorus of snitches' singing directions. What if they fuck this up?' I ask.

'Then we finish the job. Later. On our terms.'

She doesn't look at me when she says it. It could be another trick in a galaxy of carefully crafted tricks.

But something urges me to believe her. Something connected to my brain or my dick? Who the fuck knows any more.

My lone wolf howls louder as I drag El Topo's limp body across the floor, zip-tie his hands, grab the folder of ledgers and keys, and snap photos of the wall safe. There are no alarms, no traps. This fucker really thought he was untouchable.

And maybe he is.

Maybe I just let the devil walk. Maybe I've betrayed everything my family raised me to be.

But that reckoning can wait.

Because right now, I need to get her out of here.

We slip down the back stairs, his life ledger stuffed into a plastic bag. Weak light bleeds into the loading dock. I can almost believe we've made it out clean.

Until an engine roars.

My head snaps to the right. A rusted van screams around the corner, tyres kicking gravel. Doors fly open.

Three men in balaclavas leap out, rifles raised. One of them screams, 'Mancinelli!'

I dive for Sofiya, terrified I'm already too late.

That the inch I gave upstairs has just become a fatal fucking mile.

* * *

The shot cracks like thunder.

I throw myself to one side, adrenaline snapping taut, just as Sofiya lunges for me, our intent colliding. Straight into the line of fire.

Her body twitches. Once. The movement is too fucking familiar. Means only one thing.

My heart stops.

Cristu, she just caught the bullet meant for me!

I stare, stupefied, as a burst of heat blooms through her T-shirt. 'No. Fuck. No!'

She stumbles, but her hand slides from her sidearm to her assailant's skull. Kneecap to temple, bone-crunching, and he collapses. The other two hesitate, just long enough for me to drop them both with a single fatal round.

The street goes silent. Only my ragged breathing and Sofiya's soft gasp as she presses a bloody hand to her shoulder. I drop to my knees beside her, heart pounding in my ears.

'Sofiya.' I touch her shoulder gently, definitely ignoring my shaking fingers. '*Tigra,* talk to me. How bad is it?'

She forces out a shaky breath, sweat plastering her hair to her forehead. 'I... I'm fine. I'll live,' she says, though her lips tremble and her eyes are glassy.

I scoop her free arm around my neck and swing her into my arms. Her head drops to my shoulder, pain flickering in her eyes. I surge up, one arm under her legs, the other around her back, barrelling towards safety.

We scramble into my SUV, the dim interior light bathing her slim frame as I place her on the back seat.

'Lie down. Hold still,' I say, yanking off my tactical vest and folding it beneath her head. Blood soaks through her shirt as she presses, wincing. I rip the cloth off my T-shirt, tear it into strips, and bind her shoulder, fingers quick despite the tremor. 'I don't have time to fetch the kit to perform a proper assessment. This will have to do.'

'Sorry,' she whispers, head dropping back. 'I thought—'

'You saved my life,' I say, voice low in the sudden hush. 'I dropped the fucking ball.' Just like I had all night. Jesus. 'I didn't even see him until it was too late.' I graze a gentle thumb across her cheek, afraid of shattering her. Then I press my forehead to hers. 'You'll be okay. You have no other fucking choice but to be okay, *tigra.* You hear me?'

She presses her face against me, eyes closed, breath catching. 'I didn't want to' – she swallows, and I feel the tension coil with guilt, relief, something deeper – 'you would've died if I... I'm not ready for that, Rafaelle.' Her voice catches again, and it snags something inside me on the way.

Pulling taut. Not letting go. A grappling hook catching feelings.

My hands hover over her, unsure whether to shift gears, or lift her into my arms, or simply hold her until the world stops spinning.

Urgency drives me to move.

Slide behind the wheel. Get us the fuck outta here.

I floor the gas and we pull away, adrenaline still thrumming in my veins.

In minutes, the highway behind us stretches dark and empty, a ribbon leading to safety, or further danger.

* * *

01:45 – Deserted Back Road, Outside Palermo

I drive at psycho-speed, knuckles white on the wheel, the silence peppered with the tiny sounds of Sofiya's moans.

I endure that because it tells me she's still with me.

The blood-soaked bandage on her shoulder pulses with each mile. Early morning fog curls over olive groves and black lava stones. I know the nearest underground clinic is too far; we can't risk being traced, even with DeLuca in Sofiya's pocket.

We need to stop, clean her wound properly.

I spot a grove of umbrella pines half-hidden behind a rusted gate. I pull the Range Rover off the road, gravel grinding under the tyres. The engine's hum dies, and only the whisper of wind and distant gulls remain.

Launching out of the seat, I tear her door open. 'Okay, baby. I'll get this cleaned, then we keep going. We have packets for field dressing.' I reach for her face, brushing a lock of hair away from her damp cheek. 'You still with me, *bedda*?'

She presses her forehead against the passenger seat, breath trembling. 'Yes.'

'Good girl.'

She sends a glare my way and my heart rate kicks down a notch. 'I hate that you're seeing me bleed.'

I grin, draw her carefully to the edge of her seat. 'Is it a bad time to say I've already seen you bleed in the best way known to this red-blooded male?'

Her good arm lashes out with a punch on my arm. 'Fuck off, Rafaelle.'

'Atta girl.'

I stride to the back, open the boot and spread out the contents of the duffel of med supplies. Then I help her back and perch her on the ledge. 'Let's get this done, baby, then you hit me all you want.'

She watches me scoop out gauze, antiseptic, and spare bandages. Her eyes dart between the supplies and me, alert but vulnerable.

My hands move fast, spilling alcohol over the wound. She white-knuckles the ledge but makes me fucking proud by not shouting when I tear her T-shirt off, stitch and dress her – thank fuck, small – flesh wound.

But she hisses and I feel it in the pit of my stomach.

Once I'm done and the bleeding stops, I wrap a new dressing around her shoulder, knotting it so firmly it can't slip free. Finish off with a shot of morphine.

'You good?'

She exhales, nods, and I rest my hand against her back, feeling the tremor in her torso.

'You saved me,' I repeat softly, voice raw. 'And I'll kill every bastard who tries this again.' My fingers graze her hair, then her neck. 'But let's get one thing straight. You ever fucking try something like that again, and I'll spank your juicy ass so hard you won't sit down right for a month, you hear me?'

She rears back, eyes widening. 'W-what? What happened to having each other's backs?'

I shrug. 'Turns out it was bullshit. Turns out I can't stand seeing you in danger. So from now on, I'll have your back and you'll stay wherever I put you, *capisci*?'

She rolls her eyes. And it's so adorable, I want to kiss her. Keep kissing her until the image of the bullet twitching her body recedes.

'You know that's some major sexist bullshit, right?'

'I do. Question is, what are you going to do about it?' I dare, stoking her fire so it'll burn some of this bone-deep terror from my veins. But the other possibility creeps around the back of my skull. 'Is this where you leverage me for other things?'

She frowns. 'Other...' she starts, then her face tightens. Chills. 'You think I threw myself in front of a bullet to get you to open the gates to that secret club you refuse to name?'

'Did you?' I ask, paying far too close attention to her wound, distancing myself from the roar building in my ear. The one that says her answer is way more important than it should be.

She exhales a bitter laugh, her voice sharp and hoarse. 'I should say yes, shouldn't I? Make you really think I'm a heartless bitch.'

'Are you going to?'

Her eyes lock on mine, biting cold and screaming *fuck you*. 'What do you think?'

I exhale, a curious relief spiking through my blood. And I blurt out words I should maybe keep to my fucking self. 'I think if that's your version of ambition, *bedda*, I've seen worse. Hell, I've done worse. But... jumping in front of a bullet? That's not strategy. That's instinct. And in my experience, instincts don't lie.' I reach out, brushing a lock of blood-matted hair from her cheek. 'So no, I don't think you did it to climb the ladder. I think you did it for me. And maybe that's the part that's fucking me up.'

She looks away. Exhales too. 'Stop talking now, Salvatore. You're making me dizzy.' She presses her eyes shut, the cool breeze threading through her hair. 'I'm useless if I faint.'

I press my lips to her temple. Her cheek. The corner of her mouth. 'You're not useless. You're the reason I'm still breathing.'

Her body falls forward, collapsing into my chest. I wrap my arms around her, holding tight.

She's shaken, soul-deep, and I feel fragile that she trusts me enough to let it happen. I bury my face in her hair, the scent of her still clinging to the cloth soaked in salt and cedarwood. The ache in my chest twists me inside out. 'Fuck, Sofiya. Fear isn't part of any mission for me. But you terrified the fuck out of me tonight.'

Minutes stretch until she tilts her head back, face lifted to mine. 'I know. I'm sorry.'

I press a kiss to her trembling lips. 'I'm waiting for that promise, *bedda*.' My voice thickens. 'You did exactly what you needed to. You saved me.'

Her eyes glisten in the half-light. 'Best I can do is say I'll think about it. Good enough?'

'You aiming to drive me crazy, *tigra*?'

One brown arches. 'Don't you mean crazier?'

I don't laugh. I breathe deep. Stare into her eyes. I press my forehead to hers. 'How can I thank you?'

Her eyes hook into mine. 'I can think of a way,' she returns huskily.

Atta. Girl.

* * *

I bury my hands in her hair, tilting her head so our lips meet. The kiss is slow, fierce, nothing like the controlled violence of our fights.

I taste the salt of her rare tears she let slip, the tang of adrenaline still on her lips.

She clutches my tattered shirt as I step closer, pushing her back until she's lying on the rough carpet of the boot, her legs dangling.

The scent of resin and wet earth builds around us. My body hums, furious and tender. Shaken like I've only ever been once in my life. A time that twists around what happened tonight so fatefully, it boggles my mind.

I press my hip to her thigh, brush her knee, and feel her flutter beneath my touch. She's still shaking, still caught in adrenaline and relief and receding pain, her breath catching in ragged moans as I trail my hands down her sides.

'Rafa,' she whispers, voice broken. 'Are we... out here—'

'You're safe.' I cradle her jaw, forcing her to meet my gaze. 'Only with me.'

I unzip her pants, draw them down her legs, then off.

She's a fucking glorious sight in her thong, bra, moonlight and bandaged shoulder. Black boots.

'My fierce baby assassin,' I rasp, enthralled more than I've ever been with anything. *Anyone.*

I kiss my way back up, past the swell of her breasts. To that luscious mouth that'll be my ruin and my salvation.

She arches into me, eyelids fluttering.

Then with a snap of power that tells me the morphine is working – or she just needs fucking really bad – she pushes me away. Rises.

'What do you need, *bedda*?' My hands roam the curve of her hips, squeezing.

She jumps down. 'Help me with these?' She indicates her bra, snaps the string of her thong.

Beyond captivated, I comply. And in under a minute she's gloriously naked, save her boots.

A blushing warrior goddess, intent on having her way.

And fuck, am I going to give her everything she wants.

I prowl towards her.

She backs away, away, away, eyes on me, hips and tits swaying, until her spine meets the rough bark of a pine tree.

My cock throbs against my cargo pants, eager to join the party.

I unzip and free myself, my breath punching out when she immediately grips me. Eyes on me, she pumps me, her breath stuttering as I grow in her hand.

'Is this what you want, *bedda*?' I rasp. 'What you need?'

She moans. 'Hmm. More. I want you to fuck my mouth, Rafa,' she whispers.

Oh. Fuck.

Are you sure?

The tiny prickle of consideration dies a horrible death when she bends at the waist, guides her trembling mouth to my hardness. She parts her lips, eyes glazing as she lowers onto me, and the world snaps to a fragile focus. Her, me, this gravity of need.

'Fuck.'

'More,' she insists. She takes me in, inch by inch, moaning my name.

Rough. Coarse. Mind-shattering.

I know what my baby needs. So I bury my hands in her hair, grip it tight, revel in her louder whimper.

I stagger back three steps to perch on the ledge of the boot of the car.

And then I give my *tigra* what she wants.

My hips push forward, impelling her deeper until we're both breathless with the shock of raw contact. Until the filthy *glurck glurck glurck* of her taking me down her throat mingles with the cicada chirps around her.

Then sound falls away, the rush of my impending nut filling my ears. With a bark of anguished pleasure, I pull away.

I steady her, pressing my hands to her shoulders, lifting her until we're strung together by need alone.

'Let me fuck you, baby,' I rasp, voice rough. 'Please. I need to be inside you.'

She glances up at me, mouth swollen, saliva and pre-cum dripping down her chin. 'I need you too.'

'God, yes.' I land a hard, filthy kiss on her mouth, her throat, suckle her nipples hard and fast, then grip her hips. 'Turn around.'

She turns back to the pine tree, braces one hand on the bark.

Back arched.

'*Diu*, you're the most beautiful thing in the world, Sofiya.' The catch in my voice is confusing as fuck. And yet so right it tunnels deep into my chest.

Over her shoulder, her eyes meet mine. 'Fuck me hard, Rafa. Please. Make me forget.'

Cristu. 'You fucking wreck me, you know that?'

I step forward, cock in hand. An eager, willing supplicant to her pleasure. I hiss when my hardness pushes an inch into her wet hole.

One fucking inch and it's already – *nearly* too much.

She trembles, swept by panic, but I catch her face, gaze steady. 'All the way. Don't stop.'

I slam inside. She screams.

I roar, frightening birds out of trees.

Hands on her waist, I fuck her hard and deep, each thrust driving me deeper into a new, different kind of psychosis.

One that whispers *mine mine mine* and *kill kill kill* to anyone who tries to take this... take *her* from me.

She saved my life tonight. Doesn't that mean she owns me now?

I kick her legs wider apart, my goddess in silk skin and black boots. She responds by bending deeper, giving me more of that ass, that addictive cunt.

We move together, her body stacked against mine, back to chest, each thrust a fractured hush. Pine needles drop onto bare skin. I press deeper anyway, filling the hollow of her, desperate to be all she needs.

She cries out, wet warmth swallowing me. 'Yes! God, Rafa, it's so good. So good.'

I match her breath, thrusting harder, chasing the orgasm that builds like a storm behind my ribs. 'Take it, *tigra*. Take it all. It's fucking yours.'

Taking hold of that permission, her slick pussy grips me tight. Tighter.

With another scream, she comes, hard. Shudders violently, teeth clenched, eyes clamped shut. My name rockets from her throat – a confession and a curse. I close my eyes, and the world narrows to her gasp and the tightening coil in my stomach.

I follow her over the edge, white-hot rapture exploding in my chest. I come deep inside her, hot and thick, bones rattled. My breath hitches. I collapse against her, chest heaving, as the pine's needles scratch into my shoulder blades.

She drifts down from the release, I catch her as she sags, stagger back to sit on the ledge once more.

Sofiya collapses against me in a tangle of limbs and sweat. A light breeze whistles through the branches above, cooling our tangled skin. I rest my face in the nape of her neck, the scent of her and pine swirling around me.

'Shh,' I murmur, voice soft. 'Just rest now. I got you.'

She wraps an arm around me, pressing close. 'You saved me,' she says, voice husky. And I know she doesn't mean the bullet. I brought her back from the edge of the unthinkable after driving her to that edge of spilling family blood.

Did I say we were fucked up? I kiss her hair. 'And you saved me.'

We remain there, in the hush of scorched earth and pine, breath stuttering in unison – two warriors undone by the same moment of mercy.

Outside, the road stretches on, waiting for us to decide if we will walk it together... or race into the next battle alone.

24

SOFIYA

Montréal, Canadian Grand Prix – Friday, Late Afternoon

The roar of Formula 1 engines echoes through the paddock, a living pulse that thrums beneath my skin. Free Practice Two is underway, and the chatter in my headset crackles with telemetry and tyre data.

Narciso's out on a hot lap, the car slicing through Turn 10 like a scalpel. He's running P6 now, just behind Renzo and Dante, holding his own in a sea of sharks.

I stand by the pit wall, headset pressed to one ear, sunglasses shielding the exhaustion I can't quite hide. My left shoulder twinges beneath my blazer. It's still healing but tender from the gunshot.

I've learned to move like it doesn't hurt, learned it long before my trainer snarled into my face that weakness means death. As a man, he didn't know, of course, that not showing weakness meant far more to me. It meant the difference between being traded like a heifer or gaining fear-soaked respect. Respect that included the higher goal of being left the fuck alone.

Today, though, every shift of muscle reminds me what I risked. What I almost lost.

What I'm still hiding.

I haven't told my father yet about what happened with Bonafacio. Not a word. And with Agent DeLuca also going radio-silent on me, I don't even know for sure if my grandfather is in Interpol custody or not.

He is. He *has* to be.

Which gives me, maybe, a few more days before the truth detonates in the family. Before Narciso finds out how close he came to being dragged into Nonno's schemes.

Bonafacio had planned on snagging Narciso into signing over the millions of crypto he'd been cut off from with the lure of a shady legacy inheritance. We discovered the plot in the papers Rafaelle took.

If he'd gone through with it, Narciso would be locked up right next to him, for months, possibly years, before he could extricate himself from Bonafacio's bullshit.

It turns my stomach.

More because while I was tucked away in Valle du Luce, happily losing my V-card, my baby brother nearly got caught in the blast radius. I exhale, thank God Bonafacio is off the board. *For now*.

But still – my nerves fray like wires in the rain.

And I know why.

Rafaelle.

I... miss him. We agreed to keep our distance here.

Rafa has Salvatore business; I have Mancinelli obligations. But distance feels like a joke when I swear I can feel him at the edges of the paddock. Just out of sight, just out of reach.

My gaze flicks to the crowd behind me. No sign of him. Nothing but sunglasses, lanyards, and corporate swagger.

Lap forty-eight.

I focus back on the screen. The Salvatore twins are lead and second now, as per fucking usual. I hear sector times relayed through the comms, strategy and counter-strategy to best an enemy that feels like enemy less and less.

And then I hear it.

His voice. 'Hey, *tigra*.' Low and rough, clipped, *hot as fuck*, barely audible over my mic. My breath stutters. I step back from the pit wall, pulse spiking. Scan the garages, the VIP balconies, the dense crowd.

Nothing.

He's gone again. I didn't imagine it. I know I didn't.

Somehow he's managed to hack my comms and I'm not even surprised.

What I am is hot. Desperate.

I sip from my water bottle, trying to calm the tremble in my fingers. At the checkered flag, Narciso crosses the line in P3. The team cheers. It stings but it could be worse. My brother could've not been here at all.

Small victories.

I step out of the garage and scan the sea of bodies for the man I can't stop looking for.

The man who fucked me against a tree in Palermo like it was our last night on earth.

The man who isn't here.

And yet I feel him. Always.

An immovable bullet just under my skin.

* * *

Hotel Suite – Saturday, 02:00

The hotel corridors are quiet except for the distant hum of partygoers winding down. My bedroom door is cracked open; I slip inside, carefully easing the lock closed behind me. The dark room is cool. My suitcase lies open, the fabric of my dress spilling onto the floor. I should be sleeping, but rest is out of reach.

Moments later, the door murmurs open. I don't need to turn to know the shape stepping inside. He closes the door so softly the walls barely register the shift in the air.

'Rafa,' I breathe, pulse hammering.

He crosses the room in three strides. His gaze is haunted, need sizzling at the base of his stare. 'I should have told you earlier,' he whispers, stepping close, too close for comfort, yet perfect. His arms clamp around me, the warmth of his body a magnet.

I press back against the bedpost. 'Told me what?' My voice trembles.

He tilts my chin up until I meet his eyes. His thumb brushes a tear I didn't know had fallen. 'You're in my blood, *bedda*. Every fucking where. I can't stay away.'

I press my lips together.

The sensible response is to push him away, to remind myself of duty, of boundaries, but his proximity erodes sense. I tilt my head, yielding, and he tugs my dress from my shoulders.

He's gentle, an irony that twists my pulse. When he drops to his knees in front of me, he unzips my heels, trailing kisses down my legs, hips, abdomen, until I'm shivering, caught between fury and fever.

He looks up, dark eyes glinting. 'Do you trust me?'

I close my eyes. Heaven help me but... 'I do.'

He spins me around, pins my back to his front. 'Tell me you've missed me too,' he croons in my ear. His erection presses into the small of my back. His hand slips under my dress to cup my pussy.

I gasp, arching into him as every nerve ignites. 'Yes. So much. Tonight,' I whisper. 'I need more.'

His mouth brushes my neck. 'Good, my insatiable assassin. That's a fucking good thing, because so do I.'

He pushes me onto the edge of the bed. My wrists brush the cool metal of the headboard. Eyes on me, he reaches into his leather jacket pocket and... gulp... produces silk-lined cuffs.

Oh fuck.

My breath flutters, heart pummelling. When I nod, he guides me so my palms rest alongside the metal, securing me in tight.

He kneels between my legs. 'If at any point you want me to stop—'

I force out, 'Never.'

Something flashes in his eyes. Smug male pleasure. Satisfaction. A touch of bewilderment?

His mouth descends, slow and worshipful down my torso, until every inch of me trembles. His tongue teases the most sensitive places, and I ache with a shudder that nearly breaks me.

It's been only two days since Palermo, but if feels like a year. So I'm not surprised when I come in minutes, my fingernails digging into the headboard.

He rises, and I hear the snap of buttons, then feel his cock, already slick pressing against my entrance.

He leans down and captures my lips in a bruising kiss before guiding himself inside in one smooth thrust. My breath stutters as the room dissolves to the press of iron, the drag of silk cuffs, the rhythm of his hips.

He picks up a steady pace, so deep, so controlled, I see stars as each movement sends jolts through me. 'So fucking beautiful when you're so open for me. So wet and tight. Fuck,' he rasps, his voice so thick, it's near incoherent.

I arch into him, reclaiming each thrust with a surge of lactic-fire release. He grips my hips and drives even deeper, faster, until I cry out, and he launches me towards ecstasy.

Only to hold me at the edge, whispering ragged praise, teasing me. Edging me. Over and over, until I'm a sobbing mess.

Only then, *together*, do we tumble over the brink.

My world fractures into stars, and I cling to him as he shudders through his own release, filling me with the pulse of his need.

He collapses beside me, pressing my bound hands against his chest.

As he undoes the cuffs, I tuck trembling fingers into his hair, holding him close until our heartbeats settle into a shuddering calm.

I fall asleep with a relentless drum beating in my chest.

I'm a Mancinelli, falling under the spell of yet another Salvatore.

* * *

Sunday – Circuit Gilles Villeneuve, After the Race

The champagne has barely dried from the podium.

Dante took P1, Renzo P2 – and Narciso crossed the line third, jaw clenched tight enough to crack his own teeth. He refused to celebrate. Stormed into his trailer without a word. Not even a glance in my direction.

I shoulder past a few engineers, stepping out of the pit lane tunnel just as my uncle Stefano cuts across the tarmac.

His face is flushed from the sun, or maybe rage. I'd groan under my breath if he was worth it. My own teeth grit when he plants himself in front of me.

Does he even know I can choke him out in seconds and barely feel it? My fingers itch to do it. Jesus, I'm turning into Rafa. My unhinged lover.

And I don't… hate it.

'You're going to tell me what the hell is going on,' he snaps before I can speak.

I lift a brow. 'Excuse me?'

'Bonafacio. No one's heard from him in weeks,' he growls. 'What are you doing to fix it? To bring him home?'

I stare him down, tone even. 'I'm handling it.'

'Does your father know that?' he bites out. 'Because he's been calling all weekend. You've been avoiding him.'

I say nothing, and he pulls out his phone and thrusts it at me.

'Time's up, *ragazza*. Talk to him.'

I take the phone with a dry swallow, the ache in my shoulder flaring. 'Papà,' I say, tone steady despite the nausea.

'Where the fuck have you been?' he snarls.

'Doing the necessary, as always.'

'Well, the necessary isn't working. I haven't heard from your grandfather. Have you?'

'Not…' I pause, hating the outright lie. 'He's moving around.' *Yeah, at the back of an Interpol van.* Hopefully. 'I'll brief you when I get back home.'

'When?' he snaps. 'Have you forgotten that there are obligations for you to carry out?'

I bite my tongue from saying *not tonight*. Bite my tongue from
screaming my pain and fury. From screaming that I know *obligations*
always mean blood or sacrifice when you're a woman in this family.
That being useful is the only way they know how to love you. If they
even know what *love* fucking means. 'Soon,' I hedge. 'A day or two.'

He exhales sharply but accepts it. For now. 'Don't keep me
waiting, Sofiya.'

I hang up, shame curdling low in my gut. Stefano's smirk is
poisonous.

'You lied to him.'

'I don't report to you,' I snap, fire sparking in my chest.

'No,' he says coolly. 'But you report to him. And you're
slipping.'

'Who the fuck do you think you're talking to?' I seethe.

'I outrank you, *ragazza*. You will do as your seniors
command, or suffer the consequences – I will not—'

I lean in, the tip of my nose brushing his. 'I will not be
dictated to. I remain loyal to this family, but I am not a child. I
protect them, yes, but on my terms. Understood?'

He blinks, once, twice, barely registering the rebellion in my
tone. Then he straightens, turning away as if the conversation is
over. 'Keep up with that and you'll—' He stops. Freezes.

The air shifts with savagery.

Rafaelle appears, silent and lethal, like he stepped out of
shadow.

He closes the space between us and before I can utter a
word, his hand closes on the back of Stefano's neck. My uncle
yelps in surprise as he's yanked backwards, into Rafa's body.

Rapt and breath held, I watch Rafa murmur something low

in Stefano's ear – too quiet for me to hear, but lethal enough to make my uncle go white. Stefano stumbles back a pace, mouth gaping. He mutters something unintelligible and hurries away.

Rafa turns to me, expression unreadable. 'You okay?'

I bristle. 'I didn't need saving.'

'I know.' His gaze lingers on mine, thumb brushing just under my elbow where my jacket covers the slow-healing wound. 'But you're bleeding through the seams. Let me help you.'

I hate how much I want to let him. So I fall back on old habits and I scoff, low and bitter. 'Help me? What, patch me up so I can be useful again? That's all I've ever been good for – being the sharp end of someone else's agenda.'

His jaw tightens. 'You think that's all I see when I look at you?'

I blink, thrown off balance by the heat in his voice. The promise in it but also the edge of hurt. 'I see someone who's survived what should've broken her. That's not utility. That's power.'

For a second – just one goddamn second – I let myself believe him. And it soothes every single ache, present and past.

Rafa notices, the damn clever Enforcer.

His hand brushes mine again, a slow, grounding touch, like he's trying to steady the tremor in my chest he shouldn't know is there.

I step away. 'People are watching.'

He smirks. 'Let them.'

I take two steps before his hand closes lightly around my wrist. I resist. Far too feebly. 'I need to go and pack.'

'I know. I'll come with you. We can head to the airport together.'

'Why would I want to do that?' I scoff. Even feebler.

He smirks. 'You know why, *bedda*. You're coming on my plane,' he says, voice low, certain. 'So I can fuck you mile high, like you deserve.'

I swallow. And God help me, I nod.

It's all unravelling. And I don't know if we're headed towards victory or the abyss.

But I do know this – I'm not going into it alone.

25

RAFAELLE

Fallbrook Estate, Upstate New York – Late Afternoon

The great oaks lining Fallbrook's long drive cast knotted shadows across the gravel as I pull my Furia supercar to a halt in front of the mansion.

I could've used the family chopper but I wanted the long drive from Teterboro to get my thoughts in order. And yes, buy myself time because I'm a pussy who's terrified of his *nonno*.

Inside, a fire crackles in the foyer hearth even in mid-June; polished marble floors and the mahogany walls gleam like a cathedral to Salvatore power.

I eye the hallway leading to the kitchen, wondering if I have time to perform my usual ritual. Visiting the sacred place I shared with Mama in her favourite place in Fallbrook. Her kitchen.

My uncle Bagio, Orazio's senior capo, striding down the hallway with his beady eyes fixed on me, kills that notion.

'He's been waiting for an hour. You best not keep him

waiting any longer,' he says, not without a hint of glee in his tone.

Fucker. Neither my father nor his two brothers rose as high in the mafioso hierarchy as they would've liked. These days Pops is mired so deep in his grief very little touches him, but my uncles never fail to exhibit their disgruntlement. Or their petty barbs that barely break skin.

Nevertheless, I turn away from my desired destination, head for the opposite direction.

At the door to Orazio's study, I steel myself.

Enter.

He's pacing. No surprises there.

His frame is still imposing at eighty-one, shoulders squared, hands clasped behind his back.

Cesare stands a few paces off, arms folded, wearing that trademark half-smirk that means he's both curious and amused. I swallow and enter.

My brother's eyes drill into mine, digging out news like the impatient fucker he is. The only reason he hasn't ridden my ass like a fucking racehorse is because he has his hands full with Maddie.

'Rafa!' Orazio's voice rolls like thunder across the study. He spins, face red, eyes blazing. 'What the fuck have you been doing?'

I twirl my remote car key on my finger, forcing calm. 'The usual. Extending our reach, Nonnu. You saw the ledgers—'

He cuts me off with a scowl. 'Ledgers don't mean shit if the bastard's still breathing! His head on my platter! That's what you promised me. That's why you've plastered yourself to that unstable Mancinelli one, isn't it? And you what?' He throws his arms up and wide. 'Let him slip through your fingers? I raised you to be an *enforcer*, not a pissing contest loser!' He paces closer, every syllable jagged.

I feel Cesare's eyes on me, studying, waiting for the flash of anger I can no longer hide. I straighten my spine, let Orazio's tirade wash over me. 'Nonnu, we have him exactly where we want him—'

'Bullshit!' His fist thumps the antique desk. 'You better not be going the way of your brother with those Mancinelli women.' He jerks his head towards Cesare, who arches a dark brow. 'You're following Cesare's footsteps, falling in love, losing yourself, and soon I'll be reading about Salvatore diaspora in the fucking papers.'

Cesare chuckles, then steps forward, hands in pockets. 'Easy, Don. You know Rafa's not made for retirement. He just needs a little more time to settle the score.' His smirk flickers as he eyes me up and down. 'Besides, I've seen him more whipped than a spaniel.' He laughs, a soft, mocking rumble.

The words hit like ice. I flare with anger, thumb brushing the holster at my side. 'Try me, Cesare. One more word like that and I'll—'

Cesare's smile widens at my tension. 'Planning to shoot your big brother over a joke?' He shakes his head, amusement dancing in his eyes. 'And here I thought you were getting soft.'

Orazio strides between us, voice booming. 'That's enough! Both of you! This estate has seen more blood than any fuckin' cathedral. No one dies here, not on my watch.' He waves a hand with theatrical exasperation. 'I don't care if you two want to punch each other bloody. Keep it out of my sight and out of my business. And Rafa, if you come home empty-handed again, you'll be sleeping in the sty with the pigs. Is that understood?'

It's on the tip of my tongue to tell him what went down in Palermo. But explaining that I let El Topo live without verifying the location and size of the cage he's rotting in is *not* in my best interests.

I'm expecting my next Aegis assignment any second now. But I might make time to pay Agent DeLuca a visit. Impress some manners into the fucker for ignoring Sofiya's attempts at contact.

'I asked you a question, *nupito*,' Orazio snaps.

I grit my teeth and nod. '*Sì*, Nonno.'

Cesare claps me on the shoulder. 'Maddie wants you to come to dinner p.m. Tuesday, without fail. That means, I want you there. Without fucking fail. *Capisci?*'

The old man dismisses Cesare's remark with a grunt and storms out, the heels of his Ferragamos clicking across the floor.

Cesare watches him go, then pivots back to me. 'Hell of a family,' he mutters. 'But you know how he is.' He offers me an arm and steers me towards the door. 'Come on – go find your Salvatore sunbeam. You look like you need it. And I won't even ask whatever else it is I know you're keeping from us.'

I exhale, muscles relaxing the fraction a heartbeat. 'Thanks, *fratuzzo*.'

He smirks, pressing an arm across my shoulders.

I release him and head down to the kitchen. The June air is cool, scented with lilac and rain to come.

My phone buzzes with a text from Sofiya:

Need you. Immediately. 41.0262°N, 73.6282°W.

I glance at the GPS coordinates. It's the Mancinelli Connecticut compound. My heart skitters with something close to relief.

I walk around the kitchen once, touching her copper pots,

her apron, the bottles of home-made chilli oil that still sit in the pantry, untouched all these years later.

'*Ciao,* Mama.'

I wait. Breath held. Praying my faltering in Palermo won't cost me this too. After an age, the soft voice of my favourite ghost echoes in my ear.

Ciao, bello.

Tears prickle my eyes as I stride back out, slide behind the wheel, gut instincts buzzing but drowned by a deeper pull.

Sofiya.

Sofiya.

Damn it, I need her too.

So fucking bad.

* * *

Connecticut – Mancinelli Compound Gate, 21:30

The compound is a fortress, heavily reinforced through sheer panic by Matteo Mancinelli, Sofiya's father, last year after getting their asses handed to them when they attacked Fallbrook.

Six-foot gates of black iron, cameras perched like vultures along each corner. Security lights sweep lazily over manicured hedges and vintage sports cars.

I kill the engine two blocks away, slip into black tactical pants and a slim hoodie. My boots are soft-soled – 'ghost mode', I call it.

I vault the perimeter wall, land in a crouch on the other side, and slither along the building's shadow. The Mancinellis don't use attack dogs like us, on account of grandfather and father both being allergic to canine hair.

Weak-ass pussies.

The windows are dark, except for one upstairs, a faint glow behind sheer curtains.

My pulse hammers as I slip to the second-floor balcony. I hook my leg over the railing, swing myself onto Sofiya's balcony, and carefully unbolt the window.

The drapes are light enough to slip through. I pause inside her room. Moonlight pools on crisp sheets. There's a small writing desk, a battered leather duffel tossed at the foot of the bed's chair.

I risk a glance at her sleeping form curled under blankets, one arm clutched to her side. Even in sleep, sorrow and strength play across her brow.

I swallow and step forward. *'Tigra.'* The name resonates deep and far too profound inside me. Almost as profound as my other favourite, sacred term. Mama.

Cristu. What... seriously, *what the fuck* is happening right now?

She stirs, lashes fluttering. 'Rafa?' She sits, hair tangling around her face. 'You came.'

I cross to the bed, perching on the edge. 'You texted. I couldn't not.' An admission that scrapes something raw and urgent inside me.

She slides the sheet lower and pats the mattress. I lie beside her, heart pounding at her warmth.

'Why did you send coordinates? You think I don't know where you are?' *Every minute of every fucking day?*

She folds her arms around her knees. 'I wanted you to get here fast.' Her eyes search mine, and she swallows. 'I need you.' It's a hushed confession, impacting harder for its softness.

'I'm here, baby,' I murmur, brushing a thumb along her

cheek. Her skin is still damp from a recent shower, cool in my palm.

She goes from timid to bold in an instant, launching herself at me, fingers tangling in my hair. I meet her with the power and glory she deserves, not a hint of tentativeness about it.

She parts her lips and her thighs, and just like that, we're ignited, hungry and trembling.

Her robe falls at my knees as my hands move over the curve of her waist and the slick line of her thigh. At her throat, I nibble a harsh line, then whisper, 'I've missed you.'

Her eyes blaze. 'I've missed you more.'

'How's the shoulder, baby?'

She shakes her head impatiently. 'It's fine. I'm fine. Well, I'm not. I want you. Inside me. Please.'

Damn. A man could get addicted to that.

Aren't you already?

I ignore the voice. Press her back against the headboard, straddling her hips. Her hands tangle in my shirt as I unhook my belt, metal snapping in the stillness. She bites her lower lip, watching as I lower my pants to the floor.

Her voice is soft but fierce. 'I want you... rough.'

A lash of desire turns to cold gratitude. 'My pleasure.' I lift her so her legs wrap around my waist. I lean in, mouth brushing over her collarbones, trailing down her ribs to the waistband of her silk panties. My fingers rip through fabric. She shivers, skin sensitised by the moonlit room.

She grips my shoulders as I tug my cock free, slick with need. Beneath her, the mattress creaks. I ease into her, slow and careful, so she can find me. Her gasp is sharp, taste of want.

I press my mouth to hers, tongue seeking, as I drive into her. Harder, deeper. The headboard rattles against the wall behind us. Our breathing merges, staccato and raw.

She wraps her arms around my neck. 'Rafa—'

I cut her off with a fierce kiss, one hand at her throat pressing her head back. My other hand grips her hip, slamming into her until her nails dig into my chest. 'Is this what you want? What you've needed?'

'Yes! Fuck, yes,' she moans above me, breath hot.

I pull back just enough to see her eyes, wild and eager. I curse under my breath and bury my face in her throat. My strokes become a relentless rhythm. Thrust, pull back, thrust again, owning her, claiming her in every pulse. Driving her to the edge only to pull back.

Stepping away to her snarling protests, I bend her over the edge of her bed like I own the place. Like I've owned this moment since the first time her eyes narrowed at me across that rooftop, daring me to underestimate her.

She braces herself on the mattress, knees sinking into the comforter, spine bowed in submission she won't admit to. *Yet.*

And then I slam inside.

One long, slow thrust that buries me to the hilt. Her whole body shudders beneath my grip. *Fuck.* She's a goddamn miracle I have no business taking, but I do anyway.

'This what you needed, *picciridda*?' I rasp, my fingers digging into her hips. 'You don't want sweet or slow, do you? You want this, right here. Taking what you'll never give anyone else.'

She moans, and it's not pain. It's something purer. Hungrier. The kind of raw sound that peels open every violent instinct I've spent years perfecting and turns them into something I don't know how to name.

I thrust harder, deeper. Dammit, I want to leave a mark. I want it burned into her skin and her memory. *Forever.*

'Come for me,' I rasp, voice thick. 'Let me hear it.'

And when I slide my hand between her thighs, stroke her

just right, she closes her eyes, moaning as her body tenses. Then she falls apart with a cry that hits me in the chest harder than any bullet ever has.

Tremors ripple through her, and she shudders around me, catching her release. I follow, muscles clenching as I spill inside her, both of us riding out the last crest of our need.

We collapse on the bed together with the faint hum of distant crickets lulling us. I brush my lips along her jaw. 'God, *tigra*... every time I think I know you, you surprise me.'

She presses her face to my shoulder. 'We're both surprises now.'

I hold her, feeling her pulse slow beneath my cheek. As much as I relish some carnage, for now the Mancinelli compound mustn't know I was here, so I'll slip out before dawn.

But right now, in the hush of her bed, I know something irrevocable has started.

As her breathing evens out, I step gingerly off the bed. She opens one eye and watches as I pull on my pants.

I pause, contemplate the very foolish thing dancing on the edge of my tongue. 'Got something on the horizon soon... You wanna come with?'

Her eyes widen. Then, 'Yes, please,' she breathes.

You're neck-deep in it now, fucker. I ignore the voice mocking me. Nod. 'Good. We leave after dinner with Cesare and Maddie? Yeah?' I murmur, voice thick with longing.

'Yes,' she whispers.

I press a last kiss to her temple, gentle, as if she might vanish at the slightest violence, despite just reaming her like her pussy held the holy fucking grail. 'Don't forget to leave a review.' I wink. 'Full throated.'

The smallest giggle escapes. My first earned laugh from my enemy's granddaughter. 'For the ninja moves or the booty call?'

'For both. I expect ten stars and at least five paragraphs.'

She's giggling again when I slip through the window, heart hollow with hope and fear.

Outside, the night holds its breath.

I climb down the ivy-coated wall and vanish into the shadows. The world is turning again, and I have a family back in Fallbrook demanding results.

But for these hours, I've revelled in a shiny new discovery.

Peace within the arms of a woman who challenges me, disarms me, and still begs me to come back for more.

26

SOFIYA

I'd barely shaken the sleep from my eyes when the text came in from Cesare.

> Maddie's going into labour now – she's asking for her sisters. Don't disappoint her.

I blinked at the screen, half annoyed at the heir's asshat assumption that I'd let my sister down, half excited but terrified because Maddie's due date wasn't for another week.

One second I was imagining dinner at their Upper East Side condo, with the expectant grilling that came with each meeting with my big sister, the next I was thrown into a frantic rush to the car with my younger sister Jacinta and Mother, who admittedly had been equally curious about the whispers swirling around a certain sighting with Rafa in Montréal.

But bless them, they'd kept their questions to themselves.

Whatever Stefano had griped about once he was done shitting himself after Rafa's treatment was also making its rounds on the family grapevine.

Thankfully, Maddie's news was a good distraction that even

my father seemed to be grudgingly interested in. Although he'd elected to stay home, almost sneering at the thought of breathing the same air as the Salvatores.

I didn't say out loud what I really thought about that. That my father was plain terrified of our enemies.

He was still in the dark and worried about Nonno's whereabouts, and since I had that news to break, I was happy to leave him to his sneering. One less headache to deal with.

We barrelled onto the FDR at dawn, weaving between empty cabs, until the horizon bled from night black to pale gold.

Sirens wailed as we peeled into the private hospital's entrance.

Now we enter like a procession, Jacinta, Mama, and me, flanked by three Mancinelli capos trailing close behind, their suits tight over the bulges of holstered weapons.

Their eyes sweep every corner of the maternity wing, expressions grim and twitchy, as if someone might try to whack us between contractions.

We rush past nurses whose eyes flit between the familiar faces of Salvatore and Mancinelli, a rare togetherness they suspected they'd never see again.

Soon enough the whispers drill down into the topic more salacious than the arrival of the future Salvatore heir – *the Salvatore enforcer and* another *Mancinelli*.

It doesn't help that he's the first thing I see when we step onto the private floor the heir booked exclusively to usher in the arrival of his first born.

He's leaning against the far wall, arms crossed, expression unreadable – until his gaze lands on me. Then it changes. Darkens. Sharpens and heats.

He makes no effort to hide the blatant interest in his eyes as he looks me over, slow and deliberate. Like he's already undressing me in his head, reliving everything he did to me a few short hours ago.

Cheeks flushing, I glare.

Fucking stop.

Make me, tigra, his gaze fires back as he smirks and keeps looking, fully aware it'll fuel the gossip now simmering in every corner of the hospital.

I silently vow to make him pay for it later. But the truth twists inside me, giddy and unstoppable. A part of me... a very big part, is *thrilled*.

No one has ever looked at me like that without wanting something impossible from me. Without a snapped command before I've even taken a breath.

The way Rafa looks at me... it's like I *belong* to him.

Like I'm the answer to an important question he's searched for for a while.

For the first time, maybe I'm beginning to understand why Maddie threw caution to the wind last year.

Because sometimes being claimed by the right person... the right *man*, feels like the best high in the world.

Even if that man's the very last person on earth you should allow such a privilege.

* * *

His expression loses shades of playfulness, though, as we approach, sterile light giving way to the softer hush of the birthing suite.

And he's in full *mafiosi* enforcer mode when he steps into our path, arms crossed, brown eyes hard and lethal.

'Only the women go in,' he says flatly, gaze locking on the

capos like he's already counted how fast he can flatten each of them. From experience, I know not long at all.

One of my bodyguards shifts forward, puffed up and scowling. 'We have orders. No one goes in unescorted—'

'You want to bring guns into a delivery room?' Rafa's voice drops, all calm ice. 'Sure. Let's traumatise the baby before it even opens its eyes. Real legacy move.'

The capo bristles. I step between them, hand raised. 'It's okay. We've got this. Wait outside.'

Rafa doesn't look away from the man, but his mouth crooks in a warning smirk. 'Blink again like that and I'll think you're asking me to babysit your funeral.'

Tension clings like smoke even after the men fall back, and the three of us slip through the door. Inside is a world away from the outside.

A serene Maddie lies in a crisp white gown, belly round under the thin sheet, watching, half-amused, as Cesare paces like a caged lion at the bottom of her bed, jaw taut, hands clenching and unclenching.

His alpha composure cracks with every beep of the monitor and every contraction-induced moan Maddie tries to suppress.

As I shut the door behind us, he drops to one knee beside her, frantically pressing a kiss to her hand like she's the last sacred thing in a ruined world. 'Goddess, tell me what I can do?' he murmurs, voice rough.

Jacinta mutters, 'Yikes, he looks like he's half a second from storming into her womb and charging out with the baby himself.' She masks it with a cough.

Before I can smother my own laugh, Maddie shoots us both a glare between contractions. 'Unless you're offering ice chips or back rubs, zip it with the smartass remarks.'

Jacinta raises both hands in surrender, grinning. 'Yes, ma'am.'

Maddie exhales through her nose like a dragon in labour. 'Damn right.'

Cesare doesn't miss a beat, his dark grey eyes flitting over us, lingering longest on me. 'Laugh it up now. When your time comes, I'll be there – with snacks, insults, and a stopwatch.'

I glare at him, but he just lifts a brow and gives me a mock-sweet smirk that practically says *You'll fold too, Principessa.*

Before Jacinta can fire back, Cesare's gaze sweeps across the room like a storm system. 'This is a birth, not a circus. One more word out of either of you and I'll personally have you reassigned to diaper duty for the next five years.'

His tone is cool steel, quiet but lethal. The room goes silent.

Maddie grunts, grabs his wrist and mutters, 'My hero.'

'You want me to stay?' the heir mutters, back to worshipping his wife.

The room is warm, humming with tension and love, the air thick with perfume, antiseptic, and the weight of legacy. Maddie exhales loudly, then shakes her head. 'It's okay, I need a moment,' she says, voice tight but clear. 'With my sisters and my mom.'

Cesare kisses her knuckles, then his dark eyes sweep over all three of us like a security check he doesn't trust. 'You have five minutes. Then I want my wife back.'

Then he's gone, the door clicking shut behind him.

As he steps into the hallway, Rafa falls into step beside him.

Maddie leans back against the pillows, her face flushed and damp, but there's a rare peace in her eyes.

Jacinta props herself on one side of the bed. 'I should ask if he's always like that but I'm not sure I want to know the answer,' she half-jokes under her breath.

I sit on the other, brushing damp curls from her temple, and she leans into the touch like it anchors her. Between us, our mother, Vittoria, clasps Maddie's hand with fingers that – miraculously – don't tremble today.

'I prayed for strength,' Vittoria says softly, her voice thready but steady, 'but I never knew it would come through you.' She smiles, and there's pride in it, and it's not the apologetic kind I'm used to, but the quiet kind that carries meaning. 'You've carried all our broken pieces and made something whole.'

Maddie blinks hard. Her voice breaks as she whispers, 'I just want to do better – be better – for him.' She places a hand over her belly.

Jacinta kisses her cheek.

I lean in and press my forehead to hers. For one fragile second, there are no guns, blood feuds or ghosts. We're simply sisters and a mother, breathing in borrowed peace. We're the Mancinelli women; the ones our men mistakenly believed were weak without them.

Then the machines spike – beeping loud and fast.

The door slams open, and Cesare barrels in, jaw clenched, eyes wild. 'Out. Now.'

We scatter, hearts thudding but fuller than they were a minute ago.

But maybe that moment doesn't need to be lost forever.

Maybe... another path, however dangerous, through this Mancinelli-Salvatore war zone is possible.

* * *

When Nicolo Gaetano Salvatore's first wail echoes, more than one set of eyes mists on the hospital floor.

And when, a long ten minutes later, Cesare opens the door,

his face etched in awe and raw adoration, a lump builds in my throat.

Maddie is radiant and my nephew is perfect. Perfect fingers and toes, a tuft of dark hair and a chest already rising and falling in tiny, determined breaths.

A whole new life, wriggling and blinking against the weight of the world, utterly unaware of the bloodshed that made his existence possible.

And maybe it's selfish, but for just a second, I want to believe he'll never have to carry the legacy carved into the bones of our families. That maybe this boy, born in a flash of light and love, might be spared the dark.

Cesare leans into Maddie's sweat-slicked shoulder, and I can't help but stare, more than a little mesmerised, and yeah, a touch jealous at this family in its fullest, rawest form.

Cesare catches my eyes across the bed. In his glance, I see pride, relief... and something else that makes my spine tingle.

I'm not surprised at all when he orders, 'Give us the room, please. Rafaelle. Sofiya. You stay.'

Shit. Shit shit shit.

Rafa eyes me, a touch of puzzlement in his own eyes not quite eroded by his perennial smirk as he tips his head towards me. 'What'd you do now, *picciridda*? Steal the baby's trust fund already?'

I open my mouth, but Cesare speaks before I can.

'Maddie and I decided. We want you two to be Nico's godparents.'

Shock holds me still, then I swallow hard, adrenaline kicking in. 'What? No, not him!' I throw a thumb Rafa's way. 'He's a psychopath.'

Rafa's expression says 'ouch' so clearly my chest aches. He shrugs, half-laughing. 'Takes one to know one, *tigra*.'

Maddie's eyes widen, then go speculative, like she's calculating what's going on and coming up with way more than I want her to.

I rush into speech before she can drill where there's no gold. 'Fuck off with that, Maddie. If I'm not pissing on him if he's on fire, I sure as hell am not co-god-parenting with him.'

Rafa's voice cuts the tension like a scalpel. 'Now there's an image I won't be getting out of my head anytime soon.' He grins, deep relish in his tone.

'Mind your language in front of my son,' Cesare growls.

'You mean the son who's neck deep in a milk coma?' Rafa asks, nodding down at the baby at her breast. We all watch, arrested, Nico's blissed-out face, his eyelids fluttering as he drifts towards post-milk nirvana.

'Doesn't matter,' Cesare warns, voice low. 'Studies show they pick up all sorts of things even from birth.'

'You're gonna be one of those parents, aren't you? Jesus fucking—'

'What was that?' Cesare demands.

The Enforcer freezes – probably more terrified right here in this room with these feral newborn parents than he's been on a kill mission – then tosses both his hands up in mock surrender.

After a moment, he clears his throat, smoothing a stray hair back from his forehead. 'I think he's saying it's time he left,' I slide in, wondering why I'm bothering and totally not wanting to know.

'Trying to get me alone, *tigra*?'

It's my turn to curse. 'Jesus, do you ever stop?'

Rafa throws me a mock-offended look. 'For you? Never.' He winks, and I can't help the smile tugging hard at my lips. Even if my heart hammers with guilt and pride all at once.

Cesare's gaze swings wildly between us, attempting to decipher the undercurrents of our situation.

'We'll take it as a yes to the godparenting, shall we?' he rasps.

I clench my jaw, a new terror unravelling through me. What if I ruin it? What if I taint this perfect little thing with the curse of being mine? I've never protected anything without maiming or blood, never been trusted with a future that didn't come with crosshairs attached. The thought of holding that title – of being someone's safe place instead of their shield – twists like panic in my gut.

But Maddie is extending a trembling hand to me. 'Sof? Please. Will you do it?'

I meet her gaze, see her unwavering trust and love. Her belief. And, throat clogging, I nod. 'I'll do it. For – I mean, with him.' I nod to Rafa, who looks far too smug, if a little green at the gills.

* * *

Rafaelle
Two Days Later

I enter the hospital wing near midnight and pause in the dark corridor.

Outside the family area off the private suite, I hear the lieutenants and capos gather, murmuring.

The news that Sofiya and I will be godparents has already rippled through the family like wildfire, and this is as good a time as any to take the pulse of that revelation.

Luca 'Two-Fingers' Moretti whispers to a hovering capo, 'Mancinelli as godmother? Salvatore as godfather? The kid's destiny is sealed – international gangster or fugitive.'

'Shut up, Luca – he's only two days old,' the other capo mutters.

Luca just shrugs, unfazed. 'Beware what you set in motion.'

I enter the room, the presents I brought for Mommy and baby tucked in my back.

It takes a second before they see me.

'You got opinions on things, Luca?'

He sputters before he hauls his three-hundred-pound body upright. 'N-no... um, no boss.'

I smirk. 'Didn't think so. And don't knock things you'll never get to try in this lifetime.'

I smile harder at the ominous silence I leave behind as I head to the door at the end of the corridor.

A quick knock and I enter at Cesare's tired, gruff order.

Maddie's asleep, impossibly fresh-faced considering the eight-hour labour she's just been through.

Cesare's beside her, cradling Nico like he's holding the whole damn world. The kid's barely the size of a loaf of bread, but my brother looks like he'd shiv God Himself if anyone so much as breathed wrong near him.

I place the gift bag quietly on the table – a baby-sized racing onesie and a gold charm bracelet Maddie can add to with every win, every milestone.

Sentimental as fuck, yeah. I'm blaming the hormones in the air.

Cesare doesn't take his rapt attention off his son. 'You gonna keep staring like a creep or say something useful?' my brother rasps.

'Just trying to figure out how you made something so... clean.' I nod towards Nico. 'With that mug of yours.'

He snorts. 'Maddie's genes did the heavy lifting. Obviously.'

There's a long beat of silence. One of those rare ones where it feels like we're just brothers again, not two men carrying too many bodies between us.

'You'll be good at this,' I say quietly, surprising even myself.

He glances at me then. Something soft and ancient flickers across his face. 'I already am.'

Of course he is. *Smug prick.*

I scrub a hand over my jaw. 'He's gonna change everything.'

'Already has,' he murmurs, rocking Nico gently. Then, glancing at me sideways, 'Speaking of change... You and Sofiya.'

I stiffen. 'What makes you think there's a me and Sofiya?' I counter sharply.

He lifts a brow. 'Right. Let's roll with that. Pretend like there was no Maddie and me once upon a time too. Look, you're a dumbass, but you're not blind. And I've seen the way she looks at you. Like she might actually believe in you.'

I snort. 'Poor taste.'

He chuckles low, then he grows serious. 'I know what I said before about not wanting a war. But...' He looks over at his wife, and something wild and toxic and – yep, it's fucking jealousy – grips my insides. 'The war might be worth it. If she's the one,' he finishes on a softer tone.

My mouth goes dry. I don't want to think about that. Don't want to name whatever's happening between me and Sofiya.

Because naming it means I have to acknowledge it. Analyse and, fuck, maybe protect it. Keep it alive.

Love it?

The door opens, tearing my attention from that concussion-causing thought.

Orazio strides in like he owns the hospital; probably has the administrator deep in his pocket.

Cesare looks up, grins. 'Nonno, come meet your great-grandson.'

Perfect exit cue.

I'm already halfway to the door when Cesare says, not unkindly, 'Think about it, Rafa. Don't let fear dress up as purpose.'

I grunt, non-committal, and disappear down the hall before I'm forced to admit he might be right.

* * *

I don't start the engine right away when I return to my car.

I sit there, hands locked on the wheel, the silence pressing in like a loaded gun to the ribs. There's still a trace of baby powder on my sleeve, and I'm not sure why I'm fucking staring at it instead of removing it.

My jaw tightens. Once. Then again.

One breath in. Slower on the way out.

Get it fucking together.

Since when does a baby throw you for a loop?

Since I started to imagine a different baby... a different mother that looks exactly like Sofiya Mancinelli.

Cristu.

I tap the steering wheel twice, willing the return of calm long fled, and keep my eyes fixed on the dark street ahead.

For a second, the streetlights smear. I blink. Meticulously list why that single, infuriating, searing thought is right up there with aliens on Mars. Or world fucking peace.

When I reach two dozen, I start the engine. Pull away.

I don't get three blocks before my encrypted line pings.

NIGHTOWL

Fractures saints and short shadows lingering.

I stare at the message, a chill bleeding through the heat

crawling under my skin. I read it again. And again. It means fuck all. Looks like Nightowl is back to his cryptic best, leaving twisted breadcrumbs from a ghost who likes dangling strings I shouldn't follow.

'Fuck.' I slam my fist against the dash, breath snarling through my teeth.

I need to hunt something. End something. Or fuck someone until the noise in my skull cuts out. But there's only one person I want beneath me. Around me.

I know the source of my dark and morbid mood. I don't even need to look at my phone to know she hasn't replied to any of my texts.

For two fucking days, Sofiya's gone dark.

Two days. No calls. No replies. Not even a fucking read receipt.

Maybe it's time to dig out the cuffs again.

And maybe this time, I won't bother bringing the keys.

27

SOFIYA

They locked me in a safehouse I sourced myself and kitted out two years ago. It would be funny if it wasn't so fucking exhausting. Infuriating. Humbling and pathetic.

As it is, the irony tastes bitter, like the blood I've bitten from my tongue.

It's nestled in the backwoods of northern New Jersey, surrounded by dormant pine. From the outside, it looks like a cosy hunting lodge. Inside, it's a tomb. No signals or exits unless you know where to look.

They've stripped me of everything but my clothes. Tied me to a chair. The same men who used to drive me to school. Granted, they were men I knew I couldn't trust, but still...

My father is pacing the floor like a caged bull.

Stefano is leaning against the wall, arms crossed, that ever-present smirk bleeding cruelty. And two other Mancinelli men I don't recognise, but who all radiate the same brand of tension.

I fucked up, got distracted with being dicked down by Rafaelle Salvatore to do the necessary.

El Topo has slipped the net. Again. And he's now a half-step ahead of me.

Somehow, some way, he escaped during his handoff from Interpol to the FBI. I don't know the details – yet. But the moment the handoff was blown wide open, the accusations started flying. And now here I am. Shackled, being questioned by men who couldn't find their balls if you handed them to them gift-wrapped and labelled 'fragile'.

My father stops pacing long enough to look at me. Really look. The disappointment in his face shouldn't sting, but it does, soft punch or not.

'You don't have to be his dog forever,' I say coldly, chin high. 'Papa, for once – listen. You *know* I'd never sell out my blood. But maybe I'm done bleeding for men who don't deserve it.'

Fury rolls over his face. 'That's what you have to say for yourself after betraying your own grandfather? This is how you repay this family?'

'You mean the family I've bled for since I was fifteen?' My voice is glass-edged. 'While you sat in palazzos and played godfathers, I was out there stopping your enemies from choking us in our sleep.'

'You betrayed us,' my father says, deadly quiet. 'You let blood outweigh blood.'

A cruel thing, the truth. Especially when it's twisted like this.

'I *am* blood,' I say, straightening slowly. 'And for years you treated me like a weapon you could break and rebuild at will. You never asked if I wanted this life. You never cared if I broke trying to hold it all up. But I did it. I did it all. And still I'm not enough.'

'You're not,' Stefano says, stepping closer. 'Not if you're whoring for Salvatore scraps.'

I ignore him, knowing he'll hate that.

'I gave Nonno the chance to stop dragging this family through hell. He chose not to take it.'

'And who the fuck are you to think you can call the shots? Your sister tried the same thing,' he mutters. 'Before she ran off with Cesare Salvatore. Before she brought disgrace to our name.'

I stiffen. 'Maddie didn't betray us. You and Nonno betrayed her first.'

That earns me a backhand. Fast, sharp. But not from my father.

Fucking Stefano.

'Watch your mouth,' he sneers.

I smile, bloody-lipped. 'Still trying to make up for the fact you've never been relevant?'

The second crack across my face comes. My body reels. Salt floods my mouth. Rage surges.

But I don't fall.

I straighten. Breathing slow. Focus narrowing.

'I'm done.' My gaze sharpens to a blade. 'With all of you. With this bullshit loyalty that only ever flowed one way. I want better. I *deserve* better.'

'And you think that unhinged Salvatore's going to give it to you?' my father sneers.

I don't answer. But yes. *Yes, I do.* Even if it's not a promise Rafaelle has made. It's the way he *sees* me. The way he touches me like I'm more than broken glass. Like I'm fire he wants to burn for.

Stefano's face twists. 'I always knew you were an ungrateful little—'

Before he can strike again, Matteo raises a hand.

That's when the call comes.

He steps aside, answering his burner with the gravitas of a

pope receiving absolution. I don't even need to guess who it is when his eyes flick to me.

It's him. Interpol didn't lose him by accident. I know Agent DeLuca triple-crossed me. No worries, he'll get what's coming to him.

My father turns to me and hits the speaker button. Bonafacio sounds slurred and slippery. Unhinged enough that he's hardly making sense. But I catch the menace and the intent sure enough.

And every word cuts deeper than the last.

'My own flesh and blood,' he's ranting, 'sold me out. First Maddelena. Now her. You raise them to be killers and they stab you in the back. Maybe it's time to wipe the slate clean.'

Silence.

My eyes dart to my father's face. His nostrils are pinched but there's a resolute light building in his eyes.

No. He's fucking not— 'What are you talking about?' I blurt.

Then the kicker.

'What do you say, *figghiu miu*?' my grandfather cajoles, his voice oiled evil. 'You've been the one I've been most proud of. The exception to the rotten rule. What do you say we start over. With the boy? He'll be a new beginning for all of us.'

A new beginning. The boy.

Maddie's son.

My godson.

Something cold and wretched and furious detonates inside my chest. It takes a second for my brain to catch up, to process what I just heard. My legs nearly give out, even though I'm still seated.

I watch my father, silently imploring, hoping for a crumb I already know I'm not going to find.

Bonafacio rants on some more. And my father doesn't object. Not once.

'You can't seriously be listening to this? Have you gone ins—'

Another backhand. Pain radiates from my jaw to my left eye. I grit my teeth, suck in a slow, long breath. Still I ignore Stefano, for now. I'll deal with him later.

I lock eyes with my father as he listens to *his* father prattle on as if he's ordering a round of grappa instead of mass familicide.

My heart shreds and sinks into the floor when I realise he's actually *considering* it.

That's when I know.

There's no more reasoning with insane men. No more trying to save them from themselves. The loyalty I've bled for this family? Means nothing. I'm just a spent weapon to them. A tool they want to bury now I don't serve their purpose. But I'm not going quietly.

No more.

I hunch into myself, pretend to be nursing my sore cheek with my bound hands. But I slowly fish out the pin from the hair tie wound around my wrist – blessedly missed in their search.

Narciso's name is tossed into the mix and fresh sheets of ice unravel over me. Apparently not even the male descendant is to be spared their cold-blooded intent.

I slide the pin into the lock at the back of my cuff.

Three seconds. I cover the click with a cough. Then I wait. Count breaths. Let the rage sharpen to a blade.

Then I move.

The first man drops with a knife to the neck. *Mine.* Recovered from under the lip of the table. The second is slower, clumsier. My elbow cracks his nose as he draws his gun. I knee him in the balls the good old-fashioned way and when he drops the gun to nurse his not-quite-crown jewels, I catch it. Fire.

Stefano darts around frantically, then too stupid to spot the hidden door three feet away, he dives, narrowly avoiding the next shot. But I wing his leg. He shrieks like the weasel he is and goes down.

Matteo – because I'm never calling this man Papà ever again – shouts for the capos outside.

I wait, pick them off as they barge through the door.

One by one, they fall. Until they wise up. I know there are two or three outside but for now...

I turn back, panting, vision ringing at the edges. Only Matteo and Stefano remain.

Matteo stares at me like *I'm* the stranger. 'You won't kill me,' he states with bravado so false I'm stunned he's not pissing himself.

Coward.

'You're right. I won't kill you. But someone will, soon enough. All I need to do is tell Cesare Salvatore what you planned here for his newborn son and...' I click my fingers.

He flinches.

'Your *nonno* is right. We should've drilled better manners into you decades ago. Or better still, killed you in your fucking sleep,' he rasps, bloodied.

Sadness shrouds me but I lock it down, hard. 'Yeah,' I say. 'You probably should've. You should've done a lot of—'

His gaze flicks behind me then moves away quickly in the laughably obvious universal gesture of *nuthin-to-see-here.*

My insides clench and I brace for the worst, already moving to protect myself as I turn. To see Stefano, still on the floor raising his gun, aiming at me.

Fuck.

I brace—

The shot comes. But it's not from Stefano. Nor as deafening as I imagined it would be.

A single crack that barely shatters the glass through the window from which it arrives.

Stefano's head snaps back, then he slumps like a sack of flour.

Matteo lunges for me.

Another shot takes out his right knee. He drops to the floor in a sickening heap, wailing like a wounded animal.

Sniper.

I stagger to the window, my breath lightly fogging as I look out.

There, within the dense foliage, I spot the glint of a scope I wouldn't have if he didn't want me to. Then a figure. Black coat. Familiar gait.

Rafaelle Salvatore.

My sidekick, this time. Not my leader.

He lifts two fingers in a lazy salute, leans against the tree. Then my phone pings. I retrieve it from the drawer one of the men tossed it into.

> Come on out. It's time to go now, my brave, beautiful, badass tigra.

I'm covered in my family's blood, clutching a borrowed gun with my face throbbing.

But I've never been happier in my life.

And as I step outside of the carnage I didn't create, I let my heart unfurl. To embrace all the reasons why.

* * *

Rafaelle

She comes to me smelling of blood and cordite and copper and sweat.

But beneath it, her. My glorious *tigra*.

Wild and stubborn and painfully, beautifully alive.

I meet her halfway, stepping over a body – one of the dozen fucks who thought they could cage her. His neck's been opened like a fruit rind.

It's messy and desperate but with zero hesitation.

Good girl.

She's breathing faster than I like, gripping a Beretta in one hand.

There's something feral in her eyes. A ragged, dangerous focus. Until they find mine.

Then she focuses. And breaks.

She doesn't cry but her shoulders sag like she's finally been given permission to feel the weight of everything she's done.

I walk forward and pull the gun from her hand. Toss it behind me. Then I cup her face, the side the fucking bastard – the now delightfully fucking *dead* bastard – hit, and I kiss her like I've been dying for it. Because I have.

Every second she went dark on me. Every fucking hour I didn't know if I was tracking a body or the woman who became mine when she pumped two bullets into my chest, then fucking bit me.

Her fingers twist into my shirt. The kiss turns brutal. Salt and copper. A moan I feel deep in my spine.

She's shaking when I pull back. Her voice is hoarse. 'How did you find me?'

'Let's save that for when you can be appropriately outraged, hmm,' I rasp. 'Let's just say, I found out what DeLuca did and I knew him triple-crossing you would lead to excited tempers.' I nod over her shoulder. 'Guess I was right?'

She flinches. 'I had to do it. I didn't have a choice.'

I nod. 'I can tell.'

I drag her closer and brush hair off her face. 'Be kind to yourself. We were both born into a battlefield. And you, you've adapted beautifully.'

She lets out a breath. 'Don't say things like that to me.'

'Why, because you'll kill me?'

'Because I'm scared I'll like it. Too much. And I can't afford to.'

And isn't it the fucking hell of a thing that I want to afford it for her? Offer it to her on all the silver platters she can handle. And the million more she can't?

My thumb drags over a smear of blood on her cheek. 'I'm taking you home with me. You can tell me on the way, yeah?' Then, quieter, because neither of us needs loud right now, 'And maybe we can start to bury the past.'

* * *

Sofiya

We can start to bury the past.

The words echo in my mind as I stand in the middle of Rafa's suite in the Fallbrook Estate, a place I'd sneered and resisted coming to just a year ago, while Maddie was gleefully planning her wedding to the heir and we were on the brink of war.

A floor lamp casts warm light across the Venetian walls.

White sheets are peeled back on a wide, low bed and dark silk drapes spill onto the floor like liquid shadow. My pulse

thumps so hard I can feel it behind my collarbone. I breathe in –
deep, slow – trying to steady the tremor I always feel before we
cross that threshold from hunter and prey back to... whatever
this is.

Rafaelle emerges from the bathroom, hair damp, his bare
chest silhouetted by the warm glow behind him. He wears black
silk trousers, low-slung, narrow hips that have driven me to
madness more than once.

I swallow, aware of how my own body responds – heat
pooling low as always when he stands bare and certain.

He crosses the room, each step measured, and stops an arm's
length away. The ache between us is a familiar thing. Especially
tonight. He flirts with my boundaries like a predator, and I let
him because I crave his restraint as much as I fear it. Tonight, it
tastes like fresh adrenaline on my tongue.

I toss aside the cold compress he gave me for my face and let
my robe slip off my shoulders, silk rustling to the floor. He
inhales sharply as my bare skin is revealed – the high swell of
my breasts, the hollow of my throat, the faint scar at my right
hip I earned during training myself to be what it turned out
wasn't good enough for my grandfather.

The debrief to the Salvatores of what happened tonight and
over the past two days after my father's men snatched me, was
brutal.

Cesare's face as he listened to my hushed accounting, the
proposal to 'wipe the slate clean' by starting over with Maddie's
newborn son, made every bone in my body go cold.

And made me ecstatic I wasn't his enemy. Not any more.

Rafa's flinty look and the string of snarled Sicilian under his
breath told me that, and heaven help me, I've seized that lifeline
with both hands.

As for Orazio... he came into the Fallbrook library blazing, half enraged, half in awe as I repeated the story, yet again. Threw a glass against the wall. Called Stefano a *disgraziato figlio di puttana* and Matteo a traitor's shadow with a coward's spine. Then he looked at me, dead in the eye.

'Rest easy, girl. You've done what I never could. Cleaned the rot. The war's not done, *picciridda*. But I'm glad you struck first.'

I'm still shaking when Rafa steps behind me. His hands graze the inside of my arms, ghosting up to cup my shoulders, possessive and rough. Just the way I've discovered I like. No, *love*. Because it's the way only he can be.

'The Salvatores are taking the Mancinelli compound,' he murmurs against my neck. 'Cesare's moving in official assets. Whatever's left of your grandfather's reign dies tomorrow.'

I nod, not trusting my voice.

He tilts my chin until our eyes lock in the mirror. 'But tonight? Tonight, you're not a weapon. You're fucking mine. Say it.'

'I'm yours.'

And when I turn into him now, when our mouths meet, slow and bruising and right, I pray to God to let that be enough.

Rafa's voice is low, thick with need. 'Every inch of you is mine.'

My breath hitches, throat tight. 'Show me,' I whisper, though a part of me knows it already happened long ago.

His lips brush my shoulder, then the hollow of my neck. I shudder as stubble scrapes against my skin. Each breath is uneven, erratic, edged with the exhaustion of what we've both survived – and the raw hunger that's never gone away.

'Turn around,' he growls.

I do. And when I face him, his eyes darken like a storm at sea. One hand cradles my jaw, the other traces the bruise blooming near my collarbone. Gently. Reverently. But there's nothing soft in the way his body crowds mine.

'They put their hands on you.' His voice turns to gravel. 'Tried to break what belongs to me. Tried to fucking erase you.'

'They didn't. Nobody can erase me,' I murmur.

His gaze flashes. 'Too fucking right, *picciridda*. You erase *them*.' Then he crushes his mouth to mine.

It's the most decadent, delicious claiming yet. Punishing and worshipping at once. I open to him instantly, arms winding around his neck, fingers dragging through damp hair. He backs me towards the bed, only breaking the kiss to yank his trousers off, to pull me with him as he kneels between my legs.

His hands roam my body like a man memorising his only religion. 'You're a fucking work of art,' he mutters into my breast as he takes it into his mouth. I arch up, a gasp escaping me as he sucks hard, then soothes with his tongue. 'Every inch. I will ruin anyone who touches you. I *almost* missed my shot tonight, Sofiya. Almost lost you.'

'You didn't,' I say, and I mean it with more than just tonight in mind.

He groans, the sound vibrating against my skin. 'Don't do that again. Don't disappear on me. You want to fight? Fine. But let me watch your back while you do it.'

I nod. There's no point telling him it wasn't intentional. My instinct tells me he needs to say the words. So I let them wash over me, dizzy with heat, with the press of his hand sliding down my stomach, between my thighs. One stroke – slick, slow over my swollen clit – and I'm already shaking.

'You're soaked,' he says with a smug growl. 'Fuck. I haven't even—' He breaks off, sliding two fingers into me. Deep. Possessive. Curling just right. 'This wet for me?'

'You know it is,' I gasp.

He shifts me down the bed with one hard tug, spreading my thighs around his hips. Then he's there. Hot and thick and hard, rubbing the blunt head of his cock against my entrance until I'm whining with need.

'Say it again,' he demands, voice hoarse. 'Say you're mine.'

I stare up at him, at the man who's killed for me. Bled for me. Found me in the ashes of the only family I've ever known and didn't flinch.

'I'm yours.'

With a ragged exhale, he sinks into me.

We moan in unison, him for the tight heat, me for the heady, indescribable feeling of *home*. He holds still for a beat, forehead resting against mine, his breath hitching like he's on the edge of something deeper than sex.

Then he moves.

Powerful. Relentless. His thrusts drive everything else away. The blood. The ghosts. The betrayal. All that remains is the slap of skin, the heat coiling low, the way I sob when he grips my hips and fucks me harder.

'I've got you,' he pants. 'You don't have to be strong now. Not with me.'

I break.

He flips us, pulls me on top of him, one hand fisting in my hair, the other gripping my ass as he thrusts up from below. I ride him like I was made for it, sweat-slicked and shaking, nails raking his chest.

When I shatter, it's with a scream I can't swallow. He comes seconds later with a brutal groan, arms wrapped tight around me, like letting go isn't an option.

We lie there for a long time after. Tangled, spent, silent.

His hand strokes my spine, lazy. But there's a line between his brows, one I've come to recognise. Thought. Strategy. Worry. The war isn't over.

'It's not over,' I whisper. 'He won't stop.'

'I know, *duci*,' he says, voice flat. 'But neither will we.'

I rest my cheek on his chest, hear the solid drum of his heart. The man I used to want dead has become the only place I feel safe.

Irony of ironies. Turning out to be the night for them.

Which irony will involve the heart that's beginning to beat only for Rafaelle Salvatore?

28

RAFAELLE

Three weeks.

That's how long it's been since Sofiya killed half her bloodline and collapsed into my arms like she hadn't just walked through hell and burned the fucking place down on the way out.

I give up trying not to stare at the wind teasing strands of her dark hair beneath the billowing canopy of our private box at the British Grand Prix. Her fingers curl loosely around mine, her body draped against my side, and yet I'm the one who feels anchored.

I try not to breathe her too deeply like a fucking lunatic and instead stare at the track. Out there, the world still spins fast... well, today, with Narciso refusing to give up his seat despite what Matteo nearly allowed to happen. Despite their grandfather's mass murder threat.

Hell, the kid grinned when I asked him if he was insane. Said he'd take death at 220 mph before he cowered from an unhinged old man.

I kinda respect him for that.

But as much as I hate it, we're back to living on tenter-fuck-ing-hooks.

For race weekends, Sofiya and I are keeping an eye on the twins – who ditto snarled their own versions of *fuck no* and *bring it* at the news of El Topo's threats – and on the baby brother she adores.

Cesare's locked Maddie and Nico in Fallbrook. Tripled security. Hired more soldiers than the entire fucking military support of a small country. Reinforced every door with steel and prayer. So far, thank God, no movement from even the wounded Mancinellis.

Just tension so thick even the fucking air vibrates with it.

After the meeting at Fallbrook, my father called, a rarity that deserved the respect I gave it, if not the content of the conversation, not that I can blame him.

In a voice far more broken than I wanted to witness, he asked what the hell I was doing with a Mancinelli, much like I'd asked Cesare last year. At the back of my mind, I appreciated that I owed my brother an apology. *Maybe.*

Orazio keeps sending quiet warnings that I'm walking the same line Cesare did. And all I can say is this – they're fucking right. I am. And I don't care.

I don't see an enemy when I look at her any more.

I see what's mine. What I intend to keep.

Sofiya stands straighter as the engines scream on the start-finish straight below us, gives an excited yelp as Narciso passes Dante on track. I let her celebrate the win because she's bouncing on the tips of her toes, her mile-wide smile digging in soft places inside me I didn't know existed.

Fuck, she's gorgeous.

Even more so in one of the sexy little numbers I dropped into her shopping bag in Monaco and coaxed her into wearing today. The material frames her tits and ass just right. The only thing I didn't account for is how much I'd hate the attention she's getting.

Exhibit fucking C.

She glances back, catches some suit in an orange McLaren polo leering at her ass. Her lips part like she's about to say something, but I'm already on it.

I don't say a word – just shift enough to meet the fucker's eyes and let my deranged expression do the talking. He pales and looks away fast.

'You're going to get us banned from every paddock in Europe,' Sofiya mutters.

'Good. Less competition.' I kiss her temple, then her cheek, and because I'm fucking gone for this woman, I linger at the corner of her mouth. Any more and I'll need to find the nearest janitor's closet to fuck her in. *Cristu*, I've fucked her so much these past few weeks, I'm stunned *I* can still walk, never mind her. But my girl has fallen into her sexual awakening era like a sinner discovering silk sheets and deciding confession can wait till Monday. 'And fewer pricks looking at what's mine.'

She doesn't answer right away, just curls her fingers through mine again. There's softness there. Vulnerability. The kind she never shows anyone else.

It should scare me, how much I want to protect it.

Instead, it makes me crave more.

But it's not all adrenaline and tenderness and living on the edge of our nerves. The other thorn in my side is Nightowl's incoherent messages – riddles dressed up like intel, always two steps from useful and three from sane until I work it out. And either I'm losing my touch or the pussy-whipping has addled my brain because the latest ones have been ball-scratchers.

The last one came at 2 a.m. this morning.

NIGHTOWL

Dove il vetro sanguina e i cipressi vegliano.

Where glass bleeds and the cypress keeps watch.
Another location for El Topo?
It has to be.

I've paid outrageous sums to the two MIT kids we keep on retainer and even more to shady individuals on the dark web to dig deeper. So far, nothing.

The question is, do I tell Sofiya any of it? She's stopped asking about Aegis and I passed the last mission to someone else. But for the first time in my life, keeping secrets is beginning to feel... not fucking nice.

I know it's because she's not just some asset or enemy I need to keep an eye on any more.

She's the woman I wake up craving. The one who haunts my thoughts when I should be focusing on anything else.

And yeah, she saved herself back in that safehouse. Wreaked sweet fucking carnage and came out blood-slicked and unbroken.

But that doesn't mean I want her anywhere near another goddamn ambush.

She's my fucking *tigra*. But even tigers bleed.

So maybe keeping a few secrets isn't the end of the damn world? I'm protecting her. Like I've done my whole life for those I lo—

Cristu.

Yeah, like fucking hell I'm admitting that thought. I clamp my jaw so tight I'm stunned it doesn't crack. Because I'm terrified it's a thought I won't be able to unthink if unleashed.

Pussy ass and pussy whipped.

Maybe, but still, I back the fuck away.

Then I glance at Sofiya again, wondering... hoping she didn't catch any of that.

So why am I not relieved she's watching the track? Maybe it's because I know her well enough now to see the tension in her jaw, the flicker of unease she thinks she's hiding.

She's waiting for the other shoe to drop.

Because we both know it will.

I pull her tighter against me. Let the roar of engines mask the shift in my pulse.

For now, I don't tell her.

But I will.

Soon.

Maybe.

* * *

The race is over but the roar of Silverstone hasn't yet faded, the air still thick with the tang of rubber and gasoline. The podium glints under British summer haze – what little sun managed to survive the cloud cover – and Dante lifts his trophy like a man born to dominate.

Narciso, all smug grin and camera charm, flashes a wink from second place, and Renzo glares daggers from third, jaw clenched so tight I bet his molars crack before the after-party.

Good. It doesn't hurt to be knocked down a notch or two on occasion. Keeps a man on his toes.

Speaking of which, I'm not here for the fucking show. I'm watching Sofiya's lush body and lips I've already tasted three times since the checkered flag dropped. She's biting back a smirk as my sister Bibi and the race engineers flank her, watching the celebration. Yeah, she's in the Salvatore camp now.

Narciso steps over, brushing past a crew member, wiping at

sweat with his branded towel. 'Do I need to be seeing this?' he mutters, nodding at me and Sofiya as I tug her close, unapologetically brushing my lips against the hinge of her jaw.

I smirk, flicking him a glance like a blade. 'Close your eyes then, *cucciolo*. Or I'll start describing it.'

'Christ,' he mutters. But his chuckle is genuine. Almost. I don't miss the flicker of something else – last year's ghost, Vegas and the shitty antics he pulled that almost got Cesare killed – still drifting between us. I let it sit. A reminder. His jaw clenches but he pales a little.

Message received.

Later, over a toast and a round of cheers in the private suite with Bibi and a few loyal crew, I catch Sofiya watching me. That sharp, assessing gleam in her eye that says she's cataloguing every tension in the room.

She knows something's coming. I do too.

We slip out just before sundown, roaring down the M1 into the sticky quiet of a London summer night. My Furia supercar growls low and sexy as it invades the leafy streets, engine purring under my palm like it knows we're both trying not to explode.

Sofiya slides a hand to my thigh as I shift gears, eyes glinting under the streetlights. 'You know England has the highest CCTV coverage in the world?'

I grin, tugging her closer with one arm. I thoroughly devour her mouth when I stop at a red light. 'So they'll get good footage when we get arrested for indecent exposure.'

She laughs, breath warm. 'And then what?'

I lean in, nipping at her bottom lip. 'Then I fuck a girl with a rap sheet in a prison cell before we bust our way out, Bonnie and Clyde style. My kind of fairy tale.'

Her hand splays on my chest and she parts her lips for

another filthy kiss. When we part, she looks horny and fucking beautiful. 'You say the nicest things, Enforcer.'

I'm laughing when I floor the gas.

* * *

I'm definitely *not* laughing fifteen minutes later.

De Luca looks like shit.

They always do when the mask slips and he had fuck all to be working with in the first place. I lean against the wall of the abandoned flat we've blacked out, lit only by a lamp that hums with an old bulb and the anticipation of what's about to happen.

Sofiya walks in behind me, quiet as a knife unsheathed. Her eyes never leave the bastard's face.

He spits blood, then forces a smile. 'Sofiya. You look radiant.'

'I'd look better with a little less betrayal in the room,' she replies.

His laugh is thin, mouth leaking red. 'It was just intel. Nothing personal.'

'Right,' she says. 'Except it was deeply personal. It unravelled a shitty set of motions that put some... admittedly deserving men in the ground. But it also put a few people I love in danger. So tell me, what do I do about that?'

Fuck, she's breathtaking. Her eyes don't flash. They don't need to. The cold tundra is worse.

I step closer to be in her space but also to move things along. I need my *tigra's* tight cunt before the hour ends or I'll go feral.

I crouch beside him so he can see the truth in my eyes. 'You were a shitty inside man. You'll make a shittier corpse but, alas, that can't be helped.'

He opens his mouth again. I'm done listening.

I toss Sofiya the blade. 'Do your worst, baby. Make it quick. I have better plans that don't involve keeping traitors breathing.'

She catches it mid-air like the weapon was born in her palm. No hesitation. She steps to the squealing rat and drags two clean, precise cuts on his forehead – twin Xs. A brand for a rat as it squeaks and begs.

'Now we're even, you double-crossing fuck,' she says softly, and before she steps back, I'm yanking her to me, tongue-fucking her mouth because it's fucking glorious seeing her back in her element.

I drag De Luca out a moment later, my own blade finding its way into his ribs while she waits in the next room.

* * *

Sofiya

I'm cleaning my knife when I hear the thud of De Luca's body hit the floor. My lungs exhale like I've been holding them hostage. The heat that follows isn't guilt – it's hunger. Relief, yes because for a while there in the past couple of weeks I wondered whether the incident in the safehouse had shattered me forever. It didn't.

But now I have a craving. One I know only Rafaelle can satisfy.

He steps into the side room, blood barely dry on his gloves, and I'm already reaching for his belt.

'We celebrating?' he growls, mouth hard on mine.

'I didn't lose my touch,' I whisper, pushing him against the wall. 'Let me show you how much I've missed it.'

His laugh is a low rumble, primal and real. 'Let me show you what I do to girls who make me hard with a single look.'

He lifts me to the table. I wrap my legs around his waist. And the rest?

The rest is vengeance and victory, written in skin and sweat, in the echoes of a life we're no longer running from – but charging straight into.

* * *

Rafaelle
London, 03:19

The suite is silent, save for the soft tick of the grandfather clock and the low, erratic beat of my heart.

Glass and shadow rule the room – floor-to-ceiling windows catch the city's glow like a trap. The penthouse smells of lavender and gun oil, of blood barely washed from my hands before we were on each other, fucking like the world was ending.

Sofiya sleeps tangled in sheets the colour of old champagne, her bare back kissed by slivers of moonlight.

My phone vibrates on the table. One sharp pulse. Then another. I know who it is before I reach for it. And I make a vow. One day I'll make the fucker pay for toying with the Enforcer.

NIGHTOWL

Traitors dance in old flaming ruins and snakes
in rafters.

Fuck.

I sit up, drag a hand over my face, then stand. The cold marble bites into my soles as I pace across the polished floor. Shutting the double doors to the bedroom, I prowl into the living room, typing furiously.

> Enough riddles. Give me the fucking intel.

I'm barely done hitting send when another message pings in.

> NIGHTOWL
>
> Genesis 3:19. Black soil. Eve weeps where she waits to forget her name.

God-fucking-dammit.

I turn ready to launch my phone... or myself... at the wall. Only to find her watching me from the doorway. Eyes drowsy but sharp.

'What's going on?'

'Just a job that needs doing,' I lie, low and smooth. 'Nothing urgent.'

She cocks a brow. 'Rafaelle—'

I shake my head. 'It's nothing,' I insist, walking over to take her hand. 'The family's safe. We're safe. That's all that matters. Come back to bed, *tigra*.'

She lets me coax her down, band her tight in my arms just the way I know she likes.

She sleeps. I don't.

Because that last message about Eve?

It's got my mind spinning.

* * *

Sofiya

It's not a feeling I expected to feel again this soon, and not with Rafa, but... I can't shift the hollow in my belly.

Something's going on. Maybe good. Maybe bad.

But he's keeping secrets. And fuck... that hurts more than I want to admit.

Maybe he's protecting you?

I throw a silent finger at the voice because that's bullshit. Rafa, more than anyone else on this earth, knows I can take care of myself. Hell, he nearly burst with pride and into applause watching me carve up fucking DeLuca.

No, he's hiding more than he's protecting this time. And I sense it involves that mysterious owl and green code on his phone.

I haven't gone snooping and I don't plan to.

Honour among thieves or, in our case, assassins? Maybe.

Am I burying my head in the sand? Also maybe.

The thing I can't bury for much longer though? The way I feel about him. The way my heart cracks wide open when he walks into the room. When he smirks and winks and catches me around the waist like I'm the only thing tethering him to this world. Like I'm danger and salvation wrapped in one reckless, breathless little package.

There might be a hard reckoning down the road but for now I'm choosing to douse myself in his growly '*You're mine*' when he's deep inside me.

When his face cracks with lust and awe and savage hunger. When he pants like he's running out of oxygen and would gladly die just to be inside me.

With me. Holding me.

I jump when my phone pings a familiar sound. Then my heart follows. My contact. My eyes widen when I read the message.

'Rafa!'

He prowls into the room all swagger and sin, muscles cut from menace and a mouth built for ruin.

I almost forget why I called him until he starts to smirk, one eyebrow quirking. Mentally slapping myself, I show him my phone.

His smile vanishes. 'The intel is solid? You trust your source?'

I shrug. 'If he wants to get paid, it better be.'

He nods. 'Let's fucking go then.'

* * *

We dress in silence.

I tug on my tactical pants, pockets heavy with spare mags, while he loosens his silk-collared shirt and swaps it for a black anti-stab T-shirt, sleeves pushed up to reveal the sexy ink on his forearms. Each garment is a second skin, essential armour against the coming storm.

Our eyes meet across the bed. A silent vow.

All in. No holding back this time.

I slip a leather harness over my torso then attach the throat mic to my neck, smoothing the strap across my collarbone. Rafa picks up his Kydex holster and belts it on; metal glints as he checks his Beretta at his hip.

I consider the faint line where my scar meets unbroken skin. Tonight, I'll cross El Topo's threshold and end this. I look up and the look in Rafa's eyes holds me there. Fierce with determination, blazing with protectiveness.

He stalks to me and grips my hand, calloused thumb brushing my knuckles. 'Ready, *tigra*?'

I rest my forehead against his, breathing in the scent of him now imprinted on my heart. 'Ready.'

He crouches and slides a blade into my boot sheath.

I nod. It's time.

* * *

Rafaelle
Outside Limassol, Six Hours Later

The rental car hums over cracked coastal asphalt, moonlight a sliver of silver above the sea. My beauty sits beside me with her eyes closed but I know she's not sleeping. Her presence is steadying the wild pulse in my throat. We move like we always do – stealthy, synced. Ghosts on a mission.

The city lights are dying behind us as we push deeper into old country. I know what's waiting up that hillside. A half-forced villa belonging to El Topo's Cypriot mistress.

Fucking Nightowl and his fucking 'Traitors dance in old flaming ruins and snakes in rafters.'

I mutter a curse under my breath, gripping the wheel tighter. 'Old mistresses in ruins and fucking traitors.' If he'd just said Cyprus, we could've been here days ago. This would be over by now.

Sofiya glances at me. The corner of her mouth twitches, her eyes sharp but sombre. As necessary as this is, it's still not a light undertaking. 'You talking to yourself there, killer?'

I know she didn't hear me, but I still stiffen, and I loathe the knots building in my gut. *More fucking secrets.*

I vow to tell her about Nightowl... as soon as I decode the other message.

I shake my head, grab her hand and kiss her knuckles. 'Not now you're looking at me with those beautiful eyes. You good?'

Those said eyes dim a little and I'm not sure if it's because of my clear evasion or because of what's about to happen in the next ten minutes.

She nods after a moment. 'You think Cesare will get the men here in time?'

I nod, my trust in my brother unquestioning. 'He will. And the FBI too. If El Topo's there, he's not getting away this time. Trust me.'

Is it my imagination or does her smile waver just a tiny fraction? A conscience I haven't met since childhood rears its head and gut-punches me. *Hard.*

I realise I'm holding my breath until she breathes softly, 'I do.'

Those two words reverberate through my skull. And long after the dilapidated villa appears in the distance – a fitting tomb for an old monster, ruined, half-swallowed by vines, a relic on a wind-blasted hill – I'm thinking about those words.

With a fat ring attached to it. My name engraved on her heart. A Salvatore in her belly.

She reaches over and takes my hand. No words. Just a quiet, firm squeeze. My breath shudders out as my thumb brushes her knuckles.

And for a second, the pressure in my chest eases. For a second, the world stills.

'Whatever happens,' she murmurs, 'I'm glad it's you.'

I look at her. At the woman who saved herself and still lets me pretend I'm her protector. 'Me too.'

* * *

It goes like clockwork.

The best fucking aria in the world.

Bonafacio Mancinelli, a wraith of the man whose evil and greed murdered my mother, is bound in chains within one hour and I didn't even have to draw my gun. A few shuriken and a couple of viper steels end four ageing capos.

Moonlight slants through the trees, catching the dull gleam of his battered silver hair. He leans on a rusted iron gate in his silk pyjamas, eyes alive with hate.

I draw a sharp breath, heart hammering against my ribs. I've done this a hundred times – lined men up, put one bullet in their brains, walked away whistling. But this is different. This is the man who took away the woman who taught me how to cook, who taught me how to love my family, myself. Even love the woman who stands beside me.

Solid and loyal.

Sofiya's rifle is pressed into her shoulder, her gaze on me, not him. I feel her eyes, calm and fierce. Even as her grandfather curses her in brutal Sicilian.

'*Traitrice! Putana! Figghia di malanova!*'

She says nothing, her attention steady on me. Her presence is the strange comfort I didn't know I needed.

Bonafacio sees me raise my gun and howls, staggering straighter even though he's clearly bearing the signs of heavy drinking. 'Shoot me, if you dare! But remember, I'm the snake who taught *her* how to strike!'

I swallow, finger tracing the trigger. One squeeze – brain matter, and it could be over. My mother's ghost will sleep easy.

I feel Sofiya's breath on my jaw, soft and urgent.

I hesitate. The rage in me bleeds out.

'Life or death. Your call, *tesoru*,' she whispers.

Bonafacio continues to spit blood-red curses, foaming with venom as if they could still hold weight. I flick my gun downward and squeeze the trigger once. A thunderclap cracks the night wide open, followed by a wet crunch of bone as the bullet rakes through his right knee.

He screams. Not just in pain, but in rage, defiance, disbelief. He topples onto his side, flailing like a gutted dog. I stride forward and plant my boot over his ruined kneecap. He bucks. Tries to crawl.

I press harder.

'Stay down,' I growl.

He manages to brace on one elbow, chest heaving, lips slick with blood. Still reaching. Still arrogant.

I slam him back to the floor, pinning him with my foot on his chest, then I lean close, my voice as quiet as a confession. 'Show some respect to your granddaughter, you old bastard.'

His bloodstained grin splits wide. 'Do it. I dare you. End me now, Salvatore.'

It's not bluster. He *wants* it. Like a coward who wants to die before he faces everything he's wrought.

Which is why I don't.

Instead, I grin right back, deranged and deliberate, and yank my phone from my back pocket. I dial the direct line.

Cesare picks up on the first ring.

'How close are they?' I ask, not taking my eyes off El Topo.

'Ten minutes,' Cesare says. 'Our man from Interpol is en route – Orazio vetted him personally this time. No more fuckups.'

I exhale through my nose. 'Good.'

In the background, I hear movement, voices – Fallbrook is alive with tension. And then, Orazio's voice cuts in, sharp and hungry.

'Is he there?' he demands. 'Put me on video.'

I do.

'Bonafacio,' Orazio snarls, and the air thickens with decades of venom. 'You motherless *figghiu di buttana*. Look at you now. Pinned like the rat you are.'

Bonafacio laughs wetly. 'You finally sent one of your mongrel grandsons to do what you couldn't.'

Orazio ignores the barb. 'You know I used to call you *brother*? You remember that? Before Valentina?'

Bonafacio's smile falters. Just a flicker. Enough.

'She chose me,' he rasps.

'No, you *took* her,' Orazio says, voice rough. 'Like you took everything. The business. The alliances. The trust. And then you broke it all because you couldn't stand not owning everything in the room.' He pauses, voice lowering. 'I know you killed her, Bonafacio.'

Silence. Except the faint wheeze of blood in El Topo's throat.

Orazio continues, a bitter sigh wrapped in a choked whisper. 'You let everyone believe she ran. But I knew. I *always* knew. Maybe now she'll rest in peace, you miserable son of a Sicilian whore.'

I cut the call.

Bonafacio's chest rises and falls beneath my boot, his mouth twitching like he wants to spit again but can't find the energy.

I crouch beside him, pistol lowered. 'You don't get to die yet, old man. Not until you bleed. Not until she's buried with the truth.'

I cock my head, listening to the approaching rotor blades.

'The start of your reckoning is almost here. And you're going to live long enough to rot.'

He doesn't laugh this time. Just closes his eyes like he's already starting to fade.

Too bad for him. I've got more bullets.

* * *

We wait until the authorities swarm the crumbling ruins. Until more shackles are added to the ones I put around my mother's killer.

As they haul him away, I step into the moonlight, heart pounding.

Sofiya is beside me, shoulders trembling. 'She would be proud of you,' she murmurs.

Tears sting my eyes and I realise I am... broken open by her, by this moment. By seconds and minutes and hours that look like the kind of forever I never dreamed of.

29

RAFAELLE

It was fitting that I bring her back here. Only here.

Valle di Luce.

That I draw a bath and wash the night... the past from our bodies.

Now I rise onto one elbow, watching her in the flicker of candlelight. My voice is rough. 'Can I?'

She nods, breath catching.

I lean in, pressing my mouth to hers, slow and searing, letting her taste the truce, the bargain, the barely contained need. Her arms wind around my neck, fingers tangling in my hair as I deepen the kiss, teeth grazing her bottom lip until she sighs against me.

I slide down her body, hands trailing along her ribs to the hem of her silk slip. She lifts her hips to meet my palm, urging me higher. I tease the fabric upward, revealing the curve of her waist, the hollow of her belly, the swell of her breasts. My thumb draws a light circle around one nipple through the thin silk. She gasps, hips lifting.

Gently, I peel off her slip, letting it fall to the floor. The cool night air brushes her skin. I capture one hardened peak in my mouth, sucking and tugging until she trembles beneath me. My hands knead the other, teasing tight circles, trading places until her back arches and her nails rake down the sheets.

I rise, lips brushing the valley between her breasts, then drift down her torso until I stand between her legs. I hook a finger under her panties, sliding them down with deliberate care. She parts her thighs, restless, and I press a soft kiss to her hip before lowering my mouth to her centre.

My tongue traces slow, hungry patterns along her inner thigh, drawing out that tension until she buckles beneath me. When I finally part her pretty pink pussy with a gentle flick, she grips the mattress, head thrown back, voice low and ragged. 'Rafa—'

I pull back, brushing my lips against her thigh. 'I need you, baby. So fucking much. Do you need me?'

She nods, voice thick. 'Yes, God, yes... please.'

I stand and unbutton my jeans, pressing in slowly, testing, as her eyes flick open and lock onto mine. She nods again, urging me deeper. I pause, chest against hers, the hush between us crackling, then begin to move, first barely, then building in feral rhythm.

Her arms coil around my back, pulling me flush against her. Candlelight flickers across our sweat-slicked skin as I thrust.

She matches me, sliding her hips up and down, grounding me in the relentless give and take of our magic.

I lean close, voice low and rough. 'You were fierce tonight, even in your silence. I'm so fucking proud of you.'

She gasps, nails scraping down my shoulders. 'So were you.'

We drive each other towards the edge, breath and tension coiling tighter. When she breaks first, her cry rips the shadows apart. I follow seconds later, chest heaving.

We collapse together, breath mingling, the aftermath a raw stillness in which neither of us speaks. I drag a hand through her hair, planting a feather-light kiss on her temple.

But even as her lashes lower and her fingers curve sleepily around my wrist, my mind refuses to quiet.

The latest message from my mysterious source pulses like a hidden vein.

NIGHTOWL

Genesis. Eve. Fading.

Three words. A whisper beneath the skin of everything. I know Nightowl doesn't mean El Topo this time.

I suspect what they mean. *Who* they mean.

Giada Mancinelli.

So why haven't you told Sofiya yet?

I tell myself I'm protecting her. That I'm giving her space to breathe from all the fucking chaos. To spare her if shit goes sideways, as they do, even with the best intentions.

But as I stare up at the ceiling, my arm curled around the woman I'd kill the world for, the guilt gnaws deeper.

Because secrets rot, especially if they're not buried deep enough. And the higher they rise, the louder they tend to scream.

* * *

Rafaelle
London – Two Days Later

'The old bastard's been caught. It's over... for the next five minutes. So you two coming home now?'

Cesare's voice crackles over the line, thick with exhaustion and bone-deep satisfaction. There's laughter in the background – Maddie, probably. The kind of domestic bliss I never thought would suit my brother until he fell into it like he was made for it.

I drag a hand through my hair, then rest my forearm on the glass railing, eyes trained on the glittering London skyline. 'Not yet. *Frate*, need a favour.'

'Shoot.'

I spell out what I want. Every detail. No hedging.

Silence crackles on the other end. Then a long exhale. My gut is clenched the entire time. 'You sure about this?'

Am I? Fuck no. But my gut is leading the way on this. And when my gut leads, I follow. Even if it's all tangled together in one relentless pull.

Shouldn't you be using an organ higher up? Heart? Brain, even?

'No... I mean, yeah.' I exhale through gritted teeth. 'Shit, I sound dumber than a porn star in a priest costume.'

I'm expecting Cesare to laugh, to throw it back at me like he always does. But he just sighs. Long and heavy. 'I know you're going on your gut, and normally I'd say follow it into hell. But brother... I'd hate for you to FUBAR this.'

My jaw tightens. I swallow a lump in my throat. I've never been this fucking torn. Never felt this exposed. But then I remember the promise I made by a gravestone under cypress trees. Remember what's at stake. What I owe. 'Noted. I'm sure. Do it.'

He doesn't push again. Just murmurs, '*Buona fortuna*,' and hangs up.

Before I can take a breath, the burner on the counter buzzes. Maddie's name flashes.

'Rafaelle, tell me you haven't stolen Sofiya again.'

I smile, just a little. 'Not this time. She's in the shower.'

'Good. Because I need her. I'm drowning in guest lists and

the twins just volunteered a fire-eater for the christening and Orazio's threatening to disown us if we invite more Americans than Sicilians while insisting he wants a separate seating section for Sicilians only.'

'Sounds about right.'

'I need Sof. She has taste. She has ruthlessness. She'll put Orazio in his place.'

I chuckle. 'So what you're saying is... you're begging?'

'I'm threatening,' Maddie corrects, voice sharp. 'Seriously, if she doesn't come help me plan this thing, Nico's going to be christened in a wading pool with cannoli as holy wafers. I need her to murder my guest list and tell the caterer where to shove the fifth dessert option. I need someone who can handle Cesare's ego, Vittoria's passive-aggressive critiques, and Orazio's obsession with gold-encrusted christening favours.'

I glance towards the bedroom where the shower's still running. Part of me doesn't want to let her go. Hell, I *hate* the idea of being apart. It sits like cold steel in my gut. Especially now. But I engineered this.

And Sofiya? She'll probably like the excuse to be useful. To feel part of something that doesn't involve bloodshed.

'She'll come,' I promise. 'I'll get her to the airport.'

And if there's a shitload of guilt tucked behind my words, only Cesare and I will be the wiser.

* * *

She sits next to me in the car, wearing black jeans and one of my old hoodies. Breathtaking enough to destroy empires. That scar above her hip peeks out beneath her top when she adjusts her seatbelt, and it reminds me how far we've come.

And how close I am to fucking everything up again.

Because even though she returns my smile, something in the set of her jaw tells me she knows I'm holding back.

I distract her the only way I know how.

'There's a new assignment.'

Her brows lift. 'For me?'

'For us. Joint op. But it's recon only. We're just watching a drop site in Marseilles. Simple surveillance. No engagement.'

Her lips twitch, but she doesn't bite. 'You sure that's all?'

'Come on, *tigra*, would I lie to you?' The statement I made to her a lifetime ago when I had her tied up on my bed in my safehouse comes back to bite me. *Hard*.

She stares out the window, chin tilted. I can feel her eyes on me even when she's not looking. As if she's searching for the crack in my voice. The lie I haven't spoken yet.

Her silence says more than words. She doesn't trust easily. Not after what her own family pulled. Not after what I *still* haven't told her.

I pull into Heathrow's VIP terminal where the Salvatore jet is waiting along with the six bodyguards accompanying her. I kill the engine. 'I'll see you in a couple days,' I murmur, reaching for her hand.

'You better.'

She kisses me. Slow, soft, but laced with something sharp – like she's marking it. Like she knows.

When she disappears behind the glass doors, I let my forehead fall against the wheel.

Just one thing.

One more secret.

Then I'm done.

30

SOFIYA

Fallbrook Estate glitters under the mid-July sun like a priceless jewel.

Shame it feels like a cage.

I'm storming down the catering tent aisle, clipboard in hand, designer heels turning turf to submission. 'No. We are not serving foie gras to a family with this many Catholics and pregnant women. Find another *amuse-bouche*. One that doesn't scream class warfare.'

The chef mutters something in French. I shoot him a glare so cold he nearly slips on his own sweat.

Cesare walks past with Nico strapped to his chest in a black baby Björn, grinning like the happiest man alive. 'Keep going, *bedda*. Maddie hasn't threatened divorce in over six hours. We're on a roll.'

I wish the cut of his jaw and that tuft of hair falling into his eyes didn't remind me so much of Rafa. And seriously, I wish he'd stop smiling altogether. I've only been here six hours and the withdrawal symptoms are brutal.

Orazio lounges nearby, drink in hand. 'You're turning out to be quite the little asset,' he murmurs. 'Unstable, *sì*. But interesting.'

What the hell is wrong with me that the weird as fuck compliment warms my heart?

Don't think about your heart. How it aches for him.

'Tell me something I don't know,' I snap, brushing past him. The twins try to flank me next, Renzo with his charming smirk, Dante's quieter but piercing interest, and Narciso's lazy swagger as he trails behind them, pretending disinterest but failing.

I bat them all away with a flick of my pen and a deadpan, 'You want to help? Go set yourselves on fire. It'll save time.'

They laugh. But my smile is mechanical, preloaded. The hollowness inside me is growing teeth.

Rafa's absence is louder than any Mancinelli threat. We texted on the plane. I've FaceTimed once. Then in the last three hours... silence.

I feel it. Something pulling taut and fraying. He didn't just let me come to Fallbrook.

He *orchestrated* it.

Maddie finds me later in the nursery, one hand toying with a floral arrangement I hate. She leans in the doorway like a woman who knows everything already.

'So,' she says, tone casual. 'You want to tell me what's clawing through your ribcage?'

I stare at the roses. 'I think I'm in love with him.'

Her eyes widen. 'Fuck. Truly?'

I purse my lips, hating myself a little for blurting that shit out. Her face softens. 'You didn't mean to say that out loud, did you?'

'Is "fuck no" too rude?'

She smiles. 'Not at all.' She draws closer, rescues the arrangement before I shred it. Then she cups my shoulders. 'So, what's the plan, Sof?' She's trying to sound calm, removed even, but I see the hopeful glint in her eyes.

I shrug. 'I want to tell him. I want to do something about it. But...' I stop, bite my lip like some B-movie actress in an erotica movie franchise.

'What if it all... unravels?' I murmur, barely recognising my own voice. 'What if I hand him my heart and he doesn't even notice he's holding a live grenade?' *Or what if the thing he's still hiding is what breaks me?*

Maddie moves in, kneels, places her hands on my knees. 'Then you have front row seat of taking him the fuck out,' she says, then giggles darkly when I gape at her. 'Sorry, I'm the wife of a mobster. I'm in my mayhem era. What I meant was, you'll survive it. Like you always do. But don't let the chance pass you by or you'll spend your life regretting it. You've fought for your family since you were much too young. It's time to fight for what matters to you.'

I nod, but it's hollow. Because deep in my gut, I know.

I'm not chasing love.

I'm chasing the truth.

And if those two don't collide...

I'm a little ashamed that I'm too chicken to finish that thought.

* * *

The wind howls through the crumbling stone of Convento di Sant'Isidoro, the monastery turned asylum turned ghost. The kind of place no one speaks about without spitting.

My boots crunch gravel. Wild rosemary and black cypress sway under a moon like bleached bone. The crucifix above the archway is rusted, warped like faith left too long in the rain.

And Rafa's here.

Alone.

Pacing the cloister with his gun drawn, scanning the ruins like he expects a ghost to leap from the shadows. Maybe he hopes for it.

His back is to me. I don't call out.

Because I know.

The whispers from the deep forums, the encrypted files I wasn't supposed to dig into. Giada was here. My sister. The one who vanished like a shadow. The one Rafa pretended was less important than El Topo.

And yet here he is. With a weapon.

To protect himself? Or to finish her?

My stomach turns to acid.

'You've been holding out on me, Enforcer.'

He spins around. And the look on his face – guilt and grief and something that tears through me – confirms everything.

The Glock lowers like it's suddenly too heavy for his sins. 'Sofiya—'

'Why are you here?' My voice is dust and cracked porcelain. 'Why are you looking for my sister? And please don't bother to deny it. And while you're at it, tell me... If you came in peace, why are you holding a gun?'

He laughs. It's a broken sound. And he looks exhausted. Weighed down with boulders he can't shift. 'Maybe that's all I am, *bedda*. A killer with a broken heart.'

That stops me, dead in my feet and in my heart. 'Is that all you want to be?'

The silence after is brutal.

I step closer. 'Tell me the truth, Rafaelle.'

* * *

Rafaelle

Her voice is ice.

But her eyes – fuck me – her eyes glitter with tears. Tears I put there.

Is that all you want to be?

The question hits harder than any slug. I drag a hand over my face, feel dust and sweat and something close to shame. 'When I've fucked up this badly? Maybe that's all I deserve.'

She takes one hesitant step closer. I can't stand seeing her look at me like a stranger, so I start talking – ripping stitches I've kept shut for too many years.

'The last time I saw my mother alive, she was smiling. Said she'd bring me cannoli from my favourite bakery, even though we both knew hers were better.' My throat tightens. 'She promised she'd be back before dinner. That smile was my first memory of love, and the last time I felt unconditional love.'

Sofiya's lips tremble. I push on.

'Maddie swore Giada was the last person to speak to Mama. I needed to know her final words. Needed to hear them from the only witness still breathing.' I swallow hard. 'So I came here. To beg, not to kill.'

She looks at the gun again.

'I brought the piece because peace never comes without a weapon in my world,' I admit. 'But I walked these ruins praying Giada would appear so I could put the gun down.'

A tear breaks free on her cheek. It guts me.

'I don't deserve forgiveness,' I rasp. 'But I can't stand another second without telling you... I fell for you in the split second you pulled a trigger and spared my life. You are the miracle my grief never knew it needed. I love you, Sofiya. Fiercely. Stupidly.

Enough to trade every drop of vengeance for one breath of your laughter.'

She covers her mouth, sob catching, and I step closer, cupping her jaw, thumbs brushing tears away.

'One more,' I whisper, voice wrecked. 'If loving you is the bullet that finally drops me, I'll thank God for the perfect aim.'

The Glock slips from my fingers, clattering on stone. She surges forward and our mouths collide, our bodies trembling. Her hands fist my shirt, hauling me in as if distance itself is an enemy.

'I love you too,' she breathes against my lips, her tears mixing with mine. 'You stupid, beautiful man.'

We stand amid shattered arches and the echo of ghosts, kissing like we can stitch our broken histories together with nothing but mouth and promise. Somewhere in the wind, I swear I hear my mother's voice, a soft Sicilian lilt, drifting through the cypress.

Be happy, figghiu mio. You finally found home.

Sofiya clings to me like she's trying to anchor us both. Like she's still not sure we're real. I don't blame her.

We kiss until the pain dulls into something survivable. Until the ghosts step back and let us breathe.

Her lips brush mine again, softer this time. Searching. Then she pulls away just enough to whisper, 'Do you still hear her?'

I nod, throat too tight for words. My hand settles at the base of her spine, pressing her flush against me. 'She told me to be happy. For once in my fucking life.'

She lets out a shuddering laugh, rests her forehead to mine. 'Then maybe listen to her.'

We stand there, two assassins soaked in sorrow and soot, surrounded by holy ruins that once promised salvation. I run a thumb down her jaw, then along her bruised collarbone. The shadows hug every curve of her body, and I want – no, *need* – to feel her again. Flesh to flesh. Not because of sex.

Well, not just that.

But because I need to remind myself she's here. That I didn't lose her.

'Let's stay,' I say gruffly, my voice cracking. 'Just for a bit.'

She nods once, and I guide her gently to the weathered steps at the altar's edge. She sits, legs folding beneath her. I lower myself beside her, our knees brushing.

Wind stirs her hair. I tuck a strand behind her ear, letting my fingers linger against her temple. Her eyes are still shining with something deeper. That bottomless soul of hers. *My tigra.*

'You scare the shit out of me,' I murmur.

She arches a brow. 'Because I showed up with truth instead of violence?'

'No.' I touch her bare wrist where the vein flutters beneath my thumb. 'Because I'd burn the whole fucking world to keep you safe. And part of me is still learning that you don't need me to.'

She leans her head on my shoulder. 'But maybe I want you to. Sometimes.'

I exhale slowly. 'Fuck, that's even worse.'

We sit in silence, without bullets or enemies. Two souls on sacred ground, letting the night fold around us. My hand finds hers. I trace the calluses on her fingers, the roughness that matches my own. A match cut from the same blade.

'You think she's still alive?' she asks quietly. 'Giada.'

I sigh. 'I don't know. And that terrifies me more than knowing. Because it would devastate you, and I'll have to kill a whole lot of people to make you smile.'

Sofiya nods, solemn. Accepting. "We'll find her. And she'll tell you what you need to know. I promise."

My throat fills, blocking any attempt at swallowing. "I believe you. And I love you."

Then she turns her face towards mine. Her voice is low, dangerous. 'But don't vanish on me again, Rafa. A sister is bad enough. I can't fucking bear it, do you hear me?'

A shudder ripples through me at the agony in the plea. '*Si, amuri miu*. I vow it. No lies. No secrets.' My jaw tightens. A beat throbs past. 'Except the ones I haven't figured out how to tell you yet.'

She gives me a look. 'I'll decide what I can handle. You don't get to play martyr on my behalf.'

I smirk, wry and aching. 'You're the only woman who could cut me with truth and I'd beg for more.'

'Good,' she says. 'Because I love you, Rafaelle Salvatore. And I plan to be your sharpest blade.'

I reach for her, pulling her onto my lap. She straddles me without hesitation, arms looping around my neck, nose brushing mine. 'Say it again.'

'I love you.'

'Fuck.' I bury my face in her neck, inhaling her, grounding myself. 'You just stitched something broken in me I didn't know was bleeding.'

We stay like that long after the wind dies down.

Later, I'll carry her back to the car, drive us to someplace warm and private and ours. Later, we'll peel the rest of the pain from each other's skin in a bed that smells like new beginnings.

But for now, in the crumbling heart of a ruined sanctuary, we sit together, alive, in love, and no longer alone.

And Jesus fucking Christ, it's more than enough.

More than I'll ever deserve.

* * *

The storm breaks above us like a warning shot, thunder echoing through the ancient bones of the convent. But all I can hear is the rasp of her breath and the pulse between us, too loud, too alive to ignore.

Without a word, I draw her into my arms. The world narrows to her scent – heady wild jasmine and brave warrior – and the rasp of her breathing. My chest tightens. 'I love you,' I murmur, voice thick. 'So fucking much.'

Her head tilts back, surprised tears catching moonlight. She presses her lips to mine, soft, and every jagged piece of me mends, just enough.

Our kiss deepens, no longer gentle but hungry. Her hands tear at my shirt, nails grazing skin, and I lift her off her feet, pressing her against the cool stone wall. She gasps, legs locking around my hips.

'I should make you wait,' I growl into her mouth, fingers already curling under her top. 'I should punish you for showing up and reading me like scripture.'

'But you won't,' she breathes, voice shaking with need. 'Because you need this too.'

'God, Sofiya,' I rasp, voice low. 'You feel so good.'

She gasps again, nails raking down my shoulders. 'Rafa—'

I slide my cock inside her in one rough thrust, and we both shatter. She cries out, fingers gripping my shoulders, and I hold her steady as her body clenches around me.

'I could fuck you for a thousand years and still not get enough,' I whisper into her ear, each word laced with reverence and threat. 'You were made to ruin me, *tigra*. And I'll thank you for it every damn time.'

She trembles against me, moaning my name like it's both plea and curse. My pace is unrelenting, slow, deep, meant to drag every ounce of feeling from her soul to mine.

I cup her face, halting for a moment, and we share a breath, eyes locking. Words aren't needed, only the heat of our union, the promise that, together, we can endure whatever comes.

'You're mine,' I say, voice hoarse, forehead resting against hers. 'And I don't care if it damns me, I'll murder-spree every day to keep you.'

Her mouth meets mine again, desperate, messy, perfect. Her release crashes over her with a shudder, body arching, breath caught on my name. I follow with a broken sound, burying myself in her, every muscle drawn tight, every wound laid bare.

Lightning cracks in the distance, two strikes to light the darkness. I hold her tight, knowing we won't be the same, but sure of one thing. We face whatever comes – together. I trace a finger down her cheek. 'I'm so lucky I get to fuck you and love you, keep living and keep hunting with you by my side. Forever.'

And as I lower us to the stone floor, my arms still wrapped around her, our bodies still tangled, I know this isn't the end.

This is the beginning.

'And I'll be right there, *cor' miu*, spreeing right along with you. Because sometimes, love doesn't save you from the fire. It teaches you how to survive it.'

EPILOGUE
SOFIYA

It's the kind of day that sparkles. Warm, opulent sunshine spills across the lawns of Fallbrook, gilding everything in soft gold.

The private chapel has been filled to capacity with stridently vetted A-listers, politicians pretending they're not nervous, and at least two billionaires whose entourages got turned away at the gates because Orazio doesn't allow entourages. *Ever.*

Cesare stands at the altar like a man who finally believes in miracles. Maddie is radiant, in a dove-grey silk dress that moulds to her waist, hair pinned with delicate pearls.

Nico sleeps in her arms, swaddled in hand-stitched lace, blissfully unaware that his godparents are two of the deadliest people in the room.

Me.

And Rafaelle.

He's behind me now. I feel the burn of his stare before I hear the low chuckle. 'You're squeezing my hand hard enough to crack bone, *tigra.*'

I glance up at him, smirking. 'You're lucky I'm not aiming higher.'

The priest starts the benediction. Cesare murmurs something to Maddie, who smiles up at him like no one else exists,
and I blink, chest squeezing with a warmth I'm still learning to
hold.

A few rows back, Jacinta is seated beside our mother, both
dressed in fierce couture rumoured to be thoroughly vetted by
Orazio. Their matching high cheekbones and sculpted glares
could outshine the Virgin herself, but in this moment, even they
seem softened by the ceremony unfolding at the altar.

When the priest begins the blessing, the hush in the air feels
sacred, ancient.

'We vow,' Maddie says, her voice unwavering, 'to raise this
child in truth, in strength, in protection. And should he ever be
lost, may he always find his way home.'

Cesare's deep voice joins hers, echoing through the vaulted
chapel. 'In love and in fire, we'll lead him.'

We repeat the same vow, and as I murmur the words beside
Rafa, my throat tightens. Because this vow isn't just for Nico. It's
for every child born into our legacy, into blood and blades. It's
for the ones like us.

I glance down at my hand, at the ring Rafa gave me after our
first Aegis mission three days ago. The diamond is unapologetically large, cushion-cut, set in a blackened platinum band
shaped like interlocking daggers. Light catches in its depths like
secrets too dangerous to speak aloud.

My heart leaps when I look up and Rafa's watching me with
a feral look in his eyes. As if he, too, can't wait for the vows we'll
be taking soon.

* * *

Jacinta, finally back in Manhattan and practising law again, clinks her champagne glass against my mother's mimosa, murmuring something dry that makes Vittoria laugh – actually laugh.

A few seats away, Narciso is in his element, tailored to sin, swirling brandy and sparring with the Salvatore twins about Formula One rankings like they're gambling chips. He's still swagger and smirk, but even I can see it – the edge has dulled. A little. I make a note to see what's up with him.

'I can't take my eyes off you,' Rafa murmurs into my ear, voice husky.

I glance down at myself. Dior ivory silk with a slit up the thigh, neckline sharp enough to draw blood. 'Can't say I blame you. I do look expensive today.'

He smirks. 'You always look expensive. Even when you're threatening to garrotte someone in cargo pants. And soon, you'll be a better assassin than me,' he adds with a smug grin that's all wolf. Then his eyes go a little molten, a lot feral. All alpha psycho goodness I can't get enough of.

Even as I roll my eyes, smoothing a hand down his lapel. 'You're thinking about our next job, aren't you?'

He hums low in his throat. 'Only if you think me getting my fat cock into your tight little c—'

I slap a hand over his mouth, face burning. 'Rafa, there are kids here!'

He nips my palm. 'Now there's a job I wouldn't mind at all. A kid. Ours.'

Shock and elation pummel me, even as I laugh, leaning in until our foreheads touch. 'You're incorrigible.'

Halfway through the ceremony, while the crowd pours into the garden and heads for champagne towers, live cello and gold-dusted canapés Orazio wouldn't budge on, I follow Rafa through the French doors into the library.

The second we're alone, he locks the door and pulls me close. Tugs off my panties, brings them to his nose to inhale deeply before stuffing them in his pocket.

'My protégé. Soon to be my wife. And the mother of all the babies I intend to put in her belly. Letting you shoot me was the best idea I've ever had.'

'God... Rafa,' I moan, even as I melt.

He brushes his lips across mine – soft, reverent, with just enough bite to make a promise.

And then, from the garden, Nico lets out his first howl of the evening.

Rafa grins. 'Our godson has taste. Knows how to make an entrance.'

'I hope he takes after Maddie.'

He sobers just a fraction. 'He'll be safe. You hear me? We'll make this whole goddamn world safer for him. For all our babies.'

I nod.

Because the war isn't over. But for the first time in my life, I'm fighting beside the man I trust – with my blood, with my life, with the very shaky, precious thing called hope.

When he's done with me in the best possible way, we open the door and walk back into the light.

Together.

* * *

MORE FROM ZARA COX

Another book from Zara Cox, *The Savage*, is available to order now here:
  https://mybook.to/SavageZaraBackAd